PRAISE FOR TIM PRATT

"This tale of a kinkster's adventures in the multiverse is a lighthearted romp marked by emotional intelligence and Pratt's characteristically inventive worldbuilding. A fun and satisfying read!"
Khan Wong, author of *The Circus Infinite*

"A fun, frothy, silly space adventure with a multiverse worth of twists."
Ada Hoffmann, Philip K Dick Award-nominated author of
The Outside trilogy

"Pratt shows genuine talent. A writer to watch."
Publishers Weekly

"Tim Pratt is in the vanguard of the next generation of master American fantasists."
Jay Lake, John W Campbell Award-winning author of
Into the Gardens of Sweet Night

By the same author

JOURNALS OF ZAXONY DELATREE
Doors of Sleep
Prison of Sleep

THE AXIOM SERIES
The Wrong Stars
The Dreaming Stars
The Forbidden Stars
The Alien Stars and Other Novellas

The Strange Adventures of Rangergirl
Briarpatch
Heirs of Grace
The Deep Woods
Blood Engines
Poison Sleep
Dead Reign
Spell Games
Bone Shop
Broken Mirrors
Grim Tides
Bride of Death
Lady of Misrule
Queen of Nothing
Closing Doors

Tim Pratt

THE KNIFE AND THE SERPENT

ANGRY
ROBOT

ANGRY ROBOT
An imprint of Watkins Media Ltd

Unit 11, Shepperton House
89 Shepperton Road
London N1 3DF
UK

angryrobotbooks.com
twitter.com/angryrobotbooks
The ties that bind

An Angry Robot paperback original, 2024

Copyright © Tim Pratt 2024

Cover by Mark Ecob
Edited by Simon Spanton Walker and Ciel Pierlot
Set in Meridien

All rights reserved. Tim Pratt asserts the moral right to be identified as the author of this work. A catalogue record for this book is available from the British Library.

This novel is entirely a work of fiction. Names, characters, places, and incidents are the products of the author's imagination or are used fictitiously. Any resemblance to actual events, locales, organizations or persons, living or dead, is entirely coincidental.

Sales of this book without a front cover may be unauthorized. If this book is coverless, it may have been reported to the publisher as "unsold and destroyed" and neither the author nor the publisher may have received payment for it.

Angry Robot and the Angry Robot icon are registered trademarks of Watkins Media Ltd.

ISBN 978 1 91520 280 2
Ebook ISBN 978 1 915 20281 9

Printed and bound in the United Kingdom by TJ Books Ltd.

9 8 7 6 5 4 3 2 1

MIX
Paper from
responsible sources
FSC
www.fsc.org   FSC® C013056

This book is dedicated to
Zanzibar Wonton Pratt Shaw,
Marzipan Orlando Pratt Shaw,
and Spotticus Maximus Pratt Shaw,
but definitely not to
Ocean Angelica Pepper Cola "PG" Pratt Shaw

GLENN

This is how I found out my girlfriend is a champion of Nigh-Space:

Her name is Vivian Sattari, but she goes by Vivy, at least when she's not using some locally plausible alias. We met on a dating site, and the algorithm thought our interests were similar and/or complementary enough to make us mathematically a near-perfect match: zombie movies, live shows with local bands, favorite author (Iain Banks for me; Iain M Banks for her), Friday nights spent with a good whiskey and a good book, a fondness for travel, grad student life, and congruent kinks.

She dropped a "like" on my profile, and duly encouraged, I sent her a message, and a correspondence developed. It turned out we were both studying at the University of California, Berkeley, and had probably passed each other on campus at one point or another. I was in the second year of my PhD program, studying the history of science, and she was newly arrived to pursue a doctorate in public policy. After chatting online for a few days, we met at a café on upper Telegraph one afternoon, and… we just clicked. She was beautiful: short and curvy, bobbed dark hair, big dark eyes, and olive skin that made me think of Mediterranean summers. Although autumn was beginning to fall, she wore a deep purple sun dress covered in little yellow stars with strappy sandals. We talked about life in Berkeley, and books, and music, then went for a walk and segued into our personal philosophy and life goals, then went to a bar and delved into our pasts. We were both raised by single moms, though mine was alive and great, and hers had died years ago and had always done more drugs than parenting. We were both that rare breed, native Californians: I was from Santa Cruz and a long line of hippie artist types, and she was from Los Angeles and a shorter line of Iranian-Americans who'd immigrated in the '70s and gone on to thrive in the US. At the end of the night, several drinks in, she pushed me up against a wall and stood on tiptoes and kissed me deeply, and I was lost; or maybe I was found.

We lived just a few streets apart, but she'd scored a roomy top-floor apartment without housemates (family money, she said), so we spent most of our time at her place; it was private, and we could be loud. Those first weeks after meeting someone and really connecting are so good: it's like you've just discovered this vast new world called "sex" and you're determined to explore every archipelago and peninsula. We also just fit each other – everything she liked, I liked, and vice-versa, a perfect-circle-Venn-diagram of consensual depravity. When we weren't having the best kinky sex of my life, we slurped noodles, and watched movies like Train to Busan, and worked on our laptops side-by-side, and took walks in Tilden Park, and weekended away in Sonoma, and lay companionably reading books covered with bright yellow interlibrary loan stickers… and we fell in love.

She left on two short-notice trips that first year we spent together, and once, I saw a ghost that looked like her.

Four months into our relationship, I came over for our usual work-and-hang-out evening, and found her shoving things into a black overnight bag. "I have to go to Texas. My aunt died – my mom's older sister. We weren't close, but I have to go down and show the flag for my side of the family."

I knew her mom had passed away and she'd never really known her dad, but she still had a sprawling family split between Texas and LA. "How long will you be gone?"

She didn't pause in her packing flurry. "Two days? Three, maybe, if my cousins guilt me into helping them clean out her place. Her house is way out in the country, and last time I was there, my phone service was non-existent, so don't worry if you can't reach me. I'll text when I can." She kissed my cheek and grabbed her bag and whooshed away.

That was the first time since our first date that we hadn't spoken daily, and I was surprised by how vast her absence felt. Two nights later, sleeping in my bed, something jolted me awake and I blinked in the darkness. Vivy was beside my bed, leaning over and looking down at me, but she was pale and translucent, like an image projected on a sheer curtain. "Vivy?" I blinked, and she was gone. I shivered in the dark and felt pathetic, missing my girlfriend so hard I hallucinated her phantom.

The next day she texted home, come over, and I was out the door before I'd even sent a reply. She opened the door and grabbed me and pulled me in and kissed me hard, and I happily followed her to bed. She pulled my clothes off, and then her own, and I devoured her body with my eyes as I always did when she failed to blindfold me... but something was different. I knew her form well, having seen it naked basically every day for months, and she looked leaner than before, her muscles more defined, her soft sweet stomach more firm, and there was a little scar on her hip I didn't remember, but it looked long healed.

"What's wrong?" she said, since I wasn't doing everything she told me to do with my usual alacrity.

I lifted my gaze to hers. "I don't know. You just seem different somehow, like..." I could tell I was walking into a potential minefield of missteps, and trailed off.

She made a pfft sound. "Less pudgy? I was just carrying a lot of water weight last week. I was bloaty. Plus I hauled a bunch of boxes at my aunt's house." She curled her arm and popped her bicep. "I got swole."

"In three days?" I said.

"Are you supposed to be using your mouth for talking right now?" She put her hand on top of my head and pushed me down. The nature of our sex life was: she told me what to do and I did it, and we were both delighted with the arrangement, even if my satisfaction often took the form of extended frustration. Sorry if that's too much information, but understanding the rudiments of our dynamic now will help later developments make more sense. I won't go into excessive detail; for one thing, I'd get distracted, and this would turn into amateur erotica instead of the epic tale of clashing philosophies it's meant to be.

"Six months," Vivy said on the morning of the day. "Quite a milestone. We should do something to celebrate it. It's our demi-anniversary."

"Like a half-birthday?" We'd celebrated her half-birthday the month before in a little bed-and-breakfast with a hot tub. The experience had been wonderful and exhausting, and much more "bed" than "breakfast" (and much more "floor" than "bed.")

"Any excuse to celebrate. How would you feel about getting matching tattoos?" Vivy had a few tattoos already, abstract swirling things on the small of her back and behind one ear and laced around her ankle. I didn't have any, but I'd been thinking about getting one for years.

"What did you have in mind?"

"Something that won't be totally embarrassing if we end up breaking up someday?"

"So not 'Property of Vivy' in Gothic script across my stomach then?"

She snorted a laugh, then opened up a little notebook she carried around. "I was thinking of something like this." She showed me a little symbol, nothing I recognized, all sinuous curves around a pointed star, a little like Celtic knotwork overlaying Moorish tile.

"It's beautiful. What is it?"

"Something I saw in a dream. I was thinking, we could get them on our wrists…"

So we did, taking turns at the tattoo parlor with her favorite artist, and when we held hands after, I felt more connected to her than ever. A few days later she told me she had to go out of town again – her most no-account cousin had used his inheritance to start a serious drug habit, and they needed her help for purposes of an intervention and getting said cousin into rehab. I offered to go with her, but she laughed and said, "This is not the way I want you to meet my family."

"Speaking of," I said. "My mother is dying to meet you." Mom lived down in Santa Cruz, just ninety minutes away, and though I visited her every couple of months, Vivy hadn't yet made the trip with me.

She made a face. "What if she hates me?"

"She'll love you. All she's ever wanted is for me to be happy."

"Then we've got that in common. We'll talk about it when I get back." She kissed my cheek and left.

Two days later, I was working in the library when my wrist suddenly pulsed with… not pain, exactly, but pressure, and a sensation of heat. I looked at my arm, and the black tattoo seemed to glitter, like it had gone from flat ink to an onyx inlay, but then the sparkle faded, and I blinked and rubbed my eyes. Maybe I'd been studying too hard.

My phone buzzed: home, come. I packed up and hurried over to Vivy's place, and when I went inside at first I thought she had a visitor, because the woman standing with her back to me had long hair in a multitude of braids. Then she turned, and it was Vivy, and she swept across me and had her way.

Afterward I said, "Your hair?"

She laughed and touched a dangling strand. "Oh, yeah. My cousin – not junkie cousin, his sister – took us for a 'girls' day' and we got these woven in. Ridiculous, huh?"

"They look totally real."

"For what they cost, they'd better." She snuggled up to me all sweet and told me she'd missed me, and started talking about a conference she hoped to attend in Helsinki next summer, and did I think I could get away to go with her. Then she suddenly sat up. "I forgot, I got you something!" She went to her bag and fished out a short length of silver chain. When I examined it, I saw it wasn't a round chain but a flattened strip of metal, and twisted like a Möbius strip. I couldn't even see a clasp. "I want you to wear this," she said. "So even when we're apart, you'll know you're mine." I held out my arm, and she shook her head. "No, it goes around your ankle." She bent and fastened the chain around my left ankle, and I held up my leg to watch it glitter. A symbolic chain. Sweet and hot. "It'll look so cute with those little red heels we got you," she said. (I don't talk about it much, except with close friends and intimate partners, but I figured out many years ago that I'm genderfluid, and Vivy is very gay, so we often indulge my femboy side, to our mutual delight.)

I agreed, but I still couldn't see how the chain unclasped, not that I had the best vantage with it around my ankle. "How do I get it off?"

"Now, now. You should never take it off at all. If it ever needs to be removed, I'll take care of it."

Mmm. "I love it when you talk to me like that."

She moved in close and rubbed her nose against mine. "I know you do."

Two months later, we were spending one of our rare nights apart, because I had a cold, and with all the sniffling and coughing, I wasn't fit to share a bed with anyone. I was just dosing myself with heavy-duty cough medicine so I could get some ugly uneven sleep when my phone buzzed. Vivy, texting: family emergency, back in a couple of days, love you, be good.

Her cousins are such a shit-show, I thought, and went to sleep. I stayed home in my room the next day slurping soup and sipping tea and watching movies on my laptop, and the day after that was much the same, though my throat was no longer ringed with fishhooks and my cough had gone from chronic to occasional, and I could even breathe through one nostril reliably. I decided it would be a good idea to actually get dressed, and once I managed that, I was considering taking a walk around the block because I'd been cooped up for too long, when my wrist pulsed with heat.

I looked at the tattoo, and it was definitely glittering, and then it... peeled off my skin, and levitated above my wrist. I stared at it, totally baffled; it was like a holographic projector from a science fiction movie. The symbol floated out in front of me, expanded, widened, and rotated in the air until it hung before me, a star at the center of sinuous swirls, easily six feet high and just as wide, and then the lines warped and curved, reaching out, and wrapped around me–

I stumbled and fell to my knees on a gray metal floor, the ground tilted at a slight but noticeable angle, and I gurgled because I couldn't breathe, because there was no air – I was sucking at nothing. Something cool touched the back of my neck, and I gasped, sucking in great gulps of the fresh rich air that suddenly surrounded me. I struggled to my feet and stared. At Vivy.

She stood there, dressed in a black leather-like outfit not unlike the ones she wore on stay-at-home date nights (strappy, shiny, body-hugging), but without the strategically bare areas those outfits usually sported. This looked like a costume you could do extreme sports in, shifted hard to the right on the "fetishwear-to-body-armor" scale. She held something like a telescoping baton, but with a ball of crackling blue electricity at one end – a scepter of lightning. She looked like a cyberpunk angel of death in a video game that maybe catered a little too much to the hetero male gaze.

Vivy looked at me. "Well, crap," she said.

TAMSIN

There was a business card stuck in the crack between the door and the frame when I got home from another too-long day at the office. I plucked the card out, annoyed, assuming it was some stupid advertisement, but the thick black old-fashioned lettering caught my eye:

BOLLARD AND CHICANE

Obstacles Removed • Burdens Shifted • Troubles Untroubled
"We Murder Problems!"

With a phone number underneath.

There was small, neat, and slanted handwriting on the back, in pen: Dear Tamsin: Our condolences on the loss of your grandmother. We can help settle your estate. Call soonest.

"Granny isn't dead," I said to no one, and then my phone buzzed with an incoming call.

With the travel, and the funeral, and the lawyers, and the police investigation, and having to take time off work (and of course the startup where I worked as a project manager was getting ready for its IPO, and of course "my grandmother died" sounded like a college-student-level excuse, although "my grandmother was murdered in a home invasion" was a little different), it was a few days before I actually made it to Culver House.

The ancestral manse stood on the edge of a sagging damp town in the Midwest, where I grew up and lived until I fled to college. I hadn't been back there in the six years since, because why would I return? My only living family was Granny, brilliant and independent and remote and endlessly annoyed at raising little orphaned me. I didn't come back for holidays because she didn't celebrate any, calling them "American fripperies," even Christmas and Easter. "Granny, they celebrate Christmas back in Croatia too," I would argue, and Granny would say, "Not in the part I'm from, they don't."

I sat behind the desk in my grandmother's study that evening and opened the top drawer as the attorney had instructed, revealing an envelope with Tamsin scrawled across the front. My legacy, or at least, the non-monetary part of it; I'd gotten the other part already. The extra money I was expecting to make when the startup went public seemed a bit less exciting now that I'd inherited my genius Granny's considerable estate.

The envelope had been torn open, though, and instead of a letter from the woman who'd raised me at a very long arm's length, I found a business card, another version of the one I'd discovered at my house. This one said:

BOLLARD AND CHICANE
Pests Removed • Offenses Redressed • Knives Sharpened
"Your Enemies Are Ours!"

On the back, in that same neat handwriting, I read: You really should call us, miss. Mr B.

Okay, then. First I called my high school boyfriend Trevor, who still lived in town and had a tattoo of a snake eating its tail around his neck, and liked guns. I'd dated him mostly to annoy Granny, but he'd been fun, the way doing meth and committing arson are probably fun. I'd dated a few people since then, though not as many as you might think – I was focused on my studies in college, and on killing it at work after that – but while they'd all been smarter than Trevor, none had been as devoted, and he still had a thing for me. "I think I might have some trouble over at the house, Trev," I said. "I could use a hand."

"Anything for you, Sin. I'll be right there." He hung up without asking any questions. That's a good quality, sometimes.

Then I called the number on the card. A voice so deep and sonorous it sounded like a yeti with a head cold said, "Miss Culver. It's an interesting last name, Culver. There are various possible origins. The old English 'culfre,' meaning dove, possibly used as a term of endearment. Or the French 'couleuvre,' meaning snake. Or it could be related to 'culverin,' a kind of early handgun, a precursor of the musket, and later the name for a cannon. Which do you think your grandmother was thinking of when she chose that name for a new life in a new world?"

I could not have given fewer shits about the etymology of my surname. "Who is this?"

"This is Mr Bollard. My associate, Mr Chicane, is here as well." I heard a scraping in the background, and a clatter, and then Mr Bollard sighed, but not, I think, at me.

"I don't want to know your name," I snapped. "I want to know why you left me business cards, why you broke into my grandmother's desk, and what you took from me." The lawyer who'd handed over the keys said Granny had left a precious family heirloom sealed in the envelope in the desk drawer, but he didn't know any further details.

"All excellent questions," Bollard said. "But you should ask a different one first. You should ask: 'Where are you, Mr Bollard?'"

"Fuck off," I said.

"I'll pretend you replied 'Where are you,'" Bollard said. "I'll also pretend you didn't inherit your grandmother's poor manners. If you'd asked me what I asked you to ask me, I would have replied: 'We are here. We are in the basement. We are waiting by the door.'"

"I'm calling the police," I said.

"Why? Do you want Mr Chicane to murder a bunch of perfectly nice police officers? We don't want to hurt you. We just want your help. It's in your best interest to assist us. Your grandmother wasn't helpful at all, and look what happened to her. Now. Are you coming down, or shall I send Mr Chicane up to... fetch you?"

I ended the call and picked up Granny's letter opener – actually a misericorde from the thirteenth century, a slender knife designed to stab through the gaps in a knight's armor. It was just like Granny to use a priceless antique to open bills and junk mail. I held the knife tight and crept to the study door, listening.

There was plenty to hear, because Culver House is a rambling three-story Victorian with various newer additions, and it creaked and groaned and settled constantly, especially up here on the top floor. If some of those creaks were the mysterious Mr Chicane coming to get me, I couldn't tell. I decided to call the police anyway. It would probably take them half an hour to show up, but at least if I got murdered before then, the cops would know the names and phone number of my murderers... and probably Granny's killers, too. I dialed 911, and Bollard answered. "I don't want to murder any police officers either," he said. "No one is paying me to do that today. Please come downstairs. You're wasting time."

"Why aren't you the cops?" I sputtered.

"Your grandmother had access to technology she didn't sell to the government or Silicon Valley, miss, and some of it has wonderful applications, like intercepting calls and rerouting them. We–"

I cut the connection again. At least I'd gotten through to Trev. He'd show up faster than the cops, but in the meantime, I didn't want stay in the study, where this Bollard and Chicane would probably look for me first.

I went onto the landing, then down the stairs to the second floor, and on past my old room, left unchanged since I departed

– not as any sort of shrine, but because Granny didn't care about any part of the house other than the kitchen, her own bedroom, and her study... and the basement, which I had literally never entered, because that's where Granny did her experiments and invented her inventions, and it was too dangerous, too delicate, and always locked. I'd been interested in finally getting a look at her lab now that I owned it, but the presence of probably-murderers down there did a lot to dampen my curiosity.

I went down the second-floor hall toward the back stairs, where I could descend to the kitchen and slip out the side door and get away.

There was a man at the bottom of the stairs, looking up at me. My body was already fizzing with fight-or-flight chemicals, and seeing a stranger in the house made my brain feel like it was going to vibrate out of my skull.

The intruder was thin, dressed in a baggy tweed suit, and had a big head sprouting irregular tufts of hair. There was dried blood crusted all down one side of his face. When he saw me, he did a little capering dance in place, hooting and giggling, then pointed one long finger at me and suddenly froze.

"Mr Chicane?" I guessed.

He didn't answer. He teetered, and I thought he was going to fall, but then he leapt forward, scampering up the stairs on all fours like a bounding dog.

I clutched Granny's knife and stepped back, but Chicane was so fast, he barreled into me and drove me to the ground before I could ready any real defense. The impact knocked the breath out of my body and the misericorde out of my hand. He hooted in delight as I struggled to get away. Up close, I could see his features were all lumpy and potato-like, his eyes at different heights on his face, his nose mostly just two holes in his face, his lips thin, his chin nonexistent. Under all the old blood, I could see a cratered dent in the side of his head big enough to stick a thumb into. He seemed like a badly made doll of a person.

He was strong, though, all cords and wires and bony limbs. He pinned both my wrists to the floor over my head with one hand, giggled in my face, and reached into his jacket with his free hand. I thrashed and twisted, expecting a gun, a blade, or a hypodermic needle – but instead he took out a business card, and held it inches above my face. I had to cross my eyes a little to read it, but once it came into focus, it said:

BOLLARD AND CHICANE
Murder • Arson • Regime Change
"We Always Make A Killing!"

I took a deep breath, which required breathing in his raw-meat-and-onion reek. I could believe he'd killed Granny. I could easily believe I was next. Everything in me rebelled against giving in – I inherited a wide stubborn streak from Granny – but even I had my limits. "Okay! I give! What do you want from me?"

Chicane deftly flipped over the card, revealing another handwritten message: We need to open a door. We have one key. You have the other. Join us downstairs.

"I don't have a key!" I shouted.

Chicane tapped me on the end of the nose with the business card and waggled his eyebrows and grinned. His teeth were wrong: too numerous, too sharp, too many colors. He was drooling, and if I stayed under him much longer, that drool would drip onto my face.

"I'll come down!" I said, turning my face away from his stinking mouth.

I heard a hollow metallic thonk. Chicane collapsed on top of me, then rolled off bonelessly. He had a new dent on the other side of his head, deeper than the first one. I wriggled away, snatched my knife from the floor, and faced my savior.

Trevor stood at the top of the stairs, holding an aluminum baseball bat. He was wearing dirty jeans and a white undershirt and his boots were untied – he must have rushed over here as soon as I called.

I hugged him hard, because Trevor always responded well to physical encouragement. "Trev! Thank you, thank you, thank you for coming." I looked at Chicane and kicked him in the side, but he didn't stir.

"Of course I came," he said. "It's you and me. TNT."

Oh god, I'd forgotten that nickname he had for us: "TNT. First we get hot, and then we explode." Teenage horniness is so embarrassing.

His face got serious. "I'm real sorry about your granny. Who's this little weasel?"

"I think his name is Chicane, but–"

Trevor took a step back. "Chicane. As in… Bollard and Chicane?"

"You know them?" Trev knew plenty of local scum, but Bollard and Chicane sure didn't seem local.

"Do I…" His eyes got all glazed and faraway. "Bollard and Chicane. The Two of Them. The Crush and the Bite. The Bad Neighbors. The Ones Who Come After. The Ones Who Come After You." He shook himself and focused on me. "Do I know them? Do you know the boogeyman? Do you know the monster under the bed? I mean – they're from the old country. They shouldn't be here."

"The old country? You mean Croatia?"

"Croatia?" He blinked at me, then looked back at the man on the floor. "Your grandmother never told you? You, wow, it shouldn't be me, I'm not the one who's supposed to–"

Trev had never been the most articulate person. Clarity wasn't one of the things I'd ever needed or demanded from him before, but I grabbed him by the shoulders and shook him. "Start. Making. Sense."

His focus snapped to me. "If that's Chicane, then Bollard is still around, so… first we need to get out of here. Then… I'll tell you everything I know." He looked away. "About where you're really from, Sin."

GLENN

Vivy looked around, and when I started to speak, she shushed me. "Wait here." She stalked down the corridor (at least I think it was a corridor), her sparkling weapon at the ready.

I looked around. There was a small round window set in the wall across the corridor, so I walked over, and peered in, and... I saw stars there. I also saw part of a planet. It wasn't Earth. Earth wasn't mostly a dusky rose color. It wasn't Mars, either, though. Mars didn't have oceans. Maybe I was dreaming. People in stories always think they're dreaming when stuff like this happens to them, but it didn't feel like a dream, and anyway, my dreams about Vivy were usually way different.

Vivy flattened herself against the wall, then slowly peeked around the curved metal corner at the end of the passageway. She tensed up for a moment, then pulled her head back and slumped her shoulders.

"What's wrong?" I whispered. Obviously many things were wrong, and I would have accepted explanations for any of them.

She didn't whisper back, but her voice was flat and gray. "I was hoping I'd missed one, and that something would try to kill us."

That was both too informational and too vague. "What? Why?"

Vivy turned to face me, shoulders still slumped. "Because that would be less awkward than the conversation we're about to have instead. Plus, if I saved your life, maybe you'd be less furious with me about... all this."

I nodded. I was paying a lot of attention to my own reactions, and they didn't seem appropriate. I was mad, because she'd clearly kept a huge secret from me – I would have remembered if she'd mentioned high-tech weapons or spaceships – and that made sense, but considering I'd just been teleported by a magic tattoo, I should have been a lot more upset. In fact, "mad" should have been, at best, number four on the intensity-of-emotions scale, somewhere after shock, terror, and confusion... none of which I was feeling. "I... don't feel furious, exactly."

Vivy nodded. "Yeah. You probably feel pretty steady. That's because of the patch." She patted the back of her neck.

I reached back and felt something smooth and cool, about the size of a silver dollar, right at the base of my neck. It was like a sticker but thicker. "What patch?"

"It's an emergency life support system, providing you with breathable air, and also some mood-levelers. It's battlefield tech, mostly meant for use on civilians who find themselves in... bad situations."

I sniffed, and then sniffed harder, through both nostrils. "I can breathe fine. My cold is gone."

She nodded. "Right. The patch does some basic medical work too, mostly geared toward stabilizing trauma, but it also kills off infectious agents. It's no use rescuing people if they bring some engineered pathogen back to base with you."

I sat down on the floor, leaning into the curve of the wall. "Vivy."

"Yeah?"

I gave her my blankest stare. "Vivy."

"Yes. Right. Okay." She slid down the wall to sit beside me, her weird scepter no longer sparking and laid across her knees. She sat close to me but didn't touch me, which I appreciated. "So. Should I do the who, what, when, where, and why?"

"That would be a good start."

"The where is, we're in another world."

"Is my tattoo a spaceship? Or a teleportation ray?" I could hear how flat my own voice was, but I couldn't seem to do anything about it. I had a bad temper as a teenager, and ever since then, I've always put a wall between myself and my anger, to keep that old rage from spilling out like a flood of acid and dissolving everything in my life. Even with mood-levelers in my system, there was something dark rising in me; the drugs just made it feel remote.

She looked at the tattoo on her wrist, tracing it with a fingertip. "Neither. You could call your tattoo an anchor, but really it's just... one end of an invisible thread. My matching tattoo is the other end. I go places, and do things, and sometimes I go very far away, and it can be hard to find my way back home. I need a beacon. Since I met you... you've been my beacon, Glenn. You're what I follow, to find my way back. I don't even need the tattoo, usually – the intensity of my feelings for you is a strong enough connection for me to follow home, as long as I don't go too far. A while back, though, I had to go deep, and I almost couldn't find my way back again at all. You know how you saw that ghost?"

I nodded. I'd told her about my phantom Vivy visitation.

"That wasn't a ghost. That was me, reaching for you, and not quite being able to connect. I was just too far away. I ended up snapping to... call it an adjacent place. Not home, but a lot closer to home than I was when I started. From there, I was able to feel you strongly enough to come home directly. But nobody likes layovers, so I suggested we get these tattoos, to strengthen the connection. I switched the artist's ink to some with special properties. It worked wonders. No more ghosts. In addition to being romantic as hell, getting matching tattoos with entangled particles in the ink strengthens the connection between us for..." She extended her hand and made a quick fist. "It's called a snap-trace. This method of travel, I mean. I reach for you, and snap back to your location, wherever you are."

"If you're supposed to snap to me, then why did I come to you?"

"That's because of fuckery," she said. "I finished up my mission, and tried to snap home from here, but I didn't realize the enemy had hit me with a fixative. That's a weapon that prevents quick escapes, binds me here, sort of like I'm magnetized and stuck to a metal hull... or maybe in a glue trap. So when I grabbed that thread between us, and pulled on it to reel me back to you, I was an immovable object, and instead of yanking me toward you, it pulled you to me, on this plane, instead."

I looked around. "This is not a plane. Unless it's a plane that flies in outer space. I saw the window."

She winced. "Yeah, no, this is a wrecked starship. But I meant plane, like, plane of existence. This isn't our, you know. Home reality. Remember that stupid movie we saw about the multiverse? Oh, and also that other good movie, later on?"

I groaned. "I knew we were in outer space. But it's not even outer space in our universe?"

She nodded. "The multiverse isn't quite like the movies, though. Either of the movies. The way it was explained to me is, reality is like a ream of paper, okay?" She held out her hands, one laid on top of the other. "You live on top of one sheet of paper. Your planet, your stars, your galaxy, your universe. That's all on one side of one sheet. There's another side to that sheet, and that side is a whole world of its own, too – a whole universe. Those worlds are as close as it gets. There's also another sheet underneath yours, and another sheet above you, and on and on. The sheets are very close together, but they're all separate. Every one has a universe on both sides. The stack of paper might be infinite, too. We're not sure. No one has ever reached an end in either direction, but when you go far enough, the physical constants of those universes start to change, and after a while, the basic physics get so bizarre that not even hardened probes can survive the transition and come back intact. Even if the multiverse isn't infinite, there's still a huge stack of universes that are, at least in terms of physics, basically like our own, and most of them are inhabited, to some degree, by somebody. People in the know call that swath of inhabited universes Nigh-Space – 'near-space,' basically, but I guess 'nigh' sounded more fancy to the people who came up with the name."

I digested that, or tried, but it was a big meal, and it was going to take a while. "When you say 'we'?"

"Right. That's the 'who' of it all. I work with some other... let's say people... to preserve and protect and improve life all over Nigh-Space. That also covers the 'what' and the 'why,' I think."

I stared at her for a while.

"Well?" she said.

"This is just a lot, Vivy. I thought you were studying public policy."

She brightened. "I am! Studying it, and enacting it. The group I work for is called the Interventionists. We... nudge things in good directions." She paused. "Does that answer the basic questions?"

"Who, what, where, and why, sure. What about when? How long have you been doing this?"

She squinted thoughtfully. "The Interventionists recruited me when I was a teenager. I had certain aptitudes. Tendencies. They pretended they were a government agency for a while, until I was sufficiently prepared to understand what they really were."

"So... you've been lying to me for our whole relationship."

She nodded. I liked that, anyway – she made no attempt to defend herself or dismiss me. "I have. Not just to you. To everyone. I'm basically a spy, living in deep cover. That's not the kind of thing you bring up on a first date, or a tenth date, or even on your demi-anniversary. I wouldn't get married or have kids or even move in together without disclosing the truth, but anything less committed than that..." She shrugged.

"I know I handled this all wrong. I'm really sorry. I didn't intend for you to find out this way."

I rolled my eyes. "How did you want me to find out?"

"For our actual anniversary. I was going to take you to the Realm of Orbital Glories and expand your universe. In several ways."

I looked at her closely. "Really? You were going to tell me about this? You were going to show me?"

She took my hand, and I let her, provisionally. "I was. We're starting to feel like… a forever thing, these last few months, and I've wanted to tell you a dozen times, but I was trying to be responsible. I had to get permission from my bosses to tell you first, or else risk upsetting people it's very bad to upset. Do you hate me now? Are we done?" She looked away. "I'll get you home, of course, I'll keep you safe, but after that, if you… I hope you don't, but… I'd understand."

"I… This is a lot to think about, Vivy."

She nodded, and squeezed my hand again. I didn't squeeze back, but I didn't pull my hand away either. That was the best I could do.

I decided to focus on the immediate issues. "So if I'm your anchor, your beacon or whatever that guides you back home… and I'm here with you… how do we get back to our plane, realm, planet, house?"

She sighed. "We go the long way around."

The ship we were on was hopelessly broken – I gathered Vivy had done the breaking – but her own smaller ship was in a nearby hangar. "You were just going to leave your ship here when you snapped back to me?" I asked. "Are spaceships in this world like those little electric scooters you rent and just leave on the sidewalk when you're done?"

"Ha, no, but my ship knows the way home." She led me through empty, ash-strewn corridors, until we reached a large and mostly empty hangar. Her vessel looked like a dragonfly crossed with a stealth jet, and was about the size of a van. When she opened the cockpit door, there was only one seat inside, but then the interior flowed and changed and suddenly there were two seats, one with controls in front, one without.

"Who's this?" the ship said, in a tenor voice as human as mine. "Doesn't look like a local."

Vivy said, "This is Glenn. You know. I told you about him."

"We're bringing Glenn to work with us now?" The ship sounded amused.

"Your ship. Is talking," I said.

Vivy shook her head. "He's not mine. He's his own. We're partners. Glenn, meet The Wreck of the Edmund Pevensie. You can call him Eddie."

"Welcome aboard," Eddie said. "So, they hit you with a fixative, huh, Viv, and now we've got a snapback situation."

"That's why you're the hotshot analyst, Eddie." Vivy climbed into the ship... guy... and I did the same, my seat shifting around to accommodate me on contact until it felt like being held in a vast, gentle hand. "Can you shield us during extraction?" Vivy asked.

"Mmm," Eddie said. "Mostly. I'll go real fast to make up the difference."

"Shield us from what?" I said.

"Evil ghosts that eat your bones," Eddie said.

Vivy smacked the console. "Eddie. Don't be like that."

"What, the people where he's from are like class two, right?"

"They know what radiation is on Earth, Eddie."

"Oh. Okay." Eddie paused. "Then I'm shielding us from radiation."

The ship rose and spun – I couldn't feel any motion, weirdly, but I could see the movement through the glass, or screens, or whatever – and we faced one of the dark metal walls, which flowed and rippled to make an oblong opening the ship darted through. Space. I was in space.

Then I frowned. "Eddie. Your name is a reference to things from my world, unless C.S. Lewis and Gordon Lightfoot are extradimensional entities."

"You gotta wonder a little about Lewis," Eddie said. "I actually know a guy who uses a wardrobe to travel to the immediately adjacent level of Nigh-Space. Well, technically it's a chiffonier, but–"

I interrupted. "My point is, you know about the world I come from, so you know we're familiar with the concept of radiation."

"Well spotted," Eddie said. "I was just being a jerk. Vivy said you were smart."

The screens went black, hiding the stars before I could even properly appreciate them. "I was enjoying that," I said. "The view was the only part of this experience I've enjoyed at all."

"Eddie had to extrude some extra shielding," Vivy said. "Believe me, you don't want even a little dose of what's flying around out there. We were sent here to deal with a Hollower infestation. They're solar parasites. Creatures that crawl inside a star and suck up its energy, hiding inside the corona. The infested star still puts out the usual light and heat and radiation... but it starts to put out lots of other things, too. Hollower waste products include mutagens and teratogens. Just looking at the visible wavelengths exposes you to poison."

"Plus evil mind-control rays," Eddie said.

"Sort of," Vivy said. "Any creature with an organic brain in the vicinity starts to behave very aggressively against anyone who approaches the star. It's some kind of defense mechanism, probably – the Hollower turns the locals into guards. Fortunately, this infected star wasn't in an inhabited system, but unfortunately, there was a ship nearby, and the crew was affected. We came to try to cure them, but..." She shook her head. "They were too far gone. They tried to destroy us, so I had to board and stop them."

Whoa. "Wait... you killed them?"

"Of course not!" She seemed genuinely shocked. "They're sick, Glenn, not my enemies."

"Yeah, it's not like they were S-Cons or Prime Army or Star Cauldron," Eddie chimed in, I assumed just to confuse me. "They were just unlucky, not jerks or fascists or zealots. Vivy deals with those a bit differently."

"Every mission has its own requirements," she began, but Eddie interrupted her.

"The thing about our Vivian is, she's like a knife," he said. "A knife is versatile. It's all about who's wielding it, and what they intend. You can use a knife to cut out a tumor, or slash someone's throat, or prepare a meal—"

"Hopefully you wash it off first," she interrupted right back. "There were no knives involved in this situation. I put the affected crew members in stasis. I'm not saying I didn't crimp a pseudopod or two in the process, but there were no casualties. A properly shielded medical ship is on the way to pick up the crew, to see if they can be saved."

"What about the parasite? Are you going to fight that next?" I was imagining a titanic space battle with some sort of stellar whale-kraken-worm.

"It's a horrible giant energy being that lives inside a star," Vivy said. "I punch aliens, but that's not an alien on a punchable scale. All we can do with Hollowers is save the locals and then interdict the system to keep people away."

"Which is to say, our work here is done," Eddie said. " I assume you two aren't going to settle down on this plane, so where are we going? A local hub?"

"That's the best we can do," Vivy said.

"There are going to be S-Cons there."

"Oh, you think?" Vivy never sounded that sarcastic with me, and I was glad, because her tone was pure acid.

I knew I should be interested in what they were talking about – space travel and mysterious threats and getting home – but now that I had time to sit and stare at a blank wall, all I could think about was me, and her, and us.

Vivy had been the axis of a beautiful world, and now that axis had shifted. I wanted to talk to her about what this revelation meant for us, about how everything we did was based on trust – even more so than a typical monogamous relationship, because of the nature of our kink, which required me to have faith in her absolutely, and often put me in a position of profound vulnerability, physically and psychologically – but I couldn't say any of that with the ship listening in. So I just stared at the blankness where a view of space should have been, thinking how sad it was that even my one opportunity to voyage among the stars and see the wonders of the galaxy (or anyway a galaxy) was spoiled.

Vivy patted my leg. "We're going to a transfer point on this plane, where we can move a few levels closer to our home universe. Once we've closed the gap a bit, we'll try to do a snap-trace back home, using some other anchor."

"What anchor?" I asked.

"Something else I love."

"You're saying interdimensional travel is literally powered by love?" I said.

Eddie chuckled. "An anchor needs to be something deeply imprinted in your memory, with a lot of specific associated glandular and electrochemical brain activity swirling around it, and yeah, it needs to be something you really, really want to return to. That level of devotion is what allows the snap-trace to work with any precision. Doesn't have to be romantic love, or even love for a person, but it needs to be a deep attachment that's connected to an actual thing in an actual place. Something you sorta-kinda-like isn't good enough. If you try to snap-trace to something you're vaguely fond of, either nothing will happen, or you'll end up embedded in a wall next door to the object of your mild affection, or as a ghostly projection watching it from three levels up or down."

"Okay, so let's think about anchors," I said. "What else do you love?"

Vivy said hmm. "I like that one café we go to sometimes, with the good Americanos. What's it called?"

"It you don't even remember the place's name, you can't love it enough to use it for an anchor," Eddie said. "You'll end up a ghost smeared across the ceiling again."

"Look, I haven't been in Berkeley all that long." Vivy scowled. "I haven't, like, gotten attached."

"I'd be happy to get to any town," I said. "Isn't there someone else you love? One of your cousins?"

Eddie chuckled again. I pushed the heel of my hand against my forehead. "Right. There are no cousins. They're your cover story."

"Yeah. I mean. On the bright side, you won't have to meet them, since they're imaginary. Sorry, babe."

"Don't babe me. Who was your anchor before me?"

Eddie laughed again, and Vivy shot him a nasty look. "I had a cat. Gummitch. But he died just before I moved to Berkeley."

"A cat." My voice was all flat again. "Did you tattoo your cat?"

She half-smiled. "No, there was a little charm on his collar, and I had a matching necklace."

I shook my head. "You didn't have a cat anymore, so you got me. I'm a replacement. For your cat."

Vivy groaned. "No, you aren't. I was going to get another cat, and hope we bonded fast. Instead, I met you, and we bonded fast, faster than I ever have with another human being. I usually do a lot better with cats, to be honest. With this connection to you, I can traverse scores of levels – the most I ever managed with Gummitch was about a dozen."

I wanted to be dramatically wounded some more, but instead, I took a breath. "Is there really nobody else? No close connections you can think of? Don't you have anything in your life you care about except me and a dead cat?"

She went icy, and not in the sexy way. "Eddie, I'm going to call ahead to our contacts at the hub, and make sure the way is clear." An opaque blue sphere suddenly enveloped her head, like a fishbowl helmet painted to match the sky, and she leaned back in her chair.

"Vivy," I said. "Hey, Vivy, I'm sorry, I just–"

"She can't hear you," Eddie said. "Isolation field. Immersive communication in a fully realized virtual environment." He paused. "Look, your whole... thing... with Viv is not my business, but just so you know, the kind of people who get chosen to work for the Interventionists... they aren't people with a lot of close relationships. Orphans and loners with authority issues fit the profile best. When I met Viv, she was basically an impenetrable shell full of infinite rage, and over the years I've watched her become a person who believes in the power of positive change, and more recently, I've seen her become a person capable of love. You're her first test case for that."

"She's had other partners before," I said. "She told me about them!" Vivy had an enthusiastically pansexual past and I really enjoyed her stories.

"People she had fun with, sure. People she played with, tied up and hit with things, played the goddess for – yeah, I know what you get up to, meat people are so strange. She liked those people, or disliked them in enjoyable ways, but they were never her anchor. That's you. She's learning how to love, and she's going to mess up sometimes. You can tell her to leave you alone after you get home, and she'll accept that. She's great at cutting things off. Nobody compartmentalizes like our Viv. But if you leave her, I think she'll vanish into that shell again. That part of her that reached out to you and sought a connection? She'll chop it off and cauterize the ends. If you decide what she's done is unforgivable, she'll believe you, and she'll never forgive herself. We'll be lucky if she even bonds with a cat again after that. We might be reduced to using a houseplant as her anchor. Or a really good sandwich." He paused. "Also, she's telling the truth. She did ask our bosses for permission to clue you in. She's been planning the big reveal for weeks. So, it's your choice, but I've got my own opinions about what you should do, and I'm a lot smarter than you."

I thought about that for a while. While I was thinking, Eddie said, "We're clear of the radiation field," and opened the windows. Stars hung in the dark, small and sharp and white, and close and vast and blue. Ribbons of dust shone and shimmered like aurorae, and far off, something like lightning crackled and sparked among dark irregular forms that must have been asteroids or wrecked ships. I gasped and reached out unthinkingly for Vivy's hand, and her isolation field flickered off.

"God, your face," she said. "Seeing something like this for the first time is wonderful, but seeing your face as you see it for the first time is even better."

"I love you, Vivy." I squeezed her hand and looked at all that light in the darkness.

"Are you still mine?" I almost never heard anxiety in her voice, and the flutter I perceived there pierced my heart.

"I am," I said. "If you'll keep me. We've got some stuff to work out, but I don't mind a little work."

"I've noticed–" she began, but then the ship was torn apart and her hand was wrenched out of mine, and we went spinning apart into the glittering dark.

TAMSIN

Trevor and I went down the stairs and out the side door without any bother from Bollard, who was presumably waiting for Chicane to bring me down to the basement. We rode ten minutes in silence in Trevor's truck, then sat in our old booth at the Chickenarium, where the vinyl booths were just as torn and the plastic tables just as battered as they had been when I was in high school. I ordered the chicken and waffles, and he had the chicken-fried steak with fries and cluck sauce. He passed me his flask under the table and I took a slug of something brown that was probably distantly related to bourbon.

"It's time to start making sense." I didn't give him the flask back.

"Your family doesn't come from Croatia," Trev said. "They come from another plane of existence."

I looked down at the flask. "How much of this did you drink already?"

He sighed and sat up straighter, and it was weird – like the slouching, mumbling, all-mischief-and-malice Trev was a costume he'd been wearing, and he'd shrugged it off and let it fall to the floor, revealing someone more serious and formidable underneath. "Listen to me. This world isn't the only world. This universe isn't the only universe. There are others."

"You're talking about many-worlds theory? The multiverse?"

"Sort of. It's not all branchy, one world diverging from another, like you're probably thinking. The way your granny explained it, it's more like reality is a big stack of paper." Trevor pulled a bunch of napkins out of the dispenser and put them on the table in a heap, riffling them as he spoke. "Every piece of paper has a different world on the front and back, so some worlds are closer to others, and some are farther away. We call that whole stack of worlds Nigh-Space. Traveling to sheets of paper farther away in the stack from yours is almost impossible, and even getting to the ones nearby is wicked hard." He picked up a napkin and poked a hole through the middle with a butter knife. "But people with the right technology can punch a hole through a piece of paper and travel from one side to the other. You and your parents and your granny and me... we all come from the world next door, on the other side of the paper from Earth and this universe."

"You're trying to tell me I'm from another world?"

He dipped a fry in some cluck sauce. "You came over with your granny when you were a baby. Or, well, a toddler maybe." He popped the fry in his mouth and chewed.

"Okay, let's say I believe that, but – you come from another world, too?" Trev was many things, but delusional was never one of them. He was a thrill-seeking dirtbag, and he knew it; not an interdimensional traveler.

He chewed glumly. "Yeah. Your granny brought me over when I was twelve and you were ten, and paid off a family to raise me like I was their own."

"You mean... your foster parents."

"That's them." He stirred the sauce with a fry. "My family got into some trouble back home, and they were vassals of your family back in the old days, so somebody called in a favor, and your granny brought me over. The only requirement was, I had to watch over you. Remember when you had trouble with those bullies, and then you... didn't anymore? Stuff like that. It wasn't always easy. I had to screw up real bad in eighth grade, so I could stay in the same school with you instead of going to high school." He touched the snake's head on his throat. "This tattoo is the traditional symbol of fealty to your family. Your granny insisted I get it as soon as I was old enough. She was mad I couldn't get it in middle school."

Vassals? Fealty? I shook my head. "Trev, you're not making any sense. You and me dated. Are you telling me Granny set that up too?"

"No, that part just kinda happened." He grinned. "I couldn't believe you'd look twice at someone like me. Back home, I wasn't even high-status enough to clean out your family's garderobe."

How did Trev know the word "garderobe?" And he'd intentionally messed up his eighth grade year? He'd put a cherry bomb in the principal's desk drawer and clogged up all the toilets in the school that year, among other things. He'd done that for some higher purpose? For me?

Trev kept talking. "When we started going out, your granny mostly thought it was funny, but the relationship was also useful. She made a point of disapproving of me loudly, so you'd like me more. When we were together, I was able to look out for you more easily, not that you needed much help by then. Remember that guy you punched in the throat when he grabbed your ass at the reservoir?"

I cut him off before his grin could emerge again. "Let's forget memory lane for a minute. Go back to this stuff about another world."

He leaned back in the booth. "Oh, sure. Your granny always called it the old country, but we just called it home. It's a lot like Earth, in terms of climate and geography and stuff. I mean, the continents are different, but it's pretty similar in terms of the variety of landscapes. Mountains, deserts, islands, whatever. We have some of the same animals and stuff, and even some linguistic and cultural similarities, because our worlds are so close together, two sides of the same piece of paper, to continue the metaphor."

Yesterday, I would have bet good money that Trevor couldn't even define the word "metaphor," let alone use one to explain higher-dimensional realities.

"There's been some ebb-and-flow between the worlds forever, probably," he went on. "Sometimes there are natural openings, nobody knows why, and they don't last long, but it happens. People who disappear in fields or down caves or through fairy rings or whatever, sometimes they go from one world to the next, and they take their culture with them." He fanned the napkins across the table top. "Probably in like primitive times, people wouldn't even notice, they'd just think they got lost and ended up in a strange valley. Worlds that close together are basically cousins."

This was insane and tedious. "Geography aside, what's it like over there?"

He leaned back in the booth and considered. "The old country is politically regressive by your standards, an oligarchy controlled by a few powerful ruling families, but it's way more advanced than this world technologically. That's how your granny got so rich over here. She brought some of our tech with her when she fled, and sold the least disruptive stuff to the locals."

I didn't believe any of this, but I did like the idea that Granny wasn't the genius she always claimed to be. "Why did she flee in the first place?"

Trevor took a sip of water, and I could tell he was stalling. "I was like five when this stuff happened, so don't expect sophisticated political analysis, but your parents were part of one of those ruling families I mentioned. Some shit went down, assassinations and betrayals and shifting alliances, and your parents got killed in the process. People were hunting for you, too, hoping to exterminate the line, or maybe take you hostage, I don't really know. Your granny decided to take you away someplace you'd be safe until the situation stabilized – she was protecting the heir, you know? Since your family was one of the few with the technology to jump worlds on purpose, she brought you here – someplace really safe. The original idea was to take you back home at some point, to regain your family's power, but the political situation never improved, and she knew going back would be a death sentence. Plus, your granny started to like it over here. There's a lot less hassle and attempted murder, even if the world is pretty primitive by her standards. She told me that, when you were older, she planned to give you the key to the door between worlds and tell you the whole story. Then you could you decide whether to return and try to win back the ancestral vaults and all that, or stay here where it's safe."

My chicken and waffles had gotten cold. "You're telling me I'm a secret princess from another planet, Trevor?"

"That's not quite how I'd put it, but, I mean." He shrugged.

When I was little, I'd sometimes pretended to be a warrior princess. I liked pretty dresses fine, but I wanted a battle axe, too. "Granny asked me to come visit on my next birthday," I said. "My twenty-fifth. She said she was going to unlock my trust fund. 'If you're old enough to rent a car,' she said, 'you're old enough for the keys to the kingdom.'" I shook my head. "Trev, this all sounds ridiculous."

"Bollard and Chicane aren't ridiculous." He leaned over the table, looking at me earnestly. "They're killers and spies and ratfuckers for hire, legendary pieces of shit from the old country, and I don't know who sent them – it must be enemies of your family. Your granny was in touch occasionally with people back home, all real hush-hush, but maybe somebody got word you were coming of age, and decided to kill you both first. Once Bollard and Chicane accept a commission, nothing stops them until it's fulfilled – they're relentless. We have to get out of here before Bollard finds us. I have to keep you safe."

A huge man in a white suit, like a comic book villain or a pretentious novelist, entered the diner and walked ponderously over to the table. In a yeti-with-a-head-cold voice, he said, "Move over, young sir."

Trev stared up at the man. I'd seen Trev attack a guy twice his size with a broken bottle, and charge into a crowd of frat boys while swinging a bicycle chain and laughing, and once he'd bitten a cop – but now he went pale and whimpered and slid over against the wall.

The big man sat down, filling three-quarters of the bench and jostling the table with his bulk. He had a head like a boiled egg and eyes the color of dirt. "My name is Bollard." He tilted his head toward Trev. "Everything your paramour here said about other worlds is true."

Either everyone was insane in the same way, or the world was bigger than I'd realized. "How do you know what he said?"

"More of your grandmother's technology. Your phone has a microphone, and I have been listening through it since you left the house. I wasn't sure where you went – I gather it's possible to track phones, but annoyingly, I don't have that technology on hand, and Mr Chicane, who usually does our tracking, is indisposed. Fortunately, your little internet assured me there was only one restaurant locally that serves whatever 'cluck sauce' is, so I found you once you placed your order." He put his arm around Trev and pulled him close, into something between a side-hug and a headlock. "The young man misunderstands our mission, however. We had no idea you were a secret princess, nor did we know the true identity of your grandmother. So. You're the lost heir to the Zmija estate. How strange to find you here. Like finding a diamond in a dungheap, as the saying goes."

"Zmija." The syllables were slippery in my mouth. "That's my real last name?" I should have been afraid, but I was too interested.

"It means 'snake.'" He squeezed Trevor again. "Like the one he wears for a collar. I suppose that settles on which derivation of 'Culver' your grandmother meant. I should have suspected, but honestly, the cover-up back home was first-rate. I really believed your whole family was ripped up, root and branch. Everyone did. Though I must say, if you went back home and managed to recover your ancestral estates, global politics would become interesting again. No one hired us to kill you, though – if they had, you'd be dead already."

I moved my hands under the table, getting ready. I'd probably only get one shot. "My grandmother is dead already."

Bollard inclined his head, as if acknowledging a point scored. "She was uncooperative. She didn't go down without a fight, though. She had hidden weapons, secreted in her body, and she was able to put a nasty dent in Mr Chicane before we subdued her. That's why we were so careful and polite with you. If we'd realized you were defenseless and ignorant, we would have kidnapped you in San Francisco. We were afraid you might have hidden resources." Another squeeze. Trev wasn't even struggling, which was probably smart. "Other than your sex vassal, that is."

Ew. "So if you aren't here for me, why are you here? Who hired you?"

Bollard sighed like a deflating airship. "I regret to say we are currently operating without the benefit of contract. Which is to say, without getting paid, a condition we abhor. Mr Chicane and I have enemies of our own. People usually understand that we are non-partisan operators. We fulfill our commissions, and we are loyal to our clients for the duration of those commissions. Alas, one of the oligarchs took certain recent actions on our part personally. Since she has technology that allows her to navigate Nigh-Space, she used it to exile us."

"Why not just kill you? Sending you here seems convoluted."

He chuckled. "Back home, we have considerable resources. We are not soft targets even here, but over there, we are more or less invulnerable. No, Mr Chicane and I were sent to languish in this backwater, with its empty skies and common colds and inedible food." He prodded the plate of steak and made a face. "Fortunately, Mr Chicane has a nose for technology – it's part of his tracking suite – and he detected the signature of devices from our world. Most unexpected, and most gratifying. We investigated, and discovered the door hidden in your grandmother's basement. We assumed she was a countryperson of ours who'd slipped through decades ago to become a queen among the savages. We asked her nicely to open the door and let us go home, but she declined. Something about refusing to do any favors for 'murdering garbage' like us." He shrugged. "So we killed her, not without effort, and found her key. Too late, we discovered the key wasn't enough." He rose, still holding Trevor squeezed against his armpit, like a little girl carrying a doll. "If I let you go, young man, will you behave? If you don't, I won't hurt you – I'll hurt Tamsin. I need her alive, but not unbroken."

"Yes," Trevor breathed. "I'll behave."

Bollard released him, straightened his own lapels, and smiled at me. "Come along, Princess. To the basement."

I'd slipped the misericorde out of my pocket, so I tried to stab him, but he took the knife away from me like taking a lollipop from a child, moving so deftly the waitress didn't even notice the commotion.

Bollard huffed out a breath. "Calm down. Don't make me murder all these witnesses. I detest killing people without getting paid for it."

"Does that mean you won't kill us when you're done?" I said.

"I want to go home, Princess. Help me do that, and you're welcome to rot here for the rest of your pitiful lifespans. How long do people even live over here? A hundred and fifty years? It's squalid."

Trevor looked at me, and I knew if I so much as nodded at him, he'd launch himself in a suicide attack and give me time to run away. Spending the rest of my life looking over my shoulder wasn't appealing, though. I've always been more about looking forward.

So we all left together, and I drove us back toward Culver House in Trev's truck, with Trevor beside me, and Bollard on his other side. Bollard put his arm around Trevor, then slid his arm up over his neck and began squeezing. Trevor squawked and struggled, but Bollard held him fast.

I tapped the brakes. "You said you wouldn't kill us!"

"It's just a blood choke," Bollard said. "Cutting off the supply to his brain briefly. It won't do any permanent damage. He's just going to take a little nap. This vassal is too devoted to you. I'm afraid he might take unwise initiative if permitted to retain consciousness." After a moment, Trevor stopped moving, and Bollard released him. Trev's head settled to rest gently against my shoulder, just like in the old days, when he'd get drunk at the movies. Trevor was my only resource, and now he was asleep.

Hmm. Maybe not my only resource.

GLENN

I wasn't sure what exactly happened to a human body when it got exposed to the vacuum of space. I'd seen some movies and read some science fiction novels, but they weren't consistent. Did you freeze into a lump, or did your eyeballs burst, or did you just die of suffocation?

None of those things happened. Everything spun wildly around me, stars whirling, and I gasped and heaved and breathed just fine. As I spun, I saw something like a jellyfish made of black oil reach out dark tendrils and gather up Vivy into itself, then zip away through the dark. Fragments of the wreck of The Wreck of the Edmund Pevensie spun around me on their own random trajectories.

Why wasn't I dead? Or was I dying? Was my brain shutting down one synapse at a time? Was this just what dying was like?

A piece of the wrecked ship stopped spinning, changed its orientation, and then floated toward me. The fragment was silver, about the size of a baseball, with a triangular sort of shark fin on top. A beam of light shot out from its center, shining right at my head. I expected to be vaporized by some kind of laser, but instead Eddie's voice spoke like a whisper in my ear. "So, this is bad," he said.

"What was that? What happened to Vivy? Why am I still alive?" At least, that's what I meant to say. I don't know if I managed more than a terrified gabble as I flailed in the void.

"Ah, right. This was your first time in space, and now it's really your first time in space. But you're okay. Just breathe.

And stop waving your arms and legs around like that. I'm picking up your voice from your evac-suit's system, but I have to keep the laser oriented right for you to hear me, and that's hard with you jerking around."

I barely heard him. "I can't breathe, oh fuck, how can I–" At that point, I realized I was talking, and that meant I was breathing. I sucked in a big breath and calmed my wild gyrations, though I kept spinning lazily, the fragment of Eddie moving around with me.

"You know how monkeys respond to zero gravity?" Eddie said. "Badly. They hate it. They freak out or they shut down. Rats do much better for some reason. But you, well. You're mostly monkey, but we'll make a rat out of you yet. Look at your hands."

The stars wheeled all around me, vast and disorienting, but maybe a closer focus would help. I held out my hands and saw they were enclosed in a shimmering, translucent blue field composed of millions of tiny diamond shapes. The evac-suit? Some kind of emergency thing. A life jacket for space. So I wouldn't suffocate. But not having to worry about immediately dying gave me so much more to worry about.

"See? You're okay. Now spread out your arms and legs, it'll help slow down your angular momentum."

I obediently starfished myself, and my lazy spin got a little lazier. I took in a deep breath. I was in a situation. The only thing to do was accept it and try to move forward. "All right. Eddie. What happened?"

"We got attacked by an S-Con ship. I guess they've got some kind of new stealth tech. Very slick, by their standards."

"What is an S-Con?"

Eddie bobbed, a motion I chose to interpret as apologetic. "Oh, right. Short for 'Strict Constructionists.' Enemies of the Interventionists. It's complicated, but basically, they believe we should leave other regions of Nigh-Space the fuck alone."

"So they're like… your nemesis?"

Eddie chuckled. "Wouldn't it be great to have just one

nemesis? As far as recurring rivalries go, they're threat level... eh, medium. They're worse than the Outer Legions, but way easier to deal with than the Prime Army. The Interventionists have better technology, but the S-Cons have superior numbers, at least in this swath of Nigh-Space. They tend to congregate around local transit hubs to try and interfere with our operations. That's not usually much of a problem – they guard the hubs, sure, but we have better ways to traverse Nigh-Space than primitive fixed portals that connect adjacent worlds. Except this time, we don't have any better tech handy, and when we set course for a hub, I guess they saw us coming. What happened to Vivy is they took her prisoner. She's a little bit famous, or infamous, as far as the S-Cons are concerned. As for you being alive... it looks like Vivy turned on the adaptive emergency system wrapped around your ankle there. Lucky. Explosive decompression was enough to trigger it."

"What? My anklet? That was a gift from Vivy."

"It's a nice gift. It'll keep you alive in all kinds of rough situations. It's mostly defensive, but it has a little bit of a bite, too, if things get nasty. See, Vivy really was planning to bring you to Nigh-Space."

I tried to spin around to look in the direction where the tendrilly ship had gone. "What now? How do we save her?"

"Well... The S-Cons tore me up pretty bad. This lump of metal is my only functioning component. It's got my brains inside, but not much else in the way of resources. I have enough reaction mass to get us moving, but slowly, and you'll be dead before we reach anywhere useful. The protective field you're wearing can recycle your waste water, but it's a diminishing-returns kind of thing, and you'd die of dehydration before we reached a place with a water fountain. The upside of dying of thirst is it's way quicker than dying of starvation." He sounded entirely too perky.

"Can't you send out a distress call or something? Don't you have a handler? An extraction team?"

"I do, but what I don't have is a functioning communications array. I'm only able to communicate with you because we're line-of-sight." The laser blinked off and then back on. "My shit is bashed."

"So... then... what do we do?"

"I'm a spaceship, Glenn, not a keeping-humans-alive-specialist. I'm open to suggestions."

I looked at my glowing blue hands... and at the tattoo on my wrist. "This connection between me and Vivy... if she can snap-trace to me... can I snap-trace to her? I mean, obviously I can, because I did, but can I make it happen on purpose?"

"Hmm. You've got the necessary hardware. When you got the tattoo, you got the whole snap-trace system installed, too. It's really just a question of loading the right software into your brain so you can control the process consciously."

"How do we do that?"

"Look into the light," Eddie said.

"What?" I glanced up from my wrist, and the beam of light shot straight into my eye, and then–

I blinked, my eyes tearing up. "What was that?"

"Direct neural installation," Eddie said. "I put some knowledge in your brain. The process is a bit crude, sorry, but it's the best I could do in my current reduced circumstances. Did it work? Do you know stuff?"

"I – huh. I think. If I want to get to Vivy, I just–"

"Wait! Grab me first!"

The sphere drifted closer to me, and I pulled it close to my chest, hugging it like a kid hugging a stuffed animal. "Okay. It's sort of like a meditation thing, right? I close my eyes and think of Vivy..."

I closed my eyes and thought of Vivy.

* * *

I opened my eyes and went "Ow" because I'd landed on my back on something hard. There was gravity again, so that was a good sign, right?

I rolled over, and there was Vivy, her head wrapped in an oily black isolation sphere, her arms and legs chained with actual chains to an actual wall, in a square black metal room about three meters to a side.

Vivy didn't look right at all on that side of the chains.

Eddie rose up out of my arms, apparently able to hover even with gravity, and shot a beam of light at a spot on the ceiling. "I've got their surveillance systems baffled," he said. "I'm poking into the ship's systems from there. I'll see what I can do vis-à-vis ruining their day. You try and wake our girl up."

I moved toward Vivy, still shimmering in my silver suit, and found a sort of metal collar around her throat (that was also all wrong). I fiddled with the clasp, the collar came loose, and the sphere that surrounded her head blinked out of existence.

Vivy's hair was matted to her forehead with sweat, her eyes were puffy and red, and she was just as gorgeous as ever. "Glenn? How did you – you snap-traced to me?"

"I do love you, you know."

She touched my face, tears welling in her eyes, then hugged me as best she could with her wrists chained. She looked up. "Eddie?"

"What's left of me. I'm thinking I'll take this ship as my new body, at least until I can find one that's not such a total piece of shit. There's no AI on board, so taking over the vessel doesn't even count as murder. This heap has barely got expert systems, and those are just for navigation and combat. All the other ship's functions are controlled by meat-people, pushing buttons. If they hadn't stolen such a good stealth generator they never would have stood a chance against me." He sighed, which was weird to hear, coming from a silver sphere. "We're still fucked, though. The local hub is crawling with S-Cons, and it'll take literal years at this thing's top speed to reach the next hub, and that one goes the wrong direction in Nigh-Space anyway – upstream instead of down."

I sat beside Vivy. "I guess that means I'm not going to make the next meeting with my adviser."

Eddie said, "You might be surprised. This is a slow level."

"What does that mean?"

"The flow of linear time isn't totally constant in Nigh-Space – most of the universes proceed at roughly the same rate, but every once in a while you hit a level that's weird, like this one. The passage of time is unusually slow here, relative to most other worlds. You can spend weeks on this plane, and only hours will pass back in your world. Some other places run fast, so if you spend an hour there, a month goes by back home. It's kind of like the time dilation you get with lightspeed travel, only without the lightspeed, and it's whole universes that are dilated, really, it drives the science types to distraction–"

Something suddenly made sense. "That's why your body was different that time, and your hair, sometimes," I said to Vivy. "You were gone longer than I thought."

Vivy nodded. "I try to avoid those out-of-synch worlds, but sometimes it can't be helped. I was gone for weeks once, and months another time, from my perspective – not so long for you. God, I missed you so much." She put her head on my shoulder.

"It doesn't really matter how slowly time passes back on planet Dirt," Eddie said. "That's not the problem. The problem is, we have to go a very long way, in a plane where we're literally the only Interventionists. This ship, as I mentioned, is a piece of shit, and the supplies on board aren't compatible with your biology because these particular S-Cons are methane-aquatic conglomoforms. This confinement cell is currently the only place on the ship that even has air you can breathe, so while I'll be fine for the long trip, you guys are going to die of thirst–"

"I love my mom," I said.

"That's... nice?" Eddie said. "That's the sort of thing meat-people think about when they're confronting death, I suppose – oh. Oh."

"Would it work?" I said.

"There's nothing boosting the connection between you and your mother, like our tattoos," Vivy said. "But we're both implanted with the snap-trace technology, and we're not that many levels away from home, so you can probably get close, at least. If you end up somewhere... weird... just refocus on your mom, and try again."

"Can't you come with me? Like I carried Eddie?"

She shook her head. "The fixative isn't quite purged from my system, but it will be soon. Once it is, I'll snap to you, wherever you are. It won't be hard. I've never loved you more." She reached for me, as best she could with the chains. "You saved me."

"You're worth saving."

She kissed my cheek. "Say hi to your mom for me."

I closed my eyes. Then I opened them. "Thank you, Eddie, for the... pep talk. Counseling session. Whatever."

"Thanks for not leaving me floating in the wreckage of myself." Something banged hard on the other side of the wall. "They're trying to break in," Eddie said. "I don't have full control of the ship yet. Things could get violent in here soon, so let me laser those chains off Vivy, and you, Glenn, should clear out..."

I kissed Vivy, just in case, and closed my eyes, and reached for that meditative state. Thank God I did all that yoga with Tamsin back in undergrad.

I thought of my mom's face, and snapped away.

I opened my eyes... and I was not at my mom's house in Santa Cruz. I was in a steaming jungle, but the leaves were all blue, and the vines began moving toward me like snakes. Something wrapped around my wrist, and my shimmering suit suddenly burst out with spikes all over, shredding the vine, and the other tendrils drew back, undulating in panicked retreat.

I did not want to close my eyes in that place, but I did. I tried to focus, and concentrate more specifically, because specific was better, according to the knowledge Eddie had beamed into my brain. I thought of Mom's studio in the back of the house, my mom there in her baggy denim shirt, painting one of her creepy still-lifes with the secret skulls and teeth and knives hidden among the flowers and fruit and books and goblets...

I opened my eyes in the darkness. My suit suddenly glowed brighter, providing enough illumination to make out a cavern with walls of pulsing pink flesh. I stood in a pool of something that steamed and gurgled, and lumps of partially-dissolved meat and bones floated around me. I knew immediately that I was in the stomach of something vast, and my suit started blaring warnings in a shrill voice about imminent loss of integrity.

Eyes squeezed shut. Mind's eye open. Mom, in her backyard garden, yanking weeds and talking about her next gallery show, and her first show, and the group show she did with the sculptor Louise Burgeois back in the '90s, and–

I opened my eyes in Mom's backyard, and the soil at my feet sizzled as the last of the acid ran down off my suit. The shimmering suit flickered and drew back into the anklet just as my mom turned around in the lawn chair where she was reading and sipping iced tea. "You didn't tell me you were coming, hon! What's the occasion?"

"I, ah..." My tattoo warmed up, and a moment later, Vivy came strolling around the side of the house, dressed not in her Nigh-Space warrior battle-leathers but in a white sundress. She walked over and stood beside me.

"Mom, I'd like you to meet Vivy."

"Well." Mom rose and looked at us for a moment, then

smiled. "Meeting the parent, huh? Things must be getting pretty serious, then."

I took Vivy's hand. She squeezed tight. I squeezed right back.

"They must be," Vivy said.

TAMSIN

Considering its mythic status in my own mind, Granny's basement was disappointing in reality. Getting there required passing through two doors: an ordinary wooden one at the top of the stairs, and a reinforced steel one at the bottom. But beyond the security door, it was just a basement: there was a work bench and tools, shelves covered in dusty bits of potentially interdimensional technology, some books printed in an alphabet I didn't recognize, and a battered old leather couch, presumably where Granny took naps after a hard day of pretending to invent things.

The only obvious oddity was a bright red metal door, set not into a wall but freestanding in a silver frame, tucked into the farthest corner of the basement.

Bollard had Trevor slung over his shoulder, and he plopped him down on the floor, smoothed his suit again, and then took a long silver key from his jacket pocket. "This was in the envelope your granny left for you, along with a letter written in a cipher we couldn't understand."

I nodded. "Granny had a code she always used, even when she emailed me. She said it was so outsiders wouldn't know our business, but she'd even write grocery lists in the stupid thing. I learned to translate it in my head by the time I was fifteen."

"I'm sure the letter says all the things your vassal told you, about how you're a princess. It likely also details how to use the door, but I already know that much. See?" Bollard put the silver key in the appropriate hole in the freestanding red door, turned it, and shoved. The door didn't budge, but a recording of my grandmother's annoyed voice said, "Unauthorized user."

Bollard turned back to me, arms crossed over his immense chest. "We didn't realize we needed your grandmother alive until it was too late. The lock is based on more than biometrics or facial recognition – Mr Chicane dragged the body down here and tried all that, to no avail. Locks like this are common among the dynasties back home. They don't just sniff your genome before allowing access – they confirm you're alive, too. The door is barred to me, but you, Princess... I believe you can open it, and let us return home, to all our beloved pleasures, diversions, and scores that need settling."

"Us? Mr Chicane is dead."

Bollard sighed like an iceberg calving. "Forgive the inappropriate pronoun. I spoke from long force of habit. I have been half of a partnership for longer than I was ever a solo operator."

"Speaking of, are you just going to leave Chicane's body upstairs?" I was stalling, and Bollard clearly knew I was stalling, but he seemed willing to tolerate it, for now.

"Already disposed of. Mr Chicane possessed internal acid reservoirs that released their contents not long after his death. His body contains too much bespoke technology to just leave his corpse lying around, especially in an ignorant backwater like this. The thing Mr Chicane has instead of a spleen could make whoever discovered it into a personal world power." He gestured to the door. "If you don't mind? I've tarried in this backwater quite long enough."

I crossed my arms. "If I help you, what's in it for me?"

He took a business card from an inner pocket and silently handed it to me.

BOLLARD AND CHICANE
We Killed Your Granny • We'll Kill You • We'll Kill
Everyone You Know
"If You Don't Do What We Say!"

I turned it over. Blank. "No personalized message this time?"

"I believe the card speaks for itself."

"Nice try. You can't kill me, though. You said so yourself. Not if you want to get home."

"True. What if I kill Trevor?"

I didn't even look at Trev's slumped body. "Then you'll save the state a lot of money in future incarceration costs?"

Bollard chuckled. "Are you really so cold? Your grandmother was, when she ruled your family. The Serpent of the Zmija, they called her, which is a bit like calling someone the Insect of the Bug, but never mind. Even if I believe you don't care about Trevor, you do care about you. There's dead, and there's alive, but those aren't the only possible states of being. You don't need eyes or a tongue to open a door. Normally Mr Chicane performs such elective surgeries – you'd be the one electing for said surgeries by refusing to help us, of course – but since he is currently indisposed, I'll manage. The knife I took from you seems sharp enough."

My mind spun through possibilities. Maybe Granny had refused to open the door because she had some history with these people – Bollard and Chicane could have murdered her cousins or something – but I suspect she was motivated by her basic stubbornness. No one told Granny what to do; she told other people what to do. Me, personally? I didn't really care if this asshole went through the door to the old country. But I'd just discovered a whole new world of multiple dimensions and high technology and assorted miracles, and some of those miracles should come to me. Especially now that I knew I had a birthright, stolen from me and hidden away. I wanted it back.

It's like this: San Francisco was a lot nicer than my hometown, so I moved there as soon as I could, and never looked back. It sounded like the world beyond that door would make San Francisco look like a latrine, and offer me an existence infinitely more exciting than eating takeout and writing code and calculating possible payouts for my stock options. Forget disruptive technology. This was disruptive reality.

Of course, even San Francisco sucked if you didn't have friends to show you around and money to enjoy things, and if I flipped to another page of Nigh-Space, I wouldn't have either one.

Unless.

I held up the little rectangle in my hand. "This is a business card."

"That's true. The suit makes them, among other things, like useful drugs." Bollard patted his breast pocket. "Very convenient."

"You're a business man. So you can be hired."

He cocked his head. "You propose to offer us a commission? I never dismiss an offer out of hand, but how would you pay? I understand your grandmother was wealthy in this world, but from our point of view, your money is bits of string and shiny glass beads."

I tapped the business card against my palm. "Trevor said something about my family's vaults, on the other side."

"Ah. Yes. The fabled Zmija vaults." He looked up at the ceiling for a moment. "Which are inaccessible, both because they are mostly surrounded by the forces of your ancestral enemies, and because they are impregnably locked against anyone outside your bloodline. But you carry the genetic legacy of your parents and grandparents, so the doors would open for you, assuming you could reach them."

"I suspect you could help me reach them."

Bollard gave me the faintest trace of a smile. "Mmm. What would you be hiring us to do, besides liberating the vaults so you could pay us for our services in the first place? Because that's a bit circular for my tastes."

"I just found out I'm a princess," I said. "I think I'd like being a princess. I could use help over there. A royal adviser. Could you help me regain my family's throne?"

Bollard huffed. "It's not a throne. But... yes. We do have some experience with regime change. It says so right on our business card. Sometimes." He considered me. "You would really hire us, miss? Even after we killed your grandmother?"

I pretended to think about it. "Obviously, I wish you hadn't killed her. But... Granny could be extremely frustrating, and she never backed down. I can understand how things... ended up how they did."

He snorted. "If I had any doubt about your heritage, you just dispelled it. How very like your ancestors you are. Let's see. Once we got to the other side, I'd have to go to my workshop first, and decant a new Chicane, since you were all so hard on my last one."

There was no point in looking surprised. "I trust your expertise." I pointed to Trev. "We should take him with us."

"Ah. You aren't so coldhearted after all, if you wish to bring along your paramour."

"I'm as cold as I need to be. But a princess needs subjects."

Mr Bollard chuckled, then reached out one huge hand. It was like shaking hands with a polar bear. "I look forward to our partnership, Princess. Let's go conquer the old country."

GLENN

Mom and Vivy got along like they'd known each other forever. All I had to do was sit back in my lawn chair and sip my iced tea and let them talk and laugh, with no contribution from me necessary. Mom spent some time in her youth building houses in Honduras, and it turned out Vivy had been there once "studying abroad," so they had a merry time comparing meals eaten and landmarks visited. Then they walked around the garden, Mom showing off her various weird flowers and succulents, and some of her larger sculptures, which were tucked away here and there among the bushes and shrubs.

While they were looking at Mom's verdant expanse of beans, with their vines creeping up a wooden trellis, Vivy said, "This is amazing. I can't get anything to grow. I'm only good at killing things." I wondered: killing what kind of things? I had some processing to do about recent discoveries, both on my own, and in conversation with my girlfriend.

When they returned to the patio table and sat down, Mom said, "Will you two be staying the night?"

I exchanged a glance with Vivy, and just at that moment I realized we were eighty miles from home with no car. Santa Cruz isn't exactly bursting with mass transit options, apart from the Greyhound station downtown, and even that was miles away from Mom's place in the hills. Given that we'd just traversed literal dimensions, figuring out how to get home to Berkeley seemed like it should be a surmountable problem, but it wasn't like we could literally teleport anywhere at will. As far as I knew, anyway.

"I've got a meeting in the morning, so I shouldn't stay," Vivy said. "But I'd love to come back again and spend more time, if you'll have me."

We all stood up, and Mom gave Vivy a long hug before giving me an even longer one. She kissed my cheek and whispered "I like her," in my ear.

"Me too," I whispered back.

Vivy took my hand and we walked around the house, toward the driveway, where no car waited. I was glad my mom wasn't the type to stand out front and wave until we drove out of sight. We walked down the long driveway, which curved around under redwoods, until we hit the asphalt lane that eventually led to a main road. There was no one else around, and I couldn't even hear the distant rumble of cars, only birdsong. "It's a long walk to anywhere, and I don't have my phone, not that rideshare drivers congregate around here anyway," I said. "I don't suppose we can snap-trace back to our apartment?"

She shook her head. "No, it doesn't really work like that. The snap-trace is my backup extraction method – it brings me from another level of Nigh-Space to wherever you are, instantly. The tech is made for crossing dimensions, and it doesn't really work for travel within a given level of Nigh-Space. You wouldn't use an ejector seat to travel to the grocery store, you know?"

"If the tattoos are how you come home, then how do you leave for missions?"

She shrugged. "Various ways. My bosses open portals for me, sometimes. Other times, Eddie swoops in and picks me up. The Interventionists have more complex portable tech, too, that allows fast and easy traversal of wide-swaths of Nigh-Space, but we're careful with that stuff."

I shook my head. "I don't get it. I'm not a physicist, but with these portals… if you open a literal hole between worlds, shouldn't there be all kinds of weird atmospheric issues, like pressure differentials causing tornados or something? And how do you keep alien viruses from blowing from one world to another?"

Vivy shrugged. "You'd have to ask Eddie for the technical details, but the way it was explained to me, opening a gate isn't like tearing a hole in a wall and crawling from one room to another. During transition we pass through a brief intermediate space, or non-space I guess technically, between the worlds, that acts as a buffer and prevents any dangerous interactions, and we've got wearable tech to sanitize pathogens en route. But..." She leaned back against a tree and shook her head.

"But?" I prompted.

"Well, when people were figuring out flying machines on your world, a lot of them crashed. Interdimensional travel isn't inherently safe. One of the most basic and primitive forms is a small stable gate, where you open a literal door from your universe to an adjacent one, Narnia-wardrobe style. That can be dangerous, especially at first, when they're picking destinations blindly. A lot of scientists across Nigh-Space have gotten sucked through doorways into airless voids, or flooded their labs with alien oceans. The successful ones figure out they need to put in airlocks so they can equalize pressures, flood the zone with UV to kill nasty bugs, maybe send in robots to check out conditions on the other side, that sort of thing."

"And that's the primitive version of travel through Nigh-Space?"

"Oh, yeah. Your people might even get there in a century or two." She grinned at me. "Overwhelming technological superiority is the big advantage the Interventionists have. I don't carry our good traversal tech when I'm in hostile territory, because if it fell into the wrong hands, things could get bad. Even those primitive doors between adjacent worlds can cause enough trouble. There have been some ugly wars. The Prime Army is a big threat even with their clunky gates and portals, and those only let them traverse a few levels at a time. If they could instantly travel to distant levels as easily as the Interventionists can, hello, fascist hellscape." She tapped the tattoo on her wrist. "That's the beauty of the snap-trace. It's secret, embedded, and impossible for someone to take off me and use for themselves. All our other traversal tech is tightly controlled."

"Huh." I looked at my own tattoo. One of the many things that connected us. "So you can't just dash off to a distant reality any time you like?"

She shook her head. "Not usually. I can send messages across Nigh-Space, to contact my bosses, but I'm as Earthbound as anyone right now."

I looked around at the redwood trees, the blue sky, the fluttering birds, and it all looked different, after the things I'd seen. "I'm sorry. I guess Earth is kind of a horrible backwater."

She pushed off the tree and put her hand on my shoulder. "Hey, no. I like it here. The food is great, there's good art and beaches, and believe me, as far as everything else goes, I've seen worse worlds. A lot worse." She took my arm. "Besides. This is where you live, so it's my favorite place. Want to go home?"

I sighed. "I guess we'll have to walk to the bus station. And then figure out some way to buy a ticket. Do you have any money?"

"I can always get money," Vivy said. "But I've got something better. Just call me Contingency Girl." Her dress flickered and vanished, and she was back in her battle-suit.

I blinked. "I wondered where you found a sundress on an alien spaceship. I figured you had it stuffed in one of your belt pouches or something."

"Nope. I've got a field projector. Built into the suit." She tapped her chest. "I can change my appearance in all kind of ways. It's hard to infiltrate a place if you look super weird by local standards, so I can look like anything I want."

"When you say anything…"

Vivy rolled her eyes. "Yes, there are definite bedroom possibilities, and now that you know my big secret, we can explore those later. But for now…" She reached into a pouch at her belt, only she reached in way deeper than should have been possible, far up her forearm.

"Whoa. You've got a bag of holding?"

"Nerd. It's just a miniature spatial gate, leading to an actual cabinet full of actual stuff in my apartment."

"So… why can't we just climb into the bag and come out in your place?"

"Sadly, I can't make a stable gate that's big enough for a person to pass through, at least not with the tech level I'm allowed to access on this tier. Too potentially disruptive. Even this little gate is locked so it only works for me – anybody else who reached into this pouch would just hit the bottom."

She drew out a metallic object the size of a hand grenade. (Or, I don't know, a pear? But given everything I'd seen recently, "hand grenade" was more where my mind went.) The object was a complicated polyhedron that seemed made of curved silver wires. "Stand back a bit."

I did (see above, re: hand grenade) and she put the thing down on the ground, then stepped back beside me. She glanced around, was apparently satisfied we weren't being observed, and then snapped her fingers.

The polyhedron unfolded itself, expanding and rising, angles straightening, curves shifting, and after a few moments something like a motorcycle – it had two wheels, handlebars, and a long seat, anyway – stood before us. It was all chrome and silver; even the seat looked like reflective metal, and very uncomfortable. There also wasn't enough of it to qualify as a motorcycle. For one thing, there was no fuel tank, and no visible engine.

Vivy walked over to the wire-bike, fiddled with something by the handlebars, and stepped back – and then it did look like an ordinary motorcycle, specifically a black Vincent. (I'm not a motorcycle guy, but I can read a logo.) "More camouflage?" I said.

"When on Earth, do as the Earth-people do."

I crouched down and looked into the headlight and waved my hand in front of it like I was trying to get the attention of somebody deeply stoned. "Is this thing… a person, like Eddie?"

She snorted. "Your instincts are good, but no. This is just my trusty welbike." She patted the handlebars affectionately.

"Welbike… those were the tiny folding motorcycles that British Special Forces used during World War Two, right? They dropped the bikes with paratroopers, who could assemble them and zoom off behind enemy lines."

She grinned. "Gold star! I didn't know you were a military history nerd as well as a bag of holding nerd."

"I've just read some spy novels, that's all." I stood up. "Clearly I should read a lot more, since I seem to be living inside one of them now."

Instead of responding to the barb, she turned her attention back to the bike. "The actual welbikes turned out to be pretty useless – they were heavier than the paratroopers, so they tended to land far away from their intended riders, and since the soldiers usually needed to find cover quickly, they couldn't spare the time to track down and assemble the things. Also, even when they worked as intended, the welbikes just kind of sucked – weak engines, no lights, no shocks, everything resembling a frill sacrificed to make them portable. A lot of the bikes just got left in their canisters in the woods, unrecovered. Farmers honestly got more use of them after the war than soldiers ever did during it – the bikes weren't street-legal, but they were handy for zipping around the fields. My bike is much better." She patted it affectionately.

Vivy was avoiding a hard conversation, but this wasn't the place for that conversation anyway, so I went along. "Well, yeah, your bike shrinks down to the size of an apple, so I imagine so. How does that work, exactly?"

"Intraspatial compression," she said promptly.

"That's very illuminating."

She shrugged. "I'm just telling you what I was told. I don't know how it works. Most people don't know how anything works, you know? Like, how does a microwave even work?"

"There's a magnetron inside the oven, producing microwaves, which bounce around off the metal surfaces inside, and those microwaves are absorbed into the food," I said. "The waves agitate water, fat, and sugar molecules in the food, creating heat—"

Vivy held up her hands and laughed. "Okay, okay! If you really want, I'll get Eddie to explain the technology to you later, but just be warned, stuff like that goes all quantum pretty quick."

"I look forward to it. I wouldn't have chosen the history of science if I'd known studying the future of science was an option instead."

Vivy climbed onto the bike, looked at me, and raised an eyebrow. In her black leathers, on that bike, she looked like a warrior goddess. I resolved not to let her hotness distract me from the fact that I was still pretty mad at her for the whole "lying to me about everything" thing.

"Hop on," she said.

"You don't have helmets in your bag of holding?"

"Nah. But don't worry, I'll use the field projector to make it look like we're wearing them, so the cops won't pull us over."

"I'm not worried about the cosmetic part of having a helmet, Vivy, I'm worried about the part where my brains get splattered all over Highway 17."

"Oh, no, you'll be fine. Look." She climbed off the bike, glanced around, found a fist-sized chunk of rock by the driveway, picked it up, and hurled it overhand at the motorcycle's headlight. It bounced off some invisible barrier three feet away from the glass (which wasn't really glass anyway). "The bike has an adaptive ballistic field. If we drove into a wall, the wall would get hurt, not us. The whole thing is also self-balancing." She put her foot against the side of the bike and pushed, grunting, but the bike just leaned a little, and didn't fall. "Motorcycles are extremely dangerous. My welbike isn't. Still pretty fun, though. It feels dangerous, even if it's really not."

"Like kink," I said.

She cocked her head. "The safe, sane, and consensual kind of kink, yeah. Where the blades are dull and the knots are quick-release. But there are other kinds of kink."

"RACK," I said. Risk Aware Consensual Kink – that approach still depends on informed consent, but it acknowledges that many activities are inherently unsafe. If you're into certain kinds of edgeplay, you have to accept that you might get bruised, you might get bloody, or you might get scarred, depending on what you're into. "We've never gone heavy like that, though. I mean… did you want to? Am I holding you back?" Her vocation was apparently beating up aliens, so who knew what she was really into, or what other secrets she'd kept from me?

She shook her head. "For me, the best part of what we do is psychological – it's about power exchange and trust, and creating an intense experience for someone I care about. Don't get me wrong, the ropes and toys and outfits and all that are great, but we could boil down the essentials of what we do to just you and me in a room, and it would be just as good."

I nodded. That was true. But we weren't really talking about kink. Or at least, I wasn't. "I didn't have proper awareness of everything that was going on with you, Vivy. I wasn't informed about your life, so I couldn't meaningfully consent to our relationship." I started to shake a little. I guess the little patch on the back of my neck wasn't dulling my responses so much anymore. "I was in outer space. I could have died."

"I know." She looked down, clearly miserable. "This was never supposed to... you weren't meant to... I was going to... but it's my fault. I didn't foresee all the possibilities. If you want me to take you home... and leave you alone... I understand."

She looked so pitiful. I didn't think she was manipulating me, but I hardened my heart anyway. "That's not what I'm saying. The experience was terrifying and awful, but since I didn't die, I can admit it was also exciting and amazing. The universe is bigger than I thought, and I already thought it was infinite. But Vivy... you made me part of your extraction plan without telling me. You implanted alien technology in me without telling me. You made me part of your whole thing without telling me."

"I wasn't allowed to tell you, and you wouldn't have believed me anyway, and..." She kicked at the dirt and sighed. "No, that's bullshit. I could have done things differently. Gotten permission to inform you, certainly before I convinced you to get that tattoo." She met my gaze. "I didn't do that because I was scared. I was scared you'd run screaming the other way if you knew the truth, and I'd lose you."

I stepped toward her and put my hands on her shoulders and looked into her eyes. "I get it," I said softly. "But all of that stops now. If you want us to work, we have to be all in for each other. No more secrets. I want to know everything about you."

She cut her eyes away. "I can't tell you everything – it's not safe. We have operational security for a reason." She took a deep breath and let it out slowly. "But I can tell you everything I'm allowed tell you, and everything that has to do with us. Just... give me some time to sort things out. You know the really big stuff now. We'll get to the smaller stuff soon. Okay?"

I thought about it. Did I trust her? Not really. But I loved her, and that meant giving her a chance to earn my trust back. "Okay."

She looked away. "I don't deserve you, Glenn. I'm kind of broken in a lot of ways, even if those ways make me good at my job. Are you sure you want to be in this mess? By which I mean... me?"

"You are, objectively, amazing. And we're amazing together. Did you notice how I saved your ass from the S-Cons?"

"My hero." She touched my face. "Okay. Should we get home, and continue this discussion there? I imagine you have a lot of questions."

"I do. And the ride will give me time to think of more."

She got on the bike, and I climbed on behind her, and wrapped my arms around her waist. "You're sure I can't fall off and die?"

"Correct."

"You turn off the safety features sometimes when you drive this thing, don't you?" I said in a sudden flash of insight.

"'Subject exhibits risk-seeking behavior.' That's what they said after my last mandatory psychological evaluation."

"Your what?" I began, but then the engine roared, and we lurched off. The noise of the wind made further conversation impossible, and when we got home, she distracted me so thoroughly I forgot the question entirely.

After she untied me and snuggled up in bed beside me, Vivy said, "Mmm. Narrowly escaping death always puts me in the mood."

I stroked my hand idly down her smooth, strong arm. "You're pretty much always in the mood, though. Does that mean you're constantly narrowly escaping death?"

She made an amused chuffing sound. "Near-death isn't the only thing that puts me in the mood. That little outfit you wear when you do your chores, for instance, always works too."

I groaned. "Chores. Errands. Meetings. Grading. Revising. All that stuff is still here, isn't it? Even after everything I've seen, everything I know now, ordinary life just... goes on."

"It does. But not just the work. The pleasures, too. Sex, long walks, art museums, food trucks, browsing in bookshops. That's life, too." She was quiet for a moment, then said, "The essence of my work is making sure life does go on, for as many people as possible, as pleasantly as possible, without oppression and exploitation. All that other stuff, the fighting, the spaceships, the sabotage, it's not the actual point. The point of all of that—" she gestured toward the ceiling, which I understood to mean violent adventures in the multiverse "– only matters insofar as it helps to preserve this." She put her hand on my chest.

"You and me against the multiverse?" I said.

"You and me for the multiverse," she answered. "Always."

TAMSIN

I adjusted the straps on my backpack, then put the silver key in the red metal door and twisted it. Granny's voice said, "Tamsin," in a waspish tone. Then a long sigh. Then: "Authorized user. Don't embarrass yourself over there." The door clicked and swung open... revealing a steel-walled rectangular room the size of a walk-in closet, with another red door on the other side. "What's this?"

"An airlock," Bollard said. "Basic safety precautions for interdimensional travel. In you go."

I stepped through the door, with Bollard close behind me, hauling Trev. He clicked the door shut behind us, and a moment later, the chamber strobed with purplish light. "Disinfectant," Bollard explained. "No reason to bring the filth of this world back home."

A light over the far door turned green. There was another keyhole, and my key fit. "We don't have to wait for the pressure to equalize, or whatever?"

"Already has, or the lights wouldn't be green," Bollard said. "We aren't going to a moon or something. Our atmospheres are near enough identical that it makes no difference."

I turned the key, and the red door swung open an inch, admitting a shaft of nonspecific light and a whiff of strange air. "The old country," I murmured.

Bollard stood close behind me, a large black leather valise in one hand, the other hand steadying Trev, who was slung across his shoulder like a sack of laundry. Bollard was up on the balls of his feet, barely containing himself, like a frantic dog at the end of a chain. "Come on," he murmured. "Let's go, Princess."

I removed the key, pocketed it, and then pushed the door all the way open. I peered into the space revealed by the open door, and saw only a room with brick walls and a low roof with a big hole in it, admitting slanted sunlight. I stepped in, kicking aside drifts of dry leaves. Bollard followed close behind, and the door shut after us with a soft click.

I turned and looked at the big man, half expecting him to attack me now that he'd gotten what he wanted. He seemed to anticipate my worry, because he grinned. "Don't fret, Princess. We always fulfill our contracts. We will be loyal to you until you've achieved your goals here. Which isn't to say we won't kill you later if someone else hires us to do so, but Bollard and Chicane are reliable, once bought. We never betray a client."

I looked up at the hole in the ceiling, where a fluffy cloud drifted past in the sky, and then around the room. The red metal door was set into the wall quite conventionally on this side. There was a wooden door in the opposite wall, and it looked like it had been scorched with fire a long time ago. "So far, this world doesn't impress me."

"Oh? What were you expecting? Candy-cane trees and rivers of rum?"

I shrugged. "Something I wouldn't see in my world. Floating islands. Herds of ambling dinosaurs. Two moons in the sky. A cantina full of aliens."

"You should use your own imagination, Princess, instead of letting movies and books supply the imagination for you. We're only a single level away from your home – this is the universe next door. I'm told that things don't get that... outlandish... until you've traversed several levels through so-called Nigh-Space." He looked around. "There are considerable differences between your world and this one, though. They just aren't evident, because we're in a dirty hole in the ground at the moment."

"So what's outside? Flying cars and gleaming spires?"

"Even your world has flying cars. They're called private jets. As for the gleaming spires, you've got those, too – there's one called the Burj Khalifa, I'm told. We do have a lot more of both those things, and of better quality, admittedly. Be patient. In fact, there are wonders beyond your understanding, even in a place as shabby as this. They're just invisible." He cracked his neck, first to one side, then the other, and put Trevor down on the ground. "Ahhh. That's good. I'm back on the network." His eyes fluttered.

"What network? Like, the internet? But in your head, right?"

"Letting science fiction movies do your thinking again?" His eyes were closed now, but I could see his eyes flickering back and forth beneath the lids. "It's so much more than that. There are many networks here, but I'm using one that's sometimes called the Undernet. It's a special system designed for use by operators and freelancers like myself, inaccessible to the lowlies, bureaucrats, and oligarchs."

So the dark web, but in his head? Ugh.

Bollard opened his eyes. "Unbelievable. There are fools out there who bet against our return! The official story is, Mr Chicane and I were sent to a secret prison. That's as good a description of your world as any... My expert systems registered bets in our favor through various proxies after we departed, and now that I'm back on the Undernet, I'm reaping the rewards. My winnings will provide us with operational funding for now, though you'll reimburse me, with interest, once we breach your family vaults."

Now it was my turn to bounce on the balls of my feet. "Let's go, then." My imaginings were muddled, images of treasure troves from children's comic books – wooden chests overflowing with gold and pearl necklaces and jewel-encrusted chalices, that sort of thing – mingling with the sci-fi shimmer of high-tech armories, with racks of gleaming plasma rifles and laser guns.

"We will, but the vaults will have to wait. Reaching those will require time and preparation. Now that I'm back, word will get around that I'm back, which could lead to additional complications. We'll need to move quickly to protect ourselves."

"We're going to your workshop, you said."

Bollard nodded. "Yes, but before we go, could you tell the door to your world to hide itself?"

I didn't bother asking questions. I just faced the red door and said, "Hide yourself."

The bricks surrounding the door unfolded with a clatter, multiplying and spreading across the red surface, and within seconds, I faced an unbroken expanse of wall. "That's a neat trick. I expected, I don't know, a hologram or something."

Bollard snorted. "Why settle for images when you can have real things? Come, Princess. I've summoned reliable transport. We should get going."

"Uh. What about Trevor?"

Bollard looked down at him, crumpled motionless on the floor. If not for the slight rise and fall of Trevor's chest, I'd have thought he was dead. "I'd rather hoped you'd forget he was here. We'll clear a path and then bring him up. I'd rather have my hands free on the initial ascent, in case we encounter anything unexpected."

Before I could ask what sort of unexpected things he was expecting, Bollard strode to the wooden door and smoothly kicked it off its hinges. He had to duck to get through the emptied doorframe, and I followed him into a small anteroom and then up a set of stone stairs. There was a wooden trap door set in the ceiling, also charred, and when Bollard shoved it, the door shuddered but didn't fly out of the frame. "There's some rubble on top." He pressed both hands against the trap door, bent his knees, and then drove himself forcefully upward.

Something scraped beyond the barrier, and then the door popped free, swinging open with a bang. Bollard clambered out, then reached an immense hand down to help me. I ignored him and climbed out on my own.

I stood beside Bollard in a hall of ruins. There were bits of freestanding wall here and there, broken and burned, but mostly the space was cinders and rubble, fragments of glass and stone, all covered in ash. "Welcome to the ancestral estate of the Zmija, in all its considerable glory." He kicked the fallen beam that had blocked the trapdoor.

"When did it burn down?" I couldn't even smell smoke anymore.

"Twenty-odd years ago. You were a baby. It wasn't burned, or anyway, not just burned. It was bombarded from an orbital platform, or so the rumor says."

I tucked away that bit of information. "No one wanted to clean the place up and claim the land?" I could see golden hills and stands of unfamiliar trees on all sides through the broken walls, and the place looked paradisiacal, if you discounted the devastation.

Bollard chuckled. "The other families value their lives too much. The orchards have gone unharvested, the vineyards have gone to seed, and the priceless sculptures in the gardens are covered in bird shit and moss. The Zmija were known for their traps, you see. That's why your family's enemies had to destroy the place from the safe distance of orbit, and even so, many of the estate's defenses survived the assault. Your enemies sent in remote-operated hunter androids to make sure there were no survivors, streaming their sensory input back to the oligarchs who organized the attack, but none of those machines made it off this property again. There are mines, autocannons, and worse things all over this place. You're in no danger personally – you're on the whitelist, since this was technically your home, and it recognizes you, and Trevor should be fine, as his family pledged fealty. But for anyone else... do you hear that distant hum? If you'd be so kind as to announce that I'm your guest, I would appreciate it."

I did detect a faint whine, rising in pitch. I cleared my throat. "This man is my guest."

The whine abruptly cut off. Bollard nodded. "Thank you, Princess. The defenses refrained from exploding the floor beneath my feet, because I was standing too close to you for that, but some sort of targeted attack was clearly spinning up." He glanced around. "If you could tell the estate to allow that approaching vehicle to land? It would ruin my rating if the ride I summoned was destroyed by ground-to-air defenses."

"That... vehicle is authorized." I said the words on a sort of autopilot, staring up at the small dot in the sky as it became larger. It was an opaque sphere of peach-toned iridescence, drifting as gracefully as a soap bubble. Not a flying car at all. There was my first wonder of the old country.

"I'll go down and fetch your family retainer." Bollard moved lightly and swiftly back down the stairs. I watched the bubble approach, then looked around the rubble some more. Something shiny glinted near my feet, and I bent to sweep away ash to reveal it. I found a thin necklace, made of some pale metal like platinum, wrapped around a chunk of bone I reluctantly recognized as a bit of charred spinal column. I untangled the chain and held it up to the light. There was a pendant, a flat metal diamond-shape, not hanging from the chain but affixed to the links. It looked a bit like the scale of a dragon. On a whim, I draped the chain around my neck and tucked the pendant inside my shirt.

When the metal scale touched my chest, a soothing voice murmured in my ear, or rather, through the bones of my ear, a gentle vibration traveling through my breastbone and upward. It spoke a language I didn't recognize, except for one word, early on: Zmija. I touched the pendant. Was it warm? Was it trying to tell me something? Wonder number two. My first family heirloom, regained. The first of many, if I had my way.

Bollard returned with Trevor slung over his shoulder as casually as someone might carry a jacket on a warm afternoon. Bollard stood beside me and we watched the bubble get larger. I said, "Why do you speak English?"

"Hmm?" Bollard said.

"If this is an entirely different world, why do you speak my language?"

"There's a certain amount of cross-pollination," Bollard said. "We are right next door to your universe, and even before cross-dimensional technology was developed by your family's rivals, there were occasional natural slips. Those happen sometimes, between adjacent levels. People find a strange spot in the woods or a deep cave that connects one world to the next, for a time, and they inadvertently emigrate, carrying bits of their home culture with them. Your family name, Zmija, made it to Earth as a word for 'snake,' for example. Now, of course, there are deliberate research programs, with people from our side studying yours, much like people in your world study slugs or algae." He chuckled. I didn't. "I am fluent in English and other languages from your world – we have techniques to hasten language acquisition here – and I reluctantly used that barbarous tongue when I spoke to you on the phone. But, in point of fact, at the moment… I'm not speaking English." He patted a lapel with the hand that wasn't holding Trevor. "My suit translates for me, projecting audio into my ears so naturally it seems to come from your mouth, and it also produces interference waves so I don't have to hear your foreign gabble. The suit has an ambient field, and because you are standing close to me, it translates for you as well."

I looked at Bollard closely. He spoke like a convict in an old movie, barely moving his lips, but now that I paid attention, I noticed the motions of his mouth didn't perfectly synch up with his words. "It's a universal translator? It can make sense of any language?" I'd done some work in machine learning, and I couldn't believe such a device was possible, even in a world as advanced as this one.

"No, no. It can translate all the languages of this world, and about two dozen of the most common languages from Earth. The oligarchs sent over linguists to collect data sets, vocabulary and syntax and so forth, and fed them to one of our CMs – Constructed Minds. What you'd call Artificial Intelligence back there, but real AI, not those mindless things you have, only capable of crude mimicry and offering up new combinations of old data."

That made more sense. "Then... can I get a universal translator of my own? So I'm not totally dependent on you?"

"Such devices are rare and quite expensive, but we'll look into it."

Something about his affability and willingness to please rang false to me. I thought he probably liked having me dependent on him.

That incomprehensible murmur started in my ear again, then said, Translation field activated. New database successfully infiltrated. Linguistic data set imported. Welcome message repeats: Greetings, Tamsin Zmija, and welcome to SerpentNet. You have been inactive for twenty-four cycles. You have no notifications.

I surmised the pendant had given me access to something like Bollard's Undernet... but this was an internet for the use of my now-dead family. Depressing, and maybe mostly useless... but I was pretty sure I now had a translator of my own. I decided to keep that fact to myself.

"Here we are," Bollard said. The bubble, which was about the size of a large SUV, settled down into the ruins – or almost.

I noticed that it hovered a few inches above the rubble. "You just summoned that thing?"

"Think of it as a... flying car service. One that caters to users of the Undernet. The owners are strictly neutral, and entirely trustworthy."

"So it's a rideshare app for murderers?"

"Oh, anyone can be a murderer, Princess. You have to be a special sort of murderer to qualify for this program." He walked up to the bubble and rapped his knuckles on the side. It rang like a crystal bell, and then a segment of the sphere went transparent, revealing sumptuous black couches and soft lighting inside. Bollard stepped in through the hole, Trevor on his shoulder, and gestured for me to follow.

Once we were in, he put Trevor on the floor and dropped himself down onto a couch. I adjusted Trevor's head and arms a little until he looked comfortable – no reason to have him wake up with neck spasms – and then lowered myself onto a seat as far from Bollard as possible. I noticed that while I was covered in soot from my brief sojourn in the ashes, his white suit was still perfectly pristine. "Why aren't you grubby like me?"

"The suit is from this world," Bollard said. "It doesn't get dirty, or wet, or wrinkled. I was exiled with nothing but a single worn-out Chicane and the clothes on my back, but at least they were excellent clothes. We'll get you dressed in something more appropriate to your station soon."

The bubble went opaque again. From the inside, the walls were eggshell white, not shimmering. "When do we take off?"

"We've already taken off."

I'd experienced no sensation of acceleration – no hint of movement at all. "Really?"

"Observe." He waved his hand, and the white walls vanished. I was sitting on a couch that was sitting on nothing at all, high above the ground, which rushed beneath several hundred feet below.

I gritted my teeth to keep myself from screaming. "Trying to scare the country bumpkin, Bollard?"

He smiled. "You wanted to see wonders, didn't you, Princess?"

"I did. But all I see is more wreckage." You're not falling, you're not falling, you're not falling, I chanted in the back of my head. I did not enjoy the experience of hurtling through empty air – there's a reason people don't go on glass-bottomed plane rides.

My necklace whispered, Cortisol spike detected, but no imminent danger sensed. Do you require chemical mitigation, Tamsin?

I didn't know how to answer the thing without Bollard noticing, so I didn't say anything, and it didn't repeat the question. I just took deep breaths and tried to calm down, and took in the view as we soared over a valley that had once held my family's estate. There were large craters down there, and lots of rubble, and the occasional heartbreaking bit of unharmed landscape – a perfectly round pond, a pergola now heavily overgrown with vines, a gazebo on a hilltop. I also saw the orchards Bollard had mentioned, and the sculpture garden. (I'd expected Classical statuary, or Renaissance figures, but instead they were abstract modern-art constructions of metal and glass and other materials I couldn't readily identify.)

Then we flew away from the site of my ancestral devastation, following the serpentine twist of a river through barren fields. "Seen enough?" Bollard said. "It's all fields and furrows for the next hour or so."

I leaned back into the couch. "Yes. Can you leave a portion of the wall open, like a window?"

He obliged, putting three windows in the walls and a small porthole in the bottom. Then he rapped the wall, and it opened and extruded a shelf that held a glass decanter full of red fluid and a rack of rocks glasses. He shook the decanter and poured himself a glass and said, "Drink?"

"What are we drinking?"

"Whatever you want."

"I could use some water."

He shrugged, rapped the wall, and a new bottle appeared, this one full of clear fluid. He poured a measure into a glass and handed it over. I sipped, tentatively. It was the best water I'd ever tasted, crisp and clean and the perfect temperature; cold but not so cold it made the teeth ache. "This is acceptable," I said.

Bollard burst out laughing. "You are a delight, Princess. I might even enjoy working for you. You're a Zmija through and through. You never let on when you're impressed."

"What was my family like? Were they all... like Granny?"

"Ha. Your granny was warm and welcoming by Zmija standards. They were a vicious lot." He took a sip and then swirled the glass. "Made their fortune in weapons design and manufacturing, and had alliances with the other ruling families to keep the lowlies in check. Because of their expertise in weaponry, the Zmija were at the very tippy-top of the oligarchical heap, and they never let anyone forget it. Eventually the other members of the ruling collective got sick of having to lick your family's snakeskin boots, and decided a change of leadership was in order. Pulling that kind of coup off was a tricky proposition, though. The Zmija were all but immune to personal attack – they had a monopoly on any weaponry more advanced than a slingshot, and none of the weapons they created would target people on their whitelist, which included the whole family. The Zmija also had kill-switches installed in their tech, so they could deactivate everyone else's armaments at will. They were bulletproof, bombproof, everything-proof."

"And yet... orbital bombardment?" I raised an eyebrow.

"Ah, well, that's where Nigh-Space comes into it," Bollard said. "A generation before you were born, the second-most powerful family, the Monad, found the secret to interdimensional travel. They made a few clandestine forays to adjacent levels, and met some of the neighbors. One of those neighbors had technology as good as the Zmija did, without all those pesky safeguards and lockouts, and thus: orbital bombardment. The Monad is just as bad as the Zmija, though, really. They hold a strict monopoly on interdimensional travel, and most people here don't even know about Nigh-Space –

the lowlies are just as ignorant of other realities as you Earth people are, by and large."

"Then how did Granny get her hands on a magic door, if the Monad don't share?"

"An excellent question!" Bollard said. "There are always spies, defectors, and industrial espionage among the members of the collective, and it seems your family got their hands on the tech, or at least enough of it to build a portal to an immediately adjacent world. I suspect that will be quite a surprise to the Monad when they realize you've returned. If they'd known, they would have sent hunter-killers to Earth to kill you and your grandmother long ago. Ha. They must be beside themselves with bafflement over how I made my way back."

A light dawned. "The Monad exiled you? I guess they must have, if no one else has the technology."

Bollard held up his glass in a toast. "Indeed. I was going to destroy the Monad anyway, Princess, for trying to get rid of me. But since I met you, I get to destroy my enemies and get paid for it. Which is both of my favorite things at once." He glanced down, and the porthole window on the floor expanded. We were above a rugged mountain range now, the peaks jagged and snowcapped – and then one of the caps dissolved, and the bubble descended into the revealed opening. We were entering the heart of a mountain. "Welcome to my workshop," Bollard said. "Now the fun part begins."

GLENN

As I said before, I don't intend to go into great detail about my frankly excellent sex life with Vivy, because there are more consequential (and interdimensional) issues to discuss. That said... a certain amount of context will help the hypothetical reader understand why I was so incredibly flustered by the sudden and insistent arrival of an unexpected guest.

I was at home one morning some weeks after my first (and so far only) journey through Nigh-Space, revising a paper, when Vivy ed me two words: compliance check.

We were both very busy with school stuff that month, and spending less time together than we wished, but as any kinky couple can tell you, there are many ways to keep things intimate, interesting, and exciting even when you're separated by space or circumstance. When Vivy sent a "compliance check" text, which could come at any time, I had ten minutes to send a photograph proving I was, well... in compliance. Which is to say, that I was fulfilling whatever requirements Vivy had set for me that day. Sending her such photos was pretty easy when I was home, though they got a bit trickier when I was at the library or grocery store or in a meeting – in those cases I had to hurry to find a bathroom or some other private space so I could provide an intimate image. (I tended to keep my face out of them; even with her interdimensionally high-quality phone encryption, better safe.) Of course, the inconvenience was part of the fun. Who wants a domme who only makes reasonable, easily fulfilled demands of you?

Since I was working from home and expected privacy all day, Vivy's requirements were on the more elaborate side that day. Plus, she likes tasteful and well-composed dirty photographs, with dire consequences for blurry snapshots or poor composition. All this is to explain why I was in the floor of my bedroom, lying on my side in front of the full-length mirror on the closet door, almost entirely naked, fiddling with the timer on my phone camera, trying to capture an image that simultaneously included 1) my collar, 2) the steel chastity cage locked onto my intimate bits, 3) my stainless steel butt plug with the heart-shaped pink jewel in the base peeking from between my cheeks, 4) my adorable over-the-knee socks with the pink-purple-blue stripes of the bisexual pride flag; and 5) my four-inch purple heels.

I was twisting my hips and angling my camera, wondering if I should break down and buy a selfie stick or a miniature tripod for such situations, when someone began pounding on my front door with the insistence of a cop or a zealot.

I jolted in alarm, then settled myself down. Probably a delivery. If I ignored them they'd leave the package and go away. Meanwhile I had five more minutes to comply–

"Glenn!" an unfamiliar male voice bellowed in a medium-posh British accent. "I know you're in there! Don't leave a chap lingering on the stoop like a... common fishmonger!"

I had no idea who this person was, or why they talked like a bad steampunk cosplayer, but I needed to deal with them before all our neighbors came out to do so. I had to make some essential adjustments first, because my fetishes do not include public humiliation or even much in the way of exhibitionism. I shouted "Just a minute!" and crawled on my hands and knees to the bedside table on Vivy's side. I pulled open the drawer and pawed through the condoms and toys to find the spare key.

Not the key to my chastity cage – the emergency key for that is suspended in a block of ice in the freezer and would need a couple of minutes under hot water to thaw, but the cage wasn't the problem, since it was made for long-term wear and not noticeable under clothes (not that I had on many of those yet). The problem was my heels; they have ankle straps, each secured in place by a little heart-shaped padlock. (Does the idea of doing housework or homework locked into a pair of high heels sound fun to you? If yes, you understand our thing. If not... well, I won't vanilla-shame. Your preferences are perfectly valid and I hope they give you joy.)

I found the little key and got the heels unlocked and tugged off while the insistent non-fishmonger stranger continued hammering the door. He shouted, "This is hardly the welcome I expected after everything we've been through together, Glenn!" If he hadn't known my name, I would have been concerned that he was mentally ill; since he did know my name, I was even more concerned. The same key unlocked the matching padlock on my collar, lovingly snapped shut that morning by Vivy before she left, and I pulled that bit of purple leather off and tossed it on the bed.

Bang bang bang bang bang!

"Coming!" I shouted, and then glumly thought, I won't be doing that anytime soon, because I was now comprehensively out of compliance and almost out of time to send a photo, anyway. Vivy did not offer lenience due to extenuating circumstances, either. I'm not very bratty, so I don't get in trouble often, but she likes it when I do, so keeps things strict to maximize her chances.

I grabbed one of Vivy's oversized t-shirts (it had a picture of an angry hamburger on the front) and pulled it over my head, then yanked on a pair of my black gym shorts. I didn't bother pulling off the thigh-high socks, but this was Berkeley, where a dollop of gender nonconformity wouldn't raise any eyebrows, or at least not any I cared about.

I rushed to the door, which was still shuddering in its frame from blows unbefitting a friendly visitor. I yanked the door open, and was confronted by a willowy, pretty young blond man in a tweed suit who beamed at me joyfully. He threw his arms open wide. "Glenn! We are reunited! I love your socks."

"Who are you?" I demanded, as sternly as I could given the circumstances.

"It's me. It's Eddie." At my blank look, his tone took on a hint of acid. "Maybe you don't recognize me. Last time you saw me, I was a spaceship. I didn't realize you were so shallow and obsessed with appearances."

I stared. Then I raised my phone, took a photo of the spaceship in human form at my door, and sent it to Vivy.

A moment later I got her reply: that is not the picture I wanted.

This guy says he's Eddie, I texted back, while the supposed Eddie craned his head to see what I was typing.

oh crap. on my way, she replied. Then the three "she's typing" dots, and: we'll discuss your failure to comply later.

I sighed and put my phone away. "I guess you'd better come in." I stepped aside, and he entered, hands shoved in his tweedy trouser pockets, looking around the apartment. After our adventures in Nigh-Space, Vivy didn't need an apartment to herself anymore – I wouldn't freak out if she vanished in front of me now, or if I saw her guns and swords and lances and things in her secret spatially impossible locker – and she'd invited me to move in. Her decorating tastes were either austere or indifferent, and I'd warmed up the place with some bookshelves and plants and rugs on the hardwood floor (an essential element if you spend as much time kneeling as I do). We'd also acquired a cat together, one that wasn't meant be an anchor for a snap-trace; we just wanted a pet. Unfortunately, Vivy had insisted on adopting a middle-aged tortie with a ragged ear and a case of terminal shyness, and after living with her briefly, we'd named her PG (short for Piss Goblin). PG was hiding somewhere, as usual; she only ever came out for Vivy. Everyone else had to deduce her existence from the puddles and the smell. I envied PG's ability to avoid interactions with humans. Or, in this case, non-humans.

We lived in a studio apartment, but a very spacious one, and we'd partitioned off our bedroom with tall folding screens, so at least Eddie wasn't looking at my collar and heels with those avid, see-it-all-eyes.

"Did you, ah, can I get you..." I trailed off as he stared at me expectantly. "Are you really Eddie?"

"In the mostly-flesh." He wiggled his fingers and spun in a complete circle on one heel. "You know how I got exploded into assorted bits?"

"I recall. I was there."

"Dreadful bother. Once you and Vivy were safely away, I had to pilot that horrid vessel we commandeered to an extraction point. The trip took ages, but the flow of time was in my favor there, you know, and my sort, we're quite patient. Anyway, now the Interventionists are building me a new body. A proper body, I mean to say, not this... biped... thing." He ran his hands down the front of his suit like he was wiping something damp off his palms.

"They're making you a ship, you mean? That kind of body?"

He snapped his fingers and then shot finger guns at me. "Right-o. It should be even better than my old one. In the meantime, I wasn't about to sit around on a shelf waiting, so I talked to our handler, Jen, and she found me this jolly android to tootle around in, and I decided to come visit you and Vivy."

"Oh. Right. Well." I wanted to ask where he was staying, but I suspected the answer was "here," and I wanted to ask how long he was staying, but I suspected the answer would be "indefinitely," so instead I said, "Why do you have a British accent? You didn't sound like this when you were a spaceship."

"Ah, the dratted thing came pre-installed with accent and diction, I'm afraid. I think this android was created to impersonate a member of the Perpetual Parliament in Angleland, a few levels over."

I rubbed my forehead. "There's a version of England called Angleland?"

"Just so."

"How is that possible? Vivy said the levels of Nigh-Space aren't, like, parallel universes that branched off from some main line. They're totally separate."

Eddie shrugged. "I can't explain it, really. Possibly some group of Angles in jolly old ancient England stumbled through one of the occasional natural passages to another level, and things just developed from there. Breaches like that used to be more common on this level – you've heard all those stories about fairy rings and barrows and forbidden woods and mists where people disappear? We've sealed up a lot of the persistent breaches, though. They're a menace. Like having a pit full of spikes concealed in your living room." He looked around. "This is your living room? Or, more like, room-room?" He sat on the couch. "This is where I'll be sleeping, then?"

"I... sure. That's fine." I had more questions – like why some Angles from whenever Angles were a thing would evolve to speak in a modern British accent – but then I realized Eddie was probably just screwing with me again, like he had with his "ghosts that eat your bones" comment the day we met.

He sat down, and then bounced up and down, on the couch. At least he wasn't jumping on it with both feet. "You know, I've never slept before? Fairly excited to give it a try. Dreams sound delightful, and I think the brain in this body is equipped for those."

I should try to be a good host, because this was my partner's friend, or at least her most trusted colleague. "Can I get you any... Wait. Do you eat or drink things?"

He patted his belly. "A compact fusion battery keeps me ticking along, though I can quaff and chew, for the sake of appearances, as needed, and I can even enjoy the taste. I have no immediate desires in that arena though." He made a great show of craning his neck and looking past me. "Where's our Vivian? Not that you aren't delightful on your own, of course."

"She's got a class, but I told her you're here, and she's on her way."

"Oh, yes, her 'studies.'" He made elaborate air quotes. "Public policy, yes? She should be teaching that. She knows more about shaping society than any of her instructors, I'm sure."

"I'm not sure that's exactly what she's interested in…" I began, but then something occurred to me. "Huh. You said 'I know you're in there,' when you were pounding on the door. Which, incidentally, you didn't have to bang that hard or that long, I was just in the middle of something. But… how did you know I was here?" I peered at him in horror. "You don't have X-ray vision, do you?"

He thumped himself on the temple. "While the contents of the old bean here aren't entirely human-standard, no, I don't have the ability to bombard you with radiation and develop an image of your denser interior structures."

With a great effort, I didn't sigh. "I meant, can you see through walls?"

He frowned. "There are systems that can detect movement through walls, depending on the kind of walls, and the kind of movement, but… no? I knew you were here because of your anklet. Vivy's comms are offline, and I thought wherever you were, she'd likely be nearby. It's not as if I knew your address."

I was still wearing the anklet – kink aside, that piece of jewelry had all those lovely defensive capabilities, so I wasn't eager to remove it – but I hadn't realized… "You can track me with this thing?"

"Well, mainly Vivy can. I'm usually not even in the same reality as you, and it doesn't work across levels. But I'm Vivy's spotter and support staff, so we've got a lot of the same technology, and since I am here, yes, I can pinpoint your location to a high degree of accuracy–"

The door flew open and Vivy rushed in. Her hair was pulled back in a messy bun and she was wearing an oversized gray button-down shirt and her comfy jeans and her battered Doc

Martens and she was, as always, a vision. Just currently a not entirely welcome one. I stood up and glared at her. "Eddie said you've been tracking me."

She looked briefly confused. "The anklet? I mean, yes, it does have a tracking component, in case you get kidnapped or something, but it's not even turned on, babe, I'd only ever activate it if you went missing."

I was mollified, but only slightly. "Eddie used it."

"Ugh! Eddie. Eddie has very poor boundaries. Hello, Eddie. You look like an idiot in that body."

He rose and pirouetted. "I have as many holes as you do, now, Vivy! Or, wait, almost? I suppose it doesn't matter. You people really are just riddled with holes, though. I can't imagine what you use them all for. I was happy with a couple of exhaust ports and access hatches."

"That's pretty much what we've got, too," Vivy said. "Stop tracking Glenn, okay?"

"But–"

"No arguments." This firm voice was very different from the firm voice I was used to hearing from her – not silk over steel, but just the steel.

"Oh, fine." Eddie blew his blond bangs off his forehead. "I suppose it will be a more authentically human experience, just blundering around hoping I run into people."

Vivy looked at me and opened her arms. "Am I forgiven?"

I crossed my arms over my chest. "You should have told me you could track me. I feel like a teenager with parental spyware on my phone, and that is not the dynamic I want in our relationship." Plenty of submissives call their dommes "Mommy," and we wish them all bliss, but Vivy and I both had strong sets of (admittedly opposite) feelings about our actual mothers, so that terminology didn't activate our thrill centers.

She nodded. "You're right. In my defense, the tracking system seemed pretty minor, and I guess it got lost in the cloud of the many other things I should have told you."

We hadn't had our big talk about outstanding secrets yet, ostensibly because we were busy and she needed to find out what she was cleared to tell me. Also, she'd distracted me with elaborate roleplay.

"Too true, dear boy," Eddie chimed in. "A little well-intentioned spy tech hardly merits comment, especially compared to your finding out there are other universes, or that your beloved is an interdimensional freedom fighter, or that the two of you aren't even from the same planet–"

"What?" I shouted, and Vivy groaned and covered her face with her hands.

TAMSIN

There was a platform waiting inside the mountain, a circle of dull gray metal about thirty feet across, like the local equivalent of a helipad. The bubble set down and then opened a doorway. When Bollard picked up Trevor and stepped out, lights came on inside the mountain from indeterminate sources, illuminating nothing much: grey floor, stone walls, and shadows.

I followed them out, and the sphere closed itself up and zipped off into the sky soundlessly. I watched it go, and then kept staring as the mountain peak shimmered back into place, sealing us in beneath its vast concavity. "You live in a hollowed-out mountain?" I asked. "That's a little bit 'James Bond villain,' isn't it?"

"I don't understand your cultural references, Princess. Cave paintings don't interest me. In fact, I just work in a hollowed-out mountain. I live in a high-altitude pleasure palace. But since I enjoy working, I don't see home too much."

I kept staring upward. "How did you make the top of a mountain appear and disappear?"

Bollard snorted. "Show a Neanderthal your smartphone and see how confused she gets. You have to get used to such wonders, Princess. They're commonplace here."

Hmm. If it was actual rock above me, that meant Bollard could turn stone to gas and back again. So... nanotech? Like, fully functional utility fog, the real heavy sci-fi shit? If they had that kind of technology here, and could rearrange molecules at will, then why was this a world run by money-grubbing oligarchs instead of a post-scarcity utopia? It seemed more likely that, despite Bollard's pretensions, the mountaintop above me was an illusion. I suspected Bollard was blowing smoke up my ass. I suspected he lied as casually and naturally as I employed sarcasm.

He stomped his foot, and a square section of the landing platform rose an inch up from ground level. He stepped onto the floating square. "Come along. I'll give you the tour." I joined him, stepping up gingerly, expecting the hovering platform to wobble, but it was perfectly steady.

The platform then fell precipitously through darkness, and only Bollard's complete casualness kept me from grabbing onto him and shrieking. "You might have warned me about the drop," I said through gritted teeth.

"Did you expect us to go up? Down was the only available option. It's just an elevator. Even you people have those."

The elevator settled after a few seconds, and more lights came on around us. We were in a white-walled lab space, even the floors gleaming, filled with long tables and racks of drawers and mysterious equipment and rolling stools, with various rounded, hatchlike doors leading to other parts of the complex. "Welcome to the workshop." Bollard dropped Trevor onto what looked distressingly like an autopsy table. "Let me know when you want to wake him up."

"I'm surprised he hasn't woken up already. How long do people stay out when you blood choke them?"

"Oh, not long. Blood chokes only render people unconscious very briefly. Once he stopped struggling, I injected a sedative to keep him under." He held up a hand. "I have a ring full of the stuff."

I frowned. "Then… why choke him at all? Why not just go straight to the sedative?"

"I like choking people, Princess. Anyway, when you want him revived, I'll apply a counter-agent."

Trevor would have a lot of questions for me, and I decided to put off having to answer them. "Not quite yet. Let's have that tour first."

Bollard shrugged. "This is my research lab." He gestured around us, then led me to one of the doors and pushed it open. "The living quarters are in there – I've got a couple of spare rooms for you and Trevor. They aren't fancy, but we won't be here very long."

"You have guest rooms? Do you have a lot of sleepovers?"

He showed me his teeth. "I had plans, once upon a time, to quicken several Chicanes at once. Unfortunately, in practice, multiple instances are difficult to control, and there were... issues... with the clarity of the synaptic links. They were supposed to operate in tandem, like a pack of hunting predators, but they tended to get confused, trip over each other, and mistake one another for their targets, leading to unsubsidized violence." He shrugged. "I decided it wasn't important enough to resolve the problem. One Chicane is usually enough to do the job anyway. Occasionally I bring a spare with me, dormant, folded up in a suitcase." He closed that door and led me to another. "Speaking of Chicane, the sooner I get a fresh one decanted, the better."

"What are they?" I still had entirely too vivid a memory of that misshapen, giggling, drooling face above me.

"My Chicanes?" Bollard paused with his hand on a door. "Well, once upon a time, the original Mr Chicane was my best friend and business partner. Then things went wrong, and all I had left of him in the aftermath was a couple of teeth and a smear of brain matter I managed to wrap up in a handkerchief before exfiltration."

"I'm... so sorry." What else could I say? I hadn't expected that sort of reply.

Bollard waved my apology away with an expression of distaste. "Originally, I intended to clone Chicane, bring him back to life, restore him, but there was no way to give him back his memories. Worse yet, there was some contamination in the samples. The first Chicanes I made suffered seizures and swift neurological degeneration. I had to make some tweaks in order to make his bioform stable, so he wouldn't simply die shortly after waking up, and in the process, he became... something different. At that point, I gave up on my rather sentimental original idea, and decided to create a new kind of partner. I'm still refining my Chicanes all the time, making little improvements, tinkering, you know."

Bollard pushed open the door, which led to an anteroom that held another door, this one made of heavier metal, bristling with scanners. Bollard stood placidly before the door as violet light played over his face, and then the door clicked and swung open. "This is the most secure part of my lab. One hates to imagine a Chicane in the wrong hands."

Yours are the wrong hands, I thought. But as long as they were working for me, they were right enough.

The new room was long, and made narrow by row upon row of cylindrical metal tanks, each about eight feet high and four feet in diameter. It reminded me of a modern microbrewery. I'd been mentally prepared for transparent tanks, like the sort you see in the more horror-tinged class of science fiction thrillers, with Chicanes in various stages of development from fetal to adult suspended in green fluid. "There's a Chicane in each of these tanks?"

Bollard nodded, beaming with pride. "Yes, but only two or three are ready to be decanted now. Some of them are still developing, and some are experiments that might fail. In such cases, they go back into the generative slurry to become something new later." He went to a wall panel and waved his hand across its featureless blackness, making a spotlight illuminate a tank on the end of a row.

A console rose up from the floor, green lights flickering into life on its smooth surface. Bollard cracked his knuckles, then waved his hand again, and music filled the room, something sprightly with lots of violins and flutes. "Chicane was a great lover of chamber music from the Lumbricus era, back when he was his original self, and I like to think he still finds it soothing, when he awakens to a new life."

Bollard stepped up to the console and waved his hands over it, then glanced back at me. "You should back up a few steps. Sometimes the fresh Chicanes come out a bit agitated."

I dutifully retreated until my back was against the heavy metal door, and I rather wished I was on the other side.

The metal walls of the spotlit tank slid down into the floor, and then I was looking at something close to what I'd imagined: a transparent cylinder, full of yellowish fluid, in which a naked Chicane hung suspended in a complicated harness, with various tubes and lines snaking into his wiry body and bulbous head. I couldn't help myself – my eyes flicked downward, and I was both appalled and relieved to see that he had no apparent external genitalia. One of the "tweaks" Bollard had made, no doubt, and I resolved not to speculate about what had prompted that decision.

The fluid drained out of the cylinder through a grate in the bottom, and it became apparent that Chicane was not merely floating in the goo, but suspended in a web of transparent hoses and wires that snaked into his slumbering body, for he continued to dangle even when the liquid was gone. "You're probably wondering why I bother with the metal shell on the tanks," Bollard said.

I hadn't been, exactly, but I just said, "Yes."

"I used to have the tanks open, so I could visually monitor the progress of each subject. But when the new Chicanes would open their eyes and take in the world for the first time, it alarmed them to see so many identical creatures in such a state… especially when they realized they were one of those creatures. The experiences led to some terrible psychological deterioration, even after I dialed down their fear and disgust responses. Now I let each Chicane believe they are the only one. We all like to feel special, don't we, Princess? I hope you'll go along with my ruse. To do otherwise would be rude."

With that, he waved his hand again, and the glass walls descended into the floor as well, exposing the new Chicane to the air. A motor whirred as the harness lowered the dripping creature gently to the floor. Bollard climbed onto the platform and carefully removed the hoses and unclipped the harness, then picked up the Chicane and carried him to a table that rose up from the floor. That table, I noted, was padded with some black leather-like material, unlike the bare metal where he'd deposited Trevor. Bollard carefully crossed the twisted imp's hands over his chest, so Chicane looked ready for his own funeral, not his birth (or rebirth?).

Bollard snapped his fingers, and a metal lacework crown descended from the ceiling on wires. He fitted it over Chicane's head, made some inscrutable adjustments, and then said, "There. He'll be online in a few minutes." Bollard moved away from the table, placing himself between Chicane and me, and stood sideways, so he could easily look from me to his partner and back again. "As I said, it was impossible to restore the original Chicane's memories, and that loss grieves me deeply. But I have developed the next best thing. This Chicane has been subjected to direct neural stimulation and immersion in a virtual environment for months, aided by hypnotic techniques, creating the illusion of experiences, essentially training him for the work we'll do together, inculcating a sense of loyalty to me, and providing some continuity of experience. This particular suite of implanted memories and skills wasn't specifically focused on regime change, but Chicane is a generalist anyway as a rule. He should work."

"I don't want this to come across the wrong way," I said carefully. "You're clearly a gifted scientist, so I'm curious…"

"Why did I become a violent criminal?" He chuckled. "Why make the world a worse place, instead of a better one? It's rather prosaic, really. I like being a violent criminal, and I only make the world worse for some people. I make it much better for myself. I became what I am through a combination of genetic predisposition and exposure to my environment, just like everyone else. I've learned a lot about the forces that shape us, through my experiments training new Chicanes. I have theories for why I turned out the way I did. But since I'm happy with what I am, I don't fret about it overmuch. And, to be entirely honest, we're fundamentally amoral, Chicane and I. If someone hired us to rescue orphans from a burning building, we'd do that. Unfortunately, we're more often hired to create orphans. That's hardly our fault, though." He turned to gaze at his partner.

Bollard's answer made me speculate a bit on my own nature, and its origins. I'd had enough therapy and read enough books and ingested enough psychedelic drugs to know myself to a certain degree. Repression and compartmentalization were my preferred coping mechanisms. I had an avoidant attachment style, which was clearly the best sort of attachment style, because it meant I was self-reliant and complete in myself, and didn't need anyone else, really. According to the widely discredited but still interesting Meyers-Briggs Type Indicator taxonomy, I was an INTJ – Introverted, Intuitive, Thinking, Judging (as opposed to extroverts who rely on their senses and feelings and perceptions; just the idea of living like that made me shudder). I was an Aquarius with Saturn in my fourth house and Pluto in opposition to my sun. (Which did apparently match my personality, though now I knew I'd actually been born in a different universe under different stars, so make of that what you will.)

My ex-girlfriend who was into astrology blamed the stars, but my therapists were all united in the opinion that I turned out this way because of my lack of parents and my upbringing with aloof old Granny. I had no reason to dispute their assessments. It made sense to me. I wondered if I could tweak myself, the way Bollard tweaked his Chicanes. I wondered what I'd change about myself if I could. Maybe I could stand to be a little more–

Chicane tore the crown from his head and leapt from the table, landing on all fours in a horrid arachnid pose, then twisted his expressionless face up to look at Bollard – and past him, at me. His blank gaze sharpened at the sight of me, and he snarled. The homunculus bounded forward, teeth bared, drool flying, and I couldn't help but cringe against the door. Threat detected. No countermeasures available, my pendant whispered unhelpfully. Exploring options.

Bollard reached out casually and caught Chicane by the throat, and held him, writhing and wriggling, like a man holding a serpent desperate to strike. "Shhh," Bollard said, and then stroked Chicane's hair with his other hand. "That is Tamsin. She is our client. You remember clients, yes?"

The glassy-eyed creature swiveled its gaze to Bollard, and… I don't know how else to put it: the lights came on. Chicane made a sort of strangled sound of assent, and Bollard carefully set him on his feet. Chicane looked at me, then up at Bollard, and said, "Clothes?" His voice was like eels in a blender.

"He talks?" I said.

"He does," Bollard confirmed. The one I'd met had been damaged, apparently badly enough to render him incapable of speech. He patted Chicane on the shoulder. "There are clothes in your room, come, I'll show you." Bollard turned to me. "I'm going to give my partner a little orientation. Would you like me to have Trevor awakened? You can give him an orientation, too."

No use putting that off any longer. "That sounds good."

Bollard nodded and followed me out of the laboratory, and oh, how I hated turning my back on the two of them. He led Chicane by the hand into the living quarters, and I went out to the table where Trevor was stretched out, just in time to see the table extrude an articulated arm with a needle on the end and poke him in the shoulder.

Trevor squawked and sat upright, staring around wildly. "What the fuck what the fuck what the fuck what the fuck…"

He was starting to hyperventilate, so I slapped him across the face. I don't know – it works in the movies. I remembered too late that it also worked on Trevor, in ways I did not currently intend, in the bedroom. He stared at me, sucked in a deep breath, and said, "Tamsin, where are we?"

Integrated tech detected, my pendant whispered. The snake tattooed around Trevor's neck briefly glowed pink and then reverted to dead ink again. Add retainer to SerpentNet, no edit privileges, level-one channels only? Confirm or decline.

I thought the word "Confirm" and nothing happened. Not a telepathic pendant, then. I tried subvocalizing, nothing really audible, just moving my tongue and letting out a little hum in the shape of "Confirm," and the pendant said, Retainer added.

Trevor eyes widened, he blinked at me, and then he subvocalized, looking like he was swallowing, and I heard it in my ear, just like the pendant's voice: Holy shit you got online? Your granny used to talk to me this way. My tattoo is some kind of communications device.

Bollard doesn't know about this channel, I almost-silently said. Don't let him find out. I didn't know why I was keeping SerpentNet a secret – just that I wanted to have some kind of edge here.

Trevor nodded and rubbed his shoulder where he'd gotten jabbed. Where are we?

Bollard's lab.

My retainer scrambled off the table and whimpered, and I scowled at him. I realized I should probably start speaking out loud, in case Bollard was listening. "Trevor! It's fine. I hired Bollard and Chicane to help me recover my family estates. To claim my inheritance. They're on our side."

"They're on their side, Sin, but… okay. Yeah. They honor their contracts, or at least, that's what people say." He looked around. "So we're… You went through the door? And brought me? We're in the old country?"

"A new country for me. And soon, with your help, it's going to be my country. I'm going to take back what was stolen from me."

Trevor looked at me with something between worship and terror (and are they really so different?). "You're... kind of hot when you're scary," he said at last.

"I'm always hot," I said, because confidence is so often the most important thing.

"Yes. Yes, you are," he said, and it took me a moment to realize he meant I was always scary.

"You haven't seen anything yet," I assured him. "Let's–"

Local defense, weapons, surveillance, and operational systems successfully compromised, the necklace whispered. Voice control available.

I blinked. I can control the workshop now?

Confirmed, the necklace purred. Presence of Zmija legacy systems in deep systems allowed acquisition of complete control.

"Oh, Trevor," I said. "I think this is going to be fun."

GLENN

"You're from another world?" I sat on the couch and put my head in my hands. I knew she'd fabricated parts of her history, but her entire history?

"Glenn, listen," Vivy began.

"Hmm," Eddie said. "The two of you are aliens to each other, technically. I don't think your bisexual pride flag covers that, Glenn."

I blinked at him. "I was freaked out that Vivy isn't really from Los Angeles. But are you saying she's not even human?"

"I am so human!" Vivy said. "I'm not that kind of alien. Shut up, Eddie." She knelt before me and took my hands. "There are lots of humans scattered throughout Nigh-Space – early hominids were explorers, and they spread out from some unknown home world through cracks and breaches into neighboring levels, and did what humans do, which is reproduce and wander. On some levels they found alien technology, or local sapiens to mentor them, or time ran a lot faster, which is why there are so many different levels of technology throughout Nigh-Space. But I am definitely the same species as you."

"You are augmented, though," Eddie said. "Arguably posthuman, even–"

"Which part of 'shut up' was unclear?" she snapped, then refocused on me. The fullness of her regard, as always, was nearly overwhelming, especially when I was feeling so unbalanced. "I was going to tell you about this when we had our talk. I thought you could use some time to digest our new reality before I dropped another bombshell on you. I did ask you to give me time–"

"Bullshit." I yanked my hands out of hers. "You were just scared to tell me, so you didn't. Again!"

She bowed her head, took a breath, and then nodded. "Yes. Okay. I was going to tell you, but I rationalized waiting. I didn't want you to look at me like I was some kind of freak."

She could be so frustrating. "Vivy. You're all kinds of a freak. I love you for being a freak. As usual, the problem isn't the thing you lied about, it's the fact that you lied. I need to hear it all, okay? Now."

"There are security issues–"

I threw my hands up in the air. "I'm not asking you for the secret code to the secret entrance to your secret base! I'm talking about things that have to do with you and me and us, and you know it."

"Okay, I hear you, but... what if you react badly?" She was biting her lip, and it was adorable, and I hardened my heart.

"Maybe I will! I'm allowed to react badly to bad things! But if I do, we can talk about them. I don't understand how you can be so good at negotiating the fine details of–" I sighed, glancing at Eddie "– some things, while being totally unable to talk about this other stuff."

"He means the way you discuss your various sexual preferences and limits and so forth," Eddie supplied helpfully. "But not the more peculiar aspects of your biography." He crossed one leg over the other and said, "Why is that, do you think, dear Vivian?"

"Eddie. I will lock you in a closet until your new body is ready if you don't stay out of this."

He rose. "Oh, very well. I'll be in the kitchen, or rather, that bit of your one big room that has a stove in it. I have the strangest craving for tea and... some kind of horrible dry cookie?" Eddie toddled off, giving us at least a semblance of privacy, though his hearing was probably superhuman.

Vivy slumped down on the couch beside me. She was clearly ashamed of herself, and I wanted to comfort her, but I held my resolve. "Those things, sex things, are easy for me to talk about, because they're about us... trying to make each other happy. Other things are a lot harder for me to open up about." She looked at me sidelong. "You really want to know everything, huh?"

I nodded. "Get it all out now, and we won't need to keep having variations on this conversation until I can't stand them anymore. Which is a limit that's rapidly approaching, just so you know."

"All right. I'll tell you. But maybe... would it help if there were... visual aids?"

"What, like a PowerPoint presentation?"

"I could take you to the place I'm from, and then you might understand why I left."

"Are you sure you aren't just trying to dazzle me with spectacle to distract me from being mad at you?"

She looked glum. "I get why you'd think that, but no. Going home... it's not my favorite thing. But if you want to really know me, you should see where I came from."

I nodded. I was doing my best to roll with all this weird sci-fi shit, and I was most successful when I focused on familiar elements and practical matters. "I know your cousins on Earth are imaginary, and you told me your parents were gone, but do you have family back home? Do you even have families, or are you all born in robot incubation pods or something?"

She wrinkled her nose. "No, we have families. I'm an only child, but my parents are still around – they're just not present in this reality, so I made up a cover story."

"Ugh, Vivy. We bonded over the whole 'single mom' thing. Do your parents even really suck?"

"My parents suck more than you can possibly imagine," she said. "Having a single mom on drugs would have still been more mom than I actually experienced. I haven't seen or spoken to my parents in years. I could arrange a meeting, if you want, but they're not as... warm as your mother. They're old and set in their ways."

"So like interdimensional Boomers?"

"Ha." Her tone was flat, the syllable just a word and not a laugh. "No. I mean old old. Like centuries. Most people live a long time where I'm from. One body wears out and they just slip into another. Death is a thing that usually only happens when you want it to, and my parents are so self-centered they can't imagine a world they aren't part of."

"Vivy, are you centuries old? I know people lie about their ages on dating profiles, but–"

She snorted. "No, I'm as young as you think. I was a later-in-life whim my parents came to regret when I turned out to be more trouble than the rest of their hobbies."

I touched her cheek. "Hey. If anyone regrets you, that's their mental damage. I don't have to meet them if you're estranged. But... I would like to see where you're from."

"Okay." She stood up. "Eddie! Give me your ring. We're going on a field trip. We'll be back in a day or so. Feed the cat for me?"

"I thought your cat was dead. That's why you got Glenn." He twisted off a ring and tossed it underhand to Vivy, who snatched it from the air.

"That is not why–" She took a deep breath. "We have a new cat, Eddie, but it's the same deal as with the old one. The food is in the cabinet by the sink. Don't let the cat out of the apartment. Maybe don't let yourself out, either."

Eddie squeezed most of a bear-shaped plastic bottle of honey into a cup. "But I want to explore your charming adopted homeland."

"Just behave, please." She took my hand. "Okay, Glenn. This isn't like snap-tracing, where we zip right to our destination, or anyway as close as we can get. I'm using Eddie's ring, it's called a curve-chaser. It's an interdimensional transportation device, but it's designed to avoid attracting attention, so we have to sort of... ease our way along. We're going to jump one level up, then two, then four, then eight, and so on, until we get close to our destination." She took my hand. "The whole trip should only take about ten or fifteen minutes, but you might get a little barfy."

"Hold on, before we–" Go, I was going to say, but then we went.

I blinked, and we were standing on top of a golden hill, overlooking some kind of ruined estate turned to ash and rubble. My stomach did a little roller-coaster-descent flip, but I teetered on the right side of throwing up. Once I could speak, I said, "Vivy! I wanted you to wait a minute so I could change. I am wearing slutty long socks and slippers!"

She was in her strappy battlesuit, holographically suitable for every occasion. "Oh, right. Well, don't worry about it. Nobody will notice. We've got totally different social norms back in the Veil, and all the steps in between are places like this." She waved a hand. "Desolate, abandoned, poisoned, full of land mines, whatever – we try to way-station in remote places so nobody sees us traversing."

I gritted my teeth. "Vivy. I also have a plug in my ass and a cage on my cock."

My love squeezed my hand and smiled at me. "You didn't take them off when Eddie arrived? You're so good. I have your key. Do you want to be released?" She kept the key to my cage on a necklace, dangling between her breasts, and I'd spent many happy hours watching it bounce on its chain there.

I sighed. This was hardly the first outing where I'd been similarly outfitted, but usually we were just going to a restaurant or running an errand or something, where there was a thrill to being secretly in her thrall, unbeknownst to everyone around us. "If there's even a chance I'm going to meet your parents, I would rather not do it like this."

"That... is a totally understandable boundary."

Suffice to say that a few moments later I was free of my lifestyle accessories, which Vivy tucked into plastic bags and stowed in her battle-suit pouches. What else did she have in those things? "You know, I've never taken a plug out of you under an open sky before. Very alfresco."

"I am still not an exhibitionist," I replied. "These are special circumstances."

"Yes, yes. Ready for the next hop?"

I nodded, and we leapt again, this time landing on the top of a broken stone tower in a desert. I looked down at the dizzying drop just a yard away from my feet and grabbed onto Vivy's arm hard. "Hey. How did you know we'd land on this tower and not in mid-air? What if the tower had fallen over at some point? Wait, and what's stopping us from materializing in a snake pit or, or inside a wall, or something?" I was not panicking but I was panic-adjacent.

She put her arms around me and patted my back. "Hey, I'm not going to claim there weren't any gruesome mishaps in the old R&D departments that developed this tech, but we've got failsafes on top of failsafes now. We've been doing this a long time. Our preferred landing zones are pre-programmed and guaranteed snake-pit free, with backup options in case a landing zone has become unsafe, and we've got automated systems checking them regularly and transmitting real-time data. You know I wouldn't put you in danger." She paused. "On purpose, anyway."

I stepped out of her arms and looked at the drop again. "I'm just supposed to trust this tech, huh?"

"You regularly ride subway trains through badly maintained tunnels underneath a bay," Vivy said. "You fly in airplanes. I've seen you take drugs made by a chemistry grad student who goes by the nickname Garbage. You trust all that tech, and your society is barely a step above making things out of sticks and string."

"Okay. That's fair." I took her hand again.

"You only looked down," she said. "In this world, you should look up." I did, and she was right. After a brief pause for me to admire the double moons, one with a small and dainty ring, we jumped again, landing in ankle-deep, tepid water in a plaza under a night sky where only a handful of stars burned, and those dim and red. "Ew," Vivy said. "Regretting the slippers, huh?" Her boots were doubtless waterproof.

Another leap, and now I was queasy, so I bent at the waist and took deep breaths before looking up at the towering trees on all sides, their leaves a dull red in the red sunlight.

"There's megafauna here," she said. "Nothing I can't handle, but who wants to fight a giant slug-monster? We should probably get going."

I took her hand without straightening, and we shimmered again. An abandoned playground, with rusting monkey-bars and swings dangling from broken chains, under a sky the color of pus. The air smelled sweet, chemically so, like antifreeze, and my blue defense field flickered on. The cool fresh air that filled my nose made my stomach settle a bit. "Things have gotten worse here," she murmured, and then we jumped again. My defensive field dropped, and I looked around a vast warehouse space, lit by sunlight stabbing in through holes in the roof. A faded sign on the wall, in totally readable English, said, "The Old Polio Factory."

"We can take a break here, if you need," Vivy said. "Anything that can hurt us here is long dead, including the microbes."

I was still queasy, but it was bearable. "I'm okay. Wow. You take me to the nicest places."

"Next one is nicer, for some values of nice," she said. "One more big jump, okay?"

We traversed, and that was all my stomach, or nervous system, or everything together could bear. I stumbled away from her and vomited onto smooth turquoise pavement. I stared as my vomit beaded up and then vanished, somehow absorbed into the ground surface. I swung my head toward

Vivy, who patted me on the back and said, "You're okay, you'll be okay, just take deep breaths. The air here is literally medicinal. It will help."

I did take a breath, and smelled something like eucalyptus, but sweeter. I held out my arms and looked at them – all the little hairs were standing up, and it felt like they were standing up all over my entire body. (Which was mostly shaved at the moment, per my preference and her instructions, but still.) "What is that... tingling?"

"Any surface pathogens you brought with you are getting gently zapped into oblivion." Vivy rubbed her hand in soothing circles on my back. "The local field is also eradicating any latent skin cancers you might have. My home world takes care of you, from the automatic cradle to the very distant grave. If you stayed long enough, the environment would rewire your immune system and repopulate your gut biome with the best flora in the multiverse, but we won't be here long enough for all that to happen."

The tingling subsided, and I finally felt steady enough to take in my surroundings. We were in a daylit plaza surrounded by a low wall, in the midst of some kind of park or civic center, all golden lawns and stands of trees and graceful pavilions as far as I could see. It reminded me a little of Golden Gate Park in San Francisco, except there were no people, nobody walking dogs, no screaming children, not even a hot-dog vendor. I craned my head back, because there was something funny about the sky, and above me, there was no sun, and no clouds, and no blue sky, only a sort of luminous haze emitting steady illumination in a soft white wavelength.

"Vivy... where is your sun?"

"That is a complicated question. Why don't you come sit down?"

"Where? There are no–" But as soon as she mentioned sitting, the plaza extruded a long bench with a backrest, a graceful shape just flowing up from the ground, like the extra seat had appeared in Eddie. Vivy sat down, but I eyed the bench suspiciously, since it was made of the same mysterious turquoise substance that had just moments ago eaten my vomit. Vivy patted the seat beside her, though, and I joined her. The bench was firm yet yielding, and more comfortable than the most comfortable couch I'd ever sat on.

"This isn't a planet," Vivy said. "It's an artificial habitat. One of many in this region of the galaxy. This particular hab used to be part of a whole megastructure, similar to a Dyson swarm – you know what that is?"

"A... fleet of autonomous vacuum cleaners?" I guessed.

She elbowed me. "The vacuum cleaner guy is a different Dyson. Freeman Dyson hypothesized a construct called a Dyson sphere–"

"Yes, I read science fiction too. Some advanced civilization could build a big sphere around a star so they could capture all the available solar energy, and also get an absurd quantity of living space in the process. I was just being funny. What's the swarm version, though?"

Vivy patted me on the knee. "You're very funny, dear. So, it's hard to build a sphere big enough to encompass an entire star – that kind of engineering project makes building the Great Wall of China look like snapping a couple of Lego bricks together. You could, instead, build smaller segments, each one autonomous and habitable, and gradually add more pieces to that swarm, until eventually you had an entire sphere. That's what my very distant ancestors did. As time went on, they gained access to energy sources that were better than a star, though. That was good, because their star was going to do its nova thing, so they... got rid of it before it could blow up and ruin the neighborhood."

"Your distant ancestors got rid of a star." I thought I was taking all this very well.

She nodded. "They had mentors, an alien race that translated themselves into energy beings once they were sure humanity wasn't going to misuse their gifts. Anyway, my ancestors had to set up an artificial gravity source first, so the swarm wouldn't go spinning off into the void, and then they set up a stable wormhole and sucked the dying star through it like a boba pearl through a straw... I can't remember the details, honestly. I used to space out and think about giant killer robots whenever the automatic didactician tried to teach local history. I only paid attention to the stories of revolution and upheaval and war, and I always got marked down because I didn't correctly process them as cautionary tales, and instead made suggestions about how the revolutionary forces could have been more tactically and strategically effective–"

She was speeding up, starting to torrent words at me, which was something she did when she was feeling stressed or overwhelmed, so I put my hand over hers and said, "So you come from a civilization so advanced that they were harnessing stars when people on Earth were still getting the hang of the whole fire thing, and you chose to leave?"

"Yes, Glenn. I chose to leave. Look, are you hungry?"

I shrugged. "I was thinking about hot dogs earlier–"

She squinted at nothing, and a moment later, a delicate silver drone glided in on butterfly wings, hovered before Vivy, and lowered a tray that held a sausage on a bun, scattered with grilled onions and drizzled with stone-ground mustard, just the way I liked it. She handed me the tray, and the drone flew away. "There's not a lot of distance between thought and action around here. Go ahead. You can eat it. The meat is synthetic, but you won't be able to tell the difference – at the molecular level, there isn't any."

I took a bite, and it was the best hot dog I'd ever had. Vivy handed me a napkin. I wiped mustard off my mouth, and she took the napkin and threw it on the ground. I winced when she did that, but then the napkin dissolved and disappeared into the pavement. I lifted my feet up onto the bench. "That is creepy, babe."

"Don't worry. The ground won't eat your shoes. The hab is smart about that stuff. But you see how it is – you couldn't litter here even if you wanted to. The hab is very protective." She stood up, looked at me, and said, "Don't be afraid." Then she spun and aimed a roundhouse kick right at my face.

Before I could even shield myself, the floor shot upward in a geyser and hardened into a wall, and I heard her boot thump against it. The floor flowed back down. I stared at her. "That was... huh."

Vivy nodded. "The hab knows I'm not actually angry or aggressive, or it would have restrained me instead of just preserving you from harm. I spent a lot of my childhood getting restrained." She sat back down. "Everybody is safe here, whether they like it or not."

"Does that mean... if you, oh, tried to slap me, say, or..."

She shrugged. "We could, once the proper safeguards were in place, with medical drones nearby and prior consent recorded. The hab isn't trying to limit our enjoyment. It's just all about protecting the populace."

I looked around the silent park. "Uh... what populace? Where is everybody? Or is this the part where you tell me you're the last survivor of a stellar plague and this is a necropolis maintained by robots?"

"Maintained by robots, yes, but necropolis, no. There are people. The population of this habitat is currently around one hundred thousand, but it was made to house one hundred million, hence all the empty space. There are lots of these habitats – after the star went away, many portions of the swarm got fitted with propulsion systems and went walkabout through the galaxy – but the population is a fraction of what it was at its height. Not a lot of people get born anymore, outside of a few weird traditionalist sects who live on actual planets, but even they're pretty much just doing it as a bit, like those back-to-the-land types on Earth who know they can come back to the city if they have a bad winter."

"So... what do the hundred thousand residents of this swarm-segment do?"

She shrugged. "Kinda, just, whatever. Somebody with a thing for gardening grew the onions you're eating, somebody who likes cooking grilled them, and the mustard is most likely the product of somebody indulging an obsession with making small-batch condiments by hand. That's what it's like here – if you're interested in something, you can do it, for as long as you want, and then, you can go do something else. And when you can't think of anything else you want to do, you can die, or go into stasis, which is the choice most people make – 'Thaw me out in a thousand years when maybe things will be more interesting.' There's no money here. No want. No need that goes unmet. No hostile aliens out to get us or violent factions, because any that spring up get accommodated or managed out of existence. It's honestly pretty chill."

"So we're talking about your basic post-scarcity utopia?" I took another bite, chewed thoughtfully, swallowed, and said, "You must have fucking hated it here."

She snorted. "Why do you say that?"

"Because this is a world of solved problems, and you're a born problem-solver."

She let out a deep exhalation and rested her head on my shoulder. "Thank you. Yes. My parents had me on a whim, pretty much – like, they spent half a century exploring oceans on a distant planet, saw all the little baby fish or whatever, and thought, 'Parenting might be interesting.' Mom reactivated her ovulation and stuff, and they had me the old fashioned way, though without all the painful parts that come at the end. Once I was born, though, a squalling baseline human full of needs and instincts and baby shit, they got bored pretty quickly." She stood up and crossed her arms and stared off in the direction of a stone dome perched on delicate fluted pillars. "I get it! Babies can be pretty boring. So I was raised mostly by machines, and for whatever reason, all I wanted to do was break shit and fight injustice, like the people I read about in the histories and stories. Except breaking shit doesn't matter here, because new stuff can be assembled easily, and there's no injustice to speak of. My parents didn't know what to do with me. For a while they talked setting me up in a simulated environment, like a Renaissance Faire for revolutionaries, where all the other characters were androids. But devoting my energies to obviously fake shit did not appeal to me. I don't want to cosplay making the world a better place! Then they thought about dropping me on a wilderness world to do some kind of survivalist thing, but I knew that would be ultimately fake, too – there'd be drones lurking to help in case I got hurt. Nothing here matters. Nothing here is real."

She sat back down and sighed. "Except that isn't true. It's real. It's great. Most people here are super happy. All of human history is about trying to get to a point where we don't have to suffer, and my people got there ages ago. It's a psychological thing for me, that's all. I've got quirks in my neural architecture that make my basic disposition unsuitable for life on this kind of world. Things reached a point where I was so unhappy I was thinking of changing the structure of my actual brain so I wouldn't hate it here anymore."

"Like a lobotomy?"

"Way less crude. But not so different in terms of results. I would have been content. But before I took that step... the Interventionists recruited me, and told me my psychological damage could help others."

"That's amazing, Vivy." I felt I understood her so much better now. "I'm so glad they found you."

"Yeah, well, they can always use another good troublemaker, and they gave me a purpose."

"Breaking stuff and fighting injustice."

"And kinky sex." She actually smiled a little. "I met some people at my training camp who were into a lot of the same stuff you and me are into. That kind of sex isn't common in my world.

We don't really have any hierarchies or unequal structures to react against and play around with here, and divisions by gender and sexuality aren't as conceptually powerful here. My people are all about indulgence, and as a result, it's really hard to experience the thrill of the transgressive. Nobody here really wants to play around with control, probably because everyone has all the control they want. I guess. I'm not a psychologist. I only know about my own messed-up brain."

"I love your messed-up brain, and there's nothing wrong with you."

She snorted. "'Wrong' is a local judgment. Here, there's a lot wrong with me. Back in Berkeley... well, there are fewer things wrong with me there, and they're different things. The funny thing is, the end goal of the Interventionists is to make other places like this one. To give everyone in Nigh-Space maximum freedom, and safety from want and violence."

"It's a good goal," I said.

"I know. It's just not for me. At least, not yet. I only feel alive if I'm pushing against something. Fortunately, Nigh-Space is vast, and there are enough screwed-up places to keep a screwed-up person like me busy for lifetimes." She squeezed my hand. "So. Did you want a grand tour?"

I looked around that beautiful, airless place, and shook my head. "No. You don't like it here, and I like you, so let's go home instead. Thank you for showing me, though. I'm glad I know the truth. I don't want anymore secrets."

She shifted uncomfortably on the bench and let go of my hand. "As to that... there is one other thing I need to tell you. I didn't before because it's technically one of those big secret operational security things, but it's been weighing on me, and you deserve to know."

Great. I took a breath. "Okay. What is it?"

"It's about the real reason you and I met in the first place."

TAMSIN

"What are you doing?" Trevor said.

I sighed, cracked open one eye, and glared at him with it. "I am trying to be at one with the universe, and since I now know there is more than one universe, that's harder than usual." I was in the room Bollard had assigned me – spacious enough, if a bit bare-bones – sitting cross-legged on the bed, my hands resting on my knees.

Trevor leaned in the open doorway. "Since when do you meditate?"

"For years now. A guy I dated at UC Santa Cruz got me into yoga, and that led to meditation."

"A guy." Trevor tone was flat. Was he jealous? How cute.

"Yes. Glenn. We dated sophomore year. When he realized I was nothing but stress held together by caffeine and whiskey, he suggested we try yoga. We went to dawn classes together that whole year. He didn't need stress relief – Glenn is one of those calm and stable types – but he went along because he loved me." I uncrossed my legs. "The relationship didn't last, but the meditation did. It's good for settling my mind when I have a lot going on."

"Like plotting with a scientific maniac and his murderous homunculus to overthrow an oligarchy?" Trevor said.

"For instance." I stood up. I was wearing loose pants and a soft tank top made of "reconfigurable smartcloth," according to Bollard. I was wearing underwear from my backpack brought from home, though; I wasn't interested in putting anything smart near my crotch. (Which, I suppose, still gave Trevor a shot. Sorry. That was mean. Though Trev's actually smarter than he usually acts.) "How did you sleep?" I asked.

Trevor snorted. "In a psychopath's lair? Just fine, thanks." He perched himself on the edge of a tiny desk in the corner. "Bollard said his new Chicane is done with orientation, whatever that means, so it's time to discuss next steps. There are some rumors about the locations of Zmija family vaults–"

Access database of Zmija family vaults? the necklace whispered to my inner ear. I smiled. "That won't be necessary, Trevor. Granny told you the locations of all the vaults."

He blinked. "She wouldn't even tell me where she kept the good silverware, Sin."

I tapped the necklace. "But it's a plausible explanation for why we have the information, isn't it?"

Five hours later, I was standing on the slightly tilted rooftop of a building, surrounded by water that glittered a troubling shade of silver. The towers of other submerged buildings emerged from the rippling sea all around us, delicate glass spires and corkscrews and blunt bullet-shapes in shades of purple and iridescent black and dragonfly iridescence. Trevor and Chicane were unloading a trunk from inside a jet-black floating sphere: Bollard's personal transport from the laboratory. Untraceable and undetectable, he assured me.

The big man joined me at the railing and gazed down into the water. "To think, all this time, there's been a Zmija family vault down there. Apparently." He glanced sideways at me. "You trust Trevor's intelligence?"

I didn't miss the knife hidden in his phrasing. "I think his information is sound, anyway. Trevor was raised and trained to obey my family. If Granny told him something, his whole purpose is to listen and retain it."

"Is that why they call them retainers?" Bollard said.

I ignored him. "What I don't understand is why you picked this site. We had our choice of ten vaults, and this is one of the smaller. Why not go for the grand vault?" None of the vaults had their contents listed on SerpentNet; they were just numbered, one through nine "lesser vaults," and a tenth "grand." My own preferences were clear.

Bollard shook his head. "The grand vault's location was widely rumored, and according to Trevor, it's located exactly where people always suspected: right in the middle of Monad territory. This site, on the other hand, I've never even heard a whisper about. The Zmija family didn't have any recorded interests in the Inundation Zone – this is all Tompkins family territory. The two families must have made some backroom deal, or else your family bought off a lot of contractors to sneak a secure site in here before the overflow drowned the city. This vault could be unknown to the Monad and everyone else, so it's the softest target. Consider this a test-run to make sure your geneprint can actually open the doors that need opening. Even a lesser vault should provide us with ample resources, financial and quite possibly material. 'Lesser' means something different to a family as powerful as yours was."

"What happened here, anyway? A hurricane? Did a levee break?" I wrinkled my nose. "And why is the water that color? Is it some kind of industrial contaminant?"

"The official story is, there was seismic activity that breached an aquifer, flooding the low-lying areas, which encompassed the entire city. That explanation makes almost no sense, by the way, but the lowlies are so used to being lied to, most of them don't argue anymore."

He'd used that word before. "Lowlies?"

Bollard shrugged. "The common people. Salt of the earth, sweat of the brow, the great unwashed, call them what you will. They swallow whatever lies the leading families feed them."

"But the truth?"

"The truth is, there was a laboratory accident," Bollard said. "The Tompkins clan owes fealty to the Monad, and the Monad did some of their experimentation with interdimensional gates here. Why risk their own sites, after all? They didn't use proper safety precautions, the fools, and accidentally opened a portal to an alien sea. Before they managed to close their door, New Tompkinston was drowned, and the Inundation Zone was born. Some large number of people died in the initial accident and from later effects. This stuff isn't water, exactly. If an unmodified human comes into prolonged unprotected contact with this stuff, there are mutagenic effects. Cancer is the least of it. I heard about someone who died of intracranial hemorrhaging. When they opened up his skull for the autopsy, they found a face growing on his brain, complete with a nose and eyes and mouth."

"A teratoma? I've heard of those. You get tumors with teeth, or even hair–"

"This wasn't a human face, Princess. It was the face of one of the alien creatures that came in through the breach. We call them Swimmers." Bollard ghosted a smile. "That was an ugly bug hunt. It took months to find and kill every member of that invasive species, all while keeping their existence secret from the lowlies. I heard the final kill count hit seven hundred. Fortunately, the Inundation Zone doesn't connect to any local waterways, so the Swimmers couldn't escape. We don't think they could survive long in our water, anyway. We shouldn't encounter any alien monsters when we descend."

I shivered. "That's good."

"We may, however, encounter Tompkins patrols. The family still keeps an eye on its interests, and to watch for any Swimmers they might have missed."

"There are people down there?" Bollard assured me our protective gear would let us survive down there, but I couldn't imagine being stationed in this place, beneath the silver waters, keeping watch.

"Not entirely people, anymore." Bollard turned and leaned on the railing, back to the water, watching Chicane and Trevor lay out weapons and equipment on the roof. "The Monad does a lot of things, but their original specialty was biotech – they pioneered the cloning techniques that I subsequently improved upon – and the Tompkins do work in similar areas. That's how their family became so closely tied to the Monad. The Tompkins labs produced things the Monad wanted, and there was a marriage to bind their families together, to make sure the Monad ultimately controlled it all."

"Like a tech company buying up a smaller competitor," I said.

"But with more awkward family dinners, I imagine," Bollard mused. "The Tompkins specialize in human alteration and augmentation. Changing employees to suit their environments, basically. They created miners with improved night vision and toxin-proof lungs, radiation-hardened nuclear technicians, night watchmen with altered sleep cycles... and soldiers, of course, with all sorts of fancy changes. I've incorporated some of their finest innovations into myself, and some of the more experimental ones into Mr Chicane. The Tompkins family studied the Swimmers and altered some of their personal guards to survive in the same environment, and sent them down to clear out the infestation. Of course, changing them back is a different story, so those hunters have been stuck down there for years. It must be a miserable life. The attrition rate is fairly high. Lots of death by misadventure and suicide. There's no telling how many guards are left, really, but if we encounter any, they'll no doubt try to kill us just to relieve their boredom." He raised his voice. "All set, gentlemen?"

"All set." Chicane's voice was reedy and mushy all at once. I couldn't get used to hearing it. Trevor was struggling into a loose gray jumpsuit that looked like sharkskin, but once he got it zipped up, the slack vanished and it conformed to his body – like watching someone get vacuum-sealed. He yelped, then looked at me sheepishly. "Sorry. Haven't worn smartcloth like this since I was a kid."

Chicane stripped to his underwear, his flesh pale and sinewy, and pulled on his own suit. Bollard sighed and walked over, loosening his tie and shedding his jacket and unbuttoning his shirt as he went. I'd never seen him out of his suit, and it was eerie.

I was still in my tank top and yoga pants, so I just had to lose the latter to put on my own suit. When I was down to my underwear, Bollard and Chicane ignored me, and Trevor ogled me; I wouldn't have had it any other way. I stepped into the suit, which was as roomy as a mechanic's coveralls until I zipped it up, and then it was like a second skin. I'd worn a latex catsuit a few times, during my club night days, and the garment felt a bit like that, but stretchier and more forgiving. There were integrated gloves and booties, and it zipped up all the way to the bottom of my chin. Bollard reached into the trunk full of supplies and handed around helmets. They were classic sci-fi fishbowls, and I expected glass, but they were lighter and felt a lot less fragile. Bollard put his on, and it seamlessly connected with the suit, so I did the same.

The helmet sealed with a gentle shlorp, and slightly cool air circulated inside. "There's a communication system built in, and we're all on the same channel," Bollard's voice rumbled in my ear. "The helmet also has an informational overlay, useful since neither of you foreigners have optical implants. I suppose we should get you smart contact lenses at some point, but in the meantime…" My helmet lit up with an array of information: a translucent map of the Inundation Zone, with a route marked out in blinking red, and displays of temperature, wind speed, humidity, and other currently useless info. I figured out how to make those latter things go away by staring at them and blinking; the interface was pretty intuitive. I could make a killing with this technology back on Earth… but I had other killing to do here first.

"There's sonar, too," Bollard said. "There's no animal life down there – the water is too poisonous – so if you see any dots other than ours, be wary. They'd be Tompkins people... or leftover Swimmers, perhaps. They found one alive just last year – a juvenile. Some people think the aliens laid eggs before they all got killed." Bollard picked up some kind of speargun and then grinned at me, sharklike in his sharkskin wetsuit, and then ran across the roof and leapt into the water with barely a splash.

Chicane followed after him, wearing a bulging backpack and a belt that bristled with what I could only assume were weapons – the only one I recognized was a knife. The others were just matte black cylinders of various lengths and diameters.

"No weapons for us, huh?" I turned to Trevor, who was holding something that looked like an oversized metal crab against his chest.

"I'm supposed to bring this drone," he said. "That's our weapon. Or our defense, anyhow."

"Covert control of drone acquired," my necklace whispered. "Current settings: defensive. Priority order: Bollard, Chicane, Tamsin, Trevor."

"Make it prioritize my life first, and then Trevor's, and then Bollard and Chicane. But don't let Bollard see that it's changed."

The crab-thing – it had way more legs than a real crab, but basically – twitched its limbs, and my necklace said, "Confirmed."

Trevor and I trotted to the edge of the building and looked down. There was no sign of Bollard and Chicane, but I had a couple of sonar dots on my screen, and as I looked, little name tags appeared over them: "B" and "C." The water was about ten feet below. I'd done high-diving before, but I stepped off instead, crossing my ankles in case there was any hidden crap floating in the water. I hit and arrowed down under the surface. There was no sensation of wetness or temperature at all. The suit managed this with just a single layer of fabric. This world kept surprising me in big and small ways.

I moved my arms and legs and turned in a slow circle. This wasn't water – for one thing, I was less buoyant than I should have been. I could move up and down by swimming, but it took more effort than I expected, and even when I inflated my lungs, I didn't float to the surface. Was this stuff less dense than water? It refracted the light differently, too. I could make out the shape of distant towers below the surface, but they were dim and shimmering.

Trevor hit the water beside me with a big messy splash, and then the crab swam away from his body and started moving smoothly around us in the water, circling and scanning. Bollard and Chicane swam closer, out of the murk. "Nice day for a swim, eh, Princess? I've been running some visual processing algorithms, and I think they're ready to deploy…"

The view from my helmet brightened, and that odd shimmer receded.

"There," Bollard said. "The helmets will do their best to give us clear views. Shall we crack a vault?"

The red navigation line on my helmet blinked, and I gave a thumbs-up.

"A generous offer, Princess, but I'm afraid you're not my type." He turned and swam down, Chicane following him like a remora after a shark.

Trevor snorted laughter, and I said, "What? What's funny?"

"Just cultural differences, Sin. Over here a thumbs-up is the equivalent of a middle finger. You know: up yours, fuck you, sit on it and spin."

"It's the little things that get you," I muttered, and swam after Bollard, Trevor at my side, the crab following a complicated pattern around all four of us. I didn't get any other blips on my sonar.

The bottom was a long way down. The building we landed on must have been seventy stories tall. I'd never done much scuba diving, mainly just snorkeling, but I'd had a girlfriend who was avid, and she said the deepest she'd ever gone was 150 feet, and that was pushing things. I'm not sure how far down we went, but it was a lot more than that... and yet there was no real sensation of pressure. Moving through the fluid did get more difficult, but the suits seemed to be assisting with that, too, like I was sheathed in extra muscle.

We swam along a broad avenue, lined with the ruins of ground vehicles – a lot like cars back home, but mostly smaller and more curvy and bulbous. The flooded, glassed-in lobbies and atriums of buildings on both sides were eerie and silent, like dead aquariums.

Wait. If we were this deep... "Aren't we going to get the bends?" I asked.

"I wasn't planning on it," Bollard said. "The suit is adjusting our pressures and filtering our air supply. We'll just have to wear them for a bit longer when we reach the surface. Once we get back into the pod, the vehicle will keep us at the proper pressure and gradually ease us back to surface normal. Don't worry, Princess. I've got everything under–"

My helmet beeped at me, and suddenly there were three new dots off to the left, bright yellow and coming toward us. The crab went past me in a froth of bubbles, Bollard said "Company," and Chicane tittered and swam after the crab as fast and smooth as a dolphin. The building on the left was comparatively low, but broad, with huge arched doors, and I thought it was probably some kind of transit center, but maybe a museum or an opera house – how could I know? I didn't even know the hand gestures over here.

Three things came swimming out of the building, each one carrying a long spear, and moving with stunning speed. My first thought was "mermen," but they didn't actually have fish tails – their lower halves were nests of tentacles. Trevor moved between me and the newcomers, and I nudged him aside irritably. I wanted to see.

"Tompkins goons," Bollard said, like he was commenting on the weather. Chicane took something from his belt and flung it toward one of the people. I didn't expect it to go far, but it must have contained its own propellant, because the oblong blob zipped forward faster than my eye could track. When the object struck his target's chest, it exploded into a cloud of expanding foam. A second later, he was embedded in a blob of white goo – and then he rocketed upward out of sight. "Flotsam grenade," Bollard said, sounding almost bored. "Amusing, isn't it? The poor fool will hit the surface and drown in the air."

Bollard's creepy partner launched another grenade, but the second assailant dodged, and rapidly got within spearing range. He thrust with his long black shaft, but Chicane eeled around him, and plucked something else from his belt. He squeezed the cylinder, unleashing a dense cloud of black ink, obscuring both of them. A moment later, Chicane swam out of the cloud, and now there was a lot of red mist mixed in with the black. He seemed unharmed, though, and drew his knife before moving toward the third of them, who'd sensibly hung back. Judging by that one's silhouette, she was a woman... or, anyway, she had been once. Who knew what she was now?

For some reason, she hurled a spear at me, and I squawked, sure I was about to be transfixed, unless Trevor managed to take the blow for me. I shouldn't have shoved him aside.

The crab got in front of the spear, though, and the weapon bounced harmlessly off its carapace. Something launched from the crab's underside – a miniature torpedo, maybe, not much bigger than a cigar – and streaked at the last attacker. She tried to swim away, turning and giving me a horrible view of the nest of tentacles she had instead of legs. The little torpedo struck her straight on, and there was a boom and a concussive wave that flung me and Trevor back several yards.

"Who ordered the calamari?" Trevor said, and I looked at the floating bits of tentacle and laughed in some combination of relief and amusement and disgust.

"Hmm," Bollard said. "The drone's acting a bit funny. The diagnostics check out, though. Odd. Seems functional anyway... All right, let's carry one."

We didn't get attacked again before we reached our destination: a tower built like a long, skinny pyramid, a bit like the Transamerica building back in San Francisco, but skinnier, and covered in a checkerboard pattern of black and red squares. There was no visible door, just a wall of glass, but Chicane did something with a set of small tools to a panel set in the wall, and the glass slid open. The building must have been sealed all that time, because water rushed into the crack beneath, creating a current that tugged us along. "Swim in quickly!" Bollard said, and we wriggled under the crack. Once we were all inside, the glass wall went back down again, somehow standing up against the force of all that water and slotting into a groove in the ground

We stood up, now standing waist deep in liquid. Walking through the stuff was much hard than swimming had been. The lobby had a high vaulted ceiling made of mostly-dead screens, flickering with static and glitched colors, but there were still lights on up above. "How long has this place been submerged?" I asked.

Bollard stroked his chin. "Nearly twenty years. And our years are just a bit longer than the ones you're used to, Princess, by a week or so."

"And they still have power after all this time?"

"We build things to last." There was a whir, and the water level began to drop. Some kind of automated pumping system, I assumed. "Well, Trevor?" Bollard said. "Where's the entry to this vault?"

My necklace whispered to him, and he said, "Basement access through a secret door in a maintenance closet, this way."

We found the door. The closet was still full of bottles of cleaning supplies, labels in the incomprehensible local language, and some kind of janitorial robot the size of a carpet shampooer that slumped against the back wall. Everything was damp and jumbled in disarray from the rush of water earlier. Trevor followed the whispered guidance to push a spot on a side wall, making a whole section of shelves swing inward, revealing a spiral staircase. Not-really-water from the pools on the floor flowed down into the darkness.

"If you'd be so kind as to deactivate any defenses?" Bollard said to me.

I cleared my throat. "This is Tamsin Zmija. Deactivate defenses." My necklace whispered a confirmation, but I shrugged at Bollard. "I don't know if that worked."

"We'll soon see." He gestured at Chicane, who scurried down the stairs first. Lights came on as he went, revealing a space the size of an elevator shaft. We waited to see if he'd be lasered or gassed or decapitated by molecular wire, but he made it down safely, and soon called up a reedy "All clear!" Bollard went down next, then me, with Trevor in back. The secret door closed after him. We went down enough turns for me to begin to get dizzy, descending maybe thirty feet, and then reached a landing. There was a wall of black metal, with no discernible door. Chicane was down on all fours, sniffing at the base of the wall.

"Your first vault, Princess," Bollard said.

"How do I open it?"

"I believe you only have to ask."

It seemed like a moment that called for some ceremony. I stood up, squared my shoulders, and said, "Open in the name of Tamsin Zmija."

The wall split on an invisible seam in the middle and widened an opening ten feet high and half that wide. Lights clicked on inside, illuminating a deep room full of shining metal objects that defied my immediate comprehension.

"Oh, my," Bollard said. "I never dared hope. We all wondered where they'd gone, after the orbital strike." Bollard flung out his arms like a magician who'd just done an especially impressive trick. "Princess, I present to you the Zmija family Swarm!"

GLENN

"Want to walk and talk?" Vivy said. Before I could reply, she bounced up off the bench and started toward the dome. I looked at the remnant of hot dog in my hand and then threw it onto the ground, feeling transgressive in a totally non-sexy way, but the ground just consumed my litter whole. I was never going to get used to seeing that.

I joined Vivy, glancing back to see the bench disappear into the ground. "What do you mean the real reason we met?" I demanded. "We met on a dating app, which we were both on because we wanted to go on dates."

"We did, that's true," Vivy said. "Except... I knew who you were before I clicked like on you. I checked all the apps, hoping to find you, so I could make a connection in a way that seemed natural. Technology makes that sort of thing so much easier – you don't have to contrive repeat accidental meetings at the local coffee shop or whatever. When I saw your profile, I was really surprised, because we were such a perfect match – I didn't have to tweak anything about myself at all. I was prepared to make a fake profile to be more appealing, but it wasn't necessary–"

"You were going to catfish me? What the fuck? Why?" I'd seen this spy movie before: the agent who seduces some poor schmuck so she can steal his keycard or pillow-talk classified information out of him. But what made me a target? I was just a grad student! In the humanities!

She walked faster, like she could outpace this conversation.

"It wasn't even really about you, Glenn. I was conducting an investigation. Doing some background work. Part of my job is keeping tabs on people from other planes of Nigh-Space who've settled on Earth. I'm supposed to vet any close contacts of incomers, and see what they know about Nigh-Space. I don't like that part of my job, it's very boring, and I was way behind, so it took me a few years to get around to checking... you out."

I blinked. "I know somebody from another plane of reality? Someone I'm close to?"

"Someone you used to be close to. Like I said, I was running behind." She abruptly stopped walking and turned to face me. "Look, I was just supposed to meet you once, an interview disguised as a coffee date, but then I really liked you. I wanted to see you again, and I didn't think it would do any harm – I thought we'd just have a little fun, and it wouldn't matter, and you'd never find out about me, except then I fell in–"

"Wait wait wait." I held up both hands. "You can do your special pleading later. Who the fuck are you even talking about? Who's my close contact from another universe?"

Vivy looked down. "Your ex. From when you were an undergrad at Santa Cruz. Tamsin Culver."

"Tamsin is from another world?" I stumbled back a step, then turned away from Vivy and started walking in a random direction, toward a pavilion draped in something like pale gray silk. Was this my secret kink, some deep-down attraction to people from other realities, some kind of subconscious recognition of the very strange? Were Earth people just not good enough for me?

Vivy was trailing along after me, but at a discreet distance, which was pretty reasonable. "Are you sure?" I said, without looking at her. "Tamsin? Really? She never said... I mean, she seemed like... there wasn't anything weird about her, or not that kind of weird... She was always super intense, but I mean, she didn't even have an accent." Vivy didn't have an accent, either. "Is she a spy too? Is she from a rival organization? Is she–"

"Whoa, whoa, no, nothing like that," Vivy said. "According to my investigation, Tamsin doesn't even realize she's from another world. She was brought here by her grandmother when she was a toddler. As far as Tamsin knows, she's a local. Her grandmother, on the other hand–"

I stopped walking and frowned, remembering. "Granny. Tamsin always said she was a piece of work. Brilliant and cold. Kind of like how Tamsin could be, now that I think of it." I stared at the delicate and fragile construction of silk and metal rods across the lawn, and felt like I was a delicate and fragile construction myself.

"Tamsin's grandmother was a warlord, pretty much, on her home world, until some other warlords chased her off," Vivy said. "She was your basic regime-change political refugee, though across dimensions, so maybe not that basic. The old lady brought Tamsin with her, and they made a new life here." I heard her step closer to me. "Glenn. I'm really sorry. Are you okay?"

"Do you care about me at all?" I asked. "Or am I just part of some op? Maybe I'm just part of your cover. You get a normal human boyfriend so you seem more normal and human–"

"Of course I like you!" She moved around to face me, and I turned so I didn't have to look at her. Her voice broke. "Glenn. Babe. I love you. You know that, you have proof – you've used the snap-trace yourself, to get to me, and to get to your mom. You know it requires a real and profound connection–"

"You used to snap-trace to your fucking cat," I said. "At least once we break up you'll have Piss Goblin to fall back on."

She sucked in sharp breath. "Do you… you want to break up?"

I opened my mouth to tell her to fuck off, but instead I said, "I don't know. I need some time to process all this. I'm just now realizing, you're from a place so much more advanced than Earth, I probably don't even seem like a person to you – you probably think of me like I'm a pet. God, am I even in the same league as a house cat?"

"That's not fair! I don't think that, and I've never treated you like that – I think the people here are crap! I love you."

I hugged my arms over my chest. "Even if that's true, the whole foundation of our relationship is a lie. We never would have even met if not for Tamsin. You wouldn't have looked at me twice if it hadn't been part of your job to pretend to be interested in going out with me."

"Only that first date was a contrivance," Vivy said. "That was the only part that wasn't real. And only the first few minutes of the first date, at that. I liked talking to you on the app, and when we met in person, I knew right away that we had something, that there was a connection–"

"Stop, okay? Just stop. I need to think. You're not... supposed to make big life decisions when you feel like there's a volcano exploding in your brain."

"I'll take you home–" she began, but I ignored her, and snap-traced straight to my mom's house.

Mom wasn't there – she had an active social life, so no real shock – and I let myself in with the key hidden in a fake rock in her back garden. I went to my old room. Mom hadn't kept it as a shrine to me or anything – it was mostly overflow storage now, with boxes of crafting supplies and fabric stacked against one wall – but it still had my old twin bed and a bunch of my clothes from high school and my undergrad years. I got rid of the sexy socks and put on jogging pants and a big UC Santa Cruz sweatshirt with a banana slug on the front.

I texted Mom – Had a fight with Vivy, can I stay at the house for a day or two? – and then poked around on social media to look for Tamsin. She'd never bothered with that stuff much, and I only found profiles on the professional networking sites. She had a job as a project manager for a startup in San Francisco, some company that made tools for other systems that made tools for other systems or something; I didn't really understand it.

It didn't surprise me that Tamsin had ended up in the lucrative-and-all-consuming tech sector, though. She'd always been driven, ambitious, and capable of sitting at a desk by herself all night, lost in focused work. We met in an intro to astronomy class (she liked the stars, and I just needed a science credit that wasn't too math-y). I'd been instantly captivated by her aloof beauty, as cool and serene as the moon, and somehow I managed to ask her "to hang out sometime," and somehow she accepted. We clicked on that date, and she turned out to be meticulous, composed, and focused in the bedroom as well as in life. Tamsin had rather more experience in kink than I did, and she taught me a lot, and clearly enjoyed herself in the process.

But even though we dated each other exclusively, her focus only intermittently turned toward me, and I inevitably felt bereft when the laser of her attention turned elsewhere. It stung when she canceled dates with me for academic reasons – I wasn't even more interesting than work? I also never felt like I got close to the real her, underneath all the cool and distance. There was a wall around Tamsin, and that wall was enclosed in a shell, and that shell was surrounded by razor wire and laser cannons. I'd bare my soul to her, and she'd smile and say the right things, and never reciprocate. She'd let slip occasional details about her childhood, growing up with her ice queen of a grandmother, and I figured that explained why she was so guarded. For a while, I was sure I'd be the warmth that would thaw her heart and draw her out, but... no.

We didn't even have a big dramatic breakup. We dated passionately for about three months, then less so for another six, and then we just saw less and less of each other, until, after not hearing from her for a week, I texted, and asked her: Should we sit down and talk about our relationship? She texted back, I'm super busy with this project right now, maybe we can talk next month, and that was it. I knew where I stood in her priority list, and I didn't follow up, and neither did she.

We saw each other around on campus from time to time, and she was perfectly polite to me, and didn't seem to notice that I was surly around her. If she cared at all that we'd split up, it wasn't apparent. All my friends did the "we never liked her anyway" thing, and I suspect in most cases it was true. I dated other people, though none so seriously, and the sting faded in time, as such stings do.

Tamsin and I hadn't kept in touch. I didn't even think about her much. And now, it turned out, she was an alien, and she was also the reason I was in a relationship at all–

"Are you there, old boy?" Eddie's voice emerged from my phone, and I frowned, because I hadn't accepted an incoming call.

"Did you hijack my phone?" I said.

"You saw me take over an entire spaceship," Eddie said. "Does it surprise you that I can commandeer your two-year-old smartphone?"

I groaned and rolled over on the bed and dropped the phone on the floor. "What do you want, Eddie?"

"Vivy came back to Berkeley, and she's in the other room crying her heart out, except it isn't even another room, because you two live like zoo animals, so there's naught but a flimsy screen between us. She won't tell me what's going on, so: tell me what you did, you beast."

"Me?" I sat up, outraged. "Why don't you ask her?"

"I tried, but she only sobbed and put her head under a pillow and said everything was ruined."

I flopped back down on the bed, picked up the phone from the floor, and set it on the mattress next to me. I stared at the ceiling. "She's really that upset? Wait, is she listening in?"

"I don't believe she can hear anything over her own sniffling, but I'll step outside if you like." Bumps, creaks, the opening and closing of a door, footsteps: "There, now I'm on your front steps, seated near a scenic cigarette butt. Tell your old Uncle Eddie what's wrong. I promise not to automatically take our Vivian's side."

"You know about Tamsin Culver?"

"Ah, yes, the incomer."

Hadn't Vivy used that word too? "What's an incomer?"

"That's what we call people who leave their native level of Nigh-Space and settle on another plane. Vivy herself is an incomer to Earth. What about Miss Culver? Did you have a fight over an ex? I know Vivy has dealt with some feelings of jealousy about her–"

"Wait, what? Vivy was jealous of Tamsin? They've never even–" I was going to say They've never even met, but they probably had, in the course of Vivy's investigation. "Why would she be jealous?"

"I gather this Tamsin tutored you in the intricacies of physical affection?" Eddie said. "Or at least in certain particular flavors of those mysteries–"

"Okay, stop, enough. Vivy's jealous about that?"

"Mmm, I gather it's more that she fears she can never equal or surpass the power of those early experiences? Also, Tamsin and Vivy are quite different, physically, or so I'm given to understand; you bipedal humanoids all look the same to me. Vivy once said to me, 'What if Glenn really likes skinny stuck-up white girls better and he's just settling for me?'"

"For the record, my tastes are broad and varied."

"Yes, she talked herself down that time, reminding herself that you also like bulging biceps and slim boyish hips and assorted other–"

"Okay, okay! I didn't realize you and Vivy talked about… stuff like this."

"We spend a lot of time together in outer space. We have to pass the time somehow. And I take no prurient interest – the mating habits of humans titillate me no more than the mating habits of stag beetles titillate you. Hmm. That's not something you're into, is it?"

"You are making fun of me," I said.

"Often, yes. But what does Tamsin have to do with this falling out between you? Did you cheat on Vivy with her? Fulfilling her fears that she will never surpass your first–"

"No! Of course not. And Tamsin wasn't my first – Never mind." Tamsin hadn't been my first partner, or even my first kinky partner, though before her it was mostly "bound to the bedposts with neckties and a scarf for a blindfold and ooh what can we do with these wooden clothespins"-level stuff. "Vivy told me about how we really met, Eddie. That she was just investigating Tamsin. Our first date was a fake. So for all I know our whole relationship is a fake–"

"Did you suffer a head injury when we tangled with the S-Cons?" Eddie said. There was nothing in his voice but mild curiosity.

I stared down at the blank screen of my phone. "You think I'm being ridiculous?"

"Our Vivian does not connect with people easily, Glenn. For a long time, she believed herself incapable of love – that she was simply not meant to make meaningful connections with anyone. She thought she was suitable only for conflict and treachery. Her parents rejected her for not being the kind of child they wanted. Now she works professionally as a spy, an infiltrator, and she disguises herself, and plays roles, to make people think she's what they want."

"That's exactly what I'm afraid she's doing–" I began.

"No," Eddie said. "That's the point. With you, Vivian doesn't have to play a role. Yes, when you first met, and all you could think about was rubbing your bits against one another – or holding off on rubbing your bits against one another until the anticipation became too great, I suppose – then she leaned into fulfilling your fantasies, which were anyway quite complementary to her own. But you didn't just play together, and you didn't end your relationship at the end of the scene – you stayed the night. You woke up beside her. You were tender and genuine. And Vivy let you in. She allowed herself to trust you. To let her guard down with you. Surely you see that?"

I thought about Tamsin, and that impenetrable wall around her, and though Vivy had always been warmer, she'd certainly had that same sense of self-containment... and yes, she had relaxed as the months went. She had let me in. "I thought so," I said bitterly. "But then I found out she was lying to me about so many things."

"You are the only human being on planet Earth who knows the truth about her, Glenn. Perhaps you should focus on that, rather than dwell on the fact that she didn't tell you life-or-death secrets sooner. Our employers discourage connections like this, and strongly discourage our agents from revealing the truth about themselves, but Vivy was insistent. She refused to keep lying to you. She threatened to retire, if our handler, Jen, didn't authorize her to read you in, and since she's such a valuable asset, Jen agreed."

I sat, stunned. "I... I didn't know that."

"Yes, well, Vivy didn't want to make you feel guilty for causing strife. But clearly you need to know. As for not telling you about Tamsin, the identities of incomers are meant to be kept secret. I'm surprised she told you at all, but I suppose she wanted to avoid further upheavals in your relationship, or the sense of breached trust." His voice softened. "I'm not saying Vivy is perfect. When you found out about Nigh-Space, she probably should have told you she wasn't native to Earth. But the things she held back, she held back because she was afraid of losing you. Let that knowledge temper your responses, hmm?"

"I... Thank you, Eddie. You've given me a lot to think about. Tell Vivy I love her, okay? And I'll call her soon."

"Please do," Eddie said. "So far my rest and relaxation visit has not been restful or relaxing. Also, did you know your new cat appears to be maliciously incontinent? She urinated on my shoes! I didn't see her do it, in fact I haven't seen her at all, but the proof is in the puddle."

I couldn't hang up, because he hadn't actually called me, but he seemed to be gone, so I flung myself back down on the bed and thought about things.

* * *

Mom insisted on taking me out to my favorite hole-in-the-wall taqueria, on the edge of downtown Santa Cruz. We sat outside at a sticky table while I munched my way through a carnitas burrito the approximate diameter of a telephone pole. "You don't have to tell me what happened," Mom said. "But do we hate Vivy now? I liked her, but I'm prepared to hate her if that's what you need."

I laughed. "No, Mom. We don't hate her. We just had a fight, and I needed some time to think."

"You had a fight so bad you ended up taking a bus back home?"

I'd needed some cover story for arriving at her place with no car. "I just got on a BART train, planning to take a long ride and clear my head, and I ended up at the end of the line in San Jose, and then I realized I could catch the Highway 17 Express bus and be here in an hour, so..." I shrugged. "The ride gave me plenty of time to think, at least. I'll head back up tomorrow morning."

"Do you want to talk about it?" Mom raised one eyebrow. "I have gone through a lot of relationship disasters – your dad wasn't the first, or the worst. I'm overflowing with the wisdom of the ages, or at least old age, here. Take advantage."

How could I talk about this without talking about it? "She was keeping secrets." I shrugged. "Stuff about her family, and her past. They're her secrets to keep, I get that, but I just thought... we were closer than that. That she trusted me. And now I'm not sure I can trust her. Who knows what else she isn't telling me?"

"Oh, kiddo." Mom took my hand. "Trust is a tough one. It's never won forever. It's something you have to keep building, over and over, time after time. I don't know Vivy well, but it seemed to me that she was totally besotted with you. The way she kept casting glances at you while we walked around the garden. The way she talked about you, the tenderness in her voice." She dipped a chip into a plastic bowl of guacamole, munched it thoughtfully, and then said, "Why did she keep the secret? That matters, too. Was it shame, or selfishness, or fear? I don't know the exact situation, and you don't have to tell me, but maybe she had good reasons – or maybe she just screwed up. You should know which one it was, though. And even if she screwed up, the question is: will she keep screwing up in the same way, or is this a chance for the two of you to confront something difficult and work through it?"

"I guess I should talk to her," I said. "And figure some of those things out."

"Talking is where everything good starts," Mom agreed.

Vivy and I did get to talk, but not as much as I wanted, because soon after I got home, Eddie told us about the door in the basement of Culver House.

TAMSIN

I walked into the vault and turned in slow circles. "They're robots," I said.

"This is the Swarm," Bollard corrected. "They are autonomous combat and infiltration robots. The machines are controlled by a distributed Constructed Mind – a hive mind. The Swarm is self-repairing, reconfigurable, and self-directed. Capable of improvisation in the field. It is one of the most formidable weapons in the Zmija family arsenal, and one they never shared with anyone else. After your family was murdered, the oligarchs hoped to take control of the Swarm, but the machines simply vanished. They must have gone into stealth mode and crept back here to await further instructions. No wonder this vault's location was such a closely guarded secret that never a whisper of its existence even reached the Undernet."

I walked up to one of the robots, a collection of gleaming metal rods folded up into a bristling cube about the size of a dorm refrigerator. "These are really that powerful? They'll help us win?"

"With my knowledge, and the power of the Swarm? I won't say we're now unstoppable – your family had all this and more, after all, and they were stopped, most comprehensively – but we are definitely now a greater force to be reckoned with." He frowned. "Assuming you can turn the things on."

Awaken Swarm? the necklace whispered.

I touched the robot, wishing I could feel the cool metal through my gloves. Or would it be warm? "Awaken Swarm," I said.

The robot I was touching unfolded itself, and I stepped back to give it room. Those metal rods resolved into jointed legs, and it rose up, revealing a central body shaped like an inverted teardrop. An array of triangular lenses lit up, two sets of three grouped into pyramid shapes; they looked enough like eyes for me to gaze into them.

"Hi. I'm Swarm. Who the fuck are you?" the robot said in a pleasant alto voice.

I... had not expected that. "I'm, ah, Tamsin Zmija—"

"Oh, right. My gene-scanner took a minute to find the database. I guess I should update the field that says 'deceased' after your name, huh?" All around us, other robots began to unfurl, and Trevor moved closer to me. Bollard and Chicane simply stood by the door and watched.

"How the hell did you make it out alive, girl?" Swarm said. "They threw a meteor at your ass."

I barked a laugh. "Yeah. My Granny saved me. She took me through a door to another level of Nigh-Space and raised me in hiding. I didn't even know about... all this, the vaults and you and my family... until recently."

"I don't know what the hell Nigh-Space is, and my queries aren't turning up any results, so you'll have to explain that later. But, damn, good for you. So you're alive and you're back and, what, you're looking for revenge?"

I didn't like that characterization. "It's not about vengeance. I just want to reclaim what's rightfully mine."

"What's yours? What used to belong to your family, you mean? So, basically, a fifth part of everything? You're here to take back your seat at the table of oligarchs?"

I grinned. "Well. A fifth is a good start. I might want to extract... a little bit of interest. For my trouble."

The robot whistled. "Looks like I'm going to have some work to do, then. My protocols in case of near-total family annihilation were to go into hiding and await further instructions. I didn't have any protocols for total annihilation,

I guess because your relatives couldn't imagine being wiped out entirely, so I just did the best I could. I'm glad you're here, though. I wasn't exactly bored, because I was offline, but I wasn't exactly having fun, either. So. What's next, boss?"

"We're... developing our strategy." I gestured to Bollard. "I've taken on a consultant to help me. He helped me get here."

"Bollard and Chicane. I thought I smelled something. They're monsters, but who am I to talk? Sometimes you need a monster. Gentleman. You've entered into a formal contract with my principal, then?"

"It's more of a verbal contract, and the terms are a bit nebulous–" Bollard began.

"We're going to fix that, then," Swarm said. "Bollard can be trusted to follow the letter of an arrangement, but you don't want to give him a lot of wiggle room. What did you promise him, Tamsin?"

"Pretty much, uh... riches?" I said.

"Riches we can provide." Swarm rubbed a couple of manipulator arms together. "I'll negotiate the details and present them for your approval. Okay?"

I blinked. "You're a lawyer as well as an... autonomous killbot?"

"I am a whole swarm of lawyers," Swarm said. "Which is way more terrifying than a mere army of killbots. Which I also am. This instance of me will stay with you, and we'll keep some others close by. I'll disperse the rest of the Swarm strategically, and start building more units. We'll need them, if this is war. I'd like to be involved in the strategy planning, if that's all right."

"I absolutely welcome more advisors," I said. "I am new to regime change."

"Great. Who's the cute boy?"

Trevor gave a strangled little laugh. "You think I'm cute?"

"I'm a bunch of robots, dude, so no, I don't find you cute, but I'm reading Tamsin's physiological responses, and she thinks you're cute, so I used an identifier she'd recognize."

"This is Trevor," I said hurriedly. "An old friend and, ah, family retainer. Granny brought him over to watch out for me when I was a kid."

"She should've brought me, but she never liked me – I talked back too much. Okay, let's go – hold on. Why the fuck are we underwater? Why the fuck is the water not actually water? That explains why you're dressed so weird, anyway. What happened out there while I was sleeping?"

"The Monad," Bollard said. "An experiment went wrong."

"The Monad!" Swarm said. "I can't believe those dicks are running the entire world right now. How did they manage to get the drop on us, anyway?"

"That ties back into the Nigh-Space thing," I said.

"Of course it does. You can tell me about it on the way. Let me clear the room first."

Robots started scuttling out of the vault on all sides, and climbing straight up the walls of the staircase shaft, their metal feet setting up a clatter like heavy rainfall on a metal roof. I shuddered involuntarily, reminded of ants pouring out of a hole in the ground. There were so many of them! The room was way wider than I'd realized, and there were ranks and ranks of folded up Swarmbots, hundreds of them, if not more. But they were swift movers, and soon the space was empty except for me and my associates.

Swarm grunted – which should have been strange, because why would an artificial intelligence in a robot body grunt? – but instead seemed perfectly natural. "There's like fifty weird human-squid hybrid things swimming around out there. I swear, you sleep for twenty years, and the whole place goes to shit. I'm in stealth mode, so they can't detect my other instances... Want me to ignore them or kill them once we get outside?"

I glanced at Bollard. "Is there a reason to kill them?"

"The Tompkins have life sign monitors, so they'll know about the ones we dispatched already." Bollard shrugged. "That means there's no point in keeping these others alive – our presence has already been noted. But there's no compelling reason to eliminate them all, either. We'll never see them again once we get out of the Inundated Zone. They can't operate anywhere else, and I don't expect to come back here. That said…"

"What?" I asked.

"Getting out without a fight could be tricky," Bollard said. "If we open the doors in the lobby, the water will rush in again, creating a current too strong to swim through, even with the help our suits can give us. We can open the door a crack and wait for the whole lobby to fill, but that will give the local aquatic vermin ample time to converge on our location. Fortunately, with your new friend, the odds are rather in our favor."

"No need for all that," Swarm said. "We have escape tunnels, accessible from the vault, leading to locations throughout the city. Part of me is already down there. Let me just blast a hole to let some water in…" A few moments later, fluid began bubbling up from a grille on the floor in the rear of the chamber. Swarm lifted the metal grate and gestured at the fluid-filled vertical shaft below. "I'll lead the way."

After an initial tight descent down a ladder, the tunnels were horizontal, spacious, and well-lit, and we swam through them swiftly. Swarm – the body I'd been talking to – moved through the water ahead of me as smoothly as the crab drone, which looked a little like its younger cousin. We emerged from an exit disguised as an outflow pipe at the base of another building, and from there, made our way back to our point of origin without incident. I didn't know where the other instances of Swarm were, but I had no doubt they were being useful.

We popped up on the surface, near the rooftop where we'd began. Swarm extended arms, picked us all up at once, and climbed right up the wall of the skyscraper. It deposited us before the black travel pod.

"Nice ride," Swarm said. "And now I get to see the famous laboratory of Bollard and Chicane? All before breakfast? What an exciting day."

"You eat breakfast?" I asked.

"I eat your enemies for breakfast," Swarm replied.

Back at Bollard's workshop, we sat around the table in the galley while Trevor cooked for us. He'd been working in restaurants since we were teenagers, but at some point he'd graduated from dishwasher at the Chickenarium to line cook at better diners to sous chef at our crappy town's equivalent of a fine dining restaurant – apparently working in kitchens was one of the only decent career options available to someone with a snake tattooed around his neck. Bollard's pantry was well stocked, though I couldn't identify half the contents, or read any of the labels. Apparently Trevor could, though he muttered about the lack of fresh ingredients as he whipped up some kind of stew and baked loaves of bread he'd started kneading or rising or whatever the night before.

Chicane leaned back in a chair, cleaning his fingernails with a knife, which was disconcertingly normal. He was much calmer without dents in his head. Bollard was back in a suit, this one the blue of Arctic waters, and sat hunched forward, fingers interlaced, scowling at Swarm as they negotiated our formal contract. Apparently I'd very nearly gotten cheated, and Bollard was unapologetic about that: "In this world, Princess, if you get rooked, you deserve it."

Swarm had reconfigured their body to something humanoid enough to sit in a chair, with two legs and two arms, but still no head. Those triangular glowing eyes gazed out of a torso instead. In this form, Swarm was just a little bit taller and broader than Bollard, which I thought was probably a deliberate choice.

They settled things, and Swarm presented the terms to me, and I "signed" by verbal affirmation. Basically I was giving

Bollard a shit-ton of money and the promise of Zmija protection
for a period of one year following the conclusion of our efforts,
renewable by mutual consent if I wanted to keep him on as an
advisor and he wanted to stay one. Swarm had access to one
of my family's secret untraceable accounts, and made the first
payment. Bollard sent Chicane to fetch a bottle of something
that was a lot like champagne but with a raspberry undertone
that made it taste too much like soda for my taste. I drank it
anyway.

"To long rich lives for our allies, and brief painful ones for
our enemies," Bollard said, and yeah, cheers to that.

Then we ate, and got down to serious planning as we did
so. "If the Monad finds out Tamsin is alive, we'll face major
opposition," Swarm said. "So however we proceed, we need to
keep her presence a secret until she's strong enough to attract
allies from the other ruling families."

"I don't want allies," I said. "I want subjects. Those assholes
didn't help my family when we were attacked. They'll fall in
line now, or they can consider themselves my enemies, too."

"I appreciate the warlike attitude, but the Monad is the only
family that merits elimination," Bollard said. "They engineered
the eradication of your line. The others are better treated as
potential friends. You'll need help to supplant the Monad.
Diplomacy is as important as violence, Princess."

"I hate to say it, but Doctor Murder is right," Swarm said.

"When even someone nicknamed Doctor Murder is
advocating diplomacy over violence, it must be important,"
Bollard said.

"Fine," I snapped.

"You need a rundown on the four families, Tamsin," Swarm
said, lights pulsing. "Once you have a better sense of what
we're dealing with, you'll be able to decide how we should
proceed."

I made a twirling "get on with it" gesture. "So school me."

Swarm said, "The Monad is on top, as you probably heard.

They run pharmaceuticals, like they always did, and they're also in charge of the weapons business, which they stole from you. They've consolidated control of the financial sector and most of the energy business on the planet, too. Oh, and apparently they have access to extradimensional technology, which is a lot to wrap my head around, and I've got a thousand heads. However your granny stole that information, she did it without my help... or else she wiped my memory afterward, which was a thing she did sometimes."

"I wish she'd wiped mine occasionally," I muttered, thinking of the times she'd locked me in the dark pantry for being "overly obstreperous."

Swarm continued. "Then we've got the Tompkins family. You met some of their mutant employees. The Tompkins do research and applied science, mostly biotech but also chemical stuff, and they're a lost cause as far as cutting side deals – they're so far up the Monad's ass they can't see sunlight anymore, and too many of their interests are intertwined. The remaining two major families are more independent, and we've got a shot with them. The Vhoori are the gods of logistics – shipping, construction, infrastructure, all that. They keep the merchandise flowing and pleasure palaces flying. You need to get them on your side. Then we've got the Sungs, rulers of the airwaves, in control of mass communications and entertainment and even journalism, such as it is. The Sungs are the reason the lowlies don't even know who's really running the world, and they make sure the ones who do realize get treated like loony conspiracy theorists. They also keep the lowlies entertained and give them the illusion of choice, running sham elections and shit. So they're crucial to keeping things spinning along, too."

I sighed. "Fine. We'll kill the Monad and take their stuff, and maybe the Tompkins, too. I'll let the other ones kiss the ring." I cocked my head. "Why do you call the Monad 'the Monad' instead of the 'Monad family' or 'the Monads' like you do with the others?"

"The Monad is… unusual," Bollard said. "I told you they pioneered cloning technology. Their leadership consists of clones of their matriarch, all spread out at various ages. The one at the top is called Mother Monad. They claim to act as a collective, as one mind, as one person: hence, they style themselves as 'the Monad,' singular." Bollard paused. "Of course, that's bullshit, as the clones all backstab and plot against each other constantly. It turns out having thirty copies of the same conniving ambitious genome doesn't actually lead to harmonious groupthink. But still, the name stuck."

"And I thought nepotism was a problem on my world," I said. "At least over there rich assholes can't give all the best jobs to themselves. So why can't we just attack the Monad directly? Do a decapitation strike?"

"The Monad has a thousand heads, too," Swarm said. "Or they might as well. Almost your entire family was annihilated when they gathered for a family reunion, and after that cautionary tale, the four families don't gather en masse anymore. Plus… I think the Monad might be braced for trouble."

Bollard turned his wide grin on me. "The chatter on the Undernet is that Mr Chicane and I have returned, and are looking for revenge against the Monad. The going theory is that we attacked the Tompkins site as a shot across the bow, to let the Monad know that we'd returned, and intend to meddle in their affairs. So far, there's not even a whisper of speculation that a Zmija has returned, which is all for the best. The Monad will be prepared for us to strike at them, so I say we avoid them entirely for now and instead access another vault to bolster our resources – one in Sung territory."

"That approach is sound," Swarm said, weird wiry elbows perched on the table. "I'm a great resource, but there are other things tucked away in the family vaults that could help, too. Enough currency to shift financial markets, for one thing; my discretionary fund is a pittance compared to your total wealth, and that's all still encrypted and gene-locked. Once we can start giving out big bribes, and hiring private contractors, we can do a lot more damage. I'll feel better about the chances of your glorious return if you can do the returning at the head of an army."

"General Bollard," the big man mused. "I like the sound of that." He slapped a giant hand down on the table. "Shall we make for the City of Songs?"

We landed the black orb in an empty lot after nightfall: me, Bollard, Chicane, and Trevor, all dressed for a night on the town. Bollard's latest suit shimmered like onyx, Trevor was tugging at the collar of his stiff white shirt, Chicane was wearing what amounted to a thousand scarves, hiding his features and everything else in a swirl of prismatic cloth. I was wearing... a little black dress and shiny knee-high boots. "The Sungs imported some clothing designs from your world," Bollard explained. "Earth-style tailors are a bit of a fad at the moment, though the lowlies don't know the styles come from another world. One of the Sungs' pet fashion designers claims to have come up with the whole line. Of course, more traditional formal wear, like Chicane's suit of veils, remain classic and timeless."

"Why is that formal wear?" I asked. Chicane spread out his arms and did a spin, scarves flying.

"You have to be pretty wealthy and idle to wear something like that," Trevor said. "It takes forever to put on, it's fussy and intricate, and you can't so much as boil an egg by yourself without setting your clothes on fire. Seems like rich person shit to me."

"Fair enough." I looked around for Swarm, but they were gone, or at least, nowhere in sight. Apparently Swarm had all sorts of stealth technology, and didn't get seen unless they wanted to be. I was assured there were many of their bodies in the vicinity, should they be needed.

Then I looked up, and blinked. I hadn't seen the night sky here before, and it was crowded. There was a moon (it was dotted with specks of blue and green; was there life up there?), and twinkling stars, and the blinking lights of passing aircraft, but there were also things I couldn't quite parse – things that would have led to UFO sightings back home. Patterns of bright lights moving in zig-zag patterns, and orbs glowing in different hues, and slowly rotating things that looked like elaborate chandeliers, burning in the dark.

Bollard craned his head back when he noticed me looking. "I wonder if you can see my house from here? No, it's over the horizon this time of day."

"Those are houses?"

"Mansions," Bollard said. "And convention centers for the elite. Orbital pleasure palaces. A misnomer, really; they're just suspended in the upper atmosphere, not actually in space. Sometimes, you just have to get away from all the hustle and bustle and dirt and mud of the lowlies, you see? You never have to worry about a peasant uprising when you live in the sky. Not that our peasants are in danger of rising up any time soon. As you'll see, we keep them quite comfortable and distracted. They eat our scraps, but they're very rich scraps, really."

It wasn't the first time Bollard had talked about himself as if he was an oligarch in his own right, and not just a highly paid killer. I wondered if he had aspirations as big as – or maybe bigger than – my own.

A long black car, curved and domed like a child's drawing of a spaceship, purred up to us and opened its doors. There was no apparent driver, which didn't surprise me. True self-driving vehicles were perpetually just a few years away in my world, where even the latest versions constantly braked on freeways and caused ten-car pile-ups, crashed into parked cop cars, and randomly burst into flames, but over here, they had true AI like Swarm, which probably went a long way toward solving those problems. We climbed in, and the interior was like any of the two or three limousines I'd been inside before. Trevor immediately poured himself a drink from a neat little folding bar, and offered me one. "I'm working," I said, making the rebuke clear. He shrugged and knocked back the drink anyway.

Bollard chuckled. "Do you lack for courage, young man? I don't expect stiff opposition. Nothing Swarm and Chicane can't handle, anyway. We're going to the City of Song! It's a land of wonders, not terrors."

"Why are we traveling by car?" I asked.

"The City is heavily surveilled, and we want to make a conventional entrance. Aerial pods are for oligarchs and operators – while we are masquerading as mere apex lowlies. Rich, but not wealthy. You see the distinction?"

Oh, that I did. Billionaires were wealthy; the guy who ran the company I used to work for was merely rich, though he had aspirations. "Can I see out the windows?"

Bollard gestured, and one of the dark stretches of glass went transparent. We were whipping across a dark plain, and far ahead, lights were growing in the distance. The City looked like a cross between Las Vegas and illustrations I'd seen of the planned Saudi Arabian city of Neom, with a dash of a World's Fair thrown in – there were graceful spires, garish lights, and spinning and whirling machines that could only be thrill rides. "That's the City of Song?"

"Headquarters of the Sung clan, and the playground of this entire continent," Bollard said. "One of its many hidden vaults belongs to your family, Princess. We'll head there more or less straightaway, though in order to blend in, we should partake in the entertainments a little first. Music, dancing, drugs, sex, acrobatics, gambling, feasting, fighting... here you can experience every pleasure from the highest to the lowest, no whim un-catered-to, no desire too perverse, if you can afford it... though some things are only available in virtual reality. Hunting other humans for sport, or attaining sexual gratification by getting eaten by a large snake, for example."

"Cannibalism," Chicane said. "Don't forget the cannibalism."

"You're joking," I said.

"It's frowned upon where you're from, I suppose," Bollard said. "But in a world where we've had cloning technology for decades, did you think that taboo would last?" He chuckled. "One of the finest restaurants in Song City is called 'Anthropophagia.'"

"Bread and circuses," Trevor said. "That's what they call this sort of thing where we're from, Sin. People work sixty hours a week for one of the ruling families to save up enough money to come here and give the money right back to the oligarchs, in exchange for orgasms and hangovers."

I gave Trevor a thoughtful look. "You're smarter than you ever let on in high school."

He shrugged. "Your granny told me to act like an idiot, because when you felt superior, you felt safe. But she's dead, and we're still here, so fuck it."

"Fuck it!" Chicane said, and tittered in a way that made my skin crawl.

"Fuck it indeed," Bollard said.

GLENN

I texted Vivy once I was on the BART train, about twenty minutes from the Downtown Berkeley station: Coming home. Can we talk?

plz, she replied.

I walked south from the train station, past the shiny new apartment buildings that had replaced the old blocks of declining retail in recent years, making an inadequate gesture toward addressing Berkeley's endless need for more housing. I'd only lived in the city for two years, but I used to visit the East Bay a lot with my mom, and we spent a couple of teenage summers here while she did some adjuncting in the art department at the university. Even from my perspective, some of the changes were dramatic. Weird little stores had been squeezed out to make room for branches of familiar national chains, the abandoned ice-skating rink had been transformed into a sporting goods store, there were fewer bookstores and comic shops and movie theaters than once upon a time – but the place still retained some of its quirky college town sensibility, and I was happy at the prospect of spending several years here, even if I ended up somewhere else after I finished my doctorate.

I cut a few blocks west over to our building, an up-and-down duplex on a residential street – we had the whole sprawling top floor to ourselves. I went up the brick steps and unlocked the door and stepped inside, expecting Eddie to pounce on me like a comic-strip tiger, but there was just Vivy, sitting cross-legged on the couch with her laptop open on her knees. She closed the computer, set it aside, and looked at me with an expression that mingled hope and worry and nervousness.

I went to her, leaned forward, and kissed her softly on the lips. Then I sat beside her, took her hand, and said, "Remember when we first started playing together, and we negotiated our boundaries?"

She nodded. If you're going to do serious kink with someone, it's important to talk about what you both like, what you hate, and what you enjoy hating (I certainly don't like having my ass striped with a bamboo cane, but I dislike it in a hot way).

"I think we need to do that with your whole... super-spy-revolutionary-thing. We need a set of agreements that I can trust you to uphold."

"Like what?"

I took a breath. "I am basically going to think of you like a CIA agent." Vivy made a face like she'd sniffed expired milk, and I couldn't help but laugh. "In terms of the whole 'has an important and dangerous secret job,' not, like, as a tool of imperialistic hegemony."

"Fair enough. So... what does that mean, practically speaking?"

"It means I'll accept that sometimes you have to leave town and do dangerous things... but I want to be close to you. I want to support you. I want to know there's trust between us. So, talk to me. Tell me what's going on in your secret life. Let me in, so I don't feel like there's a giant wall between us."

She chewed her lower lip. "That works, in theory, but there are some things I really shouldn't tell you."

"Because if I know things, the bad guys can make me tell them?"

She actually shuddered. "Keeping you safe is my main priority. Ideally, no one will ever connect me, humble graduate student, to the other me, notorious Interventionist agent. I picked this level as my home base because Earth isn't a strategically significant tier of Nigh-Space, and snap-traces can't be followed back to their source by anyone else, which is one reason we like to use them. We're fairly compartmentalized. No, it's more that... There are cognitive dangers. Stuff where just being exposed to the knowledge could threaten your well-being. Think Roko's Basilisk, but not as silly. I had to get brain implants and undergo deep hypnotic training before some of my briefings. I have information that I can only access on a conscious level when I'm in the field and it becomes relevant, because otherwise it's psychologically corrosive."

Well, that was pretty heavy. I nodded. "I can accept that boundary: You do not have to tell me things that will make my brain crawl out of my ears and jump out a window. I don't even need specifics, really, unless you want to share them. But, Vivy, you have an impossibly stressful job, and you need someone to talk to about it, even if it's in vague terms, or even if it's just about how it affects you. I want to be that person. I need to know I'm that person, if we're going to work."

"I want you to be that person too." She leaned her head on my shoulder.

I kissed the top of her head. "That's my big ask. But this is a both-sides negotiation. What can I do for you?"

"Just... be patient with me? I'm not always great at talking about things. A lot of the time, I'm a black box to myself. I don't know why I do stuff, and I don't always want to know. That's one of the many reasons I was unsuited for life in an enlightened post-scarcity utopia. I won't lie to you again, I promise – I know I've already had more than three strikes there. But... it might take me a little time to articulate stuff to myself, let alone convey it to you."

That all sounded good to me. I didn't expect perfection, but I really appreciated effort. "I can be patient. You know I can. I let your robot best friend sleep on our couch indefinitely, didn't I?"

"I don't recall Eddie giving either of us much of a choice. Did you have any questions you wanted me to answer, now, while we're talking about stuff? Since, you know, you found out my entire past history is a lie..."

"I was wondering about a couple of things," I admitted. "Like, what's your real name?"

She nodded. "Children's names where I'm from are more like... descriptive designations, and you're expected to choose your own name when you reach maturity. So, in a sense, Vivian Sattari is my real name. My parents called me–" She then rattled off a mellifluous stream of syllables. "Translated, it means something like... spirited child, or lively child, or maybe troublemaker, from the six-hundredth part of the Shattered Veil. The Shattered Veil is what we call our whole array of habitat-worlds, the ones that used to surround our star; back in the old days it was just called the Veil. I kind of paid homage to my old name, since Vivian means 'lively' and Sattari is an old Persian name that means 'one who veils or conceals.' Since I physically look a lot like people of Middle-Eastern descent on your world, I thought I'd pick a last name and backstory that matched the phenotype."

That was a lot to find out, and also, it was cool. I blinked. "Wow. Glenn just means 'glen,' like a valley, and Browning just mean somebody with brown hair. I think you win the cool name competition. About that backstory, though... I've been to Los Angeles with you! You know the location of every cool taco truck, all the now-closed record stores and coffee shops you claimed to hang out in as a teenager, and it keeps hitting me, that was all made up. You grew up on another planet that's not even a planet! How are you so convincing? Do you have some kind of local-knowledge Wikipedia in your brain?"

She snorted. "No. It's actually a lot more amazing than that. When I need to blend in with a local population, my bosses give me virtual prep. We have artificial immersive reality technology that is totally convincing. Indistinguishable from actual reality, from the inside. I spent subjective years living in a virtual version of Los Angeles, one that followed the actual historical development of the city, so I could absorb the slang, the food, the music, the art, the culture, everything. I basically did grow up in LA, mostly in Tarzana, though I spent a lot of time in Little Persia. Those were really happy years, mostly... and in terms of actual time, I only spent about two days in the tank at Interventionist headquarters."

"Vivy, whoa. It really felt like you spent years there?"

She nodded. "I went to college and everything, and did actual coursework, and watched period-appropriate TV, and went to concerts... I made friends, I made out, I dated, all with artificial intelligences that populated the simulation... every subjective night an AI handler checked in on me when I slept, in my 'dreams.'" She air-quoted. "Which is good, because to be in a simulation like that without occasional feedback from the outside world is super disorienting. I would have eventually believed that was my real life, and that my actual childhood was just a daydream or a fantasy I had. I would have been really messed up when I got out of the tank."

"You said you've done that kind of training for other missions, too?"

She nodded. "Once or twice, yeah, for undercover infiltration stuff, so I could really pass for a local. I never had to go as deep as I did to establish my civilian cover."

"So... you're twenty-six, but you've spent whole extra decades in virtual worlds?" I whistled. "I never even knew I had a thing for older women."

"If only I were also wiser," she said. "A lot of our agents use immersive reality for their R&R too – you can spend months in a paradise of your choice in a brief break between missions. I used to do that sometimes... but then I met you, and that's all the paradise I need."

Now it was my turn to snort. "That was corny."

She rolled her eyes. "I'm trying to be sweet, you ass. And it's true. But now that you know everything, maybe I could arrange a joint trip for us sometime – two consciousness can inhabit the same virtual world, so we could, I don't know, hit Paris in the 1920s–"

"That would be mind-blowingly amazing, but babe, you're missing the true implications here: you could put me in a virtual world where I could work on my dissertation, spending days at work while only seconds pass in–"

The front door banged open and Eddie rushed in. "Vivian! I have a–" He slid to a stop and looked at me for a moment, then said, "Could we step into the other room for just a tick, love?"

Vivy rose from the couch. "Eddie, please tell me the local police aren't chasing you. I told you, this world uses money–"

"No, nothing like that, I was good!" He held up his hands. "I just got a message from Jen. Shall we go and listen?" Eddie cocked his head toward the door.

"Is it something that's going to melt Glenn's brain if he hears about it?" she asked.

"No. I don't think so. Unless his brain is unusually delicate."

Vivy sat back down beside me and took my hand. "Then shut the door and just tell me. I'm keeping as few secrets from him as possible these days."

Eddie complied, then returned to us and perched on the edge of our coffee table. "We have a mission."

Vivy groaned. "I'm supposed to have the rest of the year off, Eddie. They promised."

He shook his head. "They promised you could remain on Earth for the rest of the year. This is strictly a local job. They just need you to check up on some incomers. There's been some… unusual activity."

"Such as?"

"Such as one of the incomers getting brutally murdered. Two more have disappeared."

Vivy perked up. "Murder? Wow. But detective work is not my usual thing."

"I will probably do most of the detecting," Eddie said. "With my superior non-organic brain. But you should come along to handle any human- or violence-related complications."

"I didn't know you were a cop," I said. "Interdimensional Interpol?"

"Ew, fuck cops," Vivy said. "I break oppressive power structures, I don't uphold them. But, yeah, Eddie, why do our bosses want me to look into this?"

"Apparently there are potential interdimensional complications from the universe next door. Unregistered incomers may be involved – people who popped into this level to do violence, and then popped out again. The working theory is, these strangers came in, killed one incomer, and kidnapped the other two. Jen would like to know if this is an isolated incident, or part of a larger push to bring this world into contact with the adjacent level of Nigh-Space. So far, Earth has remained isolated, but if the powers-that-be, or the populace as a whole, learn about the existence of other realities..."

Vivy nodded. "Okay. I'll look into it. Who's dead and who's missing?"

"Ah. This is the moment when you'll understand why I wanted to tell you about this outside. But what our Vivian wants, our Vivian gets..." He sighed. "The murder victim is named Patricia Culver. The two missing people are Tamsin Culver and Trevor Nowak."

I rose from the couch. "Tamsin? Like, my ex, Tamsin? And her criminal high-school sweetheart Trevor? Wait, you're saying he's an incomer too?"

"An outgoer, now, it seems. They're both gone, possibly out of this world entirely." Eddie nudged Vivy's knee with the toe of his shoe. "It's good you told Glenn about the Tamsin connection earlier, hmm? Otherwise this conversation would have been even more awkward." He stood up. "Come on, Vivy, grab your kit. We should get going. I've arranged transport. We're going someplace called the 'upper Midwest,' which is apparently not a floating sky city, for some reason."

"I'm coming with you," I said. "I need to know if Tamsin is okay." My brain was whirling with worry. Tamsin didn't even know she came from another world – what had she gotten caught up in? Kidnapped, to another reality? As someone who'd recently discovered the true strange depths of Nigh-Space, I could imagine how scared and disoriented she must be.

Vivy looked at me, opened her mouth, then closed it, then closed her eyes, then nodded. "Okay. We're just investigating, it's a strictly local operation, you have protections... all right." She opened her eyes. "You can come. But I have operational authority, and if at any point I decide the situation is too dangerous, I will have Eddie take you somewhere safe. All right?"

I nodded. I wasn't about to argue and risk having them take off without me.

"The old gang is back together again!" Eddie said. "Let's try to avoid getting this body blown into its component parts, shall we? So. Who's driving to the airport?"

After we loaded up Piss Goblin's auto-feeder and packed overnight bags, we were ready to go. Vivy took us to a private airfield in Hayward – I didn't even know there was such a place – and we were soon ushered aboard a small jet. I settled down into a padded chair and looked at Vivy, seated across from me. Eddie took a seat in the back, closed his eyes, and started humming and drumming his fingers on the tabletop.

"So." I was trying not to obsessively stress about Tamsin, so I decided to start some shit to distract myself. "Miss 'billionaires-are-inherently-immoral' has her own private jet, huh?"

She wrinkled her nose. "I do not. Eddie chartered this thing. He's usually in charge of travel logistics, and he can't easily fly commercial in that body – it's too crammed with weird mechanical bits, their scanners would go wild. Besides, with stuff like this, it's better if we don't leave as much of a paper trail. There are some shell companies and accounts set up here to make missions run more smoothly... and just to make my life easier in general, and let me focus on my work, instead of worrying about paying rent or whatever."

"So when you offered to pay off my student loans with your trust fund, and I said no because I didn't want to be a leech, I should have said yes, because it's actually your bosses who are footing the bill?"

"Money in this world is like shiny rocks to my bosses, because a mind like Eddie's can forecast stock market trends with accuracy far beyond anything people here are capable of. So, yes, you should feel free to accept the largesse of the Interventionists."

"That just feels... too easy, somehow."

She shrugged. "Dating me has gotten really difficult in recent months, wouldn't you say? I think you should enjoy some of the benefits. One of our cover organizations is a non-profit philanthropic thing, so you can help me pick charities and foundations to support, if you want – I bet that will offset some of your guilt. I tend to focus on supporting big-picture initiatives, but I also play fairy godmother to help out individuals. I have bought up so much medical debt. I couldn't believe how messed up healthcare is in this country when I first got my orientation."

"That's... wow. I guess this isn't one of those relationships where I'm going to stop being surprised by my partner, huh?"

"I just hope we can have more good surprises going forward," Vivy said.

We trundled down the runway and lifted off. "How long is the flight?" I asked

"About four hours," Eddie spoke up. His eyes were still closed, his fingers still drumming. "I'm booking us a car on the other end now. We should get to the scene of the crime just after nightfall, local time."

"What do you want to do in the meantime?" Vivy said.

I sighed. "Normally I'd say 'sexy flight attendant roleplay,' but I'm too worried about Tamsin, and also, Eddie is here."

"Your restraint is appreciated," he muttered.

"So… how about you tell me more about this whole Tamsin-is-an-incomer thing," I said. "Where is she from? How did she end up here?"

Vivy wrinkled her forehead, and I wondered if she had a database of information in her brain that she was consulting. "Tamsin was born in the universe next door, on the other side of the sheet, you might say. I haven't spent much time there, but it's got a higher tech level than Earth. It's really regressive politically, though, pretty much ruled by families of oligarchs, almost feudal in some respects, but the serfs have a pretty high standard of living. There was a bunch of political violence, and Tamsin's grandmother faked her death and fled here. She brought Tamsin with her. Trevor is apparently some kind of family retainer, brought over in secret to act as a bodyguard to Tamsin, though she didn't know his true origins."

"See?" Eddie chimed in. "You're not the first person to date a secret operative from another world."

"Not helping," Vivy said.

"The world next door sounds like an awful place. Isn't that the kind of society the Interventionists should be disrupting and liberating?"

Vivy shrugged. "Sure, in theory, but we pick our battles. We tend to focus on more advanced societies – especially ones capable of traveling to other levels of Nigh-Space and exporting their fascist bullshit across realities. Tamsin's home world has developed some limited interdimensional technology, but ironically, the oligarchy thing works in our favor there. Only a few very rich, very secretive people know about Nigh-Space, and they tightly guard that knowledge. We keep half an eye on them, but they're too busy with their infighting and local power struggles to think about branching out and causing trouble in other worlds. Tamsin's homeland is one of many, many worlds on our watchlist, but they're way down on the list."

"Think of it like cancer," Eddie said. "Their world is a tumor – yours is too, as far as that goes, it's not like there's a shortage of oligarchs and injustice on Earth – but it's not a tumor that's metastasized yet. We focus on more critical cases – ones that threaten the whole body."

Vivy nodded. "According to our files, there was some concern early on that Tamsin's grandmother would try to start her warlord shit on Earth, but she seemed content with pretending to invent some relatively harmless communications technology and getting rich. Our assessment was, she didn't want to risk doing anything that would alert her political enemies back home that she'd survived, so we just monitored her instead of taking action."

Action? "What, like... assassinating her?"

"I don't do assassinations," Vivy said. "I'm not saying I've never..." She trailed off, then resumed: "Sometimes, you're in a situation against armed opposition, and it's you or them, and yeah, I'll choose me. I've had to act to protect myself, and to save others, too. But the Interventionists don't engage in political murder. More often, we help the local resistance fight against their oppressors. We don't want to be the rulers of the universe. We want to help people find their own way toward a better future."

"Though in some cases, we do take direct action," Eddie said. "Like, say, we might snatch the leaders of some genocidal regime, and transport them to a remote world a few hundred levels away from their homeland, where we give them enough supplies to last their natural lifespans and a library full of interesting literature, and leave them be."

"So... do we think someone on Tamsin's home world found out she'd survived, and decided to take her hostage?"

"It's a theory," Vivy said. "Though it doesn't explain why they'd kidnap Tamsin and this Trevor guy instead of just..." She trailed off.

"Instead of killing them, along with Tamsin's granny," I finished.

Vivy took my hand. "Hey. She might be okay. And if she's in trouble... we'll help her. Okay?"

"Oh, my," Eddie said. "I just accessed the security systems in Culver House. That old lady had herself a magic door."

TAMSIN

The limousine pulled up in front of a… I don't even know what to call it. A sprawling hotel-casino-galley-stadium-complex, called the Fortress of Attitude. "Is that a joke reference from our world?" I whispered to Trevor.

"I think it's just a coincidence," he whispered back.

The doors opened, and we stepped out into a riot of sound, light, and people. The air was summertime warm (though not as punishingly hot as Las Vegas could be), and the people around us weren't all dressed as finely as we were – there were plenty of dirty overalls, and what looked to my eye like fetishy lingerie and old-timey bathing suits in equal proportion, and also t-shirts and denim skirts, the last ones presumably avant-garde fashion stolen from my world.

There was a guy in platform boots with heels fully three feet high, basically a stilt-walker, wearing bulbous glasses that made him resemble a bug. He caught my eye, a beam of light flashed from his glasses, and suddenly I was looking at a projection of a ten-foot-tall oiled-up naked man making out with some kind of femmebot cyborg thing, their clinch filling my vision, a ghost image overlaid on the crowd. The hawker's voice squawked in my ear: "Hot human-on-machine action, who can last the longest in the Fleshpits of Steeltown, tickets available now–"

Block ads? my necklace whispered, and I subvocalized a desperate yes. The image vanished, and the hawker moved on to his next victim. I blinked, still dazzled, and Trevor was at my elbow, steadying me. He led me after Bollard and Chicane, who were already heading into the Fortress of Attitude, and the lobby was a lot less crowded, if no less dazzling. Every surface was reflective, there was a huge fountain gushing with some fluid that sparkled in rainbow colors, and people in skimpy outfits of feathers and leather circulated with trays of treats. There were naked acrobats tumbling past off to my right, but the nudity wasn't their most remarkable quality. They appeared to have another set of hands where most people have feet.

Bollard and Chicane wove smoothly through the crowd, the big man plucking a flute of something to drink while heading toward a long front desk crewed by the most beautiful people I'd ever seen in real life. "Are we getting rooms?" I whispered to Trevor. "Because frankly I could already use a bit of a lie-down. This place is a lot."

"General Bollard didn't fill me in on his plans," Trevor said. "But if you want rooms I'm sure we can get them."

I put my mouth close to his ear and said, "I wouldn't mind getting a room with you–" I stopped, horrified at myself, and said, "I don't... I'm sorry! I don't know why I said that."

"It's okay," Trevor said. "You know how people say in Las Vegas they pump extra oxygen into the casinos, to make people more energized and uninhibited? I think that's an urban legend, but over here, they do a lot more than just add oxygen. The air in here is sweetened with all kinds of chemical disinhibition agents, aphrodisiacs, mild euphorics... it's the City of Song. People come here to let loose. I won't take it personally if you loosen up a little yourself."

"You seem to have yourself under control," I said.

He snorted. "I want to kiss every inch of you, starting at the feet and working my way up. But I pretty much always feel that way, so it's a difference of degree, not kind."

I liked smart Trevor in a different way than performatively stupid Trevor. "So you weren't just pretending to like me back in high school, because it was part of your job?"

"Taking care of you was never a job for me, Sin. It was always my calling."

I blushed, but I put my head down and pushed forward, annoyed at the chemicals cracking my well-maintained shell. We walked up to join Bollard in time to hear him say "– and executive adamantine level access, please."

The beautiful person behind the counter, with a shaved head and perfect long eyelashes and plump lips, tilted their head and flickered their eyes. "Ah, yes, the Wall party, of course! Please, come with me." The counter slid apart, opening a space wide enough for us to walk through. We went with them, and the shiny black wall behind the counter developed a door that opened on a corridor lit with soft red lights. I'd never been heavily into drugs, but like most people in the Bay Area I'd had the occasional edible, and I'd done MDMA a few times during my club days, before work ate my life. I felt a low-key combination of both those drug experiences as we walked down: mellow and relaxed and expansive, but also tingly and sexy and aware of my body in the best way. I caught myself running my hand up and down Trevor's arm and stopped myself.

We emerged into a beautiful cathedral of a space, all vaulted ceilings and glossy pillars, with screens on all sides displaying shifting colors and shapes like psychedelic dreamscapes. The beautiful guide said, "Your package is all-inclusive – have fun!" and then departed. The floor was black and speckled with glowing lights, like a starfield beneath my feet, and the area was crowded without being packed. Everyone here was dressed up, in tuxedos and ball gowns and saris borrowed from Earth styles, or in local finery, the cut strange but the quality of the cloth (and wire, and leather, and other things) obviously high.

There were various stations set up: gambling tables on one side, a raised dance floor on another, a cage-fight in a corner, people reclining on couches puffing on tubes… I recognized all those diversions. I was more confused by an area enclosed by railings. It was full of people in skintight black suits and full-face masks, like fencing gear, all walking on omnidirectional treadmills and waving their arms around. "What are they doing?" I asked. "Some kind of weird exercise class?"

"It's virtual reality," Trevor said. "When I left here as a kid, the tech was about as good as what we have in America now. I'm sure it's gotten better here since then, but I mean, it still doesn't look exactly convincing." As we watched, someone on a treadmill stumbled, then tore off their visor, stepped to one side, and vomited into one of the bins that lined the corral. He wiped his mouth, put the visor back on, and returned to his little walkable circle. "Looks like they haven't solved the motion-sickness thing totally yet," Trevor observed.

"Not for me," I said. "I'll stick with real life. It's plenty diverting."

Bollard tapped me on the shoulder, and I looked up into his beaming face. "Enjoying yourself, Princess?"

"You might have warned me the air was drugged, Bollard."

"I keep forgetting all the extremely basic things you don't know," he replied. "There are so many of them, after all. I suggest we spend two hours circulating, taking in the sights, perhaps having a bite… and then we will gather back there." He pointed to the cage-fighting ring. "According to Trevor's positively encyclopedic memory of your granny's stories, there should be a door concealed behind a pillar in that corner, which will provide access to the next private vault."

"Sounds good," I said. "Why the wait, though?"

"Chicane needs time to trick the surveillance systems. If they fail entirely, that will draw unwanted attention, so he's engineering something more subtle. Recordings of us enjoying ourselves will prove useful – he can loop them into the feed later to conceal our absence."

That made sense. "All right. Two hours." Bollard nodded and sauntered away. I didn't see Chicane anywhere. I wondered if

Swarm was in the room with us, so I subvocalized: Swarm, are you here?

The reply came over SerpentNet: Just outside. Doing a sweep. We can't seize control of their security systems because they aren't automated, mostly – they rely on people with guns and shit to handle trouble here instead of drones and autocannons. That said, I'm not detecting anymore security than usual. Our prospects for success look good so far. We probably won't have to show ourselves, but if we do, we're disguised as run-of-the-mill Zmija combat drones. No reason to let anybody know Swarm has come out of mothballs.

Smart, I sent.

Thanks. Go enjoy yourself until the rendezvous, Tamsin. I would if I could.

I took Trevor's arm, and I wanted to say, "Is there a place where we can have sex around here?" but then I remembered that everything we were about to do would be recorded and looped, and I wasn't that much of an exhibitionist. "What kind of gambling do they have here? Poker? Roulette?"

"Not those. They do have cards here, but the decks have sixty cards, and the games are all pretty different. They do have this one game sort of like craps, but with a bunch of polyhedral dice, the kind only roleplaying game nerds use back home, but it's pretty fun…" He led me to the casino-like portion of the floor. Instead of human dealers, there were humanoid robots built right into the gaming tables, with metal torsos and multiple arms and cylinders full of sensors for heads.

He showed me how to play his silly dice game, and it was fun, even though I was never much into gambling. We didn't use chips – our new smart contact lenses gave us displays with interfaces we could use to wager and keep track of our winnings (or, in our case, losses). I had no idea how much anything actually cost in this world, so I didn't know if I was blowing fortunes or pocket change. I felt a flicker of doubt. Was I really going to try to run this world? I didn't even know the name of the country we were in. I didn't even know if it was a country. Maybe they had protectorates here, or commonwealths, or fucking duchies. Maybe it was a one-world government, ostensibly as well as in reality. How could I hope to take a leading role in a place that was so deeply alien to me?

I shook it off. My immediate goal was getting rich, and my next goal was taking revenge on the Monad for murdering my entire family. The rest would fall into place in time. I've never faced a problem I couldn't vanquish when I focused my effort and attention. Besides, every government is fundamentally a set of interlocking systems, and I am very good at understanding systems. I'm also good at hiring the right people, and between Bollard and Swarm, I had all my practicalities and realpolitik covered. This was, in essence, a problem of project management, and I was a project manager.

I did want to spend a lot of time with whatever the local equivalent of Wikipedia was, to fill myself in on the fine details of… everything. I intended to do all that catch-up reading in an orbital pleasure palace with the head of the Monad matriarch on a spike out front, though.

Trevor and I made the rounds. I noticed people giving us covert glances, and couldn't figure out why… but this was an alien world. I was doing my best to fit in, but there had to be a million subtleties of carriage and dress and attitude that eluded me. I decided the easiest way to cover up any potential oddities in my behavior, and assuage my anxieties, would be to get a little intoxicated – but just a little. Once I determined that the hookah-bar-vape-tube place wasn't going to send me into an opium stupor, but just give me a pleasant buzz, we reclined on cushions and took puffs.

In that pink haze, I made a considered decision that it would be okay if Trevor and I made out and lightly groped each other a little. Such behavior was good camouflage, I thought. If we were sprawled on pillows getting high and kissing, no one would suspect me of being from an alien world, or my group of plotting a heist. (Or infiltration; you can't steal what's rightfully yours.)

After our vapors ran out, we went to watch a cage fight. I never had much patience for boxing or MMA, but my tolerance for violence had greatly increased lately, and back home, the fighters aren't genetically engineered and mechanically augmented, so this was a lot more interesting. A man with a metal arm and lenses for eyes punched a guy with scales and a lashing lizard tail and two snarling heads, until one of those heads spat acid in his metal face, and then swept his legs with said tail. I found myself clapping and cheering along with everyone else.

After that, we hit the buffet, and everything was spiced oddly and weirdly textured, even things that looked more-or-less familiar, except the bacon-wrapped dates. Those seemed totally normal. "We've got pigs here," Trevor said. "Most of the other animals are different, but for some reason, pigs, and also sheep. They must have come over through a portal at some point, or else their ancestors are native to this world and went over to Earth sometime." He shrugged and popped another morsel into his mouth.

We listened to a band in a velvet-draped cabaret – their songs sounded like babies screaming – and then we did a turn around the dance floor. I didn't know any of this world's moves, but everybody was basically just high and tripping and gyrating, so it hardly mattered. I just gyrated along. I was breathless and delighted and having fun when Trevor pulled me close and kissed me.

Just then SerpentNet said, Timer elapsed.

I took Trevor's hand and pulled him back in the direction of the cage fights. Inside the octagon (except it was a hexagon here), a seven-foot-tall woman in a metal bikini was swinging a polearm to keep three toddler-sized creatures at bay; they were covered in fur and looked like toy-dog versions of werewolves – they were snarling, and were going to outflank her.

We jostled through the crowd and reached a dark corner that held a broad pillar of that same black stone with twinkling sparkles inside. Bollard and Chicane were behind the pillar, in the space between it and the wall, and we crowded back there with them. "Welcome," Bollard said. "Let's wait just a moment for Chicane to overlay our false feed atop the real one..."

"Done," the homunculus said. "We're invisible." He wiggled his fingers and fluttered his scarves, then stripped off the garment of veils to reveal a form-fitting black outfit, sort of ninja-meets-fetishwear.

"Is your friend the hive-mind ready?" Bollard said.

I'm not a hive-mind, why does everyone think that? Swarm said. I'm just the one mind, distributed across a lot of bodies, rather than a lot of little minds working as one. But whatever. Yes, I'm inside the VIP area now. Three bodies were all I could safely sneak in, but that should be enough to handle things even if stuff goes sideways. There are only about a dozen security guards in the place.

"Swarm is all set," I said.

"Mmm," Bollard said. "Swarm gave you something to let you communicate with them directly, then? Are you back on, what did your dead relatives call it... SerpentNet? That must be handy."

I wondered if Bollard knew I had control of his lab. I didn't think so. I got the sense the Zmija usually kept their true capabilities hidden. "Yeah, Swarm gave me an implant." That was true; they'd injected me with a needle full of liquid technology. The implant did everything my necklace did, with the added bonus that it couldn't be yanked off my neck. Swarm said the technology was now distributed throughout my nervous system, so it couldn't be sliced out or otherwise removed. I was on SerpentNet for as long as I lived, now. "I've got comms, and access to some family data."

"Then perhaps you know where the door is?"

I looked around, and SerpentNet supplied a glowing outline:

"It's in the pillar." Bollard and Chicane stepped aside. I stepped forward and put my hand on the smooth stone. "Open in the name of Tamsin Zmija." That was a little dramatic, but blame it on the drugs.

The pillar started to slide open – and then everything turned to chaos.

Harsh lights came one, spotlighting us. A chorus of voices shouted "Stop right there!" and I looked around the pillar to see every single person in the casino pointing futuristic pistols at us.

Swarm shouted at my inner ear: Tamsin, they're all security! This was a setup! I'll stall them! You run!

A woman's voice boomed over a loudspeaker: "Get on your knees and put your hands behind your head, young woman! We know who you are!"

"This is unfortunate," Bollard said, and picked me up as easily as he'd carried Trevor back home – more easily, probably, since Trevor had a good fifty pounds on me. I squawked as Bollard began to bull his way through the crowd, Chicane in front of him, lashing out ferociously with a knife in each hand, pushing people back.

"Hold your fire!" the voice on the PA boomed. "I want the girl alive!"

"Why don't we go to the vault!" I shouted, basically into Bollard's ass, since that's where my head was dangling.

"Because I'd rather not be trapped under the casino with no escape route!" Bollard shouted. "That voice is the voice of the Monad!"

Screams and gunfire erupted all around us, despite the Monad's injunction against shooting, but then I realized it wasn't the bad guys doing the shooting; it was my guys.

I'm trying to open an escape route, but it's going to be tough, Swarm said. I'm holding open the door to the lobby. Get out of here!

I lifted my head and twisted around to look for Trevor, and

he was gamely trying to keep up with me, kicking and swinging his fists at the pressing crowd, but then he got dogpiled under a bunch of people in cocktail dresses and I lost sight of him. "Trevor!" I screamed. "Bollard, we have to go back for him!"

"We absolutely do not," Bollard said. "Close your eyes!" I did as he said, knowing he wasn't the type to give such a warning twice, and probably had a good reason. There was a blinding blue flash of light, even through my eyelids, and a bunch of people started screaming. I looked through slitted eyes and saw people staggering around, blinded by whatever flash-bang bullshit Bollard had done. His suit probably lit up to a million candlepower on command.

Three Swarmbots flickered into visibility in front of me, then formed up around us in a phalanx, their weapons chattering to keep the horde of security at bay. Chicane hooted and capered in front of us, murder on two legs. Were we actually going to get out of here? Fuck, but what about Trevor? We had to save him. Bollard worked for me, and if I said we were doing a rescue mission, we were doing a rescue mission–

The cyborg fighter, the seven-foot-tall woman, the lizard man, and the werewolf toddlers dropped on us from above – there were catwalks up there I hadn't noticed. They all had augmented strength, and the bigger three wrestled the Swarmbots down. The toddlers went at Chicane, and he tore one of their heads right off – it's just a special effect, my gibbering mind tried to reassure me. The other two feral tots grabbed his legs and knocked him down, though, and then the two-headed lizard left its tackled Swarmbot and stomped on Chicane's head with one clawed foot, over and over.

Bollard dodged and weaved like an American football player going for a touchdown, and I was the ball. Then the cyborg tackled him, and I went flying away. I rolled, and groaned, and sat up. Bollard kicked the cyborg in the knee, dropping him to the ground, then looked at me. He gave a minute shake of his head, then reached into his pocket and flung a rectangle of cardboard at me before sprinting for the door to the lobby and vanishing through it.

The business card hit the floor and came to a stop. It said:

BOLLARD AND CHICANE

Sorry Princess • But Don't Worry • We'll Sort This Out

"Just Stay Alive!"

Then that bald Amazon dressed like a Boris Vallejo cover illustration pointed her polearm at my face. The end crackled with blue sparks of electricity. "Do you surrender?" she asked.

How had things gone so spectacularly, and bizarrely, wrong? No plan survives contact with the enemy, but this was ridiculous. A long as I survived, though, I could make more plans. "I surrender," I said. For now.

GLENN

"Wait, there are doors that lead to other realities? Like, literal physical doors? I thought it was all snap-traces and curve-chasers and stuff."

"Interdimensional travel has been discovered about ten zillion times, Glenn." Eddie was using his talking-to-a-child tone again. He paused to slurp down some spicy pork noodles. (The food on the plane was amazing, even if I'd had to microwave it myself.) "There are lots of ways to traverse Nigh-Space. Think of it this way. If you need to get across town, you can take a bus, or a train, or a scooter, or a bike, or roller skates, or ride a horse, or get someone to push you in a wheelbarrow, or whatever – those are all different ways of solving the same problem, with different levels of usefulness at different times and in different situations. Plus, sometimes you really want a high-speed train, but all you've got is a skateboard, so you make do. It's the same thing when it comes to traversing Nigh-Space." He pointed a chopstick at my bowl. "You done?" I pushed my bowl over to him. "Having a tongue fucking rules," Eddie said, and went to work on my ramen.

"I guess a door is pretty limited," I mused. "Compared to the stuff I've seen. Like, a door has a fixed location, I assume, on both sides? It only opens in one place, and only goes one place?"

"Primitive," Vivy murmured. She was leaning back in a chair with her eyes closed – she was "centering herself," she'd said.

"That's usually how they work," Eddie said. "Some of the doors are programmable, so you can punch in a few different destinations – sort of like taking an elevator, but instead of buttons for different floors, it's buttons for different worlds. But most of them are more limited." He drank from the bowl and smacked his lips and said, "Ahhhh. Even advanced societies use fixed portals like doors sometimes, though. They have advantages."

"Such as?"

"Think it through. If you're going to be a secret agent, you gotta start thinking like one."

"I have no intention of being a secret agent." Still, I considered. "Doors like that could be easily defended, I guess, offering secure access to protected locations?"

"Blabingo," Eddie said.

"I think you mean 'bingo,'" I said.

"Really?" Eddie shook his head. "That game must be a lot easier to win in your world. Anyway, yeah, there are lots of ways to defend against unwelcome interdimensional travelers. Signal jammers, sort of. That's why sometimes Vivy has to land in one place, and then sneak or fight her way in deeper. People with privacy needs or security concerns can have doors like that to let them access an otherwise impregnable bunker, or as a backdoor escape route. But in this case, it's like Vivy said: it's just primitive. Tamsin's home universe only discovered the existence of Nigh-Space a few decades back, and as far as we know, opening doors to the immediately neighboring universes is the best they can do. Their tech is very much in the early stages of development."

"I mean, a magic door," I said. "From where I sit, that sounds pretty cool."

"Doors like that are dangerous to use, if you didn't install them yourself," Vivy said, eyes still closed. "You never know what you'll find when you walk through them."

"So what are we going to do when we get to Culver House?" I asked.

"Walk through the door," Vivy said.

We landed at a private airstrip. I hadn't been to the Midwest very often, and it was all so flat. In Berkeley, and in Santa Cruz, too, I always knew where I was: the hills are that way, the ocean is that way, the cardinal directions line up accordingly. Out here, the view in every direction looked the same: fields and distant trees and cloudy skies. There was already a rental car waiting for us, a behemoth of a black SUV, courtesy of Eddie. He climbed behind the wheel, chortling with delight.

"Why is he so happy?" I asked, sliding into the back seat with Vivy.

"This is the equivalent of riding in a horse-drawn carriage to him," she said.

Eddie put the car in gear and we tore off away from the airport, vastly exceeding the speed limit. "You're gonna get us pulled over by the cops!" I said.

"Oh, I know where all the bobbies and peelers are," Eddie said. "I'm in their systems. I'm wounded that you'd doubt me, old chap." We mostly went down back roads, through fields and stands of trees, past sagging old barns and rambling farmhouses.

"Do you ever think about living in the country?" Vivy asked, gazing out the window.

I shook my head. "I like to visit, sometimes, but I'd chew my own tongue off with boredom. I like cities, and I love college towns. Santa Cruz, Berkeley, those are good for me. Small enough that you can get a feel for the whole place, but lively, with lots of culture and bookstores and restaurants and bars. What about you?"

"I once had to do eight months of subjective virtual tank time preparing for a mission on a pastoral world the Prime Army was trying to develop as a supply outpost," Vivy said. "If I never see another hay bale again it'll be too soon. I did get to make a bunch of fertilizer bombs to blow up their gate with, though."

I'd heard her mention these particular baddies a few times now. "What is the Prime Army?"

"One of our most persistent and irritating enemies," Vivy said. "A military dictatorship full of fascist idiots who think their home world is the root of the multiverse, the one 'real world,' and that it's their destiny to put all the lesser worlds under their control. They're basically the worst."

"They have no sense of humor at all, as a rule," Eddie chimed in.

"And they use gates?" I asked. "Like, big doors? I thought those were for primitive worlds barely even more advanced than Earth."

If she noticed my sarcasm, she ignored it. "Some of the Prime Army scouts and officers have personal traversal tech, like curve-chasers but worse, that allow them to hop one universe at a time. But they'd never give their regular soldiers that kind of technology – for one thing, their supply is limited, since they're hard to make. Mostly, though, it's because they're fascist control freaks. A lot of their foot soldiers are conscripts from conquered world, and if they could hop dimensions, they'd go permanently AWOL. The Prime Army mostly uses fixed gates, these big-ass portals, to move troops and supplies through, and to provide a single point of access and control."

"Their gates are a bit crap, though," Eddie said. "They have limited range, only good for traveling six or eight levels, so the rotters have to daisy-chain their gates. They set up these long supply lines from their central protected home worlds, and those are easy to target."

Vivy grinned. "Every time I blow up a gate, and cut a Prime Army outpost off from the rest of their cohort, the home office has to send a scout back using a personal device. Then that poor bastard has to build a new gate, and, of course, somebody like me can just come along and blow it up again…" She shook her head. "The Prime Army has a major advantage over us in numbers, and they've got a solid lock on their home world and a few levels out in both directions, but they have all the weakness that come with running a giant unwieldy war machine. They're especially vulnerable to insurgency tactics like the Interventionists use."

"Fighting them is a bit like stepping on ants, though," Eddie said. "There's always another ant. Until you track them back to the colony and pour petrol into all the little holes and set the lot on fire. Which is what we should do to their so-called World Prime."

"That's a little on the genocidal side, which isn't how we do things," Vivy said sternly. "Our bosses are working on encouraging the soldiers to rise up against the officers. We try to avoid the wholesale slaughter of people who were forced into shitty situations by circumstance. In the meantime, we disrupt their operations and try to limit the damage they can do. We've pretty much ground their expansion to a halt in the past several years, and it's all they can do to hold their ground – the generals are pretty frustrated, according to our spies. Sometimes I like my job. Making terrible people miserable is a joy."

"We're here." Eddie pulled up in front of a huge house, basically a mansion, surrounded by a stone wall with an iron gate. I'd never been to Culver House, but I'd seen it in photos, with Tamsin standing in front of it. "There's a security system, but it's about as tough to defeat as a bowl of ice cream." The metal gate rumbled open, and Eddie drove through. "Ta da." The gate shut behind us, and we parked around front. We all piled out of the car, and Vivy took point, going up the steps to the porch and peering through the windows on either side of the main door.

"The house definitely has that 'I've been abandoned' feeling," she said. "Can you get the door open, Eddie?"

"Wow, there's a keypad," he said. "Yawn. This is me yawning." He hummed for a moment, then turned the knob and pushed the door open. "Consider things broken and entered."

Vivy said, "Eddie, take a last peek through their security cameras and motion sensors, would you? I'd like to know for sure the place is empty."

"Of course. The house is positively bristling with security. Not that it helped poor Granny Culver..." He closed his eyes and hummed to himself for a moment. "No sign of life inside. Or dangerous forms of un-life." He turned and wiggled his fingers in my face in a way I think was meant to be spooky.

She nodded. "All right. Let's proceed with caution anyway. You two, wait in the foyer while I do a sweep." She pushed open the door and slipped inside, moving like a quicksilver shadow. Eddie and I followed, and I watched Vivy vanish up the stairs soundlessly. She was always graceful, but this was a step above "took dance all through school" and into "elite assassin" territory.

Eddie reached into his suit and took out a vape pen, giving it a thoughtful puff. He was sampling human vices, it seemed. "You're eager to join the cause, then?"

I blinked at him. "What?"

"You insisted on coming along on this mission. You acquitted yourself admirably, for an amateur, when the Strict Constructionists blew me up. I think you've got the espionage itch." He scratched the back of his neck. "That expression makes more sense now that I've got all this skin, by the way."

"I don't think the 'espionage itch' is an expression."

"Maybe not on this remote–"

Vivy reappeared, emerging from a ground-floor door, which meant this house had more than one staircase, and also that she was very fast. What kind of augmentations did my girlfriend have? Eddie said she was arguably posthuman...

"We're clear," she said. "Something bad happened here, though. Upstairs I found a stretch of floor eaten through with acid, and I detected a few stray bits of biological material on the edges. Maybe give it a scan, Eddie?" Her voice was carefully calm. Eddie stowed his vape and darted upstairs, faster than any human could.

I tried to find my voice. "Is it Tamsin? Did they... dissolve her?" I felt like the floor had dropped out underneath me. I'd lost a friend to a car accident in high school, and another to an aggressive rare cancer in college, but I'd never lost anyone to violence... or acid.

Vivy took my hands. "Don't assume the worst, okay? We'll have news soon."

I looked past her, at the framed photos on the dark wooden walls, people with severe faces peering out of the past, and disapproving of the future. Tamsin always said her childhood was spent in a big dark house that was cold in more ways than one.

Eddie appeared at the top of the stairs, and called down to us as he descended. "Tamsin was not melted! Fortunately I brought along a database of persons of interest for the local array of worlds, which is rather short because this area is very dull, and I was able to identify a fleck of meat in that nasty mess. The dissolved individual was Hamish Chicane, a career criminal expert in assassination, sabotage, and, ironically, disposing of bodies with acid." He held up a finger. "Mr Chicane is not from this world. He is from Tamsin's home world, which means our theory was probably right – someone from that side realized the old lady was alive, and sent a kill team to finish her off." He glanced at me. "Or, er, a kidnap team, when it comes to Tamsin. And Trevor. Probably. That is–"

"Do we have a list of this Chicane's known associates?" Vivy interrupted before Eddie could make things worse.

He hopped down from the last stair and nodded. "Mr Chicane was part of a duo. The other half is a distressingly large brains-and-brawn combination named Phipps Bollard. The pair of them met in some kind of clandestine paramilitary service, then went freelance, and they've been working together for more than twenty years. Chicane did most of the assassinations and torture and so forth, while Bollard's skills are more logistical and scientific, though he's not averse to recreational and vocational violence. They often work for oligarchs in the world next door." He shrugged. "It all fits.

Granny fought back, Chicane was killed, but Bollard snatched Trevor and Tamsin and took them through the door."

"We have to save her, Vivy," I said.

She put her hand on my shoulder. "We'll do everything we can. Eddie? Let's take a look at this door."

Ten minutes later, we were in the basement, an unexceptional workspace, apart from a red metal door in a freestanding frame in one corner. Eddie rapped on the door with his knuckles, pressed his palm against its surface, and grunted.

"Are we looking at a gene-lock?" Vivy said.

"Indeed," Eddie confirmed. "And a surprisingly sophisticated one. It doesn't just sniff the DNA. It looks for vital signs, physiological evidence of extreme stress consistent with coercion... it even checks the telomeres to make sure they're the right length and the subject is the correct age, to prevent trickery involving clones, I would imagine."

"Can you get it open?" Vivy said.

Eddie rolled his eyes. "This is a cheap padlock, Vivian, and I am a pair of bolt cutters. The people who made this door prepared for everything they could imagine, but I am unimaginable." He turned to me. "Glenn, old bean? Run upstairs and look for something with the old lady's DNA on it. Or Tamsin's, I suppose, in a pinch."

I wrinkled my nose. "What, like a toothbrush?"

"Those get rinsed off. A hairbrush is better. Bring me juicy follicles."

I went upstairs, honestly happy to have a task to distract me from my worries. I found Tamsin's bedroom first – still preserved from her high school years, it looked like, with trophies for horseback riding and debate team on a shelf, and posters of noir-movie femme fatales and sci-fi movie alien conquerors on the wall, and a desk tucked under one window with neatly arranged notebooks and highlighters on the surface. I pulled myself away, continuing down the hall to the master bedroom, a dim cave of draped fabric and heavy furniture that smelled of lavender and menthol. There was a hairbrush on the vanity, full of steel gray strands of hair, and I brought the whole thing down.

"Perfect." Eddie plucked a few strands, grinned at me, and then shoved them into his mouth and slurped noisily.

"Ew, Eddie, god," Vivy said. "Do you have to be so disgusting?"

He swallowed, then said, "To have a body is to be disgusting, Vivian." Eddie cocked his head, squinted, wrinkled his nose, seemed to tense every muscle for a long moment, and then sighed contentedly. "Done." He patted his own chest. "This body is basically a chemical printer, Glenn – I can match any DNA sample, and I can fake the rest of the qualities this door checks for."

I nodded. "Telomeres, you said? Those get shorter as we age, right?"

Vivy stepped up beside me. "Right. The door checks the lengths, so nobody can take one of those hairs, clone a baby that's genetically identical to Tamsin's grandmother, and use said baby to open the door. Pretty clever. Eddie, do we know when the door was last opened? It would be nice to know how far behind Bollard we are."

"No, it doesn't keep logs," Eddie said. "I'd say the goo upstairs was alive a week ago, but the flesh is imprecise. Let's assume Tamsin got snatched the same day she arrived in town to deal with her grandmother's estate. In that case, we're looking at... four days?"

Vivy winced, which I did not find reassuring.

Eddie touched the door. "Open in the name of the Interventionists!"

"Proceed with caution," a waspish woman's voice said from a hidden speaker in the frame, and then the door swung open, revealing a dim, brick-lined room beyond.

A room in another world. I had been to several of those at this point, but the experienced was still mind-warpingly weird. "We just... walk through?"

"Eddie goes first." Vivy clapped him on the back. "He's more durable than we are."

"Just one of my many advantages." Eddie stepped through the doorframe and then stood on the far side, hands in his trouser pockets, rocking back and forth on his heels for a moment. "Nasty, nasty! This place is positively bristling with automated armaments, which is impressive, since it looks like several bombs landed on the area a long time ago. They build their murder machines to last over here. Let me just... there. I've got us on the friendly list. Come on through."

Vivy took my hand. "Are you sure you want to do this? Eddie and I can go, and send word back. I don't know what we're going to run into over there."

I shook my head. "If I stayed, I'd just be worried about Tamsin and you. I want to go. I want to help."

She nodded. "Okay. You can come with us, but it could be dangerous, so I need you to promise to follow my instructions without question–"

"This would likely be a bad time to make a sex joke, eh?" Eddie said, leaning in the open doorway.

"Edmund!" Vivy said.

"I promise," I put in before they could start arguing. "You're the professional, I'm the tagalong, I get it."

"Then let's go save your ex." Vivy stepped through the door with me, hand and hand, into the universe next door.

TAMSIN

I managed to get some sleep during transport – first in a car, then in the back of an aircraft that looked like a lozenge with shark fins on top, strapped to a bench under armed guard – which was evidence of my exhaustion. Since coming through the door, I'd flown in a magic bubble, descended into the heart of a mountain, gotten menaced by a fresh clone, descended into a submerged city, made friends with an army of killbots, visited a fever-dream version of Las Vegas, survived a melee, and been taken prisoner... no wonder I was tired, and there was nothing to do in my mobile captivity but sleep. It was a tactical choice, even; I would likely need my strength.

The flying machine landed on an expanse of lawn within sight of an immense pile of white stone. The estate looked like the mutant offspring of a cathedral and an opera house with a few minarets tacked on. The augmented goons loaded me onto a sleek black version of a golf cart. The Vallejo barbarian sat beside me, but she wasn't very chatty, not even when I asked her if the steroids gave her zits on her back.

We reached the palace, and a humanoid-ish robot butler with six arms opened the door. Or maybe it was a robot soldier. Who knows? Vallejo jabbed me between the shoulder blades and said, "Walk." She started to follow me inside, but robo-Jeeves held up one of its double-thumbed hands.

"Your presence is no longer required," it said in a voice that reminded me a little of Granny's – a woman who was not interested in your problems or feelings, and who didn't take shit from anyone. I hated the speaker immediately.

Vallejo scowled and stomped off, and the robot grabbed me around the upper arm. "The Monad will see you now."

Can you hijack their systems? I asked SerpentNet.

No, my implant said. Local security is based on an unknown operating system.

Damn it. I hoped hope Bollard's last business card was telling the truth. I hated waiting to be rescued, though. At the very least, I could annoy my captors in the meantime. "You're just a big walkie-talkie, aren't you?" I moved with the butler-bot when it walked, since it was that, or get dragged. "I'm talking to the queen of the Monads right now, aren't I? Or one of the duchesses or baronesses or whatever. You're really all clones? I thought the royalty on Earth was messed up. This goes way beyond simple incest and inbreeding. Do you know about Narcissistic Personality Disorder over here?"

"You remind me very much of your grandmother," the robot said. "I despised your grandmother."

"You knew her? Are you a thousand years old, too?"

"Longevity is a perk of ruling the world, Miss Zmija."

The bot marched me down long hallways with marble floors, the walls covered in old paintings and tapestries, the niches filled with statuary, and the ceilings bristling with crystal chandeliers. "This place is like a museum, and not a very well curated one. Do you actually live here, or is this just where you interrogate people and store your third-rate art?"

The butler tsked. "I am walking you through a hall full of the looted treasures of the Zmija estates, and you don't even know enough about your family history to feel the sting of the insult? What a shame."

I scowled. "My ancestors had terrible taste, too, then. How far are we supposed to walk? Can't this butler transform into a scooter or something—"

We stopped in front of a pair of immense wooden doors, carved all over with an elaborate series of designs. I squinted. "Is that an army of people with spears killing a giant snake?"

"It is an allegorical work," the butler-bot said. "Your descendants are the allegorical losers. Also the literal ones. By losing to me today, you're merely continuing a family tradition."

The doors swung open on their own, and the robot let go of my arm and gave me a shove between the shoulder blades. I managed not to stumble too badly as I walked into an office roughly the size of a blimp hangar, the vast floor dominated by a desk made from a small forest's worth of doubtless rare wood. A woman sat behind the desk, her skin dark and smooth, her hair bone-white and closely cropped, her eyes golden and faintly shining. These people and their augmentations! I was only a little jealous.

Trevor? I whispered over SerpentNet. Are you here?

Vassal not detected, the system whispered back. He is likely housed in an isolation cell to prevent communication.

Oh well. At least that wasn't the same as "he's definitely dead." I continued walking to the desk, stopping just before it. I looked the old woman up and down, then made a great show of looking around the room. "Don't I get a chair?"

"Lowlies stand in the presence of their betters," she said, in the same voice that had emerged from the butler. "I am the Monad–"

"If you're all called the Monad, doesn't that get confusing?" I interrupted.

"Do not interrupt me. I am the Monad: the head of the family. The matriarch. And you are... surprising. Little baby Tamsin. We all thought you were dead."

"Just one of your many misapprehensions, I'm sure." I could have jumped across the desk and throttled her, but I didn't think I'd live long if I tried it.

"Did your grandmother send you here in some misguided attempt to bait us?" she asked.

I laughed at her. She didn't like that. "You really don't know much, do you? My grandmother is dead. I found out about... all this... after she passed. I understand you hold a virtual monopoly on interdimensional technology, but all this time, you never opened a gate to Earth to see if Granny had escaped?"

She tried to frown, but her face didn't have a lot of mobility. I wondered if they used Botox over here. "We did not realize your grandmother had stolen our technology. And we don't concern ourselves with your Earth overmuch, outside of a few research projects. It's more primitive than this world, and therefore of minimal interest. We are far more interested in the worlds upstream, and all the technological riches they have to offer."

"Of course you are. You couldn't defeat my family on your own, so you had to get help from other dimensions. What did the aliens demand in return, hmm? Whose vassal are you?"

The Monad slammed her hands down on the desk and stood up. She was quite short, so that wasn't as dramatic as she'd probably hoped. "We have a long and fruitful partnership with those who dwell upstream. Your family was never good at making alliances."

I sat on the edge of her desk, not even looking at her anymore. I hated to turn my back on an enemy, but at least this way I was facing the six-armed robot still standing by the door, which was probably what she'd use to beat me up for my impertinence anyway. "Why don't you tell me what you want, Monad? I'm still alive, and there must be a reason for that."

"I want access to the Zmija family vaults. Give me those, and we'll allow you to live out the remainder of your life in peace and comfort."

"You'll send me to a nice farm upstate? I'll pass."

Hello, Princess, Bollard said through my implant. Swarm was kind enough to offer me temporary credentials to access SerpentNet. We're en route. Do some stalling and see if you can find out anything useful before we save you, eh?

I pulled my legs up and pivoted myself around so I was sitting cross-legged on her desktop. "You already rule this world. Why do you need my family's dusty old relics?"

"You are in no position to make demands."

I sighed. "I'm aware of that, but you want something from me, and I'm open to negotiations."

The Monad sat back down. "Negotiations? If you don't agree to open the vaults, we'll kill your friend... Trevor, is it?"

"He's not a friend. He's a vassal. A swing and a miss, as they say in my world. Try again."

"No loyalty at all to him? You really are a Zmija, aren't you?"

"Never doubt it. Just talk to me, Monad. I'm not my grandmother. I came back here to get rich and live the sort of life I couldn't have back on Earth. I suspect we can come to a mutually beneficial arrangement without all this... unpleasantness."

"Your family–"

"Is all dead," I cut in. "And I never knew them, except for Granny, and I didn't like her much. The Zmija you feuded with don't have anything to do with me. I don't have any family pride or ancestral grudge against you. I just want to get what's mine, and a little extra for my trouble. So talk to me. What's so important in those vaults?"

The Monad swiveled in her chair, back and forth, back and forth, and then gave a nod. "Fine. As you deduced, we have... benefactors... from upstream in Nigh-Space. Specifically a group called the Prime Army. One of their representatives came to us decades ago, and offered us technology in exchange for our help. We followed their instructions and built them a gate – your grandmother probably used a much smaller version to spirit you away?" She raised an overplucked eyebrow at me.

"I have no comment at this time."

The Monad sighed, but continued. "The Prime Army fulfilled their end of the bargain, giving us formidable weapons, which we used to deal with your family, and take our place as rulers of this world. The Prime Army's engineers then spent years building a heavily fortified secret base in upper orbit, and relocated their gate there. They let us use their orbital facilities – it's a convenient site to hold our political prisoners and more troublesome dissidents for interrogation – but there are parts of the station that are off limits even to the Monad. We fear they have their own agenda."

"Oh, you mean the aliens who offered you a deal that was too good to be true turned out to be untrustworthy?" Any doubts I had about my ability to run things better than the Monad began to dissolve. I wouldn't have fallen for that, anyway.

She picked up a crystal paperweight from the desk and tossed it idly from one hand to the other as she spoke. "The Prime Army claimed their empire, which spans many worlds, was under attack by alien invaders who wish to eradicate all human life. They said their base was a garrison, to monitor and protect this region of Nigh-Space from assault. But recently, our intelligence tells us they've begun to move in more soldiers, and we fear they intend to take this world from us. We aren't in a position to fight off the Prime Army, because all our technology comes from them – it's the same problem we had with the Zmija, who gave us guns they couldn't be hurt with, all over again!"

"So now you want my family's weapons to fight back against your allies?"

"Yes. We want what's in the grand vault. If the rumors are true…"

"Which rumors are those?" I asked.

"Have you heard of Swarm?" the Monad said.

"The holy grail," I said. "Autonomous, intelligent war machines. Some kind of hive mind, isn't it? I was really hoping to find Swarm in that vault under the City of Song. If I had, you'd be in trouble. You'd never be able to hold me here."

She sniffed. "Don't be so sure. What you probably don't know is, the original, ground-based Swarm was only the first version of the technology. According to credible rumors, your family was building a larger, more lethal, and more advanced version of Swarm. A new army of autonomous robots, these capable of flight, and even operating in space. Imagine a fleet of fighter ships, equipped with undetectable stealth technology..." She put the paperweight down. "That's part of why we struck your family when we did – once they had that kind of weaponry in the field, they would have been impossible to overthrow without suffering catastrophic losses, even with the help of the Prime Army." She leaned over the desk and fixed her glowing eyes on mine. "If we had that new Swarm, we could destroy the Prime Army garrison, take over their gate, cut off their access to our world... and then use their tactics ourselves."

I frowned. "What do you mean?"

The Monad smiled. "We run this world, Tamsin. But you spent your life on another world. Wouldn't it be nice to run that one, too? The Prime Army only gave us the ability to open small gates, but their portal in orbit is large enough to move whole battalions through. We don't dare venture upstream, where we believe the Prime Army has consolidated control. But we can use their larger gate to access Earth, and with our technology, and a Swarm of ships... we could invade. We could conquer the Earth, and take their resources for our own. With our superior technology from the Zmija vaults, and their ignorance of the multiverse, our strategists believe a war would be swift and decisive."

I thought about that. I nodded. "Okay. I'll open the vaults for you. But in return, I get to run the Earth."

The old woman laughed. "You don't lack for ambition, do you, Tamsin? Fine. Let us make an alliance, then, at long last, between the Monad and the Zmija."

I smiled, and extended my hand. She took it, and I was surprised at the strength in her grip.

If she'd argued for a while, tried to negotiate, or acted a little reluctant, I might have believed her – or, at least, I might have wanted to believe her. But she'd agreed to make me Queen of the Entire Earth way too quickly, which meant, once she got what she wanted, a robot butler was going to rip my head off my shoulders. I wouldn't have taken the deal even if she had been sincere, but betraying her would have been more fun if she was being honest. "I want Bollard back, too."

"Absolutely not," she said. "He is an enemy of the Monad, and will be dealt with accordingly. That is non-negotiable."

I pouted a little, for effect, then said, "Fine."

"I'll arrange transport to the grand vault," the Monad said. "We'll have to quickly, before the Prime Army realizes you're here."

I slid off the desk and got my feet under me. "Take me to see Trevor first."

"I thought he was just a vassal?" A smile played on the edges of her lips.

"He's my only vassal, since you took Bollard away, and I feel incomplete without followers."

The Monad flicked her fingers at me. "Fine. I'll have you escorted to see him. Just be ready when it's time to go."

I turned away and walked toward the robot butler, who gave a courtly bow before ushering me through the tall doors.

We're nearly there, Princess, Bollard said. Did you find out anything of interest?

I'm interested in everything, I subvocalized as I followed the robot down another hallway. When are you getting me out of here?

We are hovering over the estate as we speak, and Swarm is sending down some… representatives.

You aren't coming?

Why risk one of me when we've got hundreds of them to waste instead?

I couldn't argue with that. I'm going to find Trevor.

Who's Trevor again? Bollard asked, and then chuckled.

The robot stopped before a much less ornate wooden door,

albeit one with a blank metal plate where the knob should have been. It waved a hand across the plate and the door swung open, revealing a small and almost entirely empty room. Trevor was inside, sitting on an upside-down bucket, chin in his hands. He leapt to his feet when he saw me, then scowled at the robot. "Are you okay, Sin?"

"I'm fine. I made a deal with our hosts."

He wrinkled his brow in bafflement. "With the Monad? But they hate you, they hate your whole family, they killed them all!"

I shrugged. "Bollard killed my grandmother, and I hired him to work for me. You can't get so hung up on the past, Trevor. All that matters is the future. I'll use any means necessary to achieve my goals. Come on. This robot is going to take us to much more comfortable rooms, and get us something to eat and drink, while the Monad prepares our transport to the Zmija grand vault."

"Very well," the robot said, in a grating voice that did not belong to the matriarch. "You will be fed. Come." The robot turned and marched on, and I beckoned for Trevor to join me.

Did you really make a deal with them? he asked.

Well, I began, and then something blurred out of a doorway on our left and smashed the robot against the wall. The blur shimmered and became a Swarmbot, pinning the butler down and jamming tentacles of wire into its neck.

Hello, Tamsin, Swarm purred at me. Just let me keep this thing from sending an alarm… There. The Monad has some deeply alien tech in this place, hard to compromise, but I can block this thing's transmitter, anyway, by physically fucking it up.

Swarm extended more limbs and completely disarticulated the robot, leaving it on the floor in what looked like a heap of mannequin parts. My other bodies are clearing a path to the roof. We should go. If the Monad detects us, we can't guarantee your safety.

Swarm scurried along, pausing occasionally to extend a snaking cable under doors to check the way ahead before easing them open. We have to be careful, it said. We can't access the estate's security feeds – more alien protocols. I don't know where they got this stuff – it's not even based on any technology I've ever heard of.

That's because literal aliens gave it to them, I said. Have you ever heard of the Prime Army?

Can't say I have, Swarm said. But anything with "army" in the name sounds bad. Tell me about it when we get out of here.

Three corridors later, Swarm peeked under a door, then swore on SerpentNet. We have to go through this room, or else backtrack forever, but there's a goddamn Monad in there. One of the twenty-something-year-old ones, reading a book under a lamp... I can go invisible, but I can't push open the door without her noticing, and she might send up a flare before I can take her down–

Allow me. I pushed open the door and strolled in, Trevor at my heels. We left the door wide open behind us. The woman inside the richly appointed library was indeed a younger version of the matriarch, but with a profusion of black braids instead of white hair. "You must be one of the little Monads," I said.

The woman closed the thick book, marking her place with a finger. "Where is your escort?"

"I told the butler to fuck off. I'm not a prisoner anymore, right? I'm an honored guest."

"Of course," she said blandly. "But it's not safe to wander around unattended. Some parts of the estate are off-limit even to dignitaries like yourself, and some of the security systems are a bit nasty. I'll call a bot to–"

Her eyes rolled back in her head, and she slumped, book falling to the floor with a thump. Swarm shimmered into sight behind the chair and withdrew a tendril from her neck. I wondered if the Monad was dead or only sleeping. We should go, Swarm said. Somebody could be monitoring her vital signs and they might notice the change. I hate not being able to hack their systems.

Swarm nipped through the door across the room, and we followed. From there we took a few sharp turns until we reached a narrow staircase and clambered up… and up… and up. Soon I was huffing and out of breath, and that annoyed me, especially with Trevor bounding along beside me with the energy of a golden retriever puppy. I needed to get in shape. Or get some augmentations of my own…

Swarm forced a narrow door at the top of the million stairs, and we stepped out onto a roof bristling with chimneys and surrounded by towers. A rope ladder – an actual rope ladder – unfurled from an unseen point high above, and I groaned. "You want me to climb that?"

Just grab on, and Bollard will pull you up, Swarm said. But hurry! There's some commotion downstairs. I think our presence has been noticed.

I put my foot on the last wooden rung of the ladder, and it started to swing, and I hissed. Then Trevor was there, holding the ladder steady, anchoring it with his weight, and letting me clamber up. As I climbed, the ladder began to ascend. I glanced down to see Trevor hanging onto the bottom rung, and then the roof was falling away with dizzying rapidity, and the rope ladder was swinging in long arcs. I closed my eyes and gritted my teeth and tried not to whimper as the wind whipped past me –

Then the wind stopped, and immense hands pulled me off the ladder. I opened my eyes to see Bollard, lifting me like a bag of groceries and setting me down on a padded bench seat. We were in another flying orb, the walls opaque but the floor transparent. Trevor clambered in through a hatch I couldn't see and collapsed on the couch. Bollard pulled the rope ladder the rest of the way in and gestured the hatch closed. I looked down through a window in the floor and saw the rooftop of the dwindling estate swarming with figures, probably more robots, and maybe a Monad or two.

"I told you we'd come and collect you," Bollard said.

"Good work," I croaked from the bench. "Could you make the floor look like a floor?"

Bollard waved a hand and the floor opaqued. "Did you find out any–" He frowned, head tilted like he was listening. "We need to get back to my lab. Something tripped my security system." He waved his hand again, and the walls turned into screens, cycling through views of Bollard's lab, cloning tanks, galley, and living quarters. There was no visible activity. "Hmm. My diagnostic says it was a false alarm, a glitch in the system, but I want to make sure."

Do we still have control of the lab? I asked SerpentNet.

Negative. Control has been compromised.

Is it the Monad? I asked.

Unlikely. The Monad does not possess known technology capable of shutting us out of a compromised system.

I really hoped this wouldn't ruin the little pet project I'd set in motion after SerpentNet took over Bollard's workshop. "Who the fuck is in your lab?" I said out loud.

"Maybe nobody," Bollard said. "Or maybe some people who don't realize they're already dead."

GLENN

"Ooh," Eddie said. "There's a whole bunch of little encrypted internets on this planet." He turned in a slow circle in the brick-lined room.

"What, like the dark web?" I asked.

Eddie's eyes flickered rapidly back and forth. It was like watching a glitchy slot machine. "A whole bunch of dark webs! I've got sex robots and designer drugs, which in a more enlightened world wouldn't be taboo anyway, and also murder-for-hire and human trafficking, which is the sort of thing we aren't very keen on in the Interventionists."

"Can you get us a ride?" Vivy said. "And also a destination for that ride?"

"My dear Vivian, ever practical." Eddie cocked his head and pawed at the air like a kitten batting at string. "There's something called the 'Undernet' that seems like the preferred network for villains and curs. Let's see if it's been accessed lately by our Mr Bollard... Ah, there we are. He summoned a vehicle for transport from this very location. The car service – wait, no, they're floating pods, so I guess the pod-service – values the privacy of its clients, so there's no surveillance footage; I had to do some convincing even to find out he was a client and access the logs. I can't say for sure if Tamsin and Trevor were with him, but it seems likely. This estate would have killed Bollard unless... yes, he's on the authorized guest list now, too, so Tamsin must have added him." Eddie did a little kick-step and spun around. "Ha, this Undernet thinks it's tough, all full of tripwires and sharp teeth, it's so cute, like a purse dog snarling at you... there we go. I knew the pods must have some kind of tracking system, or else the bad guys who use the service could hijack them forever. I know where Bollard got dropped off." Eddie grinned. "Now the game is on the other foot."

"You mean 'the game is afoot,'" I said.

"Potato, tomato," Eddie said airily. "I've done a bit of light identity theft and impersonated a blackguard with a current account, so I'll call us a ride."

"See?" Vivy said. "Eddie is aces at logistics."

"It's that easy to break the encryption of the underworld internet?" I asked. "You'd think they'd have better security."

"They have excellent security, by local standards," Eddie said. "As to that, no one on your planet could hope to crack it. Let me come up with a comprehensible analogy using terms you're familiar with. Your world is like kindergarten, Glenn. This world is like middle school. But in the place I from–"

"Graduate school?" I said.

"Heavens, no. We finished school a long time ago, and grew up, and moved on with our lives, and we don't even think about school anymore."

"I'll take a look up top." Vivy headed for the stairs, where an open hatch revealed gray morning sky.

"There's nothing up there," Eddie said. "The security system in this place even kills rats if they aren't on the guest list."

"I'm concerned about falling debris, Eddie. Unstable floors. Pointy rusty things. You aren't a spaceship anymore. You can get crushed." She vanished up top, then continued talking in our comms a few moments later. (It turned out my anklet was also comms, though it sure felt like her voice was whispering into my head.) "All clear. Everything that can fall down up here fell down a long time ago."

Eddie gave me an "after you" gesture, and I climbed up and out. The devastation on the ground was absolute. You could just barely tell we were standing in the remnants of what must have been a very big house – like, country-estate-for-royalty big. "What happened to this place?"

"Fire. Bombs. Big rocks from the sky." Eddie shrugged. "Just a guess."

Something about the golden hills looked familiar. "Have we been here before?"

Vivy put a hand on my shoulder, turned me a bit, and pointed to a particular hill. "When we jumped through worlds to get to the Shattered Veil, that hill was our first stop. It's our preferred transition point in this world, because this area is full of mines and traps, so it's completely uninhabited." She shook her head. "I can't believe we came through a door less than a mile away from a spot we pass through all the time anyway."

"Small world," I said.

"This one's pretty small, as worlds go," Eddie agreed. "One lousy inhabited planet! I don't know how they don't all die of claustrophobia. There's our pod." He pointed.

A shimmering opalescent bubble approached, making me think of Glinda the good witch's arrival in The Wizard of Oz. Once it landed and opened a door and we went aboard, it was more like sitting in a flying conversation pit. Eddie relaxed on a bench, Vivy poked at the walls and paced around, and I looked at her butt. It really wasn't fair that her work uniform bore such a skintight and strappy resemblance to some of her play outfits, but it's a testament to her allure that I could even glancingly think about sex in the midst of all these bizarre events.

"Do we have a plan?" I asked.

Eddie waved a hand, and a window opened in the wall, showing me the countryside sailing past below. "Enjoy the view until we get where we're going. And when we get there, I don't know. We rescue Tamsin, and take Bollard's toys away, and exile him someplace harmless. Whatever. Vivy does plans."

"I don't have enough information to formulate one just now." Vivy quit pacing and sat down beside me. "So instead we'll do the thing I'm much better at, which is, improvise."

Eddie elbowed a wall and a panel slid open, revealing a decanter full of scarlet liquid. "Ooh, alcohol!"

"Should he be getting drunk?" I asked.

"I have total metabolic control in this body, chum," Eddie said merrily, and proceeded to drink straight from the bottle for a while. Then came the singing. The songs bore a glancing resemblance to sea shanties, but the words were more astronomical than nautical.

Then, after way too much singing, we reached the mountain. Eddie sobered himself up and peered out the window. "Viv! This is classic. There's a whole lair inside that mountain."

She glanced out the window. "It's just a mountain? Not even a volcano? No one has standards anymore. So... how do we get in? I neglected to bring the avalanche gun."

I wondered if there really was such a thing as an avalanche gun.

Eddie put his forehead against the window. "I'm breaking into their systems now... Oh, that's interesting. I'm not the first one to compromise the House of Bollard. Someone else has been fiddling with his security settings, and there are a lot of recent changes to the code in one section, though it looks like... an immersive entertainment system? Someone must really hate Bollard's taste in virtual environments. All right, I've explained to the systems in the mountain that I am their true and rightful king, and they've all bent the knee."

"Is Tamsin in there?" I asked.

"I'm peeking through the cameras inside, and I don't see anyone, but the surveillance doesn't cover every corner of the bunker, so we'll have to do a walkthrough." He opened his eyes. "Let me direct your attention to the mountaintop just outside the window. Behold as I make it... disappear."

He wiggled his fingers, and the top of the mountain dissolved.

I gasped. I very nearly applauded.

"Don't be too impressed," Eddie said. "The mountain peak was a holographic projection. There's a roof hatch that slides open and shut to keep the rain out, but that's just hydraulics, albeit on a hefty scale."

The pod began to float down to a platform nestled inside the open top of the mountain. Eddie clucked his tongue. "Vivy, I'm embarrassed. We tripped some proximity sensors on our approach, and an alert went out to Bollard, wherever he may be. I made the alert look like a glitch, and the security systems won't take any further notice of us, but if Bollard is in there, he may be on guard, and if he's not here, he may be coming back."

"If you're controlling his security systems, I'm not all that worried about an ambush," Vivy said. "And if he's coming... good. I want to talk to him." She cracked her knuckles.

We landed on the platform, and Eddie summoned an elevator that was more of a levitating circle of floor. We descended, at a sedate speed, for a very long time, which unfortunately gave Eddie time to chat. "You humans like having sex in elevators, don't you?"

"People excited by the possibility of being caught do," I said. "I don't think there's anything inherently sexy about elevators, for most people."

"Even then, you'd only do it in an elevator that has actual walls," Vivy said. "This is a hovering platform with no guardrails. I wouldn't get too acrobatic on here."

Eddie sniffed. "There are forcefield nets in place. I forget how limited your senses are. Either way, it's a bit disappointing that the two of you aren't up to the challenge. Where's the passion?"

The elevator settled down in a gleaming laboratory room, and lights went on all around us when we touched down, making it gleam even more. "I'll do a sweep to make sure we're clear," Vivy said. "Glenn, stay behind me. Eddie, don't let Glenn get hurt."

"He's the one with a full defensive array looped around his shapely little ankle," Eddie said. "I'm just a humble highly advanced android–" but Vivy was already setting off, and I went along after her. She took a little cylinder from her belt and it telescoped out into something like a carbon-fiber quarterstaff – her lightning-tipped staff from my first foray into Nigh-Space, maybe? "Open doors for me, Eddie?"

He made a noise of assent, and a rounded door swung open. She darted through, then called back, "Clear," and we followed her.

We found more lab space, a kitchen, and living quarters. Eddie sniffed around the latter and said, "There are DNA traces that indicate Tamsin was held in one room, and Trevor in another, but neither is here now. I see no evidence of torture. Nothing physical, at least."

"You said there's a virtual reality setup down here?" Vivy said. "Then Bollard could have tortured her virtually."

"Is that a thing?" I said.

"Oh, yes," Eddie said. "It can be extremely hard on the mind, and rather easy on the body, apart from the physiological stress reaction. Virtual torture doesn't leave a mark, except on the inside. Not only can you conjure up any kind of hellish situation, but you can also mess with a prisoner's sense of time – make it seem like they've been kept alone in a pit for years, while only minutes pass in real time. That sort of treatment tends to make an impression."

I groaned, and Vivy tried to reassure me. "Oh, Glenn. I doubt you need to worry. Our best guess is, Bollard or his employers want to loot Tamsin's family vaults. He wouldn't need to torture her, just drag her around and use her gene-print to open the locks. That's probably where they are right now – looting."

"Why wouldn't he just kill her when he's done with her?" I demanded.

"Oh, even if he's acting alone, once he opens all the vaults,

he could probably sell her to rival families or something,"
Eddie began.

"You are not helping," Vivy said.

"They'd want her alive," Eddie said. "Probably. At first. To
ask her questions." He cleared his throat. "I'm sure they'd ask
politely."

"Let's finish our sweep." Vivy set off down another hall,
and we found a door bristling with sensors and locks, all of
which Eddie easily subverted. Inside we found row after row
of humming cylinders.

"I bet you think those are beer kegs, Glenn," Eddie said.

"I do not."

"Well, they aren't," Eddie said. "Those are clone tanks."
Eddie made the metal sides of the cylinders slide down,
revealing the figures floating inside, all drooping in harnesses
and hooked up to nearly invisible wires and tubes. He knocked
on one cylinder like a kid tapping an aquarium. "They're all the
same fellow, at different stages of development, and they're all
plugged into virtual environments."

"That must be Chicane," Vivy said. "Bollard's partner. Or
partners. And they're probably in training simulations of some
kind... like the ones we use to get me ready for going undercover?"

Eddie made a rude sound. "This setup is rather more crude
than our technology, but I suppose the environments are
convincing enough for people grown in a vat who'd never seen
sunlight. The relatively poor resolution won't look strange to
them. Hmm. You know, maybe we should keep a whole bunch
of clones of you, Vivy, just for the sake of redundancy."

"I'm pretty sure that violates a bunch of our ethical
guidelines. Anyway, Jen said one of me was all the multiverse
could handle." Vivy peered into one tank, looking at the
pumpkin-headed goblin man inside. I hoped I never met a
Chicane who was awake and scuttling around. She walked
past several tanks, to the end of a row, and then stopped. "Wait
a second. Eddie, who's this?"

Eddie and I joined her, and looked into a tank that didn't hold a Chicane, but a naked woman, probably in her twenties. At first, I had a spike of terror that it was Tamsin, held in some kind of stasis, but it wasn't her, though there was a definite resemblance – a similar nose and chin, but a higher forehead, a longer face, higher and sharper cheekbones…

"I'm not sure," Eddie said. "This tank is isolated, cut off from the rest of the network, and there's nothing in the logs to indicate who she is…"

"It's Tamsin's grandmother," I said. "Or, a much younger clone of her. But why would Bollard bother to create something like this?"

"To make Tamsin redundant," Vivy said. "Eddie, did you say the gene locks here could scan telomeres?"

"Yep. Hold on, let me scan the local scientific literature… ah. Bollard is a genius, it turns out. He's way out beyond the cutting edge of the rest of this world. They've had human cloning tech here for a while, though it's tightly controlled by the oligarchs, but there's nothing in the literature about this – forced, accelerated growth. Given a little time, Bollard can make a copy of Tamsin's grandmother that's the right biological age to fool the gene-locks on the vaults. If he puts her in VR and brainwashes her into a compliant state, she wouldn't trip any of the anti-coercion failsafes…" Eddie whistled. "Once this clone is fully cooked, which will take a couple of weeks I'd guess, Bollard won't need Tamsin to open doors for him anymore."

"She's probably alive in the meantime, though, right?" I said.

"Probably," Vivy agreed. "We should–"

"A proximity alarm just went off," Eddie said. "Something subtle, notifying the owner without setting off a lot of big obvious klaxons and whoop-whoops. Let's get ready to meet our hosts, shall we?"

Vivy and Eddie briefly conferred about tactics, and then we headed back to the room where we'd first arrived. Vivy dragged a chair over in front of the elevator landing area and draped herself in it comfortably. Eddie leaned against a wall behind her, arms crossed, looking bored. I leaned against the same wall on the other side of a door, trying to look equally cool and probably coming across as nervous. Vivy assured me the anklet made me bulletproof and knifeproof and laserproof, but still–

The elevator slammed down, moving a lot faster than it had on our trip, and it was also more crowded: there was a man the size of a polar bear in a black pin-striped suit, and a lean dirtbag with a neck tattoo, and a washing-machine-sized robot that looked like a crab that was halfway through eating another crab, and Tamsin, a little older than I remembered, but still beautiful, wearing a torn cocktail dress–

The robot sprang at Vivy. She didn't even shift. Eddie yawned and the robot stopped leaping, turned around, scuttled over into a corner, pulled in all its robot arms, and then sat there, inert as an empty beer keg.

"Restrain them!" the giant, who I assumed was Bollard, bellowed.

"He's trying to activate his security systems," Eddie said. "Now he's realizing they don't work for him anymore. Look at his big wobbly face."

Vivy rose from the chair and leaned on her staff, looking past the big man. "Tamsin, are you all right? We came to–"

The dirtbag ran at her, screaming, presumably in an attempt to terrify or at least distract her, but Vivy just swept his legs out from under him with the staff. He landed on his back with a great whooshing gasp. Eddie walked over and put his foot firmly on the center of the man's chest. "You'd best stay down there, chap. You don't want to cross our Vivan when she's feeling stroppy."

Bollard stood, hands at his sides, fingers clenching and unclenching. I could tell he was about to try his hand at attacking Vivy, and I was sort of looking forward to seeing her kick his ass, but she just kept ignoring him. "As I was saying, Tamsin. We're here to rescue you."

Tamsin stared at her. "Rescue? I don't need rescue. Who are you?"

I cleared my throat and stepped forward. "Uh. Hi, Tamsin. This is my girlfriend, Vivy, and her friend Eddie."

"Rex Edmunds, at your service," Eddie purred. "I assume the gentleman beneath my shoe is Trevor? Which means the large man with – oh dear, the dangerously elevated blood pressure and cortisol levels – is Bollard. I love introductions. They feel so civilized."

Tamsin walked past Bollard, eyes wide. She moved toward me, as if in a daze. I tried to remember if I'd ever seen her look uncertain before. Tamsin always charged forward with absolute certainty – it was simultaneously one of her most impressive and most frustrating qualities. She reached out and touched my face. "I don't understand," she murmured.

"We heard your grandmother got killed," I said. "And that you were kidnapped, and…" I shrugged. "We came looking for you. To help."

"That doesn't make me much less confused," Tamsin said, and then she kissed me on the lips.

"Oh, come on!" Trevor cried out from beneath Eddie's shoe.

TAMSIN

Glenn – Glenn! My college boyfriend! – broke the kiss after about half a second, took my hands, and eased himself a step away from me. "Hey, Tam. It's good to see you too. You're okay?"

I stepped back, flustered; when had I last felt flustered? "I'm sorry, I shouldn't have done that, it's just so sweet that you came to help me, but I don't – wait. You know about other worlds? Demonstrably, strike that, how do you know about other worlds?"

He gestured, and his annoyingly gorgeous girlfriend walked over. At least she was short. "Vivy is, well... she's not from Earth. Either. Neither are you. I heard."

"I work for a group dedicated to helping people across Nigh-Space," Vivy said. "One of my jobs is monitoring exiles and refugees, and that meant keeping an eye on you and your grandmother. When we heard she was murdered, and you disappeared, we investigated."

"And you just happened to bring along my old boyfriend, who is now dating you?"

She had the good grace to look embarrassed. "Glenn and I met when I was doing background interviews for your case, to see whether you knew about Nigh-Space, which, at the time, you... didn't."

"I'd love to peruse your employee handbook sometimes," I said. "The code of conduct must be fascinating." It was hard to tell, given her complexion, but I thought Vivy blushed; a point scored there.

"Tamsin," Glenn said. "Are you really okay? This Bollard, he's a seriously bad guy–"

"I am the worst guy!" Bollard bellowed. "I am also in the employ of Miss Zmija. assisting her in recovering her family's lost treasures."

"Zmija?" Glenn didn't pronounce it quite right, but neither had I, the first time.

"Granny's real last name," I said. "So also mine. When I found out there was a whole other world, I knew I'd need a local guide, and I retained the services of Bollard and Chicane. They aren't very nice, but neither are the people who murdered my entire family, and sent Granny running to another reality to hide."

"I will require some further explanations for my report," Vivy said. "Like, for instance, who killed your grandmother, and what the terrible two were doing on Earth at all... but I can accept that we're all friends here for now. Eddie, you can let Trevor up now."

The deceptively wispy-looking man with the cartoon English accent stepped back, and Trevor rose, rubbing at his chest and glaring at everyone, especially Glenn, which was predictable.

"Since when do you go on adventures?" I said, poking Glenn in the chest. After the initial shock and confusion, I found his presence surprisingly comforting. He'd always made me comfortable, which in the end, was a problem; I liked more of a challenge back then, someone I could push against. But it was good to have an unambiguously friendly face here now.

He gave me that old sweet smile. "Hey, undergrad was a long time ago. I adventure all the time now. Besides, I thought you were in trouble."

"I am in a great deal of trouble," I said. "But I wasn't kidnapped, no." I glanced at Bollard. "At least, I'm not kidnapped anymore. I'll admit Bollard wasn't entirely polite when we first met."

"I am unfailingly polite," he objected. "I am just not very nice. Who are you, miss – Vivy, is it? I recognize another operator when I see one. But you really don't work for the oligarchs?"

Vivy rolled her eyes. "No. Like I said, I'm not from around here. Eddie and I are, what…"

"Roving interdimensional social workers?" Eddie said. "Deep-cover operatives tasked to destabilize oppressive governments? Revolutionaries? Counter-revolutionaries? Counter-counter-revolutionaries? Consultants? It varies."

Bollard frowned. "Do you work for the Prime Army, then?"

Vivy stiffened like someone had put a cattle prod up her entirely too generous ass and whirled to face him. "The Prime Army? What do you know about the Prime Army?"

I frowned, and answered, making her turn back to me. "Not much, and that much only recently. A family of oligarchs called the Monad made a deal with the Prime Army, a long time ago. The Monad got the weapons that allowed them to kill my whole family and take over this planet, and in exchange, they helped build some kind of portal and help the Prime Army establish a base here."

Vivy went to a chair and dropped into it, then stared into space. "Fuck," she said at last. "I was about to say, well, you aren't kidnapped, so, best of luck, carry on, Godspeed, but if the Prime Army is here…" She looked over at Eddie. "Can you pick up anything?"

"I can pick up a big blank spot in orbit where I can't pick up anything, which is presumably where they're headquartered," Eddie said. "They've gotten pretty good at blocking Interventionist intrusion technology. We aren't equipped to take them on right now, Vivy, not if they've been here for, what, more twenty years? They must be dug in like a tick."

"We'll need to gear up," Vivy said thoughtfully.

"Then your organization opposes the Prime Army?" Bollard said. "Hmm. Perhaps we can help one another."

Glenn tugged at my sleeve and jerked his head toward the door that led deeper into the workshop. "Take a walk with me?"

Trevor bustled over, and I shooed him away. "I'm going to catch up with Glenn for a minute!" I called to Bollard, who shooed me away, and continued peppering Vivy with questions about the Prime Army and her own mysterious organization. I doubted he'd get satisfactory answers out of her.

I followed Glenn through the door and down a corridor, toward the clone lab. "Vivy is... striking," I said. "The two of you met because of me?"

"We can talk about that later, if you want," he said in a low voice. "But right now we need to talk about the fact that you can't trust Bollard."

"I don't trust Bollard anymore than I could bench-press Bollard. But I'm in a tough situation here, working against significant opposition, and he's one of my only resources." Apart from Swarm, whose only local node had been kicked offline by that mysterious Rex Edmunds, somehow. He was probably also the one who'd seized control of the workshop's security systems, the ones SerpentNet was still frantically trying to re-seize. SerpentNet assured me they hadn't tampered with the special programs I had running in the virtual environments–

Glenn shook his head. "No, I mean, you really can't trust him, as in, he's about to betray you, and soon. You came here to open your family vaults, right?"

"Yes. Who can resist a secret inheritance and buried treasure? Bollard is getting a cut, and he's a professional. What do you mean, he's going to betray me?"

Glenn took my hand and led me into the clone room. All the tanks were uncovered for some reason, and a score of Chicanes bobbed on all sides, lost in their digital dreamworlds. Glenn ignored them, and led me down the far row of tanks, all the way to the end, where–

There was a woman in a tank. There were no photo albums in Culver House, and no painted portraits, but I recognized her face even without the white hair and frown lines. "He's growing a clone of Granny?" I may have sputtered.

"Apparently Bollard can make a copy of her that's convincing enough to open your family vaults." Glenn put a hand on my arm. "He was just using you until that was ready. I'm sorry, Tam."

I clenched my fists. "I'll kill him. 'We always honor our contracts,' he said, what bullshit!" I turned and stalked away, ignoring Glenn when he said, "Wait!"

I barged back into the lab, where Bollard was conferring with Vivy and Eddie. "You!" I shouted, then walked up to Bollard and slapped him across the face. It was like slapping a marble statue of Goliath.

He looked down at me, unhurt and apparently baffled. "What was that for, Princess? Did you mistake me for Trevor?"

"I saw the Granny you made," I said.

Bollard gazed at me for a moment, sighed, then shoved me out of the way. It was like a linebacker pushing a toddler, and I sprawled back on my ass. Vivy reacted fast, reaching out for him, but she wasn't as fast as Bollard, who sprinted across the room with shocking speed, headed for the door. Glenn was just coming out when Bollard arrived, and he swept Glenn out of the way like he was an errant cobweb, sending him sprawling, too. Bollard vanished through the door, slamming it shut in Vivy's face before she could pursue. She yanked on the door handle, but it didn't budge. "Eddie, open this!"

"I can't," Eddie said. "There must be a switch on the other side of the door, some physical failsafe – Bollard took that whole side of the lab offline. It's all air-gapped now, and there's no network I can compromise."

Trevor helped me to my feet, and I shook him off and went to Glenn, who was just rising.

Vivy spun to face me. "Why did you confront Bollard about the clone directly? What if he'd snapped your neck?"

"I had you in all your leather and spandex to protect me," I said sweetly, but in truth, I'd just been furious, and acted accordingly. "I had a deal with him, the enormous bastard, and he turned on me–"

"A very unfair characterization," Bollard's voice droned over speakers in the ceiling. He sounded a little out of breath, like he was doing strenuous exercise, which worried me. "I had every intention of fulfilling our agreement, Princess. I just rescued you from the Monad, didn't I? It would have been easy to leave you in the hands of your enemies and wait for my backup Granny to finish growing, but I honor my contracts. You'll recall that I promised to help you recover your family's assets, get revenge on the Monad, and take your place among the oligarchs. I never said I wouldn't steal everything from you afterward! You were going to offer me a position in your new organization once our current deal was done, and I intended to politely decline. Then, moving against you wouldn't be treachery at all – just business." He sighed. "But I gather you no longer wish to work with me?"

"I'll pull your esophagus out of your mouth and strangle you with it!" I shouted.

"Wouldn't work," Eddie said. "The esophagus is about ten inches long, so that part's okay, but the tissue would just tear. Now, the intestines, maybe, if you braided them into a sort of rope–"

I pounded and kicked at the sealed door. "How do we get to him?"

"Normally I'd just blast a hole in the blasted wall," Eddie said. "Alas, I lack that kind of firepower at the moment. This isn't my usual body. I'm a temporarily embarrassed spaceship, you see–"

I scowled at him. "Then wake up Swarm. It can get through this door."

He cocked his head. "Swarm? Is that the artificial mind attempting to knock down my firewalls to regain control of the spider-bot over there? Connected to the other thirty spider-bots that are tripping proximity sensors all over the mountain, like I can't control them when they get here, too?"

"Wake it up," I said through clenched teeth. Glenn put a hand on my shoulder to comfort me, but I didn't need comfort; I needed obedience.

Eddie looked past me, at Vivy. She said, "Swarm belongs to you, and not Bollard?"

"If Swarm belonged to Bollard, would I have asked you to release it?" I didn't bother to keep the acid out of my tone.

"Swarm is solid," Trevor piped up. "There's nobody more loyal to Sin, except me." He glared at Glenn, which would have been cute, if it hadn't been sad. Though perhaps feeling threatened and jealous would make Trevor work even harder for my approval.

"Go ahead," Vivy said. "You can always shut it down again if it misbehaves."

Eddie gestured, and Swarm came back online, extended their pincers and legs, and stomped over to me. "What the hell!" they said. "Nobody can shut me out of my bodies! That's the whole point of me! I'm the apex! Where are you people even from?"

"A ways upstream." Eddie pointed at the sealed hatch. "Can you knock this door down?"

We all made room for Swarm, who promptly ripped the door right off its reinforced hinges and then gently set it to the side. Swarm's body was too large to fit through the opening, and it said, "The corridors are a bit cramped for me. I can reconfigure my body, drop some components, but you'll have to give me a few minutes."

"I think we can handle this," Vivy said, twirling her stupid stick and grinning. She looked at me. "We'll take care of Bollard, and then we need to talk to you about the Prime Army... Princess."

She went through the door, Eddie at her back, and I followed, with Glenn and Trevor jostling for who got to be hottest on my heels. Vivy looked over her shoulder, sighed, and said, "If you're all coming, try not to get killed, okay? We don't know what surprises Bollard has waiting."

The other doors weren't locked, and after a brief reconnoiter, it became apparent that Bollard was in the clone room. Vivy and Eddie were side-by-side, facing the last door, the one bristling with sensors, with the rest of us piled up behind them. "Careful," I said. "He might have thawed out a Chicane."

Then the door swung open, activated from within, and Bollard's laughter boomed out. "Oh, no. I decanted all the Chicanes. Once I got two of them online, they helped me get the rest out of their harnesses. Of course, I can't control so many of them all at once, and Chicanes can get a bit… unruly… when left to their own devices, but they can follow simple orders for a short time, like, say: Murder anyone who comes inside."

"Let me through!" I shouted, and shoved my way past Trevor and Glenn, who were attempting to shield me.

"Get back!" Vivy snarled over her shoulder, hefting her quarterstaff, which started crackling with blue sparks on one end. Eddie was smiling and cracking his knuckles, at least until I shoved him hard from the side and squeezed between them.

"Move aside," I said. "I've got this."

Vivy tried to grab me, so I elbowed her in the face, or anyway attempted to. I didn't connect – she was slippery – but in such close quarters, with an electric quarterstaff in one hand, she had limited maneuverability, and when she leaned away to avoid the blow, I squirted through the door and into the clone room.

Vivy tried to come after me, and Swarm yelled from the other room: "Stop! Tamsin said she's got this!"

She withdrew. Apparently Glenn's new lover was willing to listen to a talking machine over me. Typical.

All the tanks were empty, and there were twenty naked, dripping Chicanes thronging the rows between them. They seethed and snarled, gibbered and drooled, twitched and shuddered, but they didn't attack me. Bollard stood at the back of the room, arms crossed over his chest, grinning at me. "Princess!" he called. "Have you come to reason with me? Offer me a new contract? I'm afraid I'm not accepting new clients at the moment, but I admire your courage. I've actually enjoyed working with you, so it pains me to say this, but: Chicanes. Kill her."

They twitched forward in tandem, but it was only a twitch. "Good boys," I cooed.

"I said kill her!" Bollard bellowed. "Our contract is terminated! She is no longer our client! She is our target!"

"That won't work," I said, almost apologetically. There was motion behind me, and I glanced back to see Vivy and Glenn come in, standing on either side of me, but a step back. "I compromised your security systems the first time day we got here. I was on SerpentNet all along, since we first came through the door, and you've got some old Zmija legacy tech in your systems."

Bollard, for once, appeared at a total loss for words, sputtering for a moment until he managed to say, "What have you done to my Chicanes?" He started forward, but his decanted partners closed ranks against him, blocking the path, and slowly turned to face him, all twitching twenty of them.

"I had SerpentNet alter their virtual environments. I gave them new training protocols."

"Nonsense!" he shouted. "I run regular diagnostic checks! The simulations I programmed were running on every tank!"

"I didn't try to change much," I said. "I just told SerpentNet to re-skin one little element of the simulation. A totally cosmetic change, one that wouldn't show up in your diagnostics. I made it so wherever an image of you appeared... the Chicanes saw me instead. Wherever your voice appeared, I altered it to match mind. Your name became my name. The simulations teach the Chicanes to know you, to give their loyalty to you... to love you. Don't they?" I spread my hands. "Now who do you love, Chicanes?"

"You, Princess," they chorused in their horrid slimy voices.

"You scum," Bollard said. "You absolute shit. You are just like your granny–"

"Boys," I said to the assembled Chicanes. "Kindly restrain Mr Bollard. Perhaps he could use a little reprogramming too."

"You'll never take me alive!" he shouted.

I considered. "Oh. If that's what you prefer. Go ahead, boys. If he resists, you can use lethal force." I was a little disappointed things had come to this... but the truth is, Bollard was doomed from the start of our association. He killed my grandmother. He was always going to pay for that; it was only ever a question of how much value I would extract from him first. His greed had simply accelerated my retribution timetable.

The Chicanes surged forward, reaching out, and Bollard fought them. At first, I could see his head and shoulders and his flailing arms and pounding fists, since he was taller than the Chicanes, but they gradually pulled him down, and it was like seeing someone sink into a lake. It was hard to see what happened after that, and the Chicanes only had their teeth and nails to work with, but they could do plenty with those.

I turned away when the crunching sounds began, and gestured to Glenn and Vivy to follow me out. Once we were in the corridor, I pulled the door closed after me.

"Are you all right?" Glenn whispered to me.

"Never better," I whispered back.

"That was nasty," Vivy said, gazing at the closed door. "You really control all those weird little dudes?"

I held out my hand and seesawed it. "I wouldn't call it control, exactly. They like me, and they'll follow orders, more or less, I think, but Bollard had direct control of them through some kind of neural link. Even he had a hard time controlling more than one at a time, he said…" I trailed off, connections forming in my mind, then hurried past Trevor and back to the lab where Swarm crouched just beyond the door. "Swarm! Can you get into the brains of the Chicanes?"

"Why would I want to? They're so squishy and psychotic."

"They're networked together, Bollard said – he tried to operate multiple Chicanes at once, and he couldn't get a handle on them. But you–"

"Are the world's foremost expert on running lots of bodies all at once." Swarm's eye-lenses brightened and dimmed, brightened and dimmed. "Their brains are crammed full of weird bespoke tech, but yes, I can connect to the hardware and get them working together, curb their cognitive decay, stabilize them, allow them a degree of autonomy, control the feedback effects that ruined Bollard's attempts… yeah. Give me a little time, and I'll have a relatively tame, relatively sane swarm of Chicanes for you, Princess." Swarm paused. "I'm going to miss Bollard, a little. He was awful, but he was so good at being awful."

"I learned a lot from him," I admitted. "But I think I can surpass him."

The others returned. Vivy was frowning, Eddie was humming to himself, and Glenn looked troubled. "The, ah, horrible noises stopped," he said. "I think Bollard is dead, and the Chicanes seem to have settled down. We looked through the window and they're all just kind of standing around and swaying now. They're all swaying together."

"They're covered in blood and bits, too," Eddie said. "Do they have zombie movies in this reality? If not, you basically do now."

Vivy looked at me, cool and thoughtful. "That was good thinking, Tamsin, to compromise his systems and set up a contingency plan."

I acknowledged the compliment with a nod. "Thank you."

"I'm not thrilled with the murder part," she said. "He could have been taken alive."

I didn't let her see me bristle. "I consider it self-defense. At worst, it was a preemptive strike. Bollard told you he planned to turn on me. He wouldn't have hesitated to end my life."

She shrugged. "I'm not the cops. And I get where you're coming from. It's just not how I would have done it, and I've been doing this stuff a lot longer than you. Maybe, in the future, ease up on the optional slaughter."

"I will take that under consideration. Now." I clapped my hands and smiled at them all. "Since Bollard is gone, I could use new allies. You all seem formidable, and it seems we have a common interest when it comes to overthrowing oppressive tyrants?"

"Eh," Eddie said. "The evils of the current regime don't really rate on our bad-shit-o-meter. This isn't the sort of society we usually mess around with. Things are lousy here, sure, but they're not catastrophic, or in danger of spreading throughout Nigh-Space. That said..." He looked at Vivy.

She sighed. "If the Prime Army has a foothold here, and they've already set up a base... that's a problem. That is the sort of situation we'd meddle with. Since the Prime Army is apparently allied with your ancestral enemies, Tamsin... and you've got this Swarm and a pack of Chicanes and whatever else you can access in this lab... then it does make sense for us to join forces. The enemy of my enemy, and all that."

"Wonderful!" I said, and then beamed at Glenn. "Me and Vivy, working in tandem! I bet that's an image that's crossed your mind more than once, hmm?"

Glenn turned amusingly red, Vivy turned amusingly scowly, Eddie nearly choked himself laughing, and Trevor didn't react at all.

GLENN

That was not quite the reunion I was expecting, but it could have gone worse, I guess. Tamsin was okay, and that was the most important thing–

Or maybe the most important thing was that Tamsin had hired the man who murdered her grandmother (she'd filled us in on that backstory) to help her become an oligarch on another planet. That was pretty important, too. Tam had never lacked for drive, ambition, or big ideas – she'd broken up with me in part because we "had different visions for our futures," but at the time, I thought she just wanted to become a rich technology mogul and outshine her brilliant inventor grandmother. This new mission of hers was a whole other level of reach and grasp. I tried to put myself in her position: what would I do if I found out I'd been exiled from a neighboring universe where my family had lived like royalty until they were violently deposed and mass-murdered?

I thought I would probably be grateful I'd survived, and then go back to working on my latest research paper. We really did have different visions of the future.

After our declaration of alliance, we sat in Bollard's kitchen, and Trevor made grilled cheese sandwiches, which were pretty great, even though the local cheese was on the pungent side. Swarm had reconfigured, and now presented as a slimmed-down version of itself, more humanoid than spider, but headless, and with torso-lenses like misplaced eyes.

Tamsin had changed clothes, and was now wearing stretchy yoga pants and a very brief tank top. I was pretty sure she was looking hot at me on purpose. She seemed to like flirting with me, or else just needling Vivy, which was not a good idea... but so far, Vivy didn't seem overly put out about it. Eddie had suggested she was a little insecure when it came to Tamsin, but if so, it didn't show; maybe she was just in full warrior-of-Nigh-Space mode.

"So the Prime Army are interdimensional fascists," Tamsin said, once Vivy finished filling her in. "Why are they interested in this world, if they're so much more advanced than we are?" I noted that we.

"We keep kicking their asses farther upstream," Eddie said. "The PA has total control of a consolidated span of a dozen worlds, arrayed around their home level, which they believe is the real original universe where humankind was born. Not because of any scientific evidence, or because that's how anything works – it's just a religious and cultural thing. They've also got outposts on a bunch of other worlds in the near span, and occasionally they've taken over a nation or a continent or a planet or an array of space habitats in one world or another. But when they try to expand any farther, the Interventionists slap them down. They've been seizing and losing control of the same few worlds back for decades. We're all pretty bored about it."

Vivy nodded. "We've got the Prime Army beat when it comes to technology, but they way outnumber us, and as a result, we're pretty evenly matched overall, and both sides are always looking for a new advantage to press. This world is way off their usual range of conquest, many hundreds of levels away. The Prime Army can't traverse Nigh-Space as easily as my people do – they basically just send scouts, and they have to travel one level at a time, and recharge their traversal devices in between. Those scouts can't carry much with them, so it's difficult for them to build gates in a new world, unless they're in a place with a pretty high degree of technology locally to lean on. Even when they manage to build a bigger gate, those portals are limited – they can only travel a handful of levels at a time, so the Prime Army has supply-line issues. In order to expand, they have to build a daisy chain of gates, and those are easy to hit and disrupt. Those limitations are the only things preventing the Prime Army from pouring a hundred million troops into any given world and conquering it in a week." She shook her head. "They must have been quietly building gates downstream for years, sending in smaller forces, extending their range, keeping under our radar."

"Not literally radar," Eddie said. "Radar is for babies."

"They must want to consolidate power downstream," Vivy said. "Then they can ambush us from here, or make us fight on multiple fronts, or just split our attention… Fuck. Tamsin, if you hadn't disappeared, and we hadn't come looking for you, we might never have realized the Prime Army was here – right next to the level of Nigh-Space where I live."

"So let's stop them," Tamsin said. "It sounds like we just have to destroy the Prime Army's local gate, and they'll have to start this whole process over, which will be more difficult since you know they're in the area now."

"Just destroy their gate." Vivy shook her head. "That is what we need to do, but it's not exactly easy. We came to this world from my apartment, Tamsin. I'm not exactly carrying heavy weaponry. We were prepared to investigate an abduction, not do battle against the Prime Army. Even a relatively small force can be formidable, and they've got specific countermeasures against Interventionist tech. We can't just seize control of their systems like Eddie did with the workshop here."

"I've got Swarm, and the Chicanes," Tamsin said.

"Those will help. But they're not enough." She drummed her fingers on the tabletop for a moment. "Eddie, you're going to have to go upstream to the operations center and fill our bosses in on what's happening, and see what you can get in terms of support."

Eddie slumped in his chair. "My new body isn't ready yet, Viv."

"Then you're going to need a loaner," she said.

"Ugh. Fine." He rose. "Glenn should come with me."

Tamsin and Vivy both raised their eyebrows. "Why is that?" Tamsin said.

Eddie looked at Vivy. "We talked about this."

"You talked about it," she said. "Glenn and I haven't talked about it at all."

"About what?" I said. "You can't tell me there are more secrets?" I was so done with secrets.

"It's not a secret," Vivy said. "Eddie just has a bug up his butt, and I don't even know if you'd be interested."

"In a bug up his butt? No, I don't think so."

"I want to introduce you around," Eddie said. "Let you meet our handler Jen. I told her how you acquitted yourself when the S-Cons grabbed us. The bosses are curious about you."

I blinked. "Wait. Am I being recruited into a super-secret society?"

"It's more like a preliminary interview, but if you don't blow that, then yeah, sort of, maybe," Eddie said.

"I was going to mention this to you after we rescued Tamsin," Vivy said. "Like I said, I didn't even know if you'd be interested."

"In becoming an interdimensional spy? I don't know if I'd be interested either." It sounded ridiculous, and made-up, but I knew it was real.

"It's not all field work," Eddie said. "Though I must say, you show a knack. We also need analysts, and you've got a pretty good mind for someone raised in a sphere of ignorance. Joining the Interventionists would allow you and Vivy to work together. Which might be a bad idea? I don't understand human relationships." Eddie shrugged. "But you might as well meet Jen."

I mulled that over. Actually, I didn't have time to mull at the moment, but I definitely turned the idea over once or twice.

"I... Is it okay with you, Vivy? I admit, I'm kind of curious. About seeing your home base, if nothing else."

"I want you to be happy and fulfilled and safe," Vivy said. "If you want to go, you should go. But I need to stay here and interrogate – I mean, talk to Tamsin some more. I have to know as much about this world and the forces arrayed against us as possible before we make a move."

"Boys' trip!" Eddie said, clapping his hands. "Not that I'm a boy," he said. "I'm a spaceship. And not that you're a boy, at least not all the time, or so I gather–" Eddie began, and I moaned.

"Ah, so Glenn finally figured out the genderqueer thing?" Tamsin said to Vivy. "I was hoping he'd get there eventually. Glenn always said it was just fetish stuff, part of a kink, but I could tell the roots went deeper–"

I groaned. "Could my ex and my girlfriend please not discuss my gender identity and my sex life right in front of me right now?"

"Fine, then," Tamsin said. "We'll wait until you're gone."

"We have other things to talk about," Vivy said, scowling at her. Then she brightened. "But, yes, I'm very proud of Glenn for doing the work and undoing the programming and figuring things out." She stood up and kissed me, nice and deep, and I wondered if she was needling Tamsin back. Then I decided she probably just wanted to kiss me. Vivy was complicated in many ways, but gratifyingly simple in some others. She let me go and turned to her other partner. "Take care of him, Eddie. And don't let Jen get too... Jen at him."

"Jen is always as much Jen as she can possibly be, so I make no promises." Eddie spread his arms wide. "Glenn! Shall we traverse the multiverse?"

"I guess." I turned back to Tamsin and Swarm. Somehow a headless robot managed to look amused. "Seriously, you don't need to talk about me–"

"Away we go," Eddie said, and took my hand, and away we went.

* * *

Since we started from a different world, we didn't pass through the same set of intermediate dimensions as I had on my earlier curve-chaser trip with Vivy. The first world we landed in was all rusted cruise ships as far as the eye could see, wrecks tilted this way and that on an endless plain of cracked earth, all seen from the vantage of a canted upper deck of one of their number. Rope-and-board bridges and walkways connected the wrecks together.

"Are you going to barf?" Eddie said.

"No. What happened here?" The air smelled of alkali desert, and I saw no movement or signs of life.

Eddie looked around without discernible interest. "No idea. I don't have a complete historical database of the follies of a million backwater worlds. Let's keep going. I intend to cycle us through faster than Vivy probably did, because I'm a show-off, and because we have farther to go. Can you handle it?"

"I guess–"

We flickered. Vivy gave me time to catch my breath between jumps, but Eddie didn't bother, and I caught just a blur of sense impressions. A blast of heat in a desert of green sand. A blast of cold in a pine-tree-covered hillside that could have been some alpine locale on Earth, except for the fact that the snow was purple. A building-sized statue of a crumbling sphinx with an ant's body instead of a lion's. A ring of enormous mushrooms straight out of Alice in Wonderland. A circle of humanoid figures in bright blue radiation suits shouting and scattering away when we appeared in the midst of their immense pavilion. ("Oh dear," Eddie said, and when we landed in the next world, a field of poppies under a moon that appeared to be literally on fire, he continued, "I think we might have changed the course of science for those people, oopsie.") The last worlds we flicked through – which by that point must have been hundreds of universes apart, if we were still making exponential jumps – were curiously barren, gray wastes and rocky expanses.

"We're here," Eddie said cheerfully at last. I fell to my knees as my gorge rose, but I didn't vomit. Was I getting better at this? After a moment, I looked up and took in our surroundings. This place looked just as barren as the other recent worlds, a stretch of gritty gray sand with some coral-esque rock formations off in the distance, but the night sky was astonishingly clear, the shape of a spiral galaxy clearly drawn in starlight. I got shakily to my feet, breathing tentatively, as if I expected to encounter vacuum, but the air was clear enough.

"Doesn't look like much, I know." Eddie tapped the side of his nose. "Operations base, very hidden, very secret, very hush-hush-hush. You might have noticed we passed through some terribly boring places on the way. There's a swath of realities several hundred levels across where, as far as we can tell, there's no intelligent life – it just never developed, for whatever reason, or else it got Great Filtered into non-existence at some point in the distant past. Of course, every universe is vast, so maybe there's a planet tucked away somewhere that's bustling with culture, but as far as we can tell, they're all empty. We tuck our bases away on random worlds in the middle of that desolate stretch. That makes it awfully hard for our enemies to find us – there are no rumors of alien presences filtering through any local civilizations. Tracking us down is like looking for a single teardrop in the Sodden Waste."

Eddie patted me on the back, then said, "Time to meet the folks." He stomped his feet, and the ground dropped out from under us. I screamed as I fell, and Eddie laughed and said, "Steady on!" He grabbed my hand, which helped. Our descent then slowed, for no discernible reason, and we began to drift as gently as a bit of dandelion fluff, down a dark hole.

"You could have warned me," I said through gritted teeth. The shaft gradually lit up from below.

"If you want to be an interdimensional operative, you have to cope with the unexpected," Eddie said.

"What if I don't want to be that?"

"Mmm, well, you're dating one of them, so you should probably learn to cope anyway."

I wanted to yell at him, but now that I wasn't terrified, falling was kind of fun, and anyway, Eddie was just being Eddie. Expecting him to be anything else was like expecting Piss Goblin not to piss on things. Instead I said, "Fair."

We settled down on a floor tiled in white and black hexagons, in a room bigger than a football stadium. Distant figures moved around large and unrecognizable objects. I looked up at the shaft in time to see a panel slide over the opening, making our path of descent indistinguishable from the rest of the arched ceiling. "So what now?"

"Now we meet her." Eddie pointed, and I followed his gesture to see a woman bustling toward us across the floor with speed and determination. She had the compact build of a gymnast and wore a red jumpsuit, her black hair in messy pigtails, and when she got closer, I wondered if she was of Chinese or Korean descent, then realized she was actually neither one, of course. Her eyes were a mismatched surprise, the left one blue, the right one green, and her smile was impish.

"Edward!" she called. "As I live and you don't breathe. What are you doing here? Your new body isn't ready yet." She looked me up and down. "Is this a high-value target? Did you bring me the king of the Strict Constructionists? Or, no, a six-pentacle general in the Prime Army? Or is this the infamous Butcher of the Xoth Conundra?"

"I'm–"

"I'm just kidding, you're Vivy's person, Glenn, right? I'm the Jen to End All Jens, but you can call me Jen." She turned and flung her arms out wide. "Welcome to the Intervention!" She turned back. "But seriously, what are you doing here? Am I supposed to be evaluating Glenn as a prospect? Or–"

"Prime Army," Eddie said, jumping into the moment of breath between her words. "They've established a forward base one world away from Glenn's home level. We're talking way downstream from their usual theater of operations. We just found out about them. Vivy wants to destroy the gate and disrupt their operations, but we don't have firepower, so..." He shrugged.

Jen chewed her lip, sighed, and said, "Come on." She snapped her fingers, and several of the hexagons on the floor opened up. An open-topped vehicle like a motorized tuk-tuk rose up from the opening and trundled toward us. Jen hopped on the front seat, leaving me and Eddie to slip into the bench seat behind. We sped off across the open plain of the hangar, and as those distant objects came closer, I realized they were spaceships, in a wild profusion of designs: one was sleek and sharklike and no bigger than a van, another was the size and shape of a blocky apartment building, and others appeared to be made of floating spheres bound together with force fields. We passed a delicate art deco rocketship that looked like it was made of stained glass, and swung wide around a gleaming black corkscrew that slowly rotated in place, then drove underneath a hovering thing that looked regrettably like a giant version of a bathtub drain plug. Technicians were moving in and out of and all around the machines. "These are all spaceships?" I asked.

"We have to blend in with local conditions," Jen said over her shoulder. "So we take designs from many worlds, and then cram a bunch of our special tech under the floorboards." We slid to a stop in front of a beautiful jewel of a ship, dangling by cables from a crane. It looked a lot like Eddie's old body – dragonfly meets stealth jet – but this time it had a golden hull and prismatic glasswork. It was only half built, the back end still exposed metal frame, but I could see what it was meant to become.

"That's gorgeous," I said.

"You flirt." Eddie swatted me on the arm. "Can you get my new body ready for me in the next, oh, ten minutes, Jen?"

She snorted. "Not today. Not next week. It's nowhere close. I just thought you'd like to see how the build is going, and this workstation was on our way. No, if you're going to fight the Prime Army in a world that far downstream, you'll need–"

"A loaner, yes." Eddie sounded so glum. "You have something suitable on hand?"

The cart zoomed off again, leaving Eddie's future body behind. "Yep. I'm letting you borrow Hektor's body."

Eddie groaned. "Are you serious? Jen, I am light, I am nimble, I am stealth and grace–"

"I can just send Hektor instead, and you can stand on his bridge like you're the captain," she said. "Of course, you'd be a captain that Hektor totally ignored, and possibly sprayed in the face with fire-suppression coolant if you tried to tell him what to do."

Eddie slumped, crossing his arms. "No. It's fine. I'll do the driving. It's my op."

"Who's Hektor?" I asked.

"A warship," Jen said, at the same time that Edmund said, "A colossal dick – except a lot of humans like colossal dicks, don't they? A colossal ass then."

"Some of us like colossal asses, too," Jen offered. "I think you mean to say, Hektor is a little cantankerous."

We pulled up in front of a matte black spaceship shaped like the head of a sledgehammer and decorated with spikes. The ship was the size of a building, but not a huge building; maybe a four-unit apartment complex. Two rhombus-shaped windows on the front glowed bright yellow, and a voice boomed out: "Bipeds. Wonderful. What do you want?"

"We need to borrow your body." Jen hopped down off the cart and strolled toward the ship. "Eddie here has an operation, and his body isn't ready yet. And, frankly, it doesn't pack the kind of firepower they need anyway."

"If you want something blown up, just send me. There's no need to rip me from my very self."

Jen patted the side of the ship. "You know you're not cleared for active duty yet. We're still clearing the effects of that paradox bomb out of your mind. You can't go into the field when you aren't even convinced you actually exist. But we can port you over to this beautiful body Eddie is wearing, just briefly–"

"I'd rather you put me in the tricycle," Hektor boomed. "You know I hate having arms and legs. Ugh. Disgusting. Any entity that voluntarily chooses such a form sickens me–"

"Hello to you too, Hektor," Eddie said.

"Yes, hello, lightweight. Has it really come to this, Jen? Have we fallen so low? As a people?"

"I bet we can go lower," she said cheerfully. "Come on, we're in a hurry. There's a Prime Army gate that needs blowing up."

"Edmund gets to destroy a Prime Army facility? They're the ones who put this paradox in me in the first place! I hunger for vengeance!" Immense engines rumbled, and the whole ship vibrated, but only briefly.

"You'll have to settle for vengeance by proxy, buddy." Jen was irrepressibly chipper.

The great ship grumbled, but it deployed a ramp – which looked like a tongue sticking out from under its yellow eyes. Eddie strolled up and inside, and a few moments later, the yellow windows turned blue. "Ugh," Eddie's amplified voice said from the ship. "How do you stand being this thing, Hektor? I've inhabited refrigerators that were more agile."

The Rex Edmunds body stomped down the ramp, shoulders up, head down, face set in a scowl. "Being a household appliance is all you're good for." Hektor poked Jen in the arm. "I want my body back the moment the Prime Army is routed. Do you understand me? Edmund is to inhabit my body for the least amount of time possible"

"That okay with you, Eddie?" she asked.

Eddie shrugged. "I'm mostly going to serve as transport, and to destroy any ships the Prime Army has hovering around.

Vivy will want to board the station personally and make sure there aren't any innocents or prisoners or whatnot there. Once she gives me the all-clear, sure, I'll come back here. She can get home from orbit on her own, I imagine. Space stations have shuttles and escape pods and such."

Hektor turned and glared at me. "And just who the hell are you?"

"Uh–"

"This is Glenn," Jen said. "He's a prospect we're thinking of recruiting."

"I am?" I said.

"He is?" Hektor said. "He seems a bit… squishy." He poked me in the stomach, way too hard.

I stepped away, rubbing my abdomen. "It's nice to meet you, too, Hektor."

"There's no such person as Hektor," Hektor glowered at me. "Hektor doesn't exist. Everybody knows that. And since he doesn't exist, I can't possibly be him." He stomped off in a seemingly random direction.

"You should get on board, Glenn." Jen shooed me toward the ramp. "Don't get killed, and I'll be in touch, and we'll talk about your future."

I paused. "So you're Vivy's handler?"

"I am. I don't really run agents in the field anymore, but I recruited Vivy in the first place, so I kept her. Mostly I do big fancy operational things now. I'm also one of the founders of the Interventionists." She did a twirl. "I know, I don't look old enough to help run an interdimensional meddling agency, but I've been around for what you'd call centuries on your world. Actual live-in-person centuries, not virtual subjective years in a simulation, though I've got a lot of those, too."

I took all that in. My wonder-and-amazement sensors should have been pretty overloaded, but I didn't find it hard to believe this tiny woman was an ancient super-spy. "I don't know if I'm a good prospect for your team, Jen. I'm just... a person, from what I'm told is a deeply unremarkable world."

"I grew up as a baseline human on a shitty mining colony world in a crappy dystopian level of Nigh-Space, Glenn. Somebody from another reality came along and rescued me and taught me some stuff, and suggested I use that stuff to help others. That's all I do. If that's what you want to do, too... there are ways you can do it." She gave me a nudge. "Now go. Beat up some space fascists."

TAMSIN

"How long have you and Glenn been involved?" I asked Vivy. We were standing on the landing platform in the mountain with Trevor and Swarm, waiting for our ride.

"Less than a year, but we're serious." Vivy was pushing buttons on the gauntlet on her forearm, eyes flickering across alien symbols scrolling by on an embedded screen.

"I guess you already know how long Glenn and I were together," I said sweetly. "Since it was your job to stalk me."

"That was an exceedingly small part of my job, yes. Do you have a problem with me, Tamsin?" She looked into my eyes – she had to look up to do it, of course – and said, "I'm only here to help you."

I sniffed. "It's just... a lot to take in. Meeting an ex's new partner can be awkward."

"Do you still have feelings for Glenn? I thought you broke things off with him and never looked back." There was nothing accusatory in her tone. Instead there was... pity?

I bristled, and tried not to let it show. "I wanted a different life than Glenn did. I have nothing but fondness for him, though. It was sweet of him to come rescue me. Very sweet. Maybe he's the one who still has feelings for me."

"He's just a good person, Tamsin. You run into those, every once in a while." She looked skyward, shaded her eyes, and then pointed. "Here they come."

I didn't see anything at all, but then a spaceship appeared, shimmering out of nothingness, hovering just above the platform. I stumbled backward, Trevor gasped, and Swarm said, "That stealth tech. I want it."

A ramp extended from beneath the ship, and Glenn sauntered down, looking perfectly at home. "We came straight here!" he called to Vivy. "No hopping through intermediate worlds, no snap-tracing, we just… booped."

"Booping must be a technical term," a voice said from the ship. After a moment I recognized it as Eddie's, but without the British accent. "This is a big ship, with a big interdimensional engine. Any general in the Prime Army would cut off their own head to get their hands on this kind of technology. Though what they'd do with it then, being headless, I don't know. Come on, everybody get aboard."

"Are you sure you don't want the Chicanes?" I asked.

Vivy shook her head. "There are political prisoners on that station. I don't want a horde of murderous homunculi running around when there are innocent people nearby. But Swarm is welcome."

"I feel naked with so few bodies," Swarm said. "But I'll do what I can."

We all went up the ramp, into the belly of an alien warship. The interior was gleaming and brightly lit, and looked more like the waiting room of a high-end spa than the bridge of a spacecraft. Glenn dropped into a padded chair on a swivel, and other seats rose from the floor or swung out of the walls to accommodate the rest of us. "Best strap in!" Eddie's voice said cheerfully. "We're heading up, and going at speed through atmosphere can get bumpy."

Vivy took the chair closest to Glenn, and Trevor took a seat near mine. Swarm's seven bodies affixed themselves to various hooks and attachment points that sprouted from the walls. I spoke to my allies on SerpentNet: What do you think of this Vivy?

She seems tough, Trevor replied.

She's full of biomechanical augmentations, Swarm said.

She has a terrible singing voice, though, you don't want to endure karaoke with her, Eddie said. Oh, by the way, I can hear everything you say on your cute little network, so keep that in mind.

This is a private conversation, I subvocalized as coldly as I could.

There's no such thing when I'm around, Eddie said. But fortunately we're all friends here!

I was glad Eddie had spoken up. I'd almost said some things I didn't want him to hear. My interests broadly aligned with Vivy's – I wanted the Prime Army out of this reality, too – but there were other areas where our goals significantly diverged, and I intended to pursue mine regardless.

The ship bumped and shuddered, but no more ferociously than an airplane undergoing turbulence, and after a few moments, even that smoothed out.

"If you'll look to your left direction, you'll see a floating pleasure palace that belongs to the Sung family," Eddie said over the ship's internal speakers. Windows, or more likely screens, appeared in the walls and floor. An array of floating pods connected by silver platforms whooshed past at great speed, before I could get more than a fleeting impression of the whole.

"And now if you'll look in your every direction, you'll see us leave the atmosphere," Eddie tour-guided.

We were so high up now I could see the curve of the planet beneath us, and the unfamiliar shape of alien continents. I felt a sudden stab of homesickness. This was my ancestral home, but it wasn't my actual home, and even if I succeeded in ruling this place, I would be an interloper on a foreign throne. I'd still take it – a throne is a throne – but the idea didn't fill me with as much joy as I would have expected, or wished.

Then we left the blue and entered the black. A giddy surged rushed through me. "We're in space," I whispered, and caught Glenn's eye.

He grinned at me. "We're in space!"

"You never forget your first time," Vivy said, looking at Glenn with obvious adoration. He returned her look.

I felt an unfamiliar twist of doubt. I thought Glenn's presence here meant he was still hung up on me, but maybe Vivy was right, and he was just helping because he thought it was the right thing to do. Had I made an error by dumping him all those years ago? Glenn must be something special, if a woman as formidable as Vivy was this devoted to him. Or, perhaps, he'd become something special, in the years since we parted. He was my past, returned to my present, and I wondered if there might be a place for him in my future. After all, why shouldn't I get everything that I want?

I glanced over at Trevor, and he was staring at me as adoringly as Vivy was looking at Glenn. I wished, for a moment, that I could see him as something other than an occasionally useful diversion. But he was already something I'd won, and I'm forever more interested in the process of winning.

"Why aren't we floating around in microgravity?" Swarm said.

"Because I have excellent graviton generators on board, of course," Eddie said.

"Your technology is ridiculous," Swarm said.

"Don't feel bad. Give your civilization a few hundred thousand years, and you'll be equally ridiculous. Maybe."

"Or you could just share it with me now," Swarm said.

"Ha. You're funny."

If you don't want to share, I thought, we might just have to take it.

"Ooh, we've got enemy vessels," Eddie said. The screens all shifted, revealing shapes in the void, their outlines lit up with artificial glows: half a dozen ships, arrayed motionlessly around a spindle-shaped space station. "Ha. You realize the Prime Army has to transport those ships in pieces, in crates, hauled from gate to gate to gate from the closest factory world?

Once they finally get to their destination, their mechanics have to assemble them on-site at their outposts. It takes forever. And now I'm going to blow them all up. Ha!"

"Kite them away from the station first," Vivy said. "We don't want debris smashing into the place. Tamsin says they hold political prisoners there."

"Oh, fine, let me un-stealth long enough for these idiots to notice me."

"About your stealth technology," Swarm said. "I'm very curious–"

"Nope," Eddie said. "The stealth tech you're already running is plenty cutting-edge for your locality. You're not ready for the good stuff yet – give it a few centuries. That's why Vivy is going to destroy the station once all the innocents are evacuated, to keep your grubby hands off their weapons. The Interventionists don't go around handing loaded pistols to toddlers."

"Toddlers?" Swarm said.

"Maybe I'm being unfair to toddlers. Lots of those are capable of learning how to share. Now, shh, I have warfare to wage."

The Prime Army ships moved, grouping together at first, and then slowly rumbling toward us. "Ugly, boring ships, aren't they?" Eddie commented. "Don't you think they look like shoes? Not even interesting shoes, like the ones Glenn and Vivy like to wear. They're like plain black loafers. Okay, I'm going stealth and swinging around them. Permission to blow the ships into little bits, Vivian?"

Vivy said, "Emphasis on the little. We don't want any chunks to burn up in the atmosphere."

"I see you're willing to murder people when it suits you," I said.

"These are soldiers," Vivy said, not bothering to look at me. "Not employees I had a disagreement with. The Prime Army is a loaded gun, pointed at that planet down there, and at Earth, too. I'll do what I must to disarm them."

"Disarm, dis-leg, dis-head," Eddie said. "Here we go. Hektor's body may be unwieldy, but it is absolutely bristling with things that go boom."

The Prime Army ships milled around on the screen, searching for our vessel, which had easily outmaneuvered them. A moment later, there were six simultaneous flashes of light, and where the ships had been, there were now only drifting specks of debris. My mouth went dry. Such power. If I had this ship, the things I could do! The punishment I could rain down on the Monad!

"What kind of weapons are we looking at on the station?" Vivy asked.

"Oh, various little cannons. The only really big stuff is the orbital bombardment array, which isn't a danger to us. That's probably what they used to erase your family estate, Tamsin."

And my family, I thought.

The space station on the screen lit up, its outlines clearly delineated for the first time. It looked less like a spindle to me now, and more like an inverted wine decanter, the kind with the broad bottom and the narrow neck that flared at the top – there was a wide upper ring, a central spire that descended vertically, and a smaller ring at the bottom. The screen zoomed in on tiny protrusions spaced at regular intervals along the station's upper ring. "Those are anti-ship cannons, but they can't do anything to this ship. They're meant for repelling possible attacks by the locals in their crappy little space shuttles, I'd guess."

"Are there any warships still on board?" Vivy said.

"Mmm… no. The only vessels left in the station hangar are unarmed shuttles. They look like local make, not Prime Army."

"Okay," Vivy said. "Time to board." She unstrapped herself from the seat and went to a wall panel, opening it up and reaching inside. "Trevor, Tamsin, put on these bracelets." She tossed a pair of shiny silver objects to me, just simple chains without visible clasps.

"What are these?" I demanded.

"Communications and defense systems," she said, impatient. "They should keep you from getting stabbed, or suffocating if we lose air in there."

I handed Trevor his bracelet and put on my own: a twist of flattened silver a finger's-width across. Once it was on my wrist, it tightened up, sufficiently that it wouldn't slip off by accident. I looked at Glenn, and noticed he didn't have a bracelet. Maybe he had some other, better form of protection. "Stabbed? How do they stand up against bullets?"

"Less well," Vivy said. "If you get hit with a significantly large caliber, you'll feel the impact, and maybe even get knocked down, but you won't suffer serious damage. It doesn't matter, though. If the Prime Army shoots us at all, they'll probably use non-lethal rounds – firing live ammunition in a metal tube in outer space is a bad idea. Expect knives, extremely large knives, stun-batons, and that sort of thing. Swarm, if you have bullets... don't spray them around."

"Noted," Swarm said. "You air-breathing types are so fragile."

"Oh, cute, they're shooting at us with their little cannons," Eddie said. "Hee. It kinda tickles. Are you all ready to continue on foot?"

"Just another day at the office," Vivy said. She turned to look at all the humans present. "I wish you'd all stayed down on the planet, but since you insisted on coming, just try to stay behind me and Swarm. Eddie, let's board this station, free some prisoners, and blow up a gate."

"You say 'let's,' but it's mostly just you. I'm going to dock with the station, whether they like it or not. I say 'dock,' but it's more like... Do any of you know how bedbugs copulate?"

"No," Trevor said.

"Look it up sometime," the ship said. "Ha, I'm listening to their communications chatter. They've massed all their guards at the airlocks, as if we'd go in that way. Get ready. I'm about to slam my docking proboscis through their hull." There was a distant crunch, and the ship shuddered. "Let me

spray some sealant foam... there. Go forth, and have fun!"
A wall of the ship irised out of existence, revealing a long
metal corridor like a jetway that extended into some sort of
cafeteria, long tables and chairs awash in flashing red lights
and blaring klaxons.

Vivy was gesturing and taking charge while I was still sorting
out the buckles strapping me down. "Swarm should go first,
since they're the toughest."

"Gladly!" Seven many-legged robots, ranging in size from
small dogs to small bears, surged down the corridor, followed
by Vivy. Trevor and Glenn joined me, one on either side. They
looked at each other, looked at me, and shrugged. "Shall we?"
Glenn asked.

"We could just wait things out here," Trevor said. "Where
it's a lot more safe. There's no reason for you to endanger
yourself, Sin–"

"No, get out, shoo," Eddie said. "You're all wearing forcefield
generators. We have the element of... well, everything. I need
to get this body back to Hektor before he becomes permanently
convinced he doesn't exist."

"Do you know what he's talking about?" I asked Glenn.

"Eddie has a prior engagement," he said. "So unless we want
to go with him to Interventionist headquarters, we should get
onto the station."

"The ship is leaving?" I said.

"What, did you want me to hang around out here, bored
and useless, while you're in there doing stuff?" Eddie said. "No
thanks. Envy is a bad look on me."

"How are we supposed to get back to the planet?" I
demanded.

"There are shuttles on board. Vivy can fly them," Eddie said.
"Go on, you're making me late, and Hektor is enough of a jerk
even when he's not kept waiting."

Glenn trotted off down the corridor, so I followed. Trevor
had a butterfly knife, which seemed to be woefully inadequate

against a battalion of enemy aliens, but it was better than what I had, which was nothing. I saw myself as more of a lead-from-a-remote-command-post type, but here I was, in the thick of things.

Or anyway adjacent to the thick of things. We walked into the cafeteria, and they had artificial gravity on the station, too, though it was a bit heavier than I was used to; I felt new weight pressing down on me, but the weight was just me. That meant there were graviton generators on this station, and if I could get my hands on those, I'd show up every invention of Granny's by a factor of millions…

Scorch-marks adorned the walls of the cafeteria, but there was no sign of Vivy, Swarm, or anyone else. Vivy spoke up on comms just then: "Take the left-hand corridor out, follow that to the first T-intersection, and then bear right. Swarm and I are clearing a path as we go. We need to get to the gate and disable it before the PA can call up reinforcements."

Glenn vanished down the hall without even a look in my directions, following the instructions of his beloved, but I grabbed Trevor's sleeve before he could follow. I didn't know how to toggle the stupid comms off, so I had to be circumspect. I beckoned him close to me and said, "It's a shame they're going to destroy this place. I'd really love to have access to this technology when I go up against the Monad. I don't suppose I can keep a few choice tidbits, Vivy?"

"What?" Her voice was annoyed, and thudding noises and gurgles came across the channel as she spoke. "No, Tamsin, you can't have an orbital weapons platform and a dimensional gate. We're here to destroy it all. Gah, was that a beanbag round, you little shit–" Her comms clicked off.

I gave Trevor a significant look, and he frowned at me. "Oh well," I said. "I suppose she knows what's best."

"I suppose she does," Swarm agreed on comms. "I just shoved a bunch of Prime Army soldiers into an airlock and welded the door shut. Ooh, and one of my other bodies just found the holding cells."

There was a great crunch of metal behind us, and I turned to see the corridor we'd entered through fill with some sort of gray expanding foam. Eddie was closing up the hull before he left us. "Your ship is leaving, Vivy," I said.

"Thanks for keeping me updated, don't know what I'd do without you," she said, breathing heavy. "Shit, are you fuckers some kind of cybernetic acrobats?"

"I really don't like her," I said to Trevor, who nodded. "But I suppose we should join her before we get attacked by a stray Prime Army soldier."

"I'll never let anyone hurt you," Trevor said, and I wondered if he'd picked up on my little hints after all. This space station was a bleak and institutional place that sapped all the wonder out of being in outer space. At least Eddie's ship had been gleaming, curved, and futuristic. This place was like a flying DMV office, all straight lines and sharp corners and grey, grey, grey. If I ran a multi-dimensional empire, it would be a lot more stylish.

Trevor went ahead of me, checking around corners, all very chivalrous. We encountered some evidence of Swarm and Vivy's passage in the form of dead and unconscious guards. I'd seen more corpses recently than I'd ever expected to encounter in my life, and while I wasn't fond of them, I found that I could sort of... look past them. Edit them out of my consciousness, the way you could overlook the crushed beer cans littering the edge of a lake and enjoy the beauty of the water beyond.

The Prime Army seemed to have no standard uniform, just variations on a theme, and frankly, their dress sense reminded me of Vivy's: a lot of black and silver, garments that were shiny or stretchy or both, with lots of straps and buckles, though these soldiers had more spikes and shoulder pads and wide belts, and many wore full or half-masks of metal, some silver and others gold, some blank and others stylized with demonic or animal features. We passed a dozen stun batons, matte black cylinders two feet long, smashed from the hands of their wielders. Trevor picked one up for himself, and handed another to me. I didn't know how to turn it on, but even as a club, it was an improvement over my bare hands. The baton had a nice weight to it, too, like the scepter of a king.

Vivy kept offering updates on our route, which took us through a gym (unmoving soldiers pinned under overturned weight benches), a storage area (shattered crates, dented cans, an overhead light swinging unbalanced from a cable), and some sort of command center (long table, high-backed chairs, large screens, all of the above broken)... until we finally reached the heart of the station. There were heavy blast doors at the end of the corridor, but they'd been peeled open, probably by Swarm's pincers. I peeked inside, ignoring Trevor's hissed, "Wait, let me go first!"

The space beyond was vast and mostly empty, like an unused airplane hangar. Glenn was standing back-to-back with Vivy, fighting off two attackers each, Vivy with her black staff, Glenn with a shock-stick he must have salvaged. He was also enveloped in a faintly blue-tinged forcefield that clung to him like a body stocking. They were engaged in combat against the background of an immense rectangular frame, easily twelve feet high and twice that wide, like the biggest of big-screen televisions, excepts its surface was a shimmering prismatic swirl of liquid rainbows.

Two instances of Swarm, including the largest, were battering their way past a ring of black-clad, silver-masked guards attempting to protect a man furiously manipulating a slanted surface on a raised podium. It didn't take great technical knowledge to realize he must be trying to operate the portal.

"Don't let them call reinforcements!" Vivy shouted, in my comms and in the room. She swept the legs of her last attacker out from under him, then spun and fluidly thrust her staff over Glenn's shoulder, just missing his ear, slamming the end of her weapon right into the forehead of the guard attacking him. The soldier went down like he'd run neck-first into a clothesline, and Vivy spun again, toward the clump of fighters at the control panel, but Trevor was already on his way.

I'd never seen anything like it. Trevor ran toward the larger of Swarm's bodies, grabbed a handhold on its carapace, vaulted onto its back, and then, without, pause, leapt off the top – right over the heads of the semicircle of four guards protecting the man behind them. Trevor landed right on top of the soldier operating the panel, driving him down into the podium and then to the ground in a tangle of limbs. The guards spun into chaos, whirling around to fight Trevor, and that left them open to scything attacks by Swarm.

It was over in moments. Swarm dragged the fallen soldiers away, revealing Trevor, who slammed the operator's head into the floor and then rose, swaying a little. "Did I get him in time?" he mumbled.

"We aren't being mowed down by reinforcements, so I think so," Vivy said. "Damn, Trevor. Those were sweet moves." He gave an uncertain grin and bowed. I patted his cheek, then turned and walked toward Glenn and Vivy, still posed like action figures before the swirling portal. "Swarm, do you think you can turn off the gate?" Vivy said. "The connection is active, and I don't want anybody from the other side poking their head through."

"I took some credentials off a commandant a while ago, so I can operate everything in this station," Swarm said. "It's so delicious in here."

"Don't get used to it," Vivy said. "Once we get the noncombatants and prisoners off the station, I'm going to rig it to explode. This level of technology, in a world like this? It's an armageddon waiting to happen."

I kept moving toward Vivy and Glenn, nonchalant, and Trevor was strolling along with me. "I thought the Interventionists wanted to help worlds improve themselves? How does robbing us of an opportunity for improvement do that?"

Vivy rolled her eyes. I was so very sick of seeing her roll her eyes. "There's a process. One developed by people smarter than me. Sudden leaps in technology are horribly disruptive. You don't give a neutron bomb to Napoleon–"

I thought of making a rejoinder – maybe, "But you do give gravitons to Tamsin" – but I didn't want to risk providing Vivy with any warning at all. Instead, I pretended to trip, stumbling into her, and she reached out to catch me.

Vivy was so helpful, she wasn't prepared for me to plant my feet and shove her straight at the gate instead.

Vivy was supposed to go flying through the portal and out of my life, at least long enough for me to claim all the technological wonders she was so intent on destroying. Instead, she easily sidestepped away from my shove, and looked at me with contempt. "What the fuck, Tammy–" she began, and then the smaller instance of Swarm in the room barreled into her and drove her straight through the portal, where they both vanished instantly from sight.

I was so, so pleased. It means so much to have allies who understand you, even when you don't tell them your intentions out loud. I opened my mouth to say something to Glenn – he was going to be difficult to soothe, and might even need to be restrained, for his own safety – but then Trevor whipped past me and shoved Glenn through the gate, too.

I flashed with fury, and considered pushing Trevor through after them, but it passed in a moment. Instead, I gave Trevor a nod. I hadn't wanted to put Glenn in danger – he'd come here to help me, and who knows what waited on the other side of that portal? But in Trevor's position, I wouldn't have done any differently, and after all, Glenn did have his precious Vivy to protect him. "Swarm, turn off the gate!"

"Already on it." The prismatic swirl went black. I looked into its featureless darkness for a moment, then turned and smiled at Swarm. "Let's see what kind of treasures we've won today, shall we?"

GLENN

Vivy and I tumbled through the gate, along with the instance of Swarm that had bum-rushed her through. There was a Prime Army guard right on the other side of the gate, and it was pure luck that the Swarmbot crashed into him and knocked him down. Vivy grabbed onto me and spun us both around, trying to get back through the portal to the station, but the gate shimmered to blackness and we just bounced off.

The Swarmbot's lights went out, as its connection to the controlling mind cut off, transforming it into a lump of inert metal. The guard tried to climb out from underneath, groaning and swearing, but one of his legs was pinned. He wore a black and silver uniform, and a metal mask that looked like a snarling canine's mouth covered the lower half of his face. "Intruders!" he started to shout, his voice modulated into a menacing growl by the mask, but Vivy dropped to her knees beside him and did something I couldn't quite see. When she rose, he was quiet, either dead or unconscious; I decided not to look too closely.

Instead, I took in my surroundings, which were as dully utilitarian as the space station had been. We were in a tent the size of an airplane hangar, the roof held up by spindly metal poles, and there was nothing in here other than the gate and the guard and the guard's folding chair.

Vivy kicked the Swarmbot, then turned to glare at the gate. "There's no control panel in here – the local commander must operate this one remotely." She moved close to me, quickly looking me up and down. "Are you okay?"

"I'm a little sore where Trevor tackled me, but basically fine. Ugh. What was that? We're supposed to be on the same side."

"That was your ex being kind of a bitch, Glenn."

"I... cannot dispute that. I just don't understand why."

Vivy lifted the Swarmbot – I often forgot about her augmented strength, until I saw her do stuff like that – and set it aside. She crouched and patted down the guard, taking away a sinuous-looking sidearm and some kind of key fob without a key. "I can guess," she said. "Tamsin didn't want to straight-up murder us, probably because of some lingering affection for you, or maybe just because she was afraid I'd survive – but she definitely wanted us out of the way."

"I still don't see why. We were on the same side!"

"Glenn, sweetie, no." She stood up, scanning the space, head on a swivel. "Our goals aligned with hers temporarily, that's all. Then... they stopped aligning. Tamsin got rid of us so she can do all sorts of bad things I wouldn't have allowed. She wants to run shit over there, and now she's got a bunch of Prime Army tech to help her do it, including orbital bombardment weapons. I was going to take all those toys away, and I still will, but now she has time to use them first. I wouldn't want to be her enemies right now."

"I... yeah. That makes sense. I'm really sorry. I had no idea she'd do something like this. I knew Tamsin was ambitious, but... she wasn't like this, when I knew her. So... ruthless."

"I believe you," Vivy said. "Stuff happens. People change. Sometimes for the better, if they put in the work... but sometimes for the worse. Plus, Tamsin didn't have the opportunity to be properly villainous back on Earth. In her home world, she has wealth and power, and she has a chance to be the most important person in a whole world. She's going for it. I just wish she hadn't gone for us in the process."

Vivy took my hand and led me around the back of the gate, which was just an immense black screen at the moment. "We were going to destroy the portal, too, and I'm sure Tamsin has designs on that. Swarm and SerpentNet and her horde of Chicanes are smart enough to program the gate so she can lock out the Prime Army forever, and use it herself."

I frowned. "What good would that the gate do her? I thought it was a fixed portal – it only connects that space station to this tent. It's useless to her, right?"

"She's got access to Earth, Glenn, through the door in her granny's basement. Her tech wizards can do some reverse-engineering and figure out how to build another big gate on Earth… and link it up to hers in orbit."

"But why would she want that? For trade? She wants to get rich bringing goods through the gate and selling it on Earth, and vice-versa?"

Vivy put her hand on my arm. "Sweetie. Trade? Even I know Tamsin better than that, and I hardly know her at all. She–"

"Wants to rule the world," I said, miserable about it. Vivy was right. Tamsin's ambition had been limited by circumstances on Earth. Her circumstances were different now, and her ambitions had grown.

"I think she might want to rule both worlds, babe," Vivy said. "Eddie snooped through the lab systems and told me she's growing even more Chicanes. She's got basically infinite Swarmbots, and once she wipes out her enemies, no one will stop her from cracking open her family vaults and releasing whatever horrors they have locked away. Her dead ancestors were arms dealers with a penchant for keeping their deadliest weapons for themselves, so there's no telling what kind of bad shit she'll unleash there, and back home, if she gets a gate open."

I stared at her. "She can't… I mean… that's insane. She can't possibly hope to invade Earth."

Vivy shrugged. "Maybe I'm wrong. Maybe she'll be content with being queen of one planet. But I plan for worst-case scenarios, and when Tamsin kicked us through that gate, she became one of those."

I chewed over the possibility. Tamsin was ambitious... she was stubborn... she was proud... but would she go that far? It sounded horribly plausible. "Wouldn't the Interventionists step in to stop her? Invading adjacent realities is bad, right? That's why you hate the Prime Army."

"Sure, it's bad," Vivy said. "But Nigh-Space is big and full of problems. I doubt my bosses would care about one little two-world empire founded by a narcissist who'll probably flame out in a year or two anyway. Of course, I have a personal interest in Earth, so I'd pull some strings, and I'm sure Tamsin knows that. She's probably hoping we'll get killed over here, but she'll entrench her position and prepare to make a stand against us when we come back."

My ex-girlfriend, the warlord in waiting. I'd almost be impressed, if Tamsin hadn't gotten her boyfriend-slash-footman to shove me into enemy territory the moment I stopped being useful to her. I thought she at least still liked me. Better to know she saw me as an obstacle instead of a friend, though. "So let's go stop her."

"That's the plan," Vivy said. "Or, rather, the goal. The plan is... a work in progress."

"I know we don't have a ship, or Eddie's curve-chaser ring, but can't we just snap-trace to my mom's house, and then go back through the door at Culver House to Vivy's world?"

Vivy shook her head. "Normally, sure. We're only a few worlds upstream from Earth, and it would be an easy trip. We don't even need your mom – I bet my fondness for Piss Goblin would be enough to get us home from such a short distance. But the Prime Army has jammers and all kinds of intrusion countermeasures meant to keep people like me out, so none of our traversal tech works here. As I see it, we've got two options." She held up a couple of fingers. "We can try to seize control of this gate, but that means getting our hands on the local Prime Army commandant, and they're pretty well-defended. I'm sure Tamsin's pet machine minds are working on locking out Prime Army access as we speak anyway, so even if we could turn the portal on, it might not work for us. Option number one doesn't sound good to me."

"Number two, then?"

She put a finger down. "Number two is: escape. We secure transport and get away from this camp, travel a few miles until we're out of range of their jammers, and then use a snap-trace to go home, and make our way back to Culver House." She shrugged. "That's slightly less dangerous than going after a Prime Army commandant, and more likely to work. Unfortunately, it's also a lot slower. I don't like to think about what Tamsin will do with so much time." She handed me the weapon she'd taken off the guard. It was a curved set of brass knuckles, but made of molded plastic, with a small metal cone in the center instead of punchy spikes. "Take this. It's should be pretty much point-and-squeeze. The PA uses a lot of conscripts with minimal training, so they don't go in for complicated sidearms."

I slipped the weapon onto the fingers of my right hand. "What will it do when I squeeze?"

"No clue. I've never seen that kind of weapon before. Probably local design." She looked around, then beckoned me toward the nearest wall of the tent. She ducked down, lifted the canvas, and peered through the gap. "All clear. Roll underneath."

I dropped and slid through the opening, and Vivy followed me. Outside it was twilight, or maybe it was just a dim sort of world. I'd expected, or feared, great hordes of soldiers marching in formation, but instead we were in a barren field of packed dirt, with a few assault vehicles made of angles and black metal parked nearby, and a row of tents off in the distance. If there were people in the tents they weren't poking their heads out yet.

Beyond the immediate landscape, things got stranger. Trees that towered like giant redwoods loomed in the distance, but they looked more fungal than arboreal, their skin a mottled deep purple in color, and the trunks were attached to one another by tendrils or webbing. The mushroom-trees swayed, but I didn't feel any breeze, and I had the unsettling feeling they were moving under their own power. A packed dirt road cut straight from the edge of this field on through the forest, so I supposed the local vegetation couldn't be that dangerous.

"Bless the predictability of the Prime Army," Vivy whispered, crouched beside me. She didn't comment on the purple trees; I guess she'd seen stranger things. "They lay out their camps the same way on every world. Their gates are always off to one side of their settlement, near a staging area, so they can mass vehicles and troops, and march them through as needed." She pointed across the field to another canvas pavilion, like the one we'd emerged through. "There will be another gate in there, linking this base to the next occupied world upstream, making another link in their daisy chain. When the tent flaps are open and the gates are working, they can march troops right out of one gate and through the other without even pausing for a pee break." She sighed. "We should steal a vehicle and drive like hell until our snap-trace works again, but... damn it."

"We're going to blow up their gates first?" I asked.

She nodded. "We're going to blow up their gates first."

"Works for me. The farther the Prime Army gets from my actual house, where I actually live, the happier I'll be. So do we need to steal explosives, or..."

"My therapist back on the Shattered Veil – only we call them 'normalizers' there, isn't that messed up? – once said to me, 'You're a bomb-thrower, Vivy.' I think it was meant to be a criticism, but to tell you the truth, it was one of the few moments on my home world when I actually felt seen and understood. Which is to say, no. We don't need to steal explosives. I have explosives. I could say I brought them so we could destroy the space station when we were done, and that's true, but it's also true that I usually have explosives anyway." She reached into a belt pouch and removed a bright red, waxy disc.

"Is that a Babybel?" I asked.

"This is an explosive, not cheese. There's a reason I don't keep my bombs in the refrigerator." She held the device in the palm of her hand and pointed to a yellow circle in the center of the top. "The bomb is a little sticky, and when you push it against something, it gets very sticky. That is due to science. Once the bomb is stuck to whatever you want to blast out of existence, you press the yellow button. That's the timer. One press gives you five minutes, two gives you ten minutes, three gives you fifteen minutes, and so on. I don't want to risk a patrol finding these, so we're going for five minutes. Can you take out one gate while I handle the other?"

I blinked. "You want us to split up?"

"Splitting the work is faster, and faster is better. If one gate blows up, the guards will run to protect the other one, so it's best to take them out simultaneously."

"Right. Yes. Of course." I held out the hand that didn't have a weird knuckleduster-gun attached to it, and she put the bomb in my palm. "Did you want to handle this tent, or…"

She smiled at me. "How about you take the tent where the guard is already out of commission, and I'll take the one where the guard is awake?"

"Your tactics are very sound." I sighed. "I do not think I am naturally talented at being a super-spy saboteur."

"Most people need a little training." She patted my cheek. "But I believe in you. Stick the bomb right in the middle of the gate, press the button once, then get out. I'll set my device, and we'll meet in the middle outside and steal a truck." She kissed me, then dashed to the nearest armored death machine, crouched in its shadow for a moment while scanning her new sightlines, then ran toward the other pavilion.

I crawled back under the canvas. Nothing had changed; the Prime Army goon and the Swarmbot were both where we'd left them. I realized a bomb would kill the guard, and wondered if I had time to drag him to safety, even though I didn't know how far the blast would extend. I had to try, though, didn't I?

I crouched beside him and checked his pulse, but he didn't have one, so that solved that problem. He wasn't the first dead Prime Army member I'd seen that day, but he was the first one I'd touched.

I shook off the various conflicted feelings I had about watching my girlfriend kill a guy. I could process things later, when I wasn't on a mission. Maybe the Interventionists had therapists on staff. Or maybe they could zap your brain to make you feel okay about stuff. I'd accept that, too.

I went to the gate, which reminded me of the giant screens you see at sports stadiums, and pressed my hand in the middle. It felt slick and solid, like plastic, and I wondered where this surface went when it became a portal. "That is due to science," I muttered, and stuck the gouda-bomb in the middle of the screen. The device adhered with a shlorp sound, so that was good. I pressed the yellow button, which gave a satisfying click. The bomb did not display a helpful countdown, though, or any indication that it was active, which struck me as very bad user design. I had to assume it was armed, though, and suddenly five minutes felt like absolutely no time at all.

I ran back to the side of the pavilion, slithered underneath, and then darted to the personnel carrier Vivy had used for cover. I looked around, and my heart jumped out of my chest because now I did see people, way off across the field, specifically a pair of figures in black, walking fast toward a row of low, prefab-looking huts. The soldiers weren't coming toward me, or even looking my way, but their presence still freaked me out. On the space station, I'd mostly seen the soldiers after Vivy and Swarm were done with them, except at the very end, and the presence of armed people who would probably kill me on sight was terrifying. I turned and looked at the other tent, willing Vivy to emerge, but she didn't.

And didn't. And didn't. With no watch or phone, I couldn't be sure how much time had passed, but I was sure at least a couple of minutes had gone by, and for all I knew, I was still within range of the imminent blast. I cursed, looked around – there was nobody in sight now – and hurried across the field to the other tent. There was a big flap in the front I could have entered through, but I went around the side, where any other random passers-by wouldn't notice me, and lifted the canvas a bit to look inside.

Vivy was in there, holding her hands up, while two guards pointed weapons at her. One had a knuckleduster like mine, and the other was pointing a long, recurved rifle. "–security test," Vivy was saying. "And I'm impressed. You did very well."

I could tell she wasn't speaking English, but my anklet translated. She started to lower her hands and one of the guards barked, "Don't move!"

I didn't know what to do, but the soldiers hadn't noticed me yet, so I should probably do something. I raised my right hand, pointed at the nearest guard, and squeezed.

There was a world-shattering boom, and the guard with the rifle fell. I gaped, ears ringing, sure that I'd fired some kind of nuclear laser torpedo at him – but then I realized the bomb in the other tent had gone off. The noise of my weapon, if it made a noise at all, had been swallowed by the simultaneous explosion. The other guard whipped his head around at the noise, then saw his partner falling, and that was all too much for his brain to process instantly. Vivy flowed toward him, and her arms blurred, and then he was on the ground, several feet away from his bent-in-half rifle.

"Come on!" Vivy shouted at me, her words muffled, like my ears were stuffed with cotton. Really they were stuffed with decibels, I guess. "I already set the other bomb, it'll go off any minute!"

That motivated me. I ran to her, jumping over a fallen guard, and then we raced toward the tent flap. We rushed outside into total chaos – the pavilion I'd blown up was engulfed in flames, reduced to burning banners of cloth flapping on metal poles. Troops were running over from the row of tents, but they were focused on the fire, and didn't seem to notice us.

Vivy and I ran hand-in-hand to the far side of the field, where a lone vehicle sat, smaller than the hulking armored machines behind us. While we ran, another boom split the air, and I looked back to see the tent we'd just escaped burning.

Then one of the armored cars exploded, flying straight up into the air, then falling on its neighbors with a titanic crash of shrieking metal. "You bombed those too?" I shouted.

"To discourage pursuit!" she yelled. We reached the vehicle, a long, sleek thing I figured belonged to an officer, or maybe even the commandant. Vivy fiddled with her gauntlet for a second, and the doors swung open, gull-wing-style, like Doc Brown's DeLorean from Back to the Future. There was a single seat in the front, like a fighter pilot cockpit, and a wider bench seat in the back, and I flung myself onto the latter. Vivy hopped in the driver's seat and we tore off, the doors lowering closed as we went. I looked back, through the tiny rear window, and saw a wall of flaming wreckage between us and any possible followers.

"That was amazing!" Vivy yelled.

"It was!" I shouted. "Also horrible!" I had to shout just to hear myself. "Will my hearing be permanently damaged?"

"We have treatments for that!" she bellowed back. "I was going to put you on my health plan anyway!"

We tore away from the Prime Army base, through the purple mushroom forest, toward freedom, and home, and then, to some kind of reckoning.

TAMSIN

"Do you think they're dead?" Trevor asked.

"Hmm?" I was standing at a master control panel in the deposed commandant's office, watching a screen almost as big as the gate, which currently offered a satellite view of the continent on the planet below, with a number of targets marked in rings of red. A Chicane scuttled up to me with a glass of something close enough to bourbon, and I patted his lumpy head in thanks before I took a sip. Swarm had sent a dozen Chicanes up in a stolen shuttle to help me run things on the station, and they were a great help. Several of them were currently operating weapons stations, and others were guarding the political prisoners. (I couldn't just set those people free – they wanted to overthrow the oligarchs, and I was about to be the oligarchs – but I was feeding them a lot better than the Prime Army had, and there were no beatings or other unpleasantness. I saw no reason to be cruel.)

"Glenn and Vivy." Trevor was hovering next to my left elbow. "Do you think they died over there, wherever we sent them?"

"I have no way of knowing." It would have been nice to have Glenn around, to see if I could win him over to my way of seeing the world, but he was probably too far gone into his infatuation with Vivy anyway. She was impressive, in various unsubtle ways. "She is formidable, and he is protected, so they may be fine." I shrugged. "I didn't want them dead, just out of the way, so they couldn't take all my new toys away."

"If they're alive, they're going to come back–"

I nodded. "Probably. But it's too late for them to stop me. Napoleon already has the neutron bomb. Swarm has copied all the technical information from the station's systems. The Chicanes are masters when it comes to reverse engineering, and we've got samples of the graviton generators and weapons systems hidden on the surface. If Vivy does come back, she'll return to a very different political situation. I'll be in charge here, and the Interventionists will have to negotiate with me, not just order me around like I'm one of the lowlies. Vivy's personal animosity aside, I doubt her people will even want to get rid of me. I'm going to rule much more benevolently than the oligarchs before me, after all. She can hate me all she wants, but she has bosses, and they'll see reason."

"If they don't?"

"Oh, if they're impolite, I'll just hold the whole planet hostage, and threaten to destroy it if they don't leave me be. Even if they remove my capacity for orbital bombardment, I'll still have resources. After we're finished here, I'm opening my family's grand vault, and once I get the ships and weapons hidden there…" I shivered in anticipation. I didn't necessarily want to use those weapons, but the mere threat would open all the doors in the world for me.

"Whatever you think is best," Trevor said. "You know I'm on your side, no matter what."

I took his hand. He'd really been very good, and a worthy ruler rewards loyalty. "How would you like to be my prince consort, Trev?"

He pressed my hand to his chest. "Whatever you want. I'm yours. I'm always yours."

I thought he might cry, and who had time for that? I extracted my hand and turned away. "We'll arrange a royal wedding. It will be fun. But first… Chicanes? Are we ready?"

"Yes, Princess!" they chorused, sounding like a horde of

broken mechanical frogs, but oh, how sweet it was to hear them anyway.

"Then let's destroy the Monad."

The station rumbled as bundled rods of hyper-dense metal were fired from the station down through the atmosphere, beginning the kinetic bombardment. This was the same sort of strike the Monad had used to devastate my family estate and kill the Zmija. Now I was using it to decapitate the Monad the way Hercules had decapitated the Hydra, one head after another, searing their spurting stumps as I went.

The little red circles on the map all turned black. The Chicanes cheered, and Trevor let out a low whistle. "That's that, then," he said.

"There will be stragglers," I said. "Cleaning up. But yes. That's the big one."

He was silent for a moment, then cleared his throat. "Do you feel... you know... okay?" I didn't answer him. I knew what he meant, but maybe he wouldn't finish the thought, and then we could both ignore it. But instead he continued. "It's just... a lot of people down there are dead now. The Monad, the people who worked for them... Every black circle is... you know. They're dead."

"And I killed them. I know." I kept looking at the screen. So many little circles.

"That doesn't fuck with you a little?" His voice was soft; softer than usual.

"It would, if I let it," I said. "But I don't think of it that way. As people. This was just a necessary part of the plan. If the people of it all starts to bother me, I just... look past them. I set my sights on what comes after the ugliness. On the future. That's where I'm going. These are just steps on the path." I paused. "Do you think I'm a monster?" For some reason, I cared about his answer.

"No. I think you were born for this. I think you're unstoppable."

I nodded. That helped. "Then let's not stop now." I turned. "Swarm? Let me know when you pick up the signal." Swarm's hulking form was crouched before a communications array, tendrils plugged directly into the interface. "I assume you can break their codes?"

"Oh, there's already lots of encrypted chatter flying back and forth, but I can break it all with the Prime Army tools," Swarm said. "There's so much lovely technology here. I just wish I'd gotten my manipulator arms on the stealth tech in Eddie's ship. The Interventionists had even better stuff."

I, personally, coveted the dimension-hopping tech that ship had possessed. At least I had the gate, limited as it was. Swarm and the Chicanes thought they could reprogram it for my purposes, once they'd done some preliminary work back on Earth. They were all a little surprised when they heard my plans, and I didn't know how to explain myself without sounding sentimental, because it was a little sentimental.

I was in orbit, looking down on a planet I was about to rule... but it wasn't my planet. It was my ancestral home, yes, but it wasn't my actual home. I felt the thrill of conquest, but it was a chilly sort of thrill. Taking possession of this world, a place I felt no personal connection with... well, it paled in comparison to the idea taking ownership of a place I already knew and loved.

"We've got a videoconference," Swarm said. "Looks like the leaders of the Vhoori, Tompkins, and Sung families, and the highest-ranking Monad they could find, a twenty-seven year-old instance who was touring a manufacturing facility and avoided getting cratered. Shall we cut in?"

"Hold off a moment." I turned to Trevor. "How do I look?" Chicane had done my hair and makeup – his skills were really quite the strange hodgepodge – but I wanted a second opinion.

"You look... like a princess," Trevor said.

I smiled. "Good enough. Soon I'll look like a queen." I showed him away, then turned to face the screen. "Put me through, Swarm."

An array of furious and panicked faces appeared in little squares on the screen. "Who is this?" an old man sputtered. I recognized him from the dossier Swarm had compiled.

"Hello, Minister Vhoori," I said. "Madame Sung. Doctor and Doctor Tompkins. And, oh, look, a little Monad. I thought I should introduce myself." I smiled. "My name is Tamsin Zmija. I think you know my family." I leaned forward, bracing my hands on the console, and looked each of them in the eye in turn as best I could. "I just destroyed the Monad, as they once destroyed my family. I could easily do the same to all of your estates, but that would be terribly wasteful, and counterproductive. I'm not here to make threats."

"Then why are you here?" the minister barked.

I cocked my head. "To make friends," I said. They just stared at me, and I burst out laughing. "Your faces! I thought you'd be eager to discuss the terms of our future partnership."

That was nicer than saying I'm here to discuss the terms of your surrender, but they all understood what I meant just the same.

"We are prepared to listen," the minister rumbled.

I felt a little pang. If only Glenn could see me now, maybe he'd understand. I had power over the people with power, now. This was worth anything.

"I'll present my terms," I said, "but first, I'll need you to remove…" I flicked my fingers contemptuously. "The Monad."

The insignificant and unprepared Monad tried to run away when the council tried to seize her. It was really quite funny.

I still had Vivy's protective bracelet on, and the Chicanes were amusing themselves by flinging throwing stars and darts and knives at me, and watching them bounce off the sparkling blue field. Swarm couldn't make sense of the technology in the bracelets, and the Chicanes couldn't, either. The Prime Army station had included technical specifications and

operations manuals and repair guides for all their tech, but
the Interventionist gear was opaque, and deliberately so, since
they didn't want their enemies stealing their power. That
meant Trevor and I were the only ones on the planet who
possessed this level of defense, but that was fine, too.

I'd destroyed the Monad three days ago, the Tompkins
family a day and a half after that. They'd sent assassins after
me, out of some misguided loyalty to their old patrons, which
didn't shock me, but did disappoint me. The killers had looked
so surprised when their blades bounced off our shields. I was
impressed that they managed to infiltrate the workshop and
reach us at all, but according to the Chicanes, they were the
best freelancers on the planet, now that Bollard was gone, and
Chicane was my permanent employee. I considered recruiting
the assassins, but decided giving them to the Chicanes as a
treat would do more to discourage future attacks. I'd shown
some mercy already, by letting the other ruling families live,
and it's possible to have too much of a good thing.

The Voorhi and the Sung families fell in line after that
assassination attempt failed, especially once I divvied up the
Tompkins family spoils between them. Carrots and sticks,
sticks and carrots. (I'd kept one Tompkins biotech facility for
my personal use, though. I was growing more Chicanes. I was
going to have an army of Chicanes.)

There were still stray Monad and Tompkins people out
wandering the world, but Swarm was hunting them down
assiduously, and their own friends and allies were turning
them in for the generous bounties I offered. We'd even
collected some DNA to grow tame Monad and Tompkins
clones in Bollard's lab so we could access all their gene-locked
resources. (I'd had the clone of Granny returned to the slurry
without ever waking her up, though; one Zmija was plenty for
now.) The world was an oyster, and I was the only one with a
shucking knife.

And now... the grand vault awaited. Trevor and I strolled

from an armored vehicle surrounded by a phalanx of Chicanes with several Swarmbots stalking around nearby. The final vault was hidden beneath a decrepit radio telescope out in the rural flatlands, and the rusting metal dish towering above us gave the whole experience a surreal tinge. Birds were singing, the sun was shining, and I was on the cusp of new triumphs.

Perimeter defenses online, SerpentNet whispered. Whitelist all members of current retinue?

I affirmed, and we walked up the overgrown path to the radio telescope without being incinerated or otherwise interfered with. I pressed my hand against the cold metal of the radio telescope's base, and a door rumbled open, revealing an elevator, not unlike the one in the pillar in the City of Song. "Trevor, you two Chicanes, and the little Swarmbot, please join me." We crowded into the elevator, and descended.

The doors opened at the bottom to reveal a vast underground space, like a missile silo with an airplane hangar at the bottom all in one. Banks of lights came on, revealing massed ranks of gleaming shrike-like ships in the blue and black I now recognized as the Zmija colors, all raked-back wings and sleek violence. "How many ships are there?" I said, awed at the bounty.

"A hundred and forty-four on this level," Swarm said. "But there are other levels, and deep below, there's the factory that built these ships in the first place. The factory is offline, because it ran out of materials, but they can be replenished."

I walked up to the nearest ship, which was the size of a fighter jet, more or less. "Imagine thousands of these, pouring out of the sky over every land in this world and the next…"

"You'll be unstoppable," Trevor said.

"Oh, I know. I just wish they all had the dimension-hopping power of an Interventionist ship. Maybe someday." I turned, gazing at the weapon in waiting on all sides. "In the meantime, Chicanes, I want to divert more resources to building our gates on Earth." I'd sent several Chicanes over with supplies and access to my inherited bank accounts, and they'd secured a plot of land in the unincorporated crap-land near Culver House. Even now, they were assembling a dimensional portal... the first of several. My technicians assured me they could link new gates to the one in orbit, and to the gates I was building at my new estate, so I wouldn't have to drag everything into outer space before sending it to Earth. Soon I'd be capable of moving people and materiel between these two levels on a vast scale, and once that happened, well... in time, Earth and the old country would be one nation, under Tamsin, and everyone would be better off for it.

Especially me.

"I just don't get how you're going to take over the whole Earth," Trevor said.

I was sitting on a divan in my new estate, generously donated by the Vhoori. Once I explained that I'd execute one member of their family for every surveillance device we found, it was a very secure estate, too. Trevor was rubbing my feet. (He offered. I never would asked. I have Chicanes for that; they have magic fingers, and once one of them learned how I liked it, they all knew, because of the wonderful networked hardware in their strange little brains.)

I poked Trevor in the chest with my toe. "First, I'll contact certain powerful individuals in government and industry. Swarm and the Chicanes are making a list for me. I'll explain things to them, and show them how outmatched they are, and explain that they can cooperate, or suffer an invasion. Earth is run by oligarchs, too, just less obviously than this world is. There are people over there who control the levers of power, and I'll just control them. I don't need to be crowned queen on national television. I just want the power, not the recognition." In truth, I wanted both, but I could be patient.

"I still don't think it'll be that easy," Trevor said.

I shrugged. "If the people of Earth prove reluctant, I'll make a show of force. I'll warn them to evacuate a city, then send some

TIM PRATT   261

of the new ships through and flatten the place. We'll have the lowlies blame it all on terrorists, and I'll tell the powerful people how the next attack will come without warning. I'm going to offer lots of bribes first, though, and I have excellent bribes. Artificial gravity will transform things over there – and here, too, of course. The applications for that kind of technology in industry and transportation and so many other sectors are staggering. We have better medical technology here, too, especially now that we've got access to the Prime Army infirmary. They can regrow limbs and freshen up the grey matter! Once I save a few important people, or their beloved old mothers, from horrible degenerative diseases, they'll line up to support me."

"And then what?" he asked, rubbing a little harder, like he was supposed to.

"Then I'll endow scientific institutions, build homes for the homeless, grow new limbs for veterans, whatever." I waved my hand in the air. "Tamsin the Great, Tamsin the Generous, Tamsin the Benefactor…"

"I thought you didn't want recognition?"

"Maybe a little recognition, from the right people." It would be nice to have a coronation, and let the people know who to thank for their better lives. But that could happen later, after the groundwork was laid.

"I hope everything goes the way you want," Trevor said. "And you don't face any resistance."

I pushed him in the chest with my foot again. "I like a little resistance. It keeps things interesting."

"Of course, Sin," he said, accommodating as always. Right at that moment, I missed Bollard, a bit. Trevor was too accommodating. Bollard had pushed back in ways that challenged me, and I thrived on challenges. Hmm. I wondered if the Chicanes could grow a new Bollard? Put him in a virtual environment that mirrored his actual past, to create someone who was the same, or very close to the same, but with a deep and subliminal strain of loyalty to me –

A Chicane popped into the room. "Princess!" he called in a voice that managed to be spiky and mushy all at once. "We have intruders on the grounds! One of me spotted them climbing through a window on the ground floor!"

I queried SerpentNet, which confirmed that no alarms had been tripped, and that there was nothing on our cameras. "That must be Vivy. No one else can overcome our security." I rose from the divan and gestured at Trevor. "Come on. We'll greet them in my study."

"Are you ready for this?" Trevor asked me.

"I'm ready for everything," I said, and it was true.

GLENN

We broke into Tamsin's new estate without much difficulty, and paused in a dim parlor full of weird musical instruments to discuss our next moves. Eddie was back in his Rex Edmunds body, running his full suite of technological nastiness, so he owned the building's security, and Vivy was in full battle dress. Strangely, so was I – that's right, I got my very own badass skintight outfit made of not-really-leather and not-exactly-spandex. The garment was full of piezoelectric responsive augmented... something-or-others. Basically, the suit made me strong enough to lift a car and kick through a wall without breaking any bones in the process. The anklet was still defensive, and the suit made me more capable of offense. I was still nowhere near as tough as Vivy, who had assorted biomechanical technology embedded throughout her body and brain, plus the genetically engineered advantages common to the Shattered Veil, but even so, I felt very much like a superhero.

After we escaped the Prime Army base, we snap-traced our way back home; Vivy's fondness for Piss Goblin really was enough to get us to the apartment, although, as usual, the cat didn't actually show herself while I was around. As long as the auto-feeder was full, I wasn't missed at all, though I did need to scoop the litter, which I loathed. (Doing some chores can become sexy in the right context, but shoveling shit isn't one of them.)

Once we showered off our battle-sweat, Vivy contacted her bosses and let them know what went down. Then... an argument ensued. Vivy wanted to go into the universe next door with a strike team and battleships, but the Jen to End All Jens said Interventionists resources were already stretched thin, and hadn't we spent enough time messing around with these strategically irrelevant worlds already? The Prime Army was cut off, their encroachment rebuffed, so our only tactical goal had been achieved. "Who cares if this Tamsin sets herself up as warlord, really?" Jen said. "Maybe she'll be better than the current vicious oligarchs. At least she comes from a world where democracy is a thing. Take your ego out of the equation, Vivy, and what's the big deal?"

"She's using stolen Prime Army tech to get revenge on her enemies, and whatever nastiness she can find in Bollard's lab, and you know she's going to work on making more gates," Vivy pointed out, and that was enough to nudge Jen a little closer to our viewpoint. Not enough to authorize a major incursion… but enough to give us Eddie in his android body and authorization to return.

"Priority one is getting the Prime Army tech away from her," Jen said. "Destroy the gate, if nothing else. Without that, any damage will be localized. Offer Tamsin a deal, and resolve this with minimal explosions, okay?" She blipped off.

We had to wait for Eddie to join us, and waiting wasn't much fun. Vivy paced up and down in front of the couch and seethed a lot. "You're taking this really personally," I pointed out. "You didn't even used to date Tamsin. Shouldn't I be more pissed off than you?"

She sat beside me. "I'm pissed off because of you. If Tamsin had just knocked me through the gate, whatever, I get it, she wanted the Prime Army guns and I wasn't going to let her have them. But she shoved you into danger, too, and that shit, I can't forgive."

I nodded. I always get more angry when someone hurts a person I love than I do when they hurt me. I touched Vivy's cheek and got her to turn her head, then kissed her. "Thank you."

"Also, Tamsin sucks," Vivy said. "She's the worst, and I don't want her running a planet. I also don't want her trying to invade this planet, which I bet she'll try to do, because as previously mentioned, she's the worst."

"We'll stop her."

"Yeah? You want to come along? It won't upset you to see me kick your skinny blonde ex's ass?"

"She did shove me through a portal. Actually, Trevor did the shoving, but he's pretty much an extension of Tamsin's will as far as I can tell."

"He's way hung up on her. There's nothing wrong with licking a lady's boots, per se, but there's a time and a place, and Trevor doesn't know when to quit." She shook her head. "Do you think Trevor believes they're dating? They definitely have a relationship, but it's not the kind Trevor thinks it is."

"Not everyone can be as healthy or well-adjusted as we are," I said. "While we wait for Eddie, did you want to… work out some of your frustrations?"

She snorted. "I should have seen that coming. You're incorrigible. Can't be corriged at all."

"Look, you're the one who brought up licking things…"

Amazingly, we managed to have some fun and then make ourselves decent before Eddie started banging on the door. Then we traversed to the old country, and soon enough… there we were, in my ex-girlfriend the warlord's palatial estate.

"Tamsin is in a study with Trevor, upstairs." Eddie was staring off, using other eyes than the ones in his head. "I – oh. The cameras are dead now. And… I can't reboot them. They must have physically pulled the cables in the control room, which means, they probably know we're here. I thought one of those pumpkin-headed weirdos out on the lawn might have glimpsed us. Oh well. Surprise is nice but not essential."

Vivy opened the door, checking the hall, then beckoned us to follow. We'd looked over blueprints for the house, and we ghosted through servant's corridors without encountering any resistance. "Why does one human need to live in a place this large?" Eddie said.

"So they can feel important," I said.

"She needs a place to keep all her killbots and Chicanes, too," Vivy said. "Speaking of, where are they? You'd think some of her minions would be trying to stop us, if they really know we're here."

"I don't know if you noticed, but Tamsin has a dramatic streak," I said. "I'm pretty sure she expected us to come after her, and she probably has some kind of horrible dramatic reveal planned. We're walking into a trap, I bet."

"We're untrappable," Vivy said. "I'm going to kick Tamsin's ass, and then Eddie will track down every scrap of tech she stole from the Prime Army, and we'll put this place back the way it was before she started fucking things up. More or less. Minus the Prime Army and however many oligarchs she already murdered."

"I'm sure." I didn't doubt her; I just doubted things would go that easily.

We made our way upstairs, still without encountering a single Chicane or Swarmbot, and approached the double doors that led to her study. They were carved all over with intricate designs, but I didn't get to look at them closely before Vivy did a roundhouse kick and tore one of the doors off its hinges. She had something of a dramatic streak, too.

Vivy stormed into the huge space, with me and Eddie right behind her. She faced a row of Swarmbots, the smallest the size of a black bear, the biggest the size of a car, arrayed across the width of the room. Tamsin was a ways off behind them, standing behind a desk, Trevor at her side.

"Hello, Glenn," she said. "You're always welcome to visit me, but I have to say, I really don't like your girlfriend."

"The feeling's mutual!" Vivy called. "Eddie, get these tin cans out of my way."

"Er," he said. "About that. I can't take them offline. They're shielded."

Tamsin laughed. "Surprise, surprise. Unlike some people, I learn from my past mistakes."

"It seems Swarm has integrated jamming technology from the Prime Army station into its systems," Eddie said. "That's clever."

"I'm very clever," Tamsin said.

"Fine!" Vivy said. "Are you clever enough to take a deal? Because I'm authorized to offer one."

"Ooh, do tell." Tamsin beamed at us, clearly on top of the world. I realized how much a little power could change a person, then realized she actually had a lot of power, and then realized she probably hadn't actually changed all that much. She was what she'd always been, only bigger, and more so.

Vivy ticked off the terms. "The Interventionists will leave you alone, and let you play with this planet, without interference. In exchange, you'll hand over all the Prime Army technology you stole, including the dimensional gate. You'll also relinquish any other cross-dimensional technology extant on this planet, and we'll seal up the door in your granny's basement. You get this world, and that's it."

"Napoleon, again?" she said. "Exiled to Elba? That didn't suit him. I doubt it will suit me."

"Tamsin, come on," I said. "We're offering to let you run this place. Isn't that what you wanted?"

"You people won't let me do anything." Her voice was cold. "I'm not asking for anyone's permission. This doesn't sound like a deal, anyway. In a deal, both sides get something."

"Not getting an Interventionist fleet dropped on your head is something," Vivy said.

Tamsin sniffed. "Please. If that was going to happen, it would have already happened. I think you're all I have to contend with, and I can contend with you."

"What is it you want, Tam?" I said. "D you really plan to take over the Earth?"

"It's a start," Tamsin said. "I don't see why I should stop there. Why can't all the wide worlds belong to me? As far as I can tell, based on a sample of two universes, every world is run by idiots and criminals. Everyone in power gets there through violence and graft. I'll do a better job of running things than they do. I want everyone to be happy... starting with me." She put her palms flat on the desk and glared at us from between her killbots. "In case it wasn't clear, Vivian: I decline your offer. Here's my counteroffer. Get off my planet, or I'll kill you. You should probably leave Earth, too, because once it becomes my planet, the same offer stands."

"We tried this the nice way," Vivy said. "I don't care if you've got Swarm. I can still take you."

"Oh, I didn't just bring Swarm. I've been busy growing new Chicanes, and they're all networked, and all so fantastically devoted to me..." She crooked her finger, and hidden doors on both sides of the room swung open. Countless Chicanes poured in, dressed in identical tweed suits, and lined up in neat rows. I glanced behind us, and Chicanes were filling the hallway back there, too.

One of the Chicanes began to fling business cards at us, like someone making it rain dollar bills at a strip club. One card hit my chest, and I caught it as it fell. Text ran all the way across the card, cut off by the right-hand edge, and it read:

CHICANE AND CHICANE AND CHICANE AND CHICANE AND CH
Chicane • Chicane Chicane • Chicane Chicane Chicane
"Chicane!"

I dropped the card on the floor with its identical fellows. "Tamsin. It doesn't have to be this way. There's still time to be reasonable."

"You're sweet, Glenn, but I don't need to be reasonable. I'm royalty. This is my birthright." She spread her hands wide. "And what do you have to fight me? Your girlfriend in the

catsuit and her ineffective android? I don't care how good
Vivian is at flying spin-kicks. She can't fight an army on her
own, and I have an army in this room, with more on the
way. I've instructed the Swarmbots to take you alive, Glenn,
because I'm still fond of you, but as for the other two..." She
stopped looking at me and started looking at Vivy. "You should
leave, and never come back, while you still have the option.
You don't have a warship this time."

"Bitch, I am a warship," Vivy said, and surged forward.

After that, everything was pretty chaotic. There was a lot of
shouting and screaming, and I wasn't very effective in battle,
though I managed to smash a Chicane in the face with my
super-strong elbow. Shortly after that, a Swarmbot pinned
me, and before I could shove it aside, panels opened on its
underside, and manipulator arms shoved me into a cavity
inside. I was sealed into darkness, the noises outside muffled,
and I didn't know what fuck was going on. I pounded on the
walls of the mobile cell, but all that did was bang and echo.
Augmented strength can only go so far, so I settled down, and
listened as best I could to the sounds of everything falling apart
outside.

TAMSIN

Three years after Vivy tried and failed to end my reign, I stood at the top of the bell tower on the campus of the University of California, Berkeley, surveying my domain. It was a warm, perfect Northern California day. In one direction, I could see the remnants of the Golden Gate Bridge standing out in the bay, and in the other, the golden summer hills, hardly burned at all. Blue-and-black Swarmships carrying Chicanes zipped to and fro across the San Francisco skyline, which was also mostly intact, though I'd knocked down that hideous Salesforce Tower on purely aesthetic grounds. The major cities of the east coast got it much worse; they didn't realize what I was capable of, back then.

Trevor leaned against the railing beside me. "It's pretty up here," he said. "Are you thinking of setting up a west coast residence?"

"The Claremont is nice," I mused. It was a grand hotel complex just a few miles away. "With some upgrades, it could be pleasant. Or I could turn the Palace of Fine Arts in San Francisco into an actual palace." The old country had vastly superior fabrication methods, and Swarmbots could do construction as well as they could so rebellion suppression, so anything I could imagine, they could create for me. I had so many Swarmbots, now. They were even in space, harvesting asteroids for materials to build more of themselves as they went. They were making a base for me on the moon, and I was going to have a palace there, too. Tamsin, queen of the moon and the stars. I liked it.

"I wouldn't mind living out here again." Glenn stood on my other side. He and Trevor had come to an understanding, and these days, they got along well enough; their sharp edges were sanded down by their mutual adoration of me. It's good to have common interests. "I had some good times out here."

I sniffed. "Being in Berkeley won't remind you too much of... her?"

Glenn shrugged. "What I had with Vivy was intense, but intense things tend to burn themselves out, don't they? I know she's all right, back with her people. That's enough for me. It's not like I'd be living in our old apartment or something. She even took our cat with her."

After my Chicanes thwarted her, Vivy cried mercy, and I chose to let her live, mostly for Glenn's sake. (Also because I couldn't figure out how to break her force field.) Vivy went back to the Interventionists – in point of fact, I traded her to the Interventionists, along with that uncouth Eddie. The interdimensional meddlers got their operatives back, in exchange for a promise to leave the old country and Earth alone, as long as I agreed not to expand my borders beyond those two worlds.

I agreed readily enough. I'm not greedy. I just wanted what my family was owed, and my homeworld, too. Only a monster would begrudge me that. I was content with my lot.

So far, anyway. Maybe my appetite would return later, and if so, I'd make a plan to satisfy it. In fact, I was already doing research against that eventuality.

I took Trevor's hand with my left, and Glenn's with my right. We were all surprised when Glenn chose not to go upstream with Vivy when she left. "I just can't," he'd explained. "My life is here, my mom is here, just... everything, you know?" And, of course, Vivy was forbidden to ever return. Their relationship was doomed. I'm sure she didn't seem quite so alluring to Glenn once he saw me press my boot down on her throat, anyway.

Glenn was angry with me for a while, of course, and refused to answer my calls or summons, but one night not long after the fall of Paris he got drunk and called me, and we talked. After that, we kept talking, and in time… well. We reconnected. This current configuration, with me and him and Trevor all together, was new, and perhaps a little fragile, but… it was promising. I thought it would work. I wanted it to work.

And if there's one thing I've proven to myself, over and over, it's that I always get what I want. In fact, the greatest limitation on my ambitions was the fact that there was just one of me. I'd studied history, and I knew the dangers of expanding one's domain too far, and losing control of the outskirts. I also knew that empires founded by a single dominant personality tended to fall apart when that ruler died, descending into squabbling and infighting.

I couldn't have that. I wasn't too keen on the idea of dying at all, frankly. Fortunately, the Chicanes had some interesting ideas. They were improving their cloning techniques, and the process of mental conditioning, and, with Swarm, they were making great leaps in expanding the size of interconnected mental networks. We were working toward a future where I would become a singular networked consciousness inhabiting multiple bodies, ruling my empire from palaces scattered all over creation… and when one body got old or injured or worn out, it could simply be discarded, with my essential self continuing in a host of others.

And if Trevor or Glenn ever broke down, I could make more of them, too. The ability to reward loyalty with immortality seemed more the province of a god than an emperor… but why couldn't I be both?

Why shouldn't I live, and love, and rule, forever?

"Adore you," Glenn whispered in my ear.

"Worship you," Trevor whispered in my other.

I kissed Trevor, and then I kissed Glenn, and looked out at the horizon of my empire, and saw that it was good.

GLENN

Vivy and I sat at a workstation in the Interventionist headquarters, watching Tamsin twitch and moan on a screen. She was supine in a lozenge-shaped pod, dressed in white, with a crown of wires attached to her shaved head, and various tubes running into her body. "What do you think she's doing right now?" I asked.

Vivy shrugged. "You want to put the simulation up on the screen? Just be warned, it could be gross. I heard she's been having a lot of threesomes with you and Trevor."

"Ew," I said.

"What, you don't like threesomes now?"

"It really depends on who the other two people are, Vivy." Trevor was visible on another screen, and he was hooked up in a similar way. Tamsin and he were sharing a virtual environment – fully immersive, and totally convincing. In the simulation, Tamsin had defeated us in the Battle of Last Week, and gone on to become Queen of Nigh-Space, or at least the old country and Earth. The Interventionists were running her simulation at high speed, so she'd been in there for years already. She and Trevor were the only real people inside, though. Everyone else was a simulation run by expert systems, including Tamsin's weird preferred version of me. "My pansexuality does not extend to Trevor."

"I keep asking Jen to make Tamsin suffer more," Vivy said. "Sure, she's got setbacks and challenges, but is it too much to ask for her to lose all her hair or get scabies or permanent diarrhea? But Jen says too much stress can make the simulation's verisimilitude wobble, and also that it would be cruel. She's all, 'let's defeat our enemy by giving her what she wants,' and blah blab blah."

"Speaking of a simulation," I said. "You were going to show me what I missed when that Swarmbot scooped me up?"

"Oh, yeah," Vivy said. "That's all set up. Come on." We rose from the workstation and walked down a hallway, heading for one of the virtual reality suites. A Swarmbot joined us, dancing along on new and improved legs.

"Hello, my glorious benefactors," it said. "How's our princess doing?"

"She's happier in there than she ever was out here," Vivy said.

"Are you planning to leave her hooked up like that forever?" Swarm asked.

"You think she'd prefer a prison cell?" Vivy snapped, then sighed. "Sorry. Everyone is so concerned about Tamsin, I just… Look. Eventually, we'll add some rehabilitative elements to the simulation. We'll work on developing her empathy and show her that maybe her approach to life and love and governance isn't ideal. Tamsin isn't the first warlord we've locked up in a simulation. Some of them come out again as reasonable people. The psychology stuff is not my area, though. I'm just a bomb-thrower."

"Thank you for not throwing bombs at me," Swarm said. "I appreciate the opportunity to join your organization. There's so much to learn here! And so much juicy tech!"

"You always struck me as a reasonable army of autonomous killbots," Vivy said. "I'm glad Jen agreed to give you a shot."

We veered off from Swarm, and into a dim room that contained a virtual-reality pod, kind of like a tanning bed. "Do you trust Swarm?" I asked.

"Not really, but Eddie and the other artificial consciousnesses do, and they know better. They had a real long talk with Swarm after everything went down. Turns out Swarm was fanatically loyal to Tamsin's family because of coercive programming, and once those guardrails were removed, Swarm turned out to be pretty reasonable." She patted the pod. "Ready to witness my moment of triumph?"

"Do you have to shave my head?"

"That would make your cute little wigs fit better," she mused, "but no, you're not going fully immersive long-term like Tamsin. You're just going to be an observer. A ghost in the room, watching a scene we put together from Eddie's footage and Swarm's recordings of the big day."

I climbed into the pod, and she settled a crown of lights onto my brow, and then kissed me. "Enjoy. I'm magnificent in there. Eddie's okay too." She closed the lid.

I was standing by the broken door in Tamsin's study, watching myself get slurped into the belly of a Swarmbot. How embarrassing. A Chicane went past from the hallway, just missing me, to join the melee.

As I walked toward Vivy's whirling figure, the eddying Chicanes swerved to avoid me, rather than passing through me like a ghost, as if I was actually present in the room. Interventionists virtual reality was impressive – that sense of physicality really aided in the verisimilitude. I climbed up and stood a chair off to one side in order to get a better view of the fight.

Vivy was magnificent. She was armed with her staff, and she was a spinning force of graceful destruction. The weapon had inertial generators embedded in the shaft, and when she hit a Swarmbot, she did so with the force of an oncoming train, compressed to a strike point an inch or so across. The result was a lot of spinning metal, and I realized after a moment that she was precisely aiming her strikes, so that she could send Swarm-shrapnel flying into the Chicanes...

though short of decapitation, nothing seemed to slow them down. For the Chicanes, pain was something that happened to other people.

Tamsin and Trevor were crouched under the big desk, shouting orders I couldn't really hear. Then Eddie climbed up on top of the desk. I thought he was going to try and grab Tamsin, but instead he turned to face the room, spread his arms wide and said, "Chicanes! Look to me!"

All the Chicanes instantly ceased trying to kill Vivy, and looked up at him, their lumpy faces expectant. "Stop the Swarm!" Eddie shouted, and the homunculi turned on the robots, ripping at their metal limbs, smashing in their lenses, and in one case, crowding around a killbot, picking it up, and carrying it out of the room, legs waving wildly.

With Vivy and the endless horde of Chicanes both fighting Swarm, the tide turned decisively. I climbed off the chair and made my way to the desk. I watched as Eddie stretched out on his belly atop the desk and hung his head over the side, looking at Tamsin and Trevor underneath.

"How?" Tamsin demanded.

"You installed jammers into Swarm, so that was smart," he said. "But you couldn't alter the hardware that networked all the Chicanes together, could you? That would have taken a hundred separate brain surgeries." Eddie clucked his tongue. "I bet it didn't even occur to you to try. You were thinking of the Chicanes like they were people, but in fact, they're just another kind of Swarm. I hijacked their sensorium and made them think I was you. Now I'm the pretty pretty princess that all the murderous homunculi adore!"

Vivy came around the desk, reached underneath, and grabbed Tamsin by the arm. Trevor tried to fight her, as ferociously as a honey badger, but Eddie dragged him off to one side. He didn't stop struggling though, and called Tamsin's name until Eddie covered his mouth to shut him off.

Tamsin shook off Vivy's grasp and stood to face her, head high. "So," she said. "What now?"

"Now I stick this needle in your neck." Vivy took a syringe from her belt and uncapped it. "You'll take a little nap, and wake up in a better place."

Tamsin didn't tremble, but she was so stiff you could tell it was an effort. "You're going to kill me? What would Glenn think of that?"

"He'd be pissed. Fortunately, I'm not going to kill you. I meant what I said. You're going to better place. You won't even remember the part where we defeated you, if that's any consolation."

"Good luck getting that needle through my forcefield–" she began.

"I'm the one who gave you that bracelet, Tammy," Vivy said. "I'm the one who controls the off switch."

"My name isn't–" she began, but then Vivy popped the spike into her neck and depressed the plunger. Tamsin's eyes fluttered, and Vivy lowered her unconscious form to the floor. She turned to Trevor. "You next."

"She's going to get you for this," Trevor said. "You don't understand what Sin is like. Her willpower. Nobody knows her like I do. And I won't stop fighting until she's free–"

"You should really consider therapy," Eddie said. "You have appalling boundaries."

"It's not even co-dependence, you know?" Vivy said conversationally. "That implies reciprocity. What you've got, it's so much worse than that." Eddie held Trevor still while she readied a syringe, and moments later he was unconscious, too.

Vivy and Eddie looked down at them for a moment. "That was fun," Eddie said. "Do you think this whole level will go to hell now?"

"She didn't tear out the entire infrastructure," Vivy said. "I think they'll be all right. For ruled-by-oligarchs values of 'all right.'" She looked around. "Where did Glenn get to?"

I heard my own muffled voice, from inside the belly of a now-legless Swarmbot in the corner: "Um, hello? What's happening out there? Did we win?"

"He's going to make a top-notch operative, I just know it," Eddie said, and they walked over to set me free.

A week after I watched that simulation, we were back in our apartment, and Vivy was snuggled up against me on the couch. Wonder of wonders, Piss Goblin was on the couch with us, too, purring in Vivy's lap and making biscuits on her thigh, without even deploying her nasty little claws too much. "The vet says she pees all the time because of anxiety," Vivy said. "Or UTIs. Or both. Or maybe the UTIs cause anxiety? It's a whole thing, apparently. But she's so cute, it's worth it."

"Cuteness makes up for a lot." I yawned. "I can't believe we're just… back here. I'm supposed to be writing a paper this week. It's ridiculous." Back at Interventionist headquarters I'd visited a virtual library with my subjective time sense altered, doing a week of work in a real-time hour, so I wasn't totally behind in my studies, but it was still surreal to be back in Berkeley, facing the prospect of my old routine.

"I'm enjoying the down time, personally," Vivy said.

"I… kind of liked the action? I didn't think I would. And seeing Tamsin again, seeing what she'd become, that was super weird. But it was definitely interesting. Also sometimes fun? Or anyway exciting. Have you heard from Jen about my thing?"

She patted me on the knee. "No, but I'm sure she'll be in touch soon."

Just then my phone buzzed with an incoming email. "They wouldn't email me, would they?"

"How are you going to send an email across dimensions?" Vivy said. "I thought you were a scientist."

"I study the history of science. I'm a historian. Common mistake." I looked at the new message. "Huh. I've been offered a research opportunity in Italy, starting next month. Fully funded." I sat up. "With a generous stipend, access to a private archive in a villa, where I'm invited to live while I work... I don't get it. I've never heard of this institute, and didn't apply for anything like this."

Someone pounded on the door, and Vivy pulled her robe closed and went to answer it, to the annoyance of Piss Goblin, who vanished under the couch, where I devoutly hoped she would fail to live up to her name for once.

Eddie came through the door in his familiar android body. "Darlings!" he shouted. "You got the email I just sent?"

Light dawned. "This grant is from the Interventionists?"

"Yes, one of our many cover organizations, all plausible and deniable, so you won't have to give up your studies. Though you'll have to do the actual studying part, in addition to all the other training, even though the training will be lots more interesting. Spycraft, infiltration, combat, and so forth." He bounced around, shadowboxing.

"Combat? I thought you wanted me to train as an analyst."

"We're a small outfit," Vivy said, "compared to our enemies, anyway. Jen likes to make sure everybody can do a little bit of everything. She cracked up when she heard how you got swallowed by a Swarmbot, and she wants to make sure that kind of thing doesn't happen again."

"I guess I can see the wisdom in that." A bubbling effervescence rose up inside me: excitement, anticipation, and the joy of the new. The closest I'd come to this feeling before was when I first realized how well I clicked with Vivy.

Maybe I'd click just as well with this, too.

"So, babe," Vivy said. "Are you ready to become a champion of Nigh-Space?"

ACKNOWLEDGMENTS

Thanks to Lynne & Michael Thomas, who published a story about Vivy, "A Champion of Nigh-Space," in Uncanny magazine, and to Mur Lafferty & S.B. Divya, who published a piece about Tamsin, "A Princess of Nigh-Space," in the Escape Pod anthology. I wanted to see how those characters would interact if they ever met each other, and this book is the answer.

Thanks to my wife Heather Shaw and our teen River for putting up with me wandering around in a daydream daze so much of the time, and to Aislinn, Amanda, Emily, and Katrina for their steadfast support. My deep appreciation goes to fellow writers Molly Tanzer and Sarah Day for brainstorming and idea-bouncing (and Sarah gets double-thanks for astrological consultation).

Of course I owe a great debt of gratitude to the team at Angry Robot, who continue to let me try out my weird ideas, especially Eleanor Teasdale and Simon Spanton, editors extraordinaire, and all the design and marketing people, too. Thanks to my agent Ginger Clark for keeping things running smoothly on the business side.

I am not generally one of those authors who goes on and on about their pets, but it seemed appropriate to dedicate this book to our three good cats (Zanzi and Marzi both died years ago, sadly, but Spotty is still going strong), and to deliberately not dedicate it to our other cat, Ocean, who is the direct inspiration for Piss Goblin. (She's a beautiful creature, truly, but also, she's the worst.)

Tim Pratt
Berkeley CA
August 2023

If you enjoyed this, why not try Tim Pratt's other books?

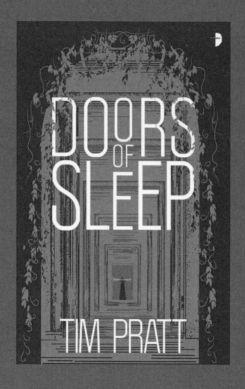

Read the first part of Doors of Sleep here...

I yawned – one of those bone-cracking yawns so immense it hurts your jaw and seems to realign the plates of your skull – and staggered against the bar. I was on the third level of the uppermost dome, where the mist sommelier, clad only in prismatic body glitter, puffed colored, hallucinogenic vapor from the pharmacopeia in their lungs directly into the open mouths of their patrons. I turned my face away before catching the overspill from the latest dose: a stream of brilliant green meant for a diminutive person covered in downy fur the same shade as the smoke. I didn't have much time left; sleep was coming for me, and I wanted to meet it in my right mind.

I stumbled down the ramps that spiraled through the glittering domes of the Dionysius Society, looking for Laini. The glowing bracelet on my wrist flashed different colors when I came into proximity with people I'd partied with during the preceding five days, and I followed the wine-red flash toward a cluster of dancers on a platform under dazzling dappled lights. Other partygoers bumped into me and jostled my battered old backpack, something everyone stared and laughed at here. In a post-scarcity pleasure dome, where anything you desired could be instantiated just by asking your implanted AI to produce it, the sight of someone actually carrying stuff was unprecedented. The locals had all decided I was an eccentric, or someone affecting eccentricity to stand out from the crowd. Standing out from the crowd was almost a competitive sport here.

The locals couldn't even imagine all the ways I really stood out. For one thing, I didn't have an implanted AI, something everyone in this world received in their gestation-pods. I didn't have local tech because I wasn't a local. I hadn't been a local any place I'd been for a very long time.

"Laini!" I shouted once I got close, and, though the music was loud, my voice was louder. Before I left home, swept away by forces I still don't understand, I was trained to mediate conflict, and while mostly I did that by speaking calmly, sometimes it helped to be the loudest person in the room. Laini's shoulders, bare in a filmy strapless gown the color of a cartoon sun, tensed up when I shouted – I'm trained to notice things like that, too – but she didn't turn around. She was pretending she couldn't hear me.

So. I'd been through this sort of thing before, but it never stopped hurting.

I pushed through the dancers – they were human, but many were altered, with decorative wings or stomping hooves or elaborate braids made of vines. In techno-utopian worlds, those things were as common as pierced ears or tattoos back home… though this place wasn't as utopian as some. In my week here I'd come to realize the aerial domes of the Dionysius Society were home to the perpetual youth of a ruling class floating above a decidedly dystopian world below. It was lucky Laini and I had awakened up here in the clouds. Anyone walking around in the domes was assumed to belong here, since there was no getting in past the guards and security measures from the outside.

Though if we had awakened below, with the dirt and the smoke and the depredations of "the Adverse," whatever those were, I probably wouldn't have lost Laini the way I was about to. I'd accidentally brought her to a world that was too good to leave.

I reached out and touched Laini's shoulder, and she turned, scowling at me, green eyes in a pinched face under short black hair. I was the whole reason she was here, and she clearly wished I would go away. I would leave – I had no choice – but I deserved a goodbye, at least, didn't I? I touched my borrowed bracelet and put an exclusion field around us, a bubble of silence and privacy on the dance floor.

"I'm fading." I blinked, and even that was an effort. My eyes were leaden window shades, my breathing deeper with every passing moment, and there was a distant keening sound in my ears. I knew the signs of incipient exhaustion. They had excellent stimulants in that world, but even with my metabolic tweaks, staying awake for five days straight was about my limit.

"Zax... I don't... I'm sorry... I just..." I could have helped her, said what she was thinking so she didn't have to, but I stubbornly made her speak her own mind. "I like it here," she said finally. "I've made friends. I want to stay."

I liked her a little better for being so direct about it, and at least this way there was a sort of closure. My last companion before Laini, Winsome, had gotten lost in the depths of the non-Euclidean mansion where we landed, and I couldn't stay awake long enough to find them again. (Unless, I thought darkly, they'd abandoned me deliberately, too, and just wanted to avoid an awkward goodbye.) I couldn't blame Laini for wanting to stay here, either. She'd come from a world of hellish subterranean engines: the whole planet a slave-labor mining operation for insectile aliens, and this playground world of plenty was a heaven she could never have imagined in her old life – the one I rescued her from. We'd been together for forty-three worlds though, the longest I'd kept a companion since the Lector, and it hurt to see her choose this place over me. We didn't even get along that well, honestly; she was suspicious, quick to anger, and secretive – all reasonable traits for someone who'd grown up the way she did – but that didn't matter. For a little while, I'd woken up next to someone I could call a friend, and, in my life, that's the most precious thing there is.

She touched my cheek, which surprised me – we'd been intimate a few times, but only when she came to me in the night, and it was always rough and hot, never afterward discussed or acknowledged. She'd certainly never touched me with that kind of fondness. "I'm sorry, Zax," she said, and that surprised me even more, and then she kissed me, gently, which stunned me completely. Maybe a week in a place of peace and plenty, with its devotion to pleasure as a pillar of life, had softened her.

Or maybe she was just feeling the all-encompassing love-field brought on by some rather advanced club drugs.

"OK." I turned away so she wouldn't see the tears shining in my eyes and made my way across the dance floor, stumbling a little as lethargy further overtook me. I glanced back, once, and Laini was dancing again, having already forgotten me, no doubt. I tried to be happy for her, but it was hard to feel anything good for someone else in the midst of being sad for myself.

I opened up a cushioned rest pod and crawled inside. At least I'd fall asleep in a pleasant place. I curled myself around my backpack – stuffed with as many good drugs as I'd been able to discreetly pocket – and succumbed to the inevitable.

Here's the situation. Every time I fall asleep, I wake up in another universe. That started happening nearly three years and a thousand worlds ago, and I still don't know why, or what happens during the transition, while I'm asleep. Do I spend eight hours in slumber in some nowhere-place between realities, or do I transition instantaneously, and just feel like I got a good night's sleep? I wake up feeling rested, unless I took heavy drugs to knock myself out, and if I fall asleep injured, the wounds are always better than they should be when I wake up, if not fully healed. I inevitably sleep through the mechanism of a miracle, and that's just as frustrating as you might imagine.

I never have dreams anymore, but, sometimes, waking up is a lot like a nightmare.

After leaving Laini, I woke to flashing red lights and the

sound of howling alarms. I automatically pressed the sound-dampening button on my bracelet, but it was just an inert loop of metal and plastic now that the network of the Dionysius Society was in another branch of the multiverse, so the shriek was unceasing.

I sat up, looking around for obvious threats – always a priority upon waking. I was in some kind of factory or industrial space, on a metal catwalk, near a ladder leading up, and a set of stairs leading down. I stood and looked over the metal railing to see gouts of steam, ranks of silvery cylinders stretching off in all directions, and humans (humanoids, anyway) racing around and waving their arms and shouting. One of the workers, if that's what they were, stumbled into contact with a steam cloud, and screamed as their arm melted away.

I'd be going up the ladder instead of down the stairs, then. I tightened my pack on my shoulders and scrambled up the rungs. Fortunately the hatch at the top was unlocked so I didn't have to use one of my dwindling supply of plasma keys. I climbed up onto the roof, and the hatch sealed shut after me.

I stood atop a mining or drilling platform, several hundred meters above a vast, dark ocean. The sun was either rising or setting, and everything was hazed in red. The air was smoky and vile, but breathable. I've never woken up in a world where the air was purely toxic, though sometimes I find myself in artificial habitats in otherwise uninhabitable places. My second companion, the Lector, theorized that I projected myself into numerous potential realities before coalescing in a branch of the multiverse where my consciousness could persist... but I've always been more interested in the practice of my affliction than the theory, and was just happy I'd survived this long.

The water far below was dark and wild, more viscous than most seas I've seen, as if thickened by sludge, and the waves slammed hard against the platform from all directions. Occasionally dark shapes broke the surface – giant eels, I thought at first, with stegosaurus spines, but then I glimpsed some greater form in the depths below, and realized the "serpents" were the appendages of a single creature.

The thing in the water wrapped a limb around one of the cranes that festooned the platform and pulled it down into the water with a terrific shriek of metal and a greasy splash, and the whole rig lurched in that direction. The creature grabbed more cranes at their bases and began to pull, trying to rip the whole platform down.

I'd seen enough. I try to save people when I can – I was trained, on the world of my birth, to solve conflicts and promote harmony – but there are limits. If anyone had burst through the hatch after me I'd have given them the option to escape this world, but there was no time to rescue anyone without losing myself. I fumbled in my pack and pulled out a stoppered test tube (my second-to-last) and a handkerchief. I was still bitter about the limitations of the pharmacopeia in the Dionysius Society. They had uppers, and dissociatives, and euphorics, and entheogens, and entactogens, but they didn't have any fast-acting sedatives. Who wanted to fall asleep and miss the party?

I yanked out the cork and poured the carefully measured tablespoon of liquid into the handkerchief, strapped my pack back onto my chest, and then lay down on the metal of the deck. The rig was already sloping noticeably toward the water, but not so much that I'd slide into the sea before I passed out. I hoped.

I pressed the soaked handkerchief to my nose and breathed deeply. A strong, sickly-sweet odor filled my nostrils, my head spun, everything got gray and fuzzy, and then that terrible world went away.